PRAISE FOR DEKKER BOOKS

BLESSED CHILD

Blessed Child is the best novel I've ever read."

LOWELL W. PAXSON, chairman, PAX-TV

"Bill Bright and Ted Dekker have written a fast-paced thriller of apocalyptic dimensions. The book will move you to wonder."

CHARLES W. COLSON

"What a beautiful picture of the love God has for us."

TIM LaHAYE

"*Blessed Child* is a letter from God's heart to every Christian! A cutting edge call to the church. It confronts us with towering truth."

JACK HAYFORD

"I enthusiastically recommend *Blessed Child*. It is a compelling story of the transforming power of the Holy Spirit."

JOSH McDOWELL

"A good novel with a strong message."

SIR JOHN M. TEMPLETON

". . . stimulating and enlightening reading . . . Congratulations . . . !"

D. JAMES KENNEDY, Ph.D.

"A real page turner . . . a captivating portrayal of God's unwavering commitment."

JAMES ROBISON

"*Blessed Child* is most inspiring and amazing . . . a must read . . ."

PAUL CROUCH

"A brilliant and heart-touching novel . . . powerful writing . . . I commend it to everyone. I believe it will have a lasting influence . . . on every reader's life!"

ORAL ROBERTS

HEAVEN'S WAGER

"[*Heaven's Wager* is] genuinely exciting . . . fast paced . . . spine-tingling . . ."

PUBLISHERS WEEKLY

"Well, well, guess what I've found. A fiction writer with a rare knack for a compelling story, an expansive reservoir of clever ideas, and a unique dry wit that makes me laugh."

FRANK PERETTI, best-selling author

"Rarely does a novel grip a reader's heart and soul the way *Heaven's Wager* does. Dekker is among a very small number of writers who have mastered the challenge of blending sound theology with knock-your-socks-off storytelling."

ROBERT LIPARULO, novelist and contributing editor of *New Man* magazine

"Readers will be lining up for the next sequel. Strongly recommended."

CHRISTIANITY.COM

"Easily one of the most visionary, gripping, and inspiring Christian novels ever written."

MARK OLSEN, author and fiction editor

"From the opening paragraphs of *Heaven's Wager*, I was caught in the human drama where life intersects with spiritual reality. It's a page-turner and I look forward to many more books from this talented writer."

W. TERRY WHALIN, best-selling author and fiction reviewer, journalist

"Not since the day a manuscript called *This Present Darkness* came to me for consideration have I come across a story as gripping and with such spiritual insight as *Heaven's Wager*."

JAN DENNIS, editor and publisher,
This Present Darkness, Piercing the Darkness, The Prophet

WHEN HEAVEN WEEPS

"*When Heaven Weeps* displays more of God's love than any other book I've read, save the Bible. It'll make anyone who is forgiven stand up and shout. It is a beautiful story . . . exquisite."

STEPHEN BLACKMON, ConsumingFire.com

"Ted Dekker is one of the most remarkable creative writers of our time . . . engrossing and spiritually inspiring . . . highly recommended!"

BILL BRIGHT, Founder and President, Campus Crusade for Christ International

"*When Heaven Weeps* is a first in Christian fiction: a bold, knock-your-socks off, four-hankie, romantic supernatural thriller. And a brilliantly written one to boot. Hang on for something brand new."

MARK OLSEN, author and editor

"Although I don't read much Christian fiction, this romantic thriller had me turning page after page."

JOSH SPENCER, editor, *Stranger Things* magazine

"Dekker is a brilliant storyteller."

JEREMY REYNALDS, Assist Communications

THUNDER OF HEAVEN

TED DEKKER

W PUBLISHING GROUP™

A Division of Thomas Nelson, Inc.

AUTHOR'S NOTE

I penned this story in the year 2000, over a year before the tragic events of September 11, 2001, although I have touched it up some since. As you read, you will understand the significance of this fact. I never quite know why particular stories come to me when they do, or who will read them. But I do know this: When you look beyond the events—when you peek behind the skin of this world—you always see things differently.

> "See, it is I who have created the blacksmith . . .
> And it is I who have created the destroyer to work havoc;
> no weapon forged against you will prevail . . ."
> ISAIAH 54: 16–17 NIV

PROLOGUE

Eight Years Ago

"It's starting again, Bill."

"Again? These things start every time we turn around."

She ignored the pastor. "I had another vision."

The line was silent for a moment.

"You're walking again?"

"No. But I'm praying. I want you to join me."

"What was the vision?"

Helen paused. "I'm not sure."

"You had a vision but you're not sure what it was?"

"Something terrible is happening, and somehow its outcome rests in my hands. In our hands."

"Our hands? God can't deal with this on his own?"

"Please don't be smart. I'm too old for games."

"Forgive me." He let out a long breath. "I'm not sure I'm ready for another round, Helen."

"I don't think anyone is this time." A tremor laced her voice. "He who is faithful in little will be given much. This feels like much. And, frankly, I'm a little scared."

The line was silent.

"Who is it?" Bill finally asked.

"Tanya," Helen said.

1

Those who know call that part of the jungle the hellhole of creation for good reason. And they call the Indians who live there the fiercest humans on earth for even better reason. It's why no one wants to go there. It's why no one *does* go there. It's why those who do rarely come out alive.

Which is also why the lone American girl who ran through the jungle really had no business being there. At least according to those who know.

Tanya Vandervan jogged to a halt atop a cleared knoll and tried to still her heavy breathing. She'd run most of the way from her parents' mission station, hidden by trees a mile behind, and in this heat, a mile's run tended to stretch the lungs.

She stood still, her chest rising and falling, hands on hips, her deep blue eyes sparkling like sapphires through long blond hair. The rugged hiking boots she wore rose to clearly defined calves. Today she had donned denim shorts and a red tank top that brightened her tanned skin.

Still drawing hard but through her nose now, she lifted her eyes to the screeching calls of red-and-blue parrots flapping from the trees to her left. Long trunks rose from the forest floor to the canopy, like dark Greek columns supporting tangled wads of foliage. Vines dripped from the canopy—the jungle's version of silly string. Tanya watched a howler monkey swing suspended by a single arm, whether provoking or protesting the parrots' sudden departure, she could not tell. She smiled as the brown mammal reached a flimsy arm out and nabbed a purple passionfruit from a vine before arching back into the branches above.

A gunshot suddenly echoed through the valley and she jerked toward the plantation. Shannon!

An image of him filled Tanya's mind and she ran down the knoll, her heart thumping steady again.

To her right, the clearing butted against hills that rose to a black cliff, looming a mile to the plantation's north. The Richtersons' large two-story white house sat still in the midday air, white like a marshmallow on a sea of green.

On Tanya's left grew fifty acres of the plantation's exotic crop: *Cavash* coffee beans, commonly regarded among connoisseurs as the finest coffee in the world. Shannon could be there working the fields, but she doubted it—he'd never taken much interest in his father's farming.

His father, Jergen, had fled Denmark and carved out this living because of his hatred toward the West. *The West is trampling out the earth's soul*, he would say in his booming voice. *And Washington's leading the charge. One of these days America will wake up and their world will be different. Someone will teach them a lesson and then they might listen.* They were just words, nothing else. Jergen was a coffee farmer, not a revolutionary.

Shannon spouted his father's rhetoric on occasion, but really, it was love, not hate, that drove his world. Love for the jungle.

And love for Tanya.

The thunder of gunfire boomed again. Tanya smiled and broke to her left, sprinting around the fields toward the firing range.

Tanya saw them when she cleared the last coffee bush—three blond Scandinavian heads bent over a rifle with their backs to her. Shannon's father, Jergen, stood on the left, dressed in khaki green. The visiting uncle, Christian, stood to the right, a brother look-alike.

The bare-chested young man between them was Shannon.

Tanya's heart jumped at the sight and she pulled up, stepping lightly.

Shannon stood tall for eighteen, over six feet, and wrapped in muscles that seemed to grow larger each day. Countless hours in the sun had darkened his skin and lightened his long blond hair. She often teased him, suggesting he take a comb to his head, but in reality she rather liked the way those loose strands fell down his neck and into those bright emerald eyes. It meant she could sweep his hair aside with her fingers, and she liked touching his face that way. His pectoral muscles flared from a rippling stomach and met broad shoulders. Today he wore only loose black shorts—no shoes on this man.

Tanya smiled at the image of being carried on those shoulders, down the mountain, while Shannon insisted she was as light as a feather.

His carefree voice drifted to her. "Yeah, the Kalashnikov's good up to a few hundred yards. But it's no good for long range. I like the Browning Eclipse," he said, motioning to another rifle on the ground. "It's good out to a thousand."

"A thousand?" his uncle said. "You can hit targets that far?"

Shannon's father spoke softly. "He can hit a quarter at eight hundred yards. He's championship material, I'm telling you. In the States he'd win anything in his class."

Tanya stopped twenty paces behind the three men and crossed her arms. For all of their manly prowess, they hadn't noticed that she was watching them from the brush. She'd see how long a woman could stand behind them without being noticed. Ten to one when they did notice her, it would be Shannon's doing. But the wind blew in her face—he wouldn't be smelling her so quickly today. She smiled and stilled her breathing.

"Show him, Shannon," his father said, holding the rifle out to him.

"Show him? Where?" Shannon took the rifle. "The targets are only two hundred yards out."

Jergen looked past his brother to the plantation's far end. "Yes, but the shed's a good way off. How far would you say that is, Christian?"

All three faced the distant structure, sitting against the tall forest. "Must be a good thousand yards. Maybe more."

"Twelve hundred," Jergen said, still looking at the small barn. "And that weather vane propped on top, do you see it?"

Christian lifted his field glasses from his chest and peered north. "That rooster? You can't expect Shannon to hit that from this distance."

"No, not just the rooster, Christian. The rooster's head."

"Impossible." He lowered the glasses. "There's no way. The best marksman in the world would have trouble putting a round there."

"*A* round? Who said anything about *a* round? That rooster there's been rusted in place for years now. I'll place money on the boy placing *three* rounds in its head from this distance."

Shannon gazed stoically at the distant target. Tanya knew he could shoot, of course. Anything to do with hunting and sport he did well. But she had to use her imagination to even see the rooster's head. There was no way this side of Jupiter a professional marksman, much less Shannon, could hit a target so far away.

The three men faced away from her, still unaware that she watched.

Shannon suddenly cocked his head over his shoulder, smiled, and winked at her.

She smiled and returned the wink. For a moment they held stares, and then Shannon returned his gaze to the rooster. Tanya took a step closer, swallowing.

"Show him, Shannon," Jergen said, glasses still at his eyes.

Shannon flipped the rifle in his hands, gripped the bolt, and chambered a round in a single smooth motion. *Kachink!*

He dropped to one knee and brought the gun to his shoulder, squeezing his eye to the scope. His bronzed cheek bunched on the wood stock. Tanya held her breath, anticipating the first detonation.

Shannon adjusted his grip on the rifle once and sank slowly to his haunches. For several long seconds nothing happened. Father and uncle stared ahead, each through their own binoculars. Tanya breathed, but barely. The air grew deathly still.

The first shot came suddenly, *Crack!* and Tanya started.

Shannon flinched with the recoil, chambered another round—*Kachink*—steadied himself briefly, and squeezed off another shot. And then a third, so close to the tail of the second that they chased each other to the target. Echoes reverberated across the valley; father and uncle stood frozen, binoculars plastered to their eyes like generals on the battlefield.

Without lowering his rifle, Shannon twisted his head and drilled Tanya with his bright green gaze. A broad smile split his face. He winked again and stood.

His uncle grunted. "My dear goodness! He's done it! He's really done it!"

Tanya walked forward and laid a hand on his arm. The breeze lifted his shoulder-length hair, and she noted the thin sheen of sweat that covered his neck and chest. He bent and kissed her lightly on the forehead.

Tanya took his hand and pulled him while his father and uncle still gazed through their binoculars. "Let's go for a swim," she whispered.

He laid the rifle against a bale and took after her.

He caught her within ten paces and together they plunged into the trees, laughing. The shrieks of howler monkeys echoed through the canopy like wailing clarinets.

"You know what the natives say?" Shannon said, slowing to a walk.

"What do they say?" she asked, panting.

"That in the jungle if you move, they will see you. Unless they're downwind, in which case they see you anyway, with their noses. Like I saw you sneaking up behind us back there."

"No you didn't!" She swung around and faced him on the path. He pulled up, pretending to study the branches. But she saw the sparkle in his emerald eyes.

Her heart swelled for him and she grabbed his head and pulled him to her mouth, kissing him deeply. The heat from his bare chest rose to her neck. She released him and glared mockingly.

"The wind was full in my face! There was no way you smelled me. Admit it, the first you knew I was behind you was when you turned around!"

He shrugged and winked. "If you insist."

She held him, wanting to kiss him again, but resisting for the moment. "Okay, that's more like it," she said, smiling, and they walked again.

"The Kalashnikov," Shannon said.

"What?"

"The Kalashnikov," he repeated, grinning slyly. "It's what I was talking about when you walked up behind us."

She stopped on the path, recalling the discussion. "Come on, you oaf." She grinned mischievously. "Beat me to the pool."

She ran past him, springing on the path ahead of him, placing each foot-fall on the squarest surface possible with each stride as he'd taught her. He could have passed her easily; could've probably taken to the trees and still reached the pool ahead of her. But he remained behind, breathing down her neck, silently pushing her to her limit. The path quickly entered thick, shadowed underbrush, perpetually damp under the canopy, forcing her to skip over the occasional stubborn puddle. Thick roots encroached on the muddy trail.

She veered to a smaller path—scarcely an indentation in the brush. The sound of crashing water grew in her ears and a haunting image flashed through her mind: Shannon standing next to the falls by the black cliffs, over a year ago. His arms had been spread and his eyes were closed and he was listening to the witch doctor's mutterings before the old bat *Sula's* death.

"Shannon!" she'd cried.

Their eyes flickered open as one—Shannon's bright green, Sula's piercing black. Shannon smiled. Sula glared.

"What are you doing?" she'd asked.

At first neither replied. Then the old bat's lips screwed into a smirk as he said, "We are talking to the spirits, my flower of the forest."

"Spirits." She shot Shannon an angry glance. "And what spirits are you talking to?"

"What is my name?" the old witch doctor asked.

"Sula."

"And where does my name come from?"

She hesitated. "I'm not sure I care."

"Sula is the name of the god of death," the old man said past his twisted grin. He waited, as if that should bring her horror. "Sula is the most powerful spirit on earth. All the witches before me took his power and his name. And I, too, have. That is why I am called Sula."

Shannon had stepped aside and was watching the man with something that hovered between intrigue and humor. He looked at Tanya and winked.

"You might think it's funny," she'd snapped at Shannon. "But I don't!" She faced the witch doctor, suppressing an urge to pick up a rock and throw it at him.

His eyes had narrowed to slits and he'd simply slipped into the forest.

She'd never told her father about the episode—a good thing because he might have come unglued over it. The *Yanamamo* tribe was known as "the Fierce Ones" for good reason—they were perhaps the most violent people on earth. And the source of their obsession with death was clearly spiritual. So her father insisted, and she believed him.

One month after the incident, Sula had died, and with him, Shannon's curiosity of his power. The tribe had buried him in the forbidden cave to three days of wailing. None in the tribe had yet worked up the courage to become Sula. To take on the spirit of death. To take on Satan himself, as her father put it. The tribe had been without a witch doctor for one year now, and as far as Tanya and her parents were concerned, that was good.

Tanya shook the memory off. It was over. Shannon was back to his old self. With Shannon still at her heels, Tanya broke from the jungle and pulled up at the cliff's edge, overlooking a waterfall that plunged twenty feet into a deep aqua pool below. Their pool.

She spun, panting. His body rushed by her, stretched out parallel, and soared over the cliff. She caught her breath and watched him fall in a swan dive before he could even see the water. If he ever miscalculated, he'd break every bone in his body on the rocks below. Her heart rose to her throat.

But he did not miscalculate. His body broke the surface silently and disappeared. For a while he didn't reemerge, and then he shot from the water and threw his long locks back with a flick of his neck.

Without a word, Tanya spread her arms and fell toward him. She broke the surface and felt the welcome chill of mountain water wash up her legs.

In that moment, free-falling into the pool's deep, she thought she had indeed come to paradise. She had been taken by her God, plucked at a young age from the suburbs of Detroit, and deposited in a jungle haven where all her dreams would come true.

She broke the surface beside Shannon. He kissed her while she still drew breath and then they struck for a sunny rock on the far side. She watched him pull himself effortlessly from the water and sit facing her, his legs dangling into the pool.

Tanya reached him and drew herself up to his knees. "Are all plantation boys as full of themselves as you?"

He suddenly reached in and lifted her from the water.

Tanya laughed and fell forward, knocking him onto his back. He put his arms over his head and lay on the warm rock. The sun glistened off tiny beads of water on his chest. She propped herself up beside him and traced the droplets with her finger.

There was nothing she could imagine as lovely as Shannon. This stunning specimen of a man with whom she was madly in love. God had brought her into the jungle seven years ago for this, she thought. To find the man she would spend her life loving. To one day marry him and bear his sons. He swallowed and she watched his Adam's apple rise and fall in his throat.

"I love you, Tanya," Shannon said.

She kissed his cheek. He drew her down and kissed her lips. "I think . . ." He kissed her again. "I really think I'm madly in love with you," he said.

"Always?" she asked.

"Always."

"Till death do us part?"

"Till death do us part," he said.

"Swear it."

"I swear it."

Tanya kissed his nose lightly.

"And I love you, Shannon," she said.

And she did. With every living cell she loved this boy. This man. Yes indeed, she thought. This was paradise.

It was the last day she would ever think it.

2

Tanya left Shannon near the pool, just after the heat's peak. She jogged most of the mile home, smothered by such contentment that she wondered if the warmth she felt came from the Venezuelan skies or her own heart.

She ran toward her parents' small mission station, and the image of a cool tumbler filled with iced lemonade filled her mind. The heat had parched her. Ahead, the tin-roofed house her father had built seven years earlier flashed with the dipping sun. Tanya had helped him paint the hardwood siding green. To blend, he'd said.

Her parents, Jonathan and Heidi Vandervan, had responded to the call of God seven years earlier when Tanya was ten. She could still see her father seated at the dinner table announcing his decision to take them to the jungle.

Her father's family lived in Germany and her mother really didn't have any family to speak of. A brother named Kent Anthony lived in Denver, but they hadn't spoken in over fifteen years. Last they heard, Kent was in jail.

Either way, leaving the United States presented no great loss for either of her parents. A year later they had landed here, in the heart of Venezuela, among the Yanamamo.

Tanya passed several buildings to her left—the radio house, a small school, a generator shed, a utility shack—and jogged to the porch.

The distant sound carried to her then, just as she stepped through the front door, a faint beating hum. She looked toward the sky to see what it was, but all she could see was the bright blue sky and a flock of birds lifting from a nearby tree. She closed the door.

Her father was leaning over a radio he'd disassembled on the kitchen table; her mother was cracking eggs into a bowl on the counter. Tanya strode straight to the refrigerator. The latent odor of kerosene fuel drifted through the kitchen, but she'd grown accustomed to the smell after so many years. It was the aroma of home, the scent of technology in a jungle hothouse.

"Hi, honey," her father called. "Want to help me put this thing back together?" He studied a coil in his right hand.

"Sorry, they don't offer electronics in my curriculum. Looks like a mess. I thought you built the toolshed for this kind of thing," Tanya said, smiling. She opened the refrigerator.

"Exactly," her mother said. "You hear that, Jonathan? The kitchen table is no place for mechanics."

"Yes, well, this isn't some lawn mower or generator here. This is a radio and radios have hundreds of very small, sensitive parts. Half of which I can't seem to find just now."

Tanya chuckled and withdrew the pitcher of lemonade.

"But they *are* here," he said. "Somewhere in this pile. If I'd torn into this mess in that shed, there's no telling where they'd run off to. You'll have your table before supper. I promise."

"Sure I will." Her mother winked at Tanya and feigned disgust.

A muffled beating flickered in the back of Tanya's mind, that same hum she'd heard just before entering. Like a moth caught in the window. She poured the yellow drink into her glass. A breeze lifted the curtain from the kitchen window, carrying with it that moth sound.

But it wasn't a moth, was it? Not at all, and that fact occurred to Tanya when the tumbler touched her lips, before she'd drunk any of the lemonade. The sound came from large blades beating at the air. She froze there, her arm cocked. Jonathan lifted his head from the radio pieces.

"What is it?" Tanya asked.

"A helicopter," her father answered. He turned to his wife. "Were we expecting a helicopter this afternoon?"

Tanya sipped at the liquid, feeling the cool juice flow down her throat.

"Not that I was aware of," Heidi said and leaned to the window, pushing the curtain aside.

It occurred to Tanya that the helicopter sounded somehow different, a higher pitch than the Hughes she'd grown accustomed to. A layered *whit, whit, whit.* Maybe two helicopters. Or more.

She lowered the tumbler to her waist, imagining five or six of the things hovering to a landing on their back lawn. Now that would be something different.

The glass in her hand suddenly shattered and she jerked. She dropped her eyes and saw that it had just crumbled like a piece of old dried lace. Glass speckled the wood floor and she thought it would have to be swept before anyone stepped there.

Then every motion fell into a surreal slowness, unfolding like dream fragments. The room shuddered, surrounding her with a rapid thumping sound as if a giant had mistaken the house for a drum set and decided to execute a long roll.

Tha-da-dump, tha-da-dump.

The counter splintered at her elbow and her father leapt from his chair. Tanya's heart slammed in her chest.

She jerked her head up and watched white holes punch through the ceiling in long ragged strings. She heard the roar of machinery scream overhead and it occurred to her that these were bullet holes in the ceiling. That bullets had slammed into the counter, ripping it apart. That a bullet had smashed her glass.

The realization fell into her mind like an anvil dropped from a high-rise crashing into concrete. She turned toward the window, stunned. An arm grabbed her midsection, throwing her to the wood floor. Her father's voice yelled above the din, but she couldn't make out his words. Her mother was screaming.

Tanya sucked at the air and found her lungs suddenly stubborn. She wondered if she'd been hit. It was as if she could see everything from an outsider's perspective and the scene struck her as absurd. She lowered her eyes to her stomach, feeling gut-punched. Father's hand was there.

"Quickly!" he was yelling. He tugged at her arm. Blood seeped from his shoulder. He'd been hit!

"Get in the cellar! Get into the cellar!" His face twisted like crow's-feet around watery eyes.

He's hurting, she thought as he shoved her toward the hall. The hall closet had a trapdoor built into its floor. He was motioning for her to climb down the trapdoor and into the cellar, as he called it. Then adrenaline reached her muscles and she bolted.

Tanya yanked the door open and shoved aside a dozen shoes littering the floor. Using her forefinger, she frantically dug at the ring her father had attached to its lip, hooked it with her fingernail, and pulled. The door pried up.

Tears ran down her father's face, past his parted lips. The chopper's engines had retreated for a moment but now they drew near once again. They were returning.

Behind Jonathan, Tanya's mother scooted along the floor toward them, her face ashen white and streaked wet. Blood dripped to the floor from a large hole in her right arm.

Tanya spun back to the trapdoor and thrust it to one side. A thought careened through her skull, suggesting that she had broken her nail while yanking on the trapdoor. Ripped it right off, maybe. Hurt bad enough. She swung her legs into the hole and dropped into darkness.

The cellar was tiny, a box really—a crate large enough to hide a few chickens for a few hours. Tanya squeezed to one side, allowing room for her father or mother to drop in beside her. The guns were tearing at the roof again, like a gas-powered chain saw.

"Father, hurry!" Tanya yelled, panic straining her throat.

But Father did not hurry. Father dropped the lid back onto the crate, *Clump,* and pitch-blackness stabbed Tanya's wide eyes.

Above, the bullets were cutting the house up like firewood. Tanya sucked at the black air and threw her arms about to orient herself, suddenly terrified that she'd come down here alone. Above, she could hear her mother screaming and Tanya whimpered below the clamor.

"Mother?"

Her father's muted voice came to her urgently, insisting something, but she could make out only her name.

"Tanya! Ta . . . ugh!"

A faint thud reached into the crate.

Tanya cried out. "Father!"

Her mother had fallen silent too. A numbing chill ripped through Tanya's spine, like one of those chain guns blasting, only along her vertebrae.

And then the hammering stopped. Echoes rang in her ears. Echoes of thumping bullets. Above her only silence. The attack had been from the air— no soldiers on the ground. Yet.

"Fatherrrrr!" Tanya screamed it, a full-throated, raw scream that bounced back in her face and left her in silence again.

She panted and heard only those echoes. Her chest felt as though it were rupturing, like a submarine hull fallen too deep.

Tanya suddenly knew that she had to get out of this box. She stood from her crouch and her back collided with wood. She reached above her head and shoved upward. It refused to budge. The door had somehow been locked!

Tanya fell back, gasping for air, stretching her eyes in the darkness. But she saw only black, as if it were thick tar instead of emptiness around her. Her right elbow pressed against a wooden slat, her left shoulder bumped a wall, and she began to tremble in the corner like a trapped rat. The musty smell of damp earth swarmed her nostrils.

Tanya lost it then, as if an animal had risen up within her—the beast of panic. She growled and launched herself elbows first toward the space through which she'd descended. Her arms crashed abruptly into rigid wood and she dropped to her knees, barely feeling the deep gash midpoint between her wrist and elbow.

Trembling, she swung her fists against the wood, dully aware of how little it hurt to smack her knuckles into the hard surface. Impulsively, as a course of reflex alone, she sprang every responding muscle and stood, willing her head to break from the grave.

But her father had built the box from hardwood and she might as well have slammed her crown into a wall of cement. Stars blinded her night and she collapsed to the floor, dead to the world.

3

Shannon Richterson had watched Tanya down the path, fighting the urge to run after her and insist she stay. She'd glanced back with those bright blue eyes twice, nearly destroying him with each look, and then she'd disappeared from sight.

She'd been gone for an hour when the distant fluttering caught his ears. He lowered the knife he'd been aimlessly whittling with and turned first one ear and then the other to the south, testing the sound carried among a thousand jungle noises. But that was just it; this beating didn't come from the jungle. It was driven by an engine. A helicopter.

Shannon rose to his feet, slipped the knife into the sheath at his waist, and jogged down the path toward the plantation, a mile south. He hadn't noticed a chopper on today's schedule, but that didn't mean anything. His father had probably drummed up something special for Uncle Christian.

Shannon covered the first half-mile at a fast run, taking time to judge his footing with each long stride. Another, harsher sound joined the beating blades and Shannon slid to a stop, a hairline chill nipping at his spine. The sound came again—a whine punctuated with a hundred blitzing detonations. Machine-gun fire!

A chill erupted and blew down Shannon's spine like an arctic wind. His heart froze and then launched him into overdrive. His legs carried him from standstill to a blind sprint in the space of three strides. He streaked over the path and covered the last quarter mile in well under a minute.

Shannon burst from the jungle fifty yards from the two-story Victorian house his father had built fifteen years earlier when they'd first fled Denmark for this remote valley. Two images burned into his mind, like red-hot irons branding a hide.

The first was the two adults who stood in the front lawn, their hands lifted to the clouds—his father and Uncle Christian. The image threw abstract details his way. His father wore khakis, as always, but his shirt was untucked. And he wore no shoes, which was also uncommon. They stood there like two children caught at play, facing west, wide-eyed.

The second image stood in the sky to his right. An attack helicopter hovered fifty feet from the earth, a stone's throw before his father, motionless except for the blur of blades on its crown. A round cannon jutted from its nose, stilled for the moment. The thing hung undecided, maybe searching the ground for a landing point, Shannon thought, immediately rejecting the notion. The whole lawn below was a landing pad.

Warning klaxons blared in Shannon's skull—the kind that go off an instant before impact, the kind that usually render muscles immobile. In Shannon's case his tendons drew him into a crouch. He stood on the edge of the jungle, his arms spread at his hips.

And then the helicopter fired.

Its first burst shifted it to the rear a yard or two. The stream of bullets cut into his father's abdomen, sawing him in two with that first volley. Shannon watched his father's upper torso fold at the waist, before his legs crumpled below him.

A high-pitched scream split the air, and Shannon realized it was a woman's scream—his mother screaming from the house—but then everything was screaming around him. The engine hanging in the sky, screaming; that nose-mounted chain gun, screaming; the jungle to his rear, screaming; and above it all his own mind, screaming.

His uncle whirled and ran for the house.

The helicopter turned on its axis and spit a second burst. The slugs slammed into Uncle Christian's back and threw him through the air, forcing his arms wide like a man being readied for the cross. He sailed though the air, propelled by the stream of lead—twenty feet at least—and landed in a heap, broken.

The entire scene unfolded in a few impossible moments, as though stolen from a distant nightmare and replayed here, before Shannon in his own back-yard. Only a small terrified wedge in his mind functioned now, and it was having difficulty keeping his heart going, much less properly processing cohesive thoughts.

Shannon stood nailed to the earth, his tendons still frozen in that crouch. His breathing had stopped at some point, maybe when his father had folded. His heart galloped and sweat streamed into his bulging eyes.

Some thoughts slurred through his mind. *Mom? Where are you? Dad, are you gonna help Mom?*

No, Dad's hurt.

And then a hundred voices began to yell at him, screaming for him to move. The helicopter suddenly sank to the ground and he watched four men roll to the ground. They came to their feet, gripping rifles. One of them was dark, he saw that. Maybe Hispanic. The other was . . . white.

The latter saw him and yelled. "The kid . . ."

It was all Shannon heard. *The kid.* In an American accent.

Something in Shannon's skull snapped then, just as the khaki-clad American lifted his rifle. He stared into that man's eyes and two simultaneous instincts flooded his mind. The first was to rush toward the bullet that AK-47 would hurl his way—speed its collision with his front teeth. He had no use for life now.

Shannon blinked.

The second instinct blasted down his spine in streams of molten fire, screaming for this man's death before his own. Shannon's muscles responded in the same instant he blinked.

He jerked to his left, snatching his knife from his belt as he moved. He lunged forward in a crouch, snarling, muttering in barely audible gutturals.

Shannon sidestepped midstride and felt the whip of slugs whirl past his right ear.

The soldier dropped to a knee and shifted his sights. Shannon dove to his left and decided there, midair and parallel to the ground, with bullets buffeting the air to his right, that it would have to be now.

At the last moment, he tucked his shoulder under, rolled topsy-turvy twice, and came to his feet with his knife already cocked. He slung the blade sidearm, carrying the momentum of his rise into the delivery.

Everything fell to slow motion then. The man's rifle still fired, following Shannon's tumble, kicking up dust just behind and below, overcompensating for Shannon's forward motion and undercompensating for his lateral movement. The knife spun, butt over blade, crossing the path of bullets, flashing once in the late sun, halfway to the man.

Then the blade buried itself in the man's chest. The soldier staggered back and struck the helicopter's opened door. The gun fell from his hands and Shannon was rolling again.

A second soldier lifted his weapon and Shannon bolted for the corner of the house—survival instincts were shouting above the other voices. He pelted full tilt, arms and legs pumping. Slugs tore into the siding an instant after he crossed into the house's shadow. Without pausing, Shannon veered to his left and raced for the jungle, keeping the house between himself and the helicopter.

Behind him a second airborne chopper began firing, its slugs tearing through the foliage ahead of him. He shifted course once, then twice, knowing that at any second one of those projectiles would smack into his back—like that, *Smack!*—and fill his spine with burning steel.

A tree just ahead and to his left trembled and splintered under a barrage of lead. He dove to his right and rolled into the forest before the gunner corrected his aim. Then Shannon was under the heavy jungle canopy, his heart slamming in his chest, sweat running down his face, but out of their reach.

Mom's in the house.

He spun back to the colonial beyond the trees. A figure inside suddenly ran past one of the rear windows, was gone for a moment, and then reappeared. It was his mother and she was wearing her favorite dress, the one with yellow daisies. Another obscure detail.

His mother's face was wrinkled with panic, lips down turned, eyes clenched. She was fumbling with the window latch.

Shannon ran four steps toward the edge of the forest and pulled up. "Mom!" he screamed.

His voice was lost in the helicopter's whine overhead.

Shannon bolted for the house.

4

Tanya quaked in the corner of the box, her mind slowly crawling from a dark dream about chain saws chewing through a bed surrounded by all of her stuffed animals, scattering white cotton fibers as it sawed. But then her parents were among the animals leaking red.

She was having difficulty knowing if her eyes were open or closed—either way she saw nothing but blackness. The memories fell into her mind, like Polaroids suspended by threads. Her glass of lemonade shattering in her hand; holes popping in the ceiling; her father crouched in the hall; her mother crawling behind on her belly; the trapdoor descending overhead.

Then darkness.

She was here, in the crate where her father had led her. He and Mother were—

Tanya snapped upright and immediately regretted it. Pain throbbed over her crown. She ignored it for a moment and reached for the ceiling. She felt the trapdoor and she shoved, but it refused to budge. It had been bolted, or something very heavy held it in place.

"Father?" she said, but the crate seemed to swallow the sound. She tried again, screaming this time. "Dad!" A breath. "Mom!"

Nothing. Then she remembered the sounds out there, before she had torpedoed into the ceiling. Smacking bullets, her mother's scream, her father's grunt.

Tanya slumped back, sucking at the stale air. "Oh, God!" she groaned. "Please, please, God."

She started breathing hard, sucking rapidly in and out like an accordion gone berserk. She clenched her eyes even tighter against the thoughts. Mucus ran from her nostrils—she could feel the trail. Tears mingled and fell on her folded forearms. Something else was wet there too, on her right arm.

She began to whisper, repeating words that seemed to still the panic. "Get a grip, Tanya. Get a grip. Get a grip."

She suddenly shivered, from her head down through her spine. And then it became too much once again and she started screaming. She arched her neck and shoved the air from her lungs, past taut vocal cords. "Help! Help!"

But nobody was listening up there because everybody was dead up there. She knew it. She groaned loudly, only it sounded more like a snort. She scrambled to her knees, gathered what strength she had, and launched herself toward the trapdoor again.

Her muscles were already thickening and she slammed into the hard wood like a sack of rocks. Tanya collapsed onto her belly.

Things went dark again.

§

Shannon cleared the tree line, headed pell-mell for his mother who had just smashed the glass with her elbow in a frenzied attempt to escape the house. She was a bloody mess.

Shannon's vision blurred and he groaned with panic. His foot caught something—a rock—and he sprawled on the edge of the lawn.

The tree at the forest edge just behind him splintered with a hail of bullets. But it didn't matter—he was down now and they could pick him off easily.

He clambered to his knees and looked skyward. The helicopter's cannon was lined up on him, ready to shoot.

But it didn't shoot. It hung there facing him.

Shannon stood slowly, quaking. Fifty meters to his right, his mom had one leg out the window, but she had stopped dead and was staring at him.

"Shannon!"

Her voice sounded inhuman—half groan, half bawl—and the sound of it sent a chill down Shannon's back. "Run, Shannon! Run!"

"Mom?"

The helicopter turned slowly in the air, like a spider on a string. Fire filled Shannon's throat. He'd seen the thing do this trick with his father and uncle. His feet wouldn't move.

He had to save his mother—pull her from that window, but his feet wouldn't move.

A streak suddenly left the helicopter. The wall above Mom's head imploded for a split second. And then the room behind his mother erupted in a thundering ball of flame.

A wave of heat from the detonation struck Shannon broadside. He stared in the face of the blast, unbelieving. The window his mom had been in was gone. Half of the house was gone; the rest of it was on fire.

Shannon whirled around and ran for the jungle, barely aware of his own movement. He ran into a tree and his world spun in lazy circles, but he managed to get back up and run on. This time he made it without a single shot. But this time he didn't care.

§

Shannon ran under the canopy, his mind numb, every sense tuned to raw instinct now. He leapt over fallen logs, dodging thorn-encrusted vines, planting each foot on the surest available footing despite his pace. He cut sharply to his right within a hundred meters. In his mind's eye, Tanya called to him from the mission, her lips screaming, stricken and pale.

Behind him, shouts rang through the trees. A sapling suddenly split in two and he jerked to the left, ducking. The staccato reports of automatic-weapon fire echoed through the jungle and he ran forward, toward the south—toward Tanya.

What if they had taken the mission out as well? How could Americans do that? CIA, DEA. His father's words about America's evils echoed through his mind. But Father was dead.

To his right, beyond the jungle's border, voices carried to him and he realized his pursuers were running along the edge of the forest, following him on even ground. They were yelling in Spanish.

Whoever they were, they were well organized. Military or paramilitary. Guerrillas possibly. They'd come intent on killing everyone on the plantation. And now he had escaped. He should turn into the jungle and run for the black cliffs. From there he could get to the Orinoco River, which snaked to the Atlantic. But he couldn't leave Tanya behind.

Then the realization struck him again—his mother and father were dead!

Tears leaked past his eyes. His vision swam and he drew a palm across his wet cheeks as he ran, barely missing a stump jutting from the forest floor. He shook his head and steeled himself against the tears.

To his right, the voices fell away and then grew again. A shot snapped through the canopy and he realized that running parallel with them was stupid. He veered to his right, leapt over a large log, threw himself to the earth, and rolled into the log's crease until his face was plastered with rotting wood and earth.

Ten seconds later they rushed by, breathing heavily. These were jungle-trained soldiers, Shannon thought, swallowing. He stood to his feet and cut straight for the mission clearing. He ran to the jungle's edge, knelt by a towering palm, and wiped his eyes again.

The mission house lay a hundred yards directly ahead. Soldiers skirted the perimeter to his far left, yelling back and forth to the others who crashed through the underbrush. He rose, intent on running across the open field to the house when he saw them: soldiers hauling several bodies through the door.

Shannon froze. He couldn't see the faces of the victims dragged to the porch, but he knew their identities already.

Shannon moved forward slowly, aware that a buzz droned between his ears. His vision blurred and he took another step.

The tree beside him smacked, and he jerked his head to the left. A slug had splintered the bark. Shouts filled the air and Shannon spun to see soldiers along the perimeter running toward him. One had dropped to his knee and was firing.

Shannon leapt back into the trees, looked back to the house once, and ground his molars. A lump filled his throat and for another brief moment he thought it might be better if they just killed him.

5

Abdullah Amir stood in what was left of the Richtersons' plantation house and stared at the smoldering hole where the bedrooms had been a few minutes earlier. He picked up a blue-and-white china bell from an end table and shook it delicately. It chimed above the crackling flames—*ding, ding, ding*. So pretty and yet so delicate.

He hurled it against the wall, shattering it.

"The Americans have no shame."

"These were not American. They are from Denmark."

He turned to see his brother, Mudah, walk through the front door. His brother had made the trip from Iran for this occasion. It made sense—the future of the Brotherhood rested in this one plan they had hatched. "God's Thunder," they had dubbed it. And it was by all measurements a plan worth a thousand such trips.

"They might say the same about you. You've just destroyed one of their trinkets without reason," Mudah said.

"And you've just killed *them*," Abdullah said.

"Yes, but for *good* reason. For Allah."

Abdullah's lips lifted in a small grin. In many ways, they were different, he and his brother. Mudah was happily married, with five children—the youngest, a two-year-old daughter, and the eldest, an eighteen-year-old son. Abdullah had never married, which was one reason he had been chosen to spearhead this mission into South America. He wasn't as devout as his brother. Mudah lived for Allah, while Abdullah lived for political reasons. Either way, they had their common enemy. An enemy both would give their lives to destroy. Materialism. Imperialism. Christianity. America.

"Yes, of course. For Allah." He looked out the window. "So now this jungle will be my home."

"For a while, yes."

"A while. And how long is a while?"

"As long as it takes. Five years. No more than ten. Worth every day."

"If it doesn't kill me first. Believe me, this jungle can drive a man mad."

Mudah smiled. "I do believe you. What I have more difficulty believing is that the CIA actually cooperated with us."

"You don't know the drug trade. I gave them enough information to indict two drug cartels in Colombia in exchange for this one small plantation. It's not so hard to believe."

Mudah was silent for a moment. "One day *they* will find it hard to believe."

Abdullah let the comment pass. They would indeed.

"Have they found the other one?" Mudah asked.

The question brought Abdullah back to their immediate concern. "If not, they will. He killed one man. And if they don't find him, I will. We can't afford survivors. It wouldn't serve any of us."

Mudah paused and looked at Abdullah. "You make Father proud, Brother. You will make all of Islam proud."

§

When Tanya found consciousness again, it was to the sound of *clunking* above her. She sat up groggily, thinking the night had ended with morning—the nightmare passed. But when she opened her eyes, darkness remained and she knew with a sinking dread that she had dreamt nothing.

The clunking though, that was new. She opened her mouth to scream out when muffled voices drifted into her box. Strange voices muttering foreign words. Her heart bolted and she closed her mouth.

Her body began to quake again. She grabbed her knees and willed it to stop.

The boots paused very near, maybe in the hall, and then they dragged something away, into the living room. She shuddered at the images the sound evoked and began to sob under her breath.

For long minutes she crouched, still, drifting between abstract thoughts. At one point the ache on her skull grew like a boulder in her mind, and she put her fingers into a gash along her crown. A sticky wetness she thought must be blood drenched her hair. She wondered what would happen if a spider laid its eggs in that gash up there. Mother had warned her a hundred times, "An insect's eggs can be much more dangerous than its bite, Tanya. You be careful in those rivers, you hear?"

Yes, Mom, I hear. But now I don't hear. I don't hear a thing 'cause you're dead, aren't you, Mother? They killed you, didn't they? She cried after that thought.

Her mind cleared slowly. A pain gnawed in her arm, and she ran her finger-tips down to a deep cut below her elbow. Now the spiders would have two places to plant their eggs. Tanya sucked deep, suddenly aware that the air in her hole was stuffy, maybe recycled already. She could suffocate—drown in her own carbon dioxide.

She reached for the ceiling again and pushed. It might as well have been a brick wall.

Her head ballooned with pain. If she had to die, a quick death would be good. But she wasn't ready to die, and the thought of dying slowly in this black box made her cry again.

A voice called from her memory—her father in his deep, confident way, "Tanya! Tanya, where are you, honey? Come to the hall; I want to show you something." It was her first week in the jungle. She'd been ten then. Father had come ahead of her and Mother to build the house. Now, after three months they'd joined him. Three months of waiting and explaining to her American friends that yes, she was leaving them for a very long time, but not to worry, she would write. She'd written three times.

"Come here, honey." She found her father looking into the hall closet and smiling proudly.

"What is it, Papa?" He'd ushered her to the spot and squatted next to her.

"It is a secret storage place," he'd said, beaming. "Think of it as a place we can hide things."

She had peered into the dark square and shuddered. "It's so dark. Why do you want to hide things?"

Her mother had intervened then. "Oh, you never mind your father, Tanya. He's just playing out his childhood fantasies. You are not to go in there. It's not safe. You understand? Never."

Jonathan had chuckled and Tanya had skipped away, giggling. There were many more interesting things in her new surroundings than a box in the ground. In fact, her father had never actually used the hiding place, at least to her knowledge.

Except now. Now he had led his daughter down in there and left her to die. The thought stung and Tanya widened her eyes despite their blindness. All right, she had to think this through or she might do just that. She might die.

For starters, she had to find a way to move in this tiny space. If she didn't stretch her joints, they would lock. Her knees were already cramping. She sniffed at the wetness covering her upper lip and ran her wrist under her nose. The walls on either side rose a mere six inches from each shoulder, and she'd established the ceiling's proximity as maybe eighteen inches above her head. She stretched her legs out. They encountered no wall and she found her first sliver of relief. She sat like an *L* with her back against one end.

Tanya reached farther with her feet, but they struck the far end of the box. She swore. Lying down straight was out. All right think. *Think!*

Heavens, listen to me. I'm stuck down in this box and I'm swearing. I don't swear. Especially when the only person who can possibly get me out of this is God. Help me, dear Father. Please, help me!

Okay, all right. What do I do? Tanya stilled and forced her mind to work logically, one step at a time.

Father, if you will let me live, I swear . . .

You'll swear what to God? As if that would make a difference.

Just let me live and I'll do anything. Anything. I swear.

The side walls were set in dirt or concrete—she didn't know which, but either way they were going nowhere. The end walls would be the same as the side walls. The floor beneath her led to even more dirt.

It was a grave.

The ceiling had already proved uncompromising, although she had only tried force. Maybe finesse would do better. Yes, finesse.

Tanya sat up and blinked in the pitch-darkness. She should explore the entire box with her fingers. Especially the ceiling—maybe she would find a lock or a crack or some simple way out of this box.

A sliver of hope brought some light to Tanya's mind. What she needed was light in her eyes, but this was a start, she thought, and she needed a start badly. She lifted her arms above her head and began walking the rough-hewn wood with careful fingertips as if she were pretending to read Braille.

"God, help me," she breathed. "I'll do anything, if you help me. Anything."

§

The thunder of a gathering storm cracked overhead as Shannon fled for his life. Less than a hundred meters to his rear, the shouts of men were drowned by the sky's booming voice.

The rain came quickly, in sheets, just as Shannon approached the steeper grades ascending to the cliffs. Now would be a good time to return home, he thought. Mother had said they were having seven-bean soup for supper and he loved seven-bean soup.

The thought struck him like a wedge to the forehead and ignited a string of images. His heart leapt to his throat and he sobbed, but quickly cut off his breath. Not now. Not now.

Shannon had run under these trees many times, often ignoring the path and scrambling through the jungle, laughing with Yanamamo Indians chasing his heels. Of course, those times had been times of play. The sun had been shining then, the jungle floor visible, and the foliage dry. Now the rain carried rivulets of mud down the steep slopes.

He glanced down the mountain and saw blurred figures no more than seventy meters behind. He veered off the path and lunged for the steep incline to his left. Through the steady downpour, he heard muffled shouts followed by a *Pop!* The weapons' fire came in close succession then, ripping through the air like a string of firecrackers.

His foot dug into the soft embankment and found a root. With the greenery around him crackling at the sound of flying bullets, he leapt into the jungle and began clawing his way up the incline. He crested the slope and launched himself forward, panting hard and shaking from exertion. The black cliffs rose above the canopy.

Heavy pounding drifted through the leaves behind him—the sound of helicopters. So they had joined in the pursuit! They would cut off the cliffs.

Shannon came to a full stop in a clearing at the base of the cliffs. The stark contrast between heavy green jungle and the sheer black shale towering above sparked an image of a tombstone rising from a cemetery lawn. The cliffs couldn't be climbed except in two well-marked passes.

He rested his hands on his knees and gasped for breath in the thin mountain air, thankful that for the moment the rain had ceased. The beating of blades warned of the heavy pursuit.

Shannon turned his tear-streaked face to the jungle below. He'd left them for the moment, but they would find him quickly. He had to think. His heart thumped in his chest like an overworked pump bleeding through blown seals.

The pond! He hadn't been to the water hole in over a year, but maybe he could hide there.

Shannon grabbed a handful of grass and quickly wiped the mud from his soles. Keeping his eyes on the trees, he ran parallel to the forest, leaping from rock to rock.

He had managed two hundred meters before the sound of chopping rotors pushed him back into the jungle. He jogged through the trees along the black cliffs without breaking pace, occasionally catching glimpses of the helicopters unloading men onto the cliffs.

He reached a small, muddy pond, dropped to his belly, pried his eyes to the sky, and then snaked out of the jungle. A clump of brush consisting of little more than twisted, broken reeds floated in the middle of the pond. Shannon slipped into the stagnant water, submerged himself, and swam for the clump. He surfaced in a small cavern formed by the brush and grasped a root.

Thin shafts of light filtered through the mass of broken reeds above. He spat at a large *Durukuli* lizard, closed his eyes, and shook his head at the swelling of tears in his eyes.

Voices barked around the water's perimeter. He held his breath and forced his muscles to relax. The feet padded by and passed into the brush. For the moment he was safe.

He swallowed hard as he stared past the unmoving lizard that sat flicking its tongue. The sound of sweat dripping from his chin and into the water echoed through his ears, like the passing of seconds leading nowhere. *Drip, drip, drip.*

Then images of the attack began to draw gauze over his mind again. He just wanted to go home, now. It was over, wasn't it? It was all over. He should go home before darkness drew the snakes.

But he couldn't move. He let more tears—streams of them—run over his face and he found some comfort in those tears. Nobody could see him. Soon though, he would have to do something.

Soon.

§

Tanya collapsed to her rear end, thoroughly stuffed with dread. She'd spent long chunks of time walking the box with her fingertips. The minutes faded into hours, but they could actually have been only seconds. It was that kind of feeling: a strange confusion staring relentlessly into midnight, but knowing morning must have come. And gone.

She had found no way out.

Besides the small crack around the trapdoor, her fingers had felt only parallel lines separating exactly eight stacked boards on all four sides of this crate. She'd estimated each board at eight inches in height. That would make the box just over five feet deep and roughly the same in length. Five by five by three, she thought. A good size for a grave. Big, actually. Now the Egyptian tombs— there were some serious graves.

But this couldn't be her grave. Not really. She was only seventeen! And her father had meant to *save* her, not bury her alive! She began to cry in steady streams. Her shoulders shook with the emotion as she wept.

Oh, God. Why? What have I or my father or my mother ever done to deserve this? Why would you allow them to die? Just tell me that, if you are so loving and so kind.

She lifted a dirt-packed nail to her lips and chewed. The dirt ground between her incisors, like tiny pieces of glass that sent shivers down her back. They were so innocent, her parents. So loving and patient. They gave their lives for others. For her.

Please, Father, save me. I will do anything.

Tanya's mind began to crumble. She had come to the end of her senses. There were no more meaningful tasks to occupy her fingers. Her nostrils were stuffed with the musty smell of decay; her ears heard only weak sobs; she could taste nothing but her own leaking mucus.

A thousand pinpricks of light flashed in her forehead, like star bursts on the Fourth of July and she thought it might be because her brain was tearing loose from its moorings. Her hands trembled like those of a very old man in desperate prayer and her eyes began to ache. They hurt because they had rolled back into her skull, from where they had a better seat for the fireworks. Her mouth yawned, exhaling stale air.

Then she heard the screaming.

It started low and distant like an approaching train blowing its horn, but quickly grew to a shrill screech, as if the train had thrown on its brakes and slid uncontrollably forward.

It occurred to her that the sound was hurting her throat and she realized that the scream came from her.

She was screaming. It wasn't a yawn at all—it *was* a scream. Sometime during that scream she fell asleep. Or passed out. They were the same down here in the box.

It was then, as she lay dead to the world, that the first vision came, like a bolt out of heaven. In a single white flash, bright sky blossomed above her. The darkness was gone. And there, huddled in the box, Tanya gasped.

She was like a bird high in the sky, circling a clearing in the jungle far below. Such relief, such contentment washed through her that she shuddered in pleasure. Silent wind rushed past her; bright sky made her squint; the smell of jungle rose wet and sweet. She smiled and twisted her head.

This is real, she thought. *I've become a bird or an angel flying high over the trees.*

A yellow bulldozer snorted gray smoke as it carved a swath of trees leading to a large square field to the north. The plantation. Shannon's plantation. And directly below, the mission.

She dipped her wings for a closer look. A stick house was being built in the center of the clearing. The tall blond-headed man working there leaned judiciously over a table saw and Tanya recognized her father immediately. His bright blue eyes glanced to the sky, smiling. He lifted a hand, as if he wanted her to come to him, and then he leaned over the saw once again.

But this was all very strange. She had never seen the mission or the house before its completion. And now through a bird's eye she saw each detail. She saw that he had carefully placed the roof joists with eighteen-inch centers for added strength; she saw that one of the windows lay cracked on the floor, waiting replacement. She saw that he had rested several large timbers against the corner and now one of those timbers slipped toward him.

With sudden alarm, she realized that the timber would smash into her father, and she screeched a warning. Jonathan pried his eyes to the sky, saw the falling timber, and dove from its path with scarcely an inch to spare. Wide eyed, he rolled to his feet. For a moment he stared at the timber in disbelief, obviously shaken badly. He lifted his eyes to the bird hovering above—to Tanya—and he smiled.

"Thank you, Father," he whispered.

And then, as if speaking directly to her, he said, "Remember, always look past your own eyes."

The sky suddenly went black, as if someone had flipped a switch.

Only no one had turned out the lights. She had just opened her own eyes. And in the box there was no light.

Tanya breathed raggedly and curled up into a ball, wishing desperately that she could slip back into the bright sky where she could look past her own eyes.

6

The small cavity under the clump grew dark as dusk settled over the mountain jungle. Relentless chopper blades passed back and forth, low over the trees. Twice he heard men arguing over how to proceed. Twice they had skirted the pond, cursing.

For the past twenty minutes the air had remained quiet. Shannon had decided that he had to get over the cliff to the river beyond, and he knew where he could climb it along a narrow crack. But another image had taken up residence in his mind. It was the old shaman, eyes black and piercing, a black jaguar's fur draped over his head, tapping a crooked cane. He was mumbling in low gutturals—reciting the old legend of how man had been formed from the blood of a wounded spirit as it fled skyward, mortally wounded.

"From blood to blood," the old man's voice croaked. "Man was born to kill. It is why the spirit of death is the strongest. Sula."

A chill ran along Shannon's spine. *You were right, Sula*, he whispered.

Then go.

Shannon blinked in the darkness. *Go?*

To the grave.

His fingers trembled and he wasn't sure if it came from the cold or from this thought whispering through his mind. The grave was strictly forbidden. It could mean death. Or it could mean power, to the next witch doctor. None of his friends had ever dared venture within a thousand meters of the cave where the tribe had buried, not only Sula, but a whole line of witch doctors before him.

Shannon swallowed. But what if he could take that power and avenge his parents' deaths? Another voice whispered through his mind. Tanya's. And it was telling him not to be a fool.

But Tanya was dead, wasn't she? Everybody was dead. He began to cry again, desperate and shaking in the cold water.

He made the decision on impulse, as much out of fear and destitution as anything else. He would go to the cave.

Shannon sucked a lungful of air, submerged into the cold water, and swam for the bank. The perimeter was clear when he surfaced and stood on the grass. He ran toward the black cliffs, pushed by a numbing determination now—a singular desire to dive into the Sula's power. For comfort or for revenge or just for his own sanity, he wasn't sure, but he ran faster as he neared the old cave.

Large fruit bats beat their huge wings in near silence overhead. Insects screeched. The looming black rock cast a foreboding shadow, even in the dark, hiding the moon.

He broke out into the clearing, thirty yards before the cave, and stopped. A human skull hung over the entrance—Sula's first victim. They had retold the story at his burial amid cries that wailed through the jungle like forlorn trumpets. The skull belonged to a woman who had wandered too far from her own tribe. Sula said she had come to cast a spell on their village and he'd taken a rock to the back of her head. He'd been fourteen.

Shannon stared into the cave and fought a sudden panic crashing around his ears. He took an involuntary step back, swallowing.

"Sula," he whispered. "Sula."

A cold breeze rustled the leaves over his head, sending a chill deep into his bones. The cave looked like a dark throat. Like the cliff was actually a face and the hanging skull was its one eye, and the cave was its yawning mouth. The natives said that the cave reached an endless abyss of black space where the spirits had first lived. Hell itself.

An image flashed in Shannon's mind, and he blinked. It was Mother, screaming past the window of the house. Begging him to run for his life.

Shannon swallowed and walked for the cave. Tears filled his vision and he marched on. He felt as though he were walking over a cliff.

"Kill me." He ground the words out past clenched teeth.

And then he was stumbling forward, his head thumping with blood.

"Kill me!" he screamed. He ran for the hole, gripped by a maniacal frenzy. He scooped up a handful of rocks and hurled them into the cave.

"Kill me! Kill me!"

Shannon stopped, legs spread. He was in the face of the cave, five feet from the mound of dirt that covered Sula. The shaman's crooked cane stuck up at the grave's head, like a dagger. A bleached jaguar's skull hung on the cane—fangs white, eyeholes black.

Shannon's muscles began to twitch with horror. It was the kind that starts deep in the marrow and spreads out to the bones and burns the flesh from the inside. He knew then that coming here had been a mistake. He was going to die.

Cold wind blew past his face, lifting his long hair. A low moan pushed it through the opening, out into the silent jungle. His legs quaked and he dropped to his knees, breathing heavy now.

"Sula . . ."

Touch the grave.

He began to sob.

Touch the cane.

Shannon spread his arms wide and lifted his face to the cave's rock ceiling. His body heaved with torturous sobs that rang through the chamber.

The cane, you spineless worm! Touch the cane!

With a final cry that sounded more like a long groan, Shannon threw himself at the grave. He scrambled over the mound and dove for the cane. His hands seized the crooked pole and he fell flat, facedown, his torso hitching in soft sobs.

The power came like an electric current, silent but unmerciful.

A wave of raw energy ripped down his back, contracting it with rapid pulses that seized his lungs and bent his spine backward like a bow. His head and his feet jerked a foot off the ground, straining to reach back and complete an impossible arc. For a full five seconds, his body convulsed, threatening to snap his back in two. He could not breathe; he could not utter a single sound; he could only drown in the power that swallowed him.

And for a moment he was sure that he was indeed drowning.

With a soft popping sound, it released him and his face thudded to the dirt. His mouth was open, and he could taste the earth, but as far as he was concerned, he was dead.

§

Tanya shriveled in the corner, unraveling. Twice now the lights had stuttered to life in her mind, each time revealing the same blue sky and the same clearing below. The images came suddenly, like the flash of a bulb hung buzzing in her brain for a minute or two and then vanishing. She imagined a monk in a monastery cellar pulling a huge switch, like on a Frankenstein movie she'd seen once at Shannon's house. Maybe that was her, Lady Frankenstein, only when the switch was pulled, her body didn't rise from the table. Instead she saw visions.

Now they came again.

Her father was down there again, working diligently, this time setting those beams that had almost fallen on him. Otherwise the scene appeared the same as the two previous episodes. A bulldozer chugged in surreal silence, the hammer swung by her father, the spinning of a saw—none with sound. And always bright blue skies and vivid green jungle. Flocks of parrots drifted above the canopy.

A voice rose to her. "Remember, always look past your own eyes." She looked down and saw that her father had lifted his chin to her. *Well, what does that mean, Father?* But she couldn't ask, because she wasn't really there with him. She was a bird or something, flying around.

But the scene had a sense of truth with it, as if she were looking at her father, months before she'd come to Venezuela. As if what she saw in the framed house was actually how he'd built it.

Now a memory joined her thoughts. She was sitting at the table of their newly constructed home and Father was telling them about how God had kept him safe those three months. And more specifically, he was telling them a story of how he'd almost been smashed by a falling beam. But a dove from the sky had screeched and he'd looked up just in time to see the beam.

It was the voice of God, he'd said.

Tanya twitched in the corner of the box and pulled her knees closer. *Heavens! That really happened,* she thought. *That wasn't part of my dream—Father told us that story. And now I'm hallucinating that it was me in the form of some bird— maybe a dove—that warned him.*

Maybe the mind played these kinds of tricks just before it died. Or maybe she was actually there, watching.

Either way, Father was telling her to *look past her own eyes.*

7

Shannon came to his senses ten minutes later. But they weren't really his senses at all, were they? Well, yes, they were his, but his senses had changed, hadn't they?

He pushed himself to his knees, and then to his feet. The taste of copper filled his mouth—blood from the fall. He swallowed and shivered with a sudden passion. At first he didn't know what had changed—he only knew that he couldn't stand waiting any longer. He had to get out of this cave and up the cliffs.

The cane still stuck out of the grave, like a big toothpick. The wind still sailed past his cheeks and his breathing still echoed in the dark chamber. But somehow it all seemed a bit simple to him. He turned around and faced the jungle.

"Sula," he whispered. It was time to go. Shannon ground his molars, spit blood to the side, and ran into the night, unable to contain the hot rage that boiled through his veins.

That was it—his sorrow had given way to a bitter fury. That was the difference in him. He stopped and looked around at the dark jungle. An image of the old witch doctor, grinning with twisted lips, flashed through his mind. It was true, then. Sula lived.

Shannon felt a finger of fear crawl up his back.

A sudden dark fog crowded his mind and he blinked in the night, disorientated. Where was he going?

Oh, yes. He was going to the cliffs. He was running away. But that hardly made sense. He should go back to the plantation and do something!

No, he should escape. Then he would do something. What, he had no idea. He was only eighteen. A mere boy. A boy with Sula.

Shannon reached the black cliff, spit into his hands, and started to climb. It rose two hundred meters into the dark sky, lighted occasionally by the moon, which peered through passing clouds. Night creatures chirped in disjointed, overlapping chorus, millions strong.

Despite the cool night air, the climb quickly coaxed streams of sweat from Shannon's pores. The thin crack he'd often studied as a possible ascent path rose like a dark scar in the dim light. Using his hands as a wedge in the thin crack, he picked his way up the rock surface. With proper climbing shoes the task would have been tricky. Only because his bare feet were calloused did he manage it now.

"Sulaaaa . . ."

He'd climbed a full hundred meters without any major problems when the crack began to thin. He paused, blinked the sweat from his eyes, and pressed on.

Within another ten meters the gap closed to a paper-thin seam that stopped at a small ledge jutting from the smooth surface above. Another hundred meters of cliff loomed above him. He couldn't back down now, not without rope. A chill ran down his spine, and he breathed deep to steady his nerves.

He walked the face of the cliff with his fingers.

Nothing.

Shannon stared again at the ledge above, his heart now pounding like a piston engine. It was one foot, maybe eighteen inches beyond the nearest hand-hold. Reaching it would require him to release the hold securing him to the face. Missing it would send him plummeting to his death.

An image stilled his breathing: a man free-falling with his arms and legs stretched to the sky, screaming. Then a sickening *thud*—a large boulder at the base breaking the fall like a fist to the back.

The image brought a twitch to his lip. He grinned softly.

"Sulaaaaa . . ." *You're a sicko, Shannon. Sicko.*

He looked at the ledge above him. He lunged upward with every last muscle sprung taut and his toes digging against the rock. He slapped his right hand against the cliff face above him.

Nothing.

He felt only flat stone. No ledge.

His body slid down the smooth cliff surface, his fingers digging hopelessly for a grip. His fingertips lost contact with the stone surface altogether. He was free-falling and his heart ran clear up into the roof of his mouth.

Then the ledge filled his hand and he locked onto it, shaking violently. Trembling so bad that he knew he would shake loose unless he found a better hold. Dangling from three fingers, he swung his left hand up as high as he could and managed to grip the same ledge.

He hung for a few moments and then edged his way along the shelf. There had to be a way up somewhere.

He inched his way farther. Again nothing. The ledge narrowed. His fingertips crowded the cliff surface. If the edge played out . . . well, if the edge played out he would die, wouldn't he? Smashed for the vultures on the rocks below. Panic spiked up his neck, threatening to erupt in his skull. He hung totally helpless. He could not go back; he couldn't descend; he couldn't climb. His life hung on this one ledge and this time the realization started his bones quaking.

Stretched to the right as far as his arm allowed, his fingers crossed a fissure and he froze. The crack? He inched his fingers a little farther and the break deepened—deep enough for him to work his hand into.

Shannon took a deep halting breath, thrust his hand into the rift, clenched his knuckles to make a wedge, and swung out into the dark abyss before him, dangling from his right fist. His hand held.

He looked down at the bottomless drop below his feet and thrust his left hand into the opening over his right to create another wedge. He hung like that for a full minute, gasping at the night air for breath. His knuckles stung and his lungs refused to fill, stretched as he was. He began hauling himself up, hand over hand.

His knuckles were bare and his hands were slippery with blood when he pulled himself over the top. Catching his breath, he rolled to his back behind a group of boulders. Pain throbbed up his arms. He lay still, numb and confused.

Muffled voices suddenly carried on the wind. Shannon bolted upright and caught his breath.

Again, a man calling and then laughing.

Shannon crept to the boulders and edged his head over its rim for a vantage point. The night scene ran into his mind in one long stream of images. A fire bending in the breeze a hundred meters ahead, west. Two dozen faces glowing in its light. Behind them, a helicopter—no, two choppers, like buffaloes feeding on the rock. Supply packs sat scattered about the camp, propping up weapons. A single man stood on guard, hands on hips, twenty meters off.

Shannon breathed deep, knowing immediately what he would do as if his whole life in the jungle had prepared him for this one moment.

A strange beckoning called. A desire, whispering in the night, urging him forward. He swallowed, still scanning the scene before him, his blood now surging through his veins. Not so much in anger, he noted with mild surprise. A craving.

A new picture rolled through his brain, slow motion. A scene of him flying parallel to the ground, hurling his knife sidearm.

The steel flashing through the air while he was still airborne.

Bet you were surprised, huh, boy? And here you thought you were going to plug me with a bullet or two. A faint smile drifted across Shannon's lips.

Sula . . .

Then the image was gone, leaving only black sky in his eyes. He pulled his head back and blinked. He scrambled across the small clearing and soundlessly leapt over its rim. He ran around the boulders, staying low to the ground. The guard stood with his back to him, bent over cupped hands, a rifle slung on his right shoulder. The outline of a knife hung loosely at his hip.

The man turned his back to the wind, facing Shannon, his head still bowed to his hands. Shannon held his breath. A flame flashed once unsuccessfully, lighting the guard's browned lips pursed around a fresh cigarette. He would later wonder what could have possibly possessed him to go then, so suddenly, with hardly a thought. But Shannon went then, just before another flame lit the man's face.

He sprinted on his toes, directly toward the glowing face, knowing the light would blind the man momentarily, knowing the wind carried away what little sound he made. He covered the twenty yards in the time it took the guard to light his cigarette and draw deep once, with his head tilted back.

Carrying his full momentum at the man, Shannon slammed his left palm under the raised chin and snatched the man's knife from its sheath in one abrupt motion. He lunged forward after the back-pedaling man, stepped into the reeling body, flipped the blade in his hand, and jerked it across the exposed neck before the man had gathered his senses for a cry.

He hadn't planned the steps to the attack—he'd simply seen the opportunity and gone. Blood flowed from the guard's jugular, spilling to the stone. The dangling cigarette momentarily lit the man's bulging eyes and then tumbled from his lips. The guard crumpled in a heap and then flopped to his back, his boots twitching between Shannon's spread legs.

What's happened to you, man? You're a sicko.

Yeah, a sicko.

Shannon reached for the man's rifle, wrenched it free, snatched an extra clip from his belt, and ran for a large boulder ten meters to his right. He slid to his knees, panting.

No sounds of pursuit carried in the night. He quickly checked the weapon in his hands, found a round chambered, and snapped the firing selection to single shot. It was an AK-47; he'd fired a thousand rounds through one like it down on the range. From long distances the weapon could only scatter hopeful fire, but within a couple hundred meters, Shannon could place a slug wherever he wanted.

He slid up the boulder and studied the camp, no more than seventy meters away. The men still talked around the fire. The helicopters were old Bell machines, identical to the one Steve Smith used to shuttle supplies to the plantation.

A spark ignited in Shannon's mind. "You know why they never used the Bell in conflict?" Steve's voice came. "Because of the fuel tank," and he'd pointed to the pod hanging on the tail boom, just under the main engine. "That there tank's made of steel." He'd smiled. "You know why steel's no good?"

Shannon had shaken his head.

"Because steel gives off sparks. It had better stop a bullet, 'cause if the bullet goes through you're gonna have one heck of an explosion. *Kaboom!*" Steve had laughed.

Shannon drew a deep breath and lined his sights up with the exposed fuel tank under the tail boom of the old Bell. He could easily place a bullet into that skin. *Kaboom!* And what if it didn't explode? They would be over him like a swarm of bees.

You just killed a man back there, didn't you? Yeah, and you still have his blood on your fingers. You're definitely a sicko.

Shannon fought a sudden surge of nausea. He closed his eyes and fought for control. The black fog swarmed his mind. For a moment he felt disoriented, and then he was okay. He glanced around in the night. Yeah, he was okay.

He snugged his finger on the trigger, but it shook badly and he took another deep breath. He applied a little pressure to the trigger.

The Kalashnikov suddenly jerked in his arms, crackling in the calm night air.

A thundering detonation lit the dark sky, mushrooming with fire. The helicopter's tail section bucked ten feet into the air, flipped once as it rose, reached its apex, and slowly fell. He removed the rifle's butt from his cheek and gazed, open mouthed, at the sight. Then the flaming wreckage crashed to the ground, and pandemonium erupted in the camp.

Shannon quickly pressed his eye back to the sights and swung the weapon to his left. Black silhouettes jumped about, scrambling for the rifles. Shannon exhaled, lined the sights with one figure, and pulled the trigger.

The gun jerked against his shoulder. The man fell to his knees and threw his arms to his face, shrieking.

Then Shannon began to shoot on count—one, two, three, four—each time pulling the trigger, as if the dancing silhouettes were clay pigeons and he in a head-to-head contest with his father. Five, six, seven, eight . . . On all counts but one—count six, he thought—a man staggered.

When he reached the twelfth count, the firing pin clicked on an empty chamber. The guerrillas fled toward the jungle now. Shannon yanked out the spent magazine, slammed another into the rifle, chambered the first round, and swung the weapon to bear on the fleeing men. He squeezed off shots in succession, barely shifting the rifle to acquire each new target. All but one lurched forward midstride and fell to the ground short of the jungle. Only one escaped, number seventeen. Two, counting number six.

Shannon's heart hammered in his chest. Adrenaline flogged at his muscles and he staggered to his feet, his eyes peeled in the night, his fingers trembling.

He blinked. Where was he? For a horrible moment he didn't know. He was on the top.

A voice groaned near the burning, twisted wreck that had been a helicopter, and it all came back like a flood. He'd killed them, hadn't he? *Sicko Sula.*

He threw the weapon down and tore for the trees. He would go now, he thought. To the river. To safety. And then he didn't know to what.

§

For the fourth time the switch to the strange visions had been thrown, and Tanya was floating above her house. Each time, her father had worked alone down there. Each time, his voice was the only sound she heard. Each time, it said, *"Look beyond your own eyes,"* as if it was information she needed.

Well now, what exactly could that mean? For starters, she could not *look* anywhere—she was trapped in her black box, dying. She could most definitely not look *beyond,* because there was no getting beyond the box. That was the whole problem. Father was saying look beyond, but he had locked the box. And as for the *own eyes* bit, well, she wasn't positive she had eyes any longer.

So the dream was nonsense. Unless it wasn't a dream. What if she were really seeing her father down there and he was really telling her to look? Imagine that! Now, what would that be? A vision, maybe?

Tanya heard a thumping below her, down on the ground near the house. Then it occurred to her that the sound came from her own chest, not from the dream or vision. Her breathing thickened and she might have shifted, but she'd lost touch with most of her body so she couldn't be certain. The parts she could feel moaned in protest. Her throbbing arm, her aching head, her bent spine.

If this were a vision or some episode of reality, then she should follow her father's suggestions, shouldn't she? She should look beyond her own eyes. Maybe look through the dove's eyes, if indeed this was a dove through which she peered. And what could she see? The clearing, her father, the house with all its framework.

Look *beyond.*

A thought struck her and she dove toward the house. Her heart now filled her ears. Why hadn't she thought of this earlier? If this were real, then she should be able to see the closet that Father had built. And the crate below. Her crate. Maybe she was already in the crate!

She swooped low and flew between the rafters—through the living room to the framed hall. The stick closet looked tiny without siding. The box rested in the floor, minus its trapdoor. Sure enough. There it was. Her box. Or an image of her box. Either way it didn't matter—she didn't see anything new here. Only a box that should have been labeled *The box in which I will lock up my only daughter until she dies.*

She hovered for a moment and then fluttered down into the closet—into the box. She might as well see the thing well lit. Knowing what kind of box sealed her fate might be a juicy tidbit, a welcome morsel in her last moments.

The box looked very much like the one her fingers had helped her imagine. Except one small detail. There was a hole in one end. *Father has not yet covered this one end,* she thought. *He'd better cover it. It won't do to have snakes crawling through that there tunnel, 'cause someday I'm gonna be in this box.*

Tunnel.

The image of a tunnel hit her head on, like a sledge to the forehead. Her head rang like a gong, setting off a vibration that hurt her teeth and buzzed down her spine.

Instantly Tanya awoke, wide eyed, gasping raggedly. For a brief moment she stared into darkness, trying to remember what had woken her. Then she jerked upright and spun to the wall at her back. The episode had revealed this wall as a door leading into a tunnel—she knew that now. It was the kind of door that snugged in place. She would have to pull at it, the one thing she had not attempted in her despairing hours.

Tanya whimpered and scratched at the stubborn wall. And what if the whole dream had been just that? Hallucinations spun by a despondent mind. She dug at the wood, willing her nails to find purchase. A long sliver ran under her right index fingernail and she gasped. Suddenly furious, she shifted back and slammed her right heel into the base of the wall.

It caved.

Warm, stale air filled her nostrils. It *was* a tunnel!

Quaking with anticipation, she ignored the passing thought that creatures might have taken up residence in the passage. She yanked at the twisted wall, slid it behind her, and scrambled into the earthen hole.

Like a wounded dog, she dragged herself on all fours away from the box. Away from that death crate. Where the passage led she lacked the strength to imagine, but her father had laid it in before the house had been completed. He wouldn't end it in a pit of snakes.

Tanya slopped through the muddy tunnel for a long time. A very long time, it seemed. Three times she encountered furry things that scurried off. Many times she heard tiny feet retreat before she reached them. But she was far past caring about minor details. Life waited at the end of this tunnel and she would reach it or die trying.

And then she did reach it, so suddenly that she thought someone had flipped that switch in Frankenstein's cellar again and initiated another episode. But the fresh air pouring over her head suggested that this was no vision. Night had fallen, the crickets screeched, howler moneys cackled, a jaguar screamed— she had reached the outside!

Tanya spilled from the tunnel, past wadded brush, ten paces from a river. The *Caura*, she thought. A small dock confirmed her guess. The tunnel had surfaced south of the mission, near their dock. Tanya stood slowly, forcing her crippled muscles to stretch past their newly memorized limits. Then she stumbled forward, to the pier, to a canoe still swaying in the water. The Caura River fed within ten miles into the Orinoco, which then ran toward the ocean. Toward people.

She rolled into the wood craft, nearly tipping the whole contraption over, and ripped the tie-knot free. The river drew her out into its current slowly and she flopped to her belly.

Then Tanya surrendered to the darkness lapping at her mind.

§

Shannon ran all night. Up from the cliffs to the top of the mountain, and then down toward the river that would take him to the sea and to safety. The Orinoco, ten miles downriver, over the mountain from the plantation.

The jungle lay heavy and the night dark, making his progress slow. But then it would also slow down any pursuit. He ran in silence, lost in the fog of the last day. His bones ached and his muscles felt shredded by the miles of savage terrain. The cruel ground had bruised his already calloused feet. But one thought pushed him forward: the thought that he would come back one day and kill them all. Every last one of them and any living soul that had anything even remotely to do with them. Shove a bomb down their throats maybe.

The sun already climbed the eastern sky when he finally burst into the clearing that bordered the gorge. The sound of thundering water exploded in his ears. He approached the deep valley and peered down at the torrential river as he placed a hand on the rope bridge to steady himself.

The Orinoco River had cut a two-hundred-foot swath into the valley floor. An old trail on the opposite side switched back and forth to the river below. The only way across was on the old rope bridge that swung precariously over the two-hundred-foot gap. He'd decided he was going to cross the swinging bridge, descend to the river, pick his way past the rapids, and then find something—a canoe, a large log, anything—to sail down the river.

He looked at the boards strapped together on the bridge. The wood appeared rotten—the hemp rope frayed. The whole contraption looked as though it might go into the water at any moment.

In fact, even as he looked a piece of wood split and sent a small fragment tumbling lazily to the river.

He watched it fall. He would have to watch his footing as he crossed. Then another board bucked, splitting to its pale core, as if an invisible ax had attacked the wood.

A chill flashed up Shannon's spine. It all sprang to his mind in a brief instant: the fact that the wood wasn't crumbling but being hit. By bullets!

He spun around.

The helicopter fired from a long distance—too far for accuracy—but it bore in quickly. The sound of its whirling blades was swallowed by the rapids, but Shannon couldn't mistake the flashes erupting from its nose.

For a moment Shannon stood shocked by disbelief, unable to move. In that moment another board fell to pieces, two meters from his planted feet. Two options streamed through his mind: He could retreat to the forest or he could race forward, across the bridge.

With a sudden roar the gunship spun overhead, climbed sharply, and kicked its tail around. It was lining up for a second pass.

Shannon leapt to the bridge. He grabbed the rope and scrambled down the sagging span, but the sudden movement caused the bridge to lurch wildly under his feet. In a moment of panic he almost missed the rope entirely and then found it quickly. To his right the attacking craft lined up on the bridge for another pass.

Crossing had been the wrong choice—he knew it then, when the first bullets took a chunk from the board at his feet. He should have run back to the forest. Now he stood in the open, helpless, with a cannon playing the planks like invisible fingers on a keyboard.

He was going to die!

The thought immobilized him.

§

The pilot watched the boards disintegrate before the boy and he eased the stream of lead to the right, knowing now that he could hardly miss.

"Finish him!" Abdullah said beside him.

The pilot quickly refocused his fire. The young man suddenly jerked back as if a huge hand had slammed into his chest. A spray of red blood glistened through sunlight. They had him!

He flipped backward over the rope that supported the bridge and tumbled lazily through the air, his hands limp like a puppet's. The fall alone would have been enough to kill a man, but neither of them could miss the gaping, bloody hole in the boy's side.

Abdullah groaned and the pilot blinked at the sound.

And then, far below, the body splashed into the current and disappeared.

"Around," Abdullah ordered. Sweat poured from his face. His black hair with its distinctive white wedge lay plastered against his skull. "Around. We have to be certain."

The pilot guided the helicopter around to look for the boy. But the pilot knew he was wasting his time.

The boy was dead.

8

Eight Years Later
Monday

"Good morning, Bill."

"Good morning, Helen. You sound good."

"I have news."

That made the pastor pause. "What kind of news?"

"It's starting," Helen said. She paused. "Evil is thick in the air and it's about to take this country by storm."

"I'm pretty sure those were your exact words eight years ago."

"I told you then and I've told you a hundred times since that the death of Tanya's parents was only the beginning."

"Yes, Helen, you did tell me. And I've prayed with you. For eight years. That's a long time."

"Eight years is nothing. God's playing his pieces in this chess match and really I think it began fifty years ago. They've been moving and countermoving for decades up there on this one."

"A chess match? I hardly think we're pawns in some game."

"Not a game, Bill. A match. The same match cast over each of our hearts. And you're right—we're not simply pawns. We have a mind of our own, but that doesn't mean God isn't telling us to move two spaces to the right or one space forward. Actually, it's more like a whisper to our hearts, but it's the thunder of heaven. It's up to us whether we will listen to that thunder, but make no mistake, he moves the match. In this case, the match started way back. And one of the moves was for Tanya's parents to go as missionaries to Venezuela. To bring truth to the Indians, yes, but perhaps even more, to bring Tanya there, so that she could become who she is."

"You honestly believe that Tanya's parents were called to the jungle, left their church with great hopes and prayers, struck off for Venezuela, lived among the Indians for ten years, and then were murdered for the effect it would have on their daughter? Who, incidentally, is not looking like a great prophet or any such thing these days."

"Yes, Bill. I do think that was one of the primary purposes in all of this. Yes, that is how God works. A missionary is called to Indonesia perhaps as much for a young boy they talk to in the airport in New York on their way out of the country, than for all the people they preach to in the next twenty years in the foreign land. Perhaps that boy is a Billy Graham or a Bill Bright. God is quite brilliant, don't you think?"

Her pastor was silent on the phone.

"But Tanya's time is coming, Bill. You will see. It's coming soon."

§

Tanya Vandervan sat flatfooted in the wooden chair, aware that her palms were sweating despite the cool air spilling from the vents mounted above. She shifted her gaze to the room's single window overlooking Denver's skyline from ten stories up, thinking that even here, within the whitewashed walls of Denver Memorial, she hadn't managed to escape the jungle. Eight years earlier she had fled a heavy jumble of green, only to be led into a tangled web of confusion in her own mind. And now she had found another jungle—these concrete structures outside her window, built up around her like a prison.

Thank God for Helen.

She moved her eyes back to the older men sitting like a panel of judges behind the long table. The medical review board of Denver Memorial Hospital consisted of these three dressed in white smocks. They knew her as Sherry. Sherry Blake. Dr. Sherry Blake, six months and counting in the hospital's intern program.

And by their frowns, six months too long, and counting far too slow. Most in the medical profession had emerged out of the stuffiness that had characterized hospitals in the seventies—these men had somehow missed the boat.

Sherry crossed her legs and nervously ran a hand behind her neck. Her hair fell in soft curls to her shoulders now—no longer blond, but brown. It swept across her forehead, above eyes no longer blue but darkened to a hazel color. The idea had been her own, five or six years ago, based on the notion that if she changed her name and her appearance, maybe then, with a new identity, she could escape her mental turmoil. Maybe then she could escape haunting memories of Shannon. The psychobabble quacks had tried to discourage her, but she'd lost confidence in them long before.

The idea had grown on her, until she'd become obsessed with altering her identity. She legally changed her name, dyed her hair, and wore hazel contact lenses. The change was so dramatic that even Helen had hardly recognized her. Comparing her high-school graduation picture to her new image in the mirror, even Tanya—Sherry—could barely see the similarities.

"What I think Dr. Park is suggesting, Miss Blake, is that there's a certain behavior becoming of doctors and other behavior that doesn't fit the image very well." Ottis Piper removed his eyes from her and peered through his glasses to the paper before him. "At least the image Denver Memorial considers acceptable. Boots and T-shirts are not part of that image."

Sherry raised an eyebrow, teetering precariously on the fence between total submission to these in white coats and bull-frank honesty.

She knew submission would bode well for her career. *Suck it up, baby. Swallow all their nasty foolishness with a yawning gullet. Tell them what they want to hear and get on with your life.*

Whatever's left of it.

Bull-frank honesty, on the other hand, might give momentary satisfaction but would most probably leave her wishing she had swallowed their nonsense after all. Unfortunately, the chill now washing over her head seemed to have frozen her mouth, and no matter how desperately part of her wanted to apologize, she could not.

"Oh? Are you dissatisfied with my work, Dr. Piper? Or is it just this image thing that has you in stitches?"

That set the gray-haired British import back a few inches. His eyes expanded.

"I'm not sure you understand the nature of this review, Miss Blake. We're here to discuss *your* behavior, not ours." His accent bit off each word precisely and Sherry found herself wanting to reach out and shove something into that mouth. A sock, maybe.

Her mind was urgently suggesting she retract herself from this insane course. After all, interns sucked up. It was a skill learned in med school. Suck-up 101.

"I apologize, Mr. Piper. I spoke too soon." She attempted a polite smile, wondering if it looked more like a snarl. "I will pay more attention to the way I dress, although in my defense, I've worn boots and T-shirts only once, last week, on my day off. I came to visit a patient who needed a hand to hold."

Director Moreland watched like an eagle from his side perch, not unfriendly necessarily, but not friendly either. Park, the last of the trio, spoke. "Just watch your dress, Miss Blake. We run a professional institution here, not a recreational park."

"Professional? Or militant? Dress isn't an issue in most hospitals anymore. Maybe you should get out a bit more."

Piper peered over the bifocals he'd mounted on his nose and cleared his throat. "It seems we have a matter of slightly greater importance to discuss. In the past two weeks you've fallen asleep three times while on duty. One of those times you missed a patient call." He paused.

"Yes," Sherry said, "I'm sorry about that."

"Oh, I don't think it's as simple as sleep, Miss Blake. I think it has more to do with the *lack* of sleep." Sherry's fingers felt suddenly cool, drained of blood. Where was the Brit headed with this?

"You see, lack of sleep is a problem with our profession. Tired doctors make mistakes. Sometimes big ones—the kind of mistakes that kill people. And we don't want to kill people, do we now?"

"What happens to me out of this place is none of your business," she said.

"Oh? You're denying you have a problem, Miss Blake?" Piper queried smugly.

She swallowed. "We all have trouble sleeping now and then."

"I'm not speaking of now and then. I'm speaking of every night, my lady."

"I'm not *your lady*, Piper. Where did you hear about this?"

"Just answer the question."

"I don't think it's any of your business whether or not I have trouble sleeping. What I do in my home is my problem, not yours."

"Oh? I see. So if you come to work sloshed, we should just turn an eye as well?"

"I'm not coming to work sloshed, am I? I intend on finishing my internship with full honors. Someday people like you will report to people like me."

"You are out of line!" Piper whispered harshly. "Answer my questions! Isn't it true, Miss Blake, that you depend on medication to keep you awake at work? For all practical purposes, you're a drug addict!"

Sherry sat speechless, trembling behind her calm facade.

"Is this true, Sherry?" the director asked from her left.

She looked past him, through the window. A horn blared in the parking lot—some patient on edge. "I'm not a drug addict. And I resent the suggestion. I've had my problems with insomnia," she said, swallowing again. For a moment she thought her eyes might water. That would be a disaster.

"But it hasn't kept me from getting this far," she said evenly.

"How long have you had this condition?"

"A while. A few years. About eight, I suppose."

"Eight years?" Park spoke again.

"How bad are the episodes?" Moreland asked.

"By what standards?"

"By any standard. How much sleep did you get last night?"

She blinked, thinking back to the restless night. An easy night, all things considering. But they wouldn't think so.

"Two hours."

"And the night before?"

"Maybe two."

He paused. "And that's normal?"

She shifted her eyes to him now. "Yes, I guess it's fairly normal."

"For seven years of medical school you've averaged two hours of sleep a night?"

She nodded. "Pretty much."

"How?"

"A lot of coffee . . . And medication when it becomes unbearable."

"So how did all this begin?" Moreland asked.

His sympathy would be her only hope now, she thought. But she'd never done sympathy well. The realization that she was lowering herself into those waters with these sharks made her swallow.

On the other hand her boat was about to capsize anyway.

"When I was seventeen, my parents were killed," she said, looking back out the window. "They were missionaries in Venezuela, among the Yanamamo. Guerrillas wiped out the mission and a plantation nearby. I was the only one who survived. They killed my mother, my father, a good friend, and his parents." She cleared her throat.

"I spent a few days locked in an underground box without realizing that it opened to a tunnel that I managed to escape through. I think I may have slept through two or three nights since." She shrugged and looked at Moreland. "The memories keep me awake. Posttraumatic stress disorder."

"I'm sorry," Moreland said. "Have you had any progress?"

"For short periods, yes. But never without relapse." Memories of therapy drifted through her mind—hundreds of hours of the stuff. Each hour spent carefully retracing her past, searching for that switch they hoped would turn all this off. They had managed to pull the shades a time or two, but never a switch.

Sherry looked at Piper and saw that his lips no longer pressed together. His eyes had softened. Maybe the human being in him was surfacing. She looked away, not wanting to see his pity.

"You lived with family after that?" Moreland asked.

"I lived with my adopted grandmother, Helen Jovic, until I went to med school. My uncle's mother-in-law, if that makes any sense. She was the most helpful despite all her antics. More helpful than all the quacks since then."

"But none of this has helped?" Moreland pressed.

"No," Sherry answered. She suddenly wondered if telling them would be her undoing. The whole hospital would be buzzing with rumors about the intern who woke up screaming each night because her parents were slaughtered when she was a kid. Poor girl. Poor, poor Sherry.

She shifted in her seat. "And if you wouldn't mind, I'd really appreciate you keeping all this to yourselves. I'm sure you understand."

"I'm afraid it isn't quite that simple." Piper, the Brit, was speaking. "I'm afraid you have more to fear from yourself than from others." Sherry faced him and saw the dispassionate look in his eyes. Heat flared up her back.

"Meaning what?" she asked.

"Meaning, irrespective of what others think or say of you, Miss Blake, the fact remains that you are a danger to your own career. And to others. A condition as severe as yours that depends on a regular dose of *uppers* will one day kill a patient, and we simply cannot have that at Denver Memorial."

"I've given my life to becoming a doctor. You're not actually suggesting—"

"I'm suggesting that you need a rest, Sherry. At least three months. We're talking about the lives of patients here, not your precious little ego. You missed a call last week, for goodness' sakes!"

Sherry felt a chill wash over her skin. Three months for what? To see one more quack? She stared at the man for a full ten seconds, thinking she was losing her mind. When she spoke, her voice held a tremor.

"Do you have any idea how many hours of study it takes to finish at the top of the class, Mr. Piper? No, I suppose you wouldn't because you finished near the bottom, didn't you?"

A twitch in his right eyebrow indicated she had struck a chord there. But it didn't matter now. She had gone too far. Sherry stood to her feet and turned to Moreland. Every bone in her body wanted her to scream, "I quit!"

But she couldn't, not after seven years in the books.

She drilled him with flashing eyes, spun on her heels, and strode from the room, leaving all three doctors blinking.

9

There was only one living soul who knew of Shannon Richterson's true fate. Only one man who knew how he'd really died eight years earlier. He knew because he, too, had come from Venezuela, farther down the same river that Shannon had fallen into after being shot. What he knew about the killers who had attacked the jungle that fateful day might have done wonders for Sherry Blake.

There was only one problem. Even if he had known about Sherry, he was not exactly the sensitive kind of guy who cared. In fact, he himself was a killer.

His name was Casius, and while Sherry was stomping out of Denver Memorial, he was standing at the end of a CIA conference table in Langley, Virginia, glaring at three seated men, suppressing a sudden urge to slit their throats.

For a brief moment, Casius saw a familiar black fog wash into his vision, but he blinked and it vanished. If they'd noticed, they hadn't shown it.

They deserved to die, and one day they *would* die, and maybe, just maybe if things fell his way, he would do the killing. But not today. He was still playing their game today.

That was all going to change soon.

He turned away from them. "Let me tell you a story," he said, walking toward the window. The thin one, Friberg, was the director of the CIA. He wore thin lips under a bald head. His eyes were dark.

Casius faced the group. "Do you mind if I tell you a story?"

"Go ahead," Mark Ingersol said. Ingersol, the director of Special Operations, was a heavyset man with slick, black hair. David Lunow, Casius's handler, just stared at him with an amused glint in his eye.

Casius met Ingersol's gaze. "Last week you sent me to kill a man in Iran. Mudah Amir. He lived in a rural house and spent most of his time with his wife and children, which made the task a challenge, but—"

"He was a monster," Ingersol said. "That's why we sent you."

Heat flashed up Casius's spine. Ingersol was right, of course, but he had no right to be right. Ingersol himself was a monster. They were the worst kind of monsters, the kind who killed without bloodying their hands. "Excuse the observation, but I don't think you know what a monster is."

"Anyone who blows up one of our embassies is a monster, in my book. Get on with it."

"You send me to kill. Does that make you a monster?"

"We don't send you to kill innocent—"

"The innocent always die. That's the nature of evil. But it doesn't take a man foaming at the mouth to fly a plane into a building. It takes a man dedicated to his war. An evil man, maybe, or a godly man. But evil is not exclusive to the Mideast. The monsters are everywhere. Maybe in this room."

"And *I'm* a monster?" Ingersol said.

Casius ignored him. He turned from them and closed his eyes. "I had to wait two days for the wife and children to leave before I killed Mudah Amir, but that wasn't the point."

He took another deep breath, calming himself. In truth if Mudah was a monster, then so was he. Yes, a monster.

"Mudah didn't die quickly." He turned back and stared at them for a few seconds. "Do you know how easily a man can be made to talk when you've removed a finger or two?" Casius asked.

"Mudah told me of a man. An Abdullah Amir—his brother, in fact. He spit in my face and told me that his brother, Abdullah, would strike out at America. And he would do it sooner than anyone might suspect. Not an unusual threat from a man about to die. But what he told me next did catch my attention. Mudah insisted that his brother will strike at American soil from the south. From Venezuela."

Director Friberg's eyes flickered, but he held his tongue.

Casius walked back to the table and rested a hand on the back of his chair. "I wouldn't bother you with the sole confession of a man about to die. But I have more."

Casius took a settling breath. "You know of a man named Jamal Abin, I'm sure."

The name seemed to still the room. For a moment they replied only with their breathing.

"It's our business to know about men like Jamal," Ingersol finally said. "There's not much to know about him. He's a financier of terrorism. What does he have to do with this?"

David spoke for the first time. "I believe Casius is referring to the reports circulated that Jamal was behind the killing of his father in Caracas."

"Your father was killed in Venezuela?" Ingersol asked. It hardly surprised Casius that the man didn't know. His history was known only by David, who'd first recruited him.

"My father was a mercenary employed in the drug wars in South America. His throat was slit in a Caracas nightclub, and yes, I believe Jamal was ultimately responsible for his death. Not personally, of course. Jamal isn't one to show his face much less kill someone himself. But now he's left a trail."

They sat there, not comprehending.

"After I killed Mudah, I searched his flat. I found a safe stashed under the bed in his room with evidence that ties Jamal to him and his brother, Abdullah." Casius pulled a folded sheet of paper from his pocket, unfolded it carefully, and slid it across the table.

"What's this?" Ingersol asked.

"A receipt for a million dollars delivered to Mudah, earmarked for Venezuela."

They studied the wrinkled sheet and passed it around. "And you're saying this *J* is Jamal's signature."

"Yes. It ties Jamal, the 'financier of terrorism' as you call him, to Mudah's brother, Abdullah. I would say that this lends some credibility to our dying man's confession, wouldn't you?"

No one responded.

"It's not really that complicated," Casius said. "Jamal is a known terrorist. I'm holding evidence that ties Jamal to Abdullah, who evidently has a base in Venezuela. I say that's a pretty strong case."

Ingersol frowned and nodded. "Reasonable."

"There's more. The safe also contained a document that detailed the location of Abdullah's base. Interesting enough by itself. But the location in question, an old plantation, was overrun by an unidentified force roughly eight years ago. A Danish coffee farmer, Jergen Richterson, and his family were killed along with some neighboring missionaries." Casius fed them the classified details and watched Friberg's eyes narrow barely.

"According to your own records, there was no formal investigation into the attack. Of course there were no survivors to push the matter either. Unusual, don't you think? I believe the information I have leads to Abdullah Amir, and I believe that Abdullah will lead me to Jamal."

Casius paused. "I want Jamal."

"Do you snoop around our files on a regular basis?" Friberg asked quietly. "Where's this document that supposedly shows Abdullah's base?"

"I have it."

"You'll turn it over."

"Will I? I want the mission."

"I'm afraid that's out of the question," Friberg said. "The fact that Jamal may have been involved in your father's death creates a personal link that precludes your involvement."

"Yes, that's your policy. Still, it's what I'm demanding. You either assign me to run a reconnaissance mission to the region, or I do my own."

"You do nothing on your own, boy." Friberg's neck flushed red. "You do what we tell you or you do nothing. Is that clear?"

"Crystal. Unfortunately, it's also unacceptable."

Casius faced Friberg down. He'd thought that it might come to this and a part of him welcomed it. He had hoped they would let him go—Jamal was a high-profile threat. But if they refused he would go anyway. That was the plan. That had always been the plan.

"Do you have the location with you?" Friberg asked.

Casius smiled, but he said nothing.

"Then you have twenty-four hours to turn it in. And don't push us."

"Is that a threat?"

"That's an order."

He had done well up until now, playing by their rules. But suddenly the heat in his head was mushrooming and the black fog was swarming. Casius felt a small tremor race through his bones.

"Good. Then I won't threaten you either." His voice was shaky and his face had grown red—he could feel it. "Just a word of caution. Don't push me, Director. I don't do well when pushed."

Silence engulfed them like hot steam. David glanced nervously at Ingersol and Friberg. Ingersol looked stunned. Friberg glared.

Casius turned and headed for the door.

"Twenty-four hours," Friberg said.

Casius walked out without responding.

It had started. Yes, it had definitely started.

10

On most nights, Sherry read until one or two in the morning, depending on the book, depending on her mood. She would then nibble on some morsel from the kitchen and climb into bed, prepared to endure the last waking hour before sleep introduced the evening's haunting dream—the same one that had presented itself to her every night for the past eight months. The beach one.

But not tonight.

Sherry's roommate, Marisa, had come home at eight and heard an earful about Sherry's review before the board. After storming out of the hospital, Sherry had roamed the park, trying to make sense of this last wrench thrown into her cogs. She'd nearly called her adopted grandmother, Helen, but then she discarded the idea. There was no living soul wiser than Helen, but Sherry wasn't sure she was ready for a dose of wisdom.

All in all, the day had been a disaster, but then so were most of her days.

Marisa had gone to bed at ten and Sherry had curled up with a novel just after that. But that was where the familiar ended and things started going topsy-turvy.

The room lay quiet below her. That was the first topsy-turvy thing. Not that it lay quiet, but that it lay *below* her.

The second topsy-turvy thing was the figure sprawled on the armchair, with arms and legs flopping over the sides like some couch potato who'd passed out after one too many beers. But the figure was no couch potato. It was her. She was sleeping on the armchair, her chest rising and falling in long draws, her mind lost to the world. A blue blanket lay across her waist. She didn't remember anything about getting herself a blue blanket.

The third topsy-turvy thing was the clock. Because it read eleven o'clock and that figure there on the couch—Sherry—was indeed asleep. At eleven o'clock. Which was impossible.

Then another tidbit struck Sherry: She was floating above it all, like a drifting angel looking down on herself, like a bird soaring overhead. Like a dove.

Like eight years ago in the box!

A warm glow surged through her belly at the thought. If she really was sleeping and not dead from a heart attack, then this episode must be a vivid dream of some kind. Most definitely not a nightmare, which was another topsy-turvy thing, because she didn't know how to dream without having a nightmare.

And yet here she was, floating like a dove over her slumbering body at eleven o'clock in the evening!

Topsy-turvy.

Then suddenly she wasn't floating like a dove over her slumbering body. She was soaring through a bright blue sky high above an endless forest like a bat out of hell. No, like an angel from heaven. Most definitely an angel.

Wind streamed past her eyes. She heard nothing, not her own breathing, not the wind. Then she was above a jungle paradise. Flocks of parrots flapped silently, several hundred meters below.

Parrots. Jungle. And then Sherry knew that she was in Venezuela again, flying over the tropical rain forest. Her heart rose to her throat and she dipped closer to the trees. Memories flashed through her mind. Images of jogging through this forest, of swimming in the rivers and running hand in hand with Shannon over the plantation. A warm contentment rushed through her veins and she smiled.

Below her, the jungle yielded to fields and she pulled up, startled. It *was* the plantation! She recognized the rows of coffee plants as if they were still there, a week before harvest, beaded red under the sun. To her right the old mansion rose white from the fields; as she swooped to the left, she could see the mission station resting in the afternoon sun, undisturbed. Neither clearing showed any signs of life.

The sight made her tremble, hanging in the air like a dove on a string. What was this? The beginning of a nightmare after all? But even her nightmares had never played this vividly.

Then a sign of life twitched at the corner of her vision and she turned toward the shed topped by the rooster Shannon had shot. The weather vane still graced the metal building, pierced head and all. But it wasn't the rooster that had moved; it was the door that now swung open, pushed by a young man who stepped out into the sun.

Sherry spun to him and immediately drew back, stunned. It was Shannon! An adolescent with long blond hair, a reincarnation of the boy she'd lost in the jungle eight years earlier. Her heart hammered in her chest and she drew shallow breaths, afraid to disturb the scene below. Afraid he might see her and turn those green eyes skyward. She didn't know if she could manage that without breaking down.

And then suddenly Shannon did turn those green eyes skyward. He smiled at her!

Her heart stopped; her breathing ceased. Whatever body she possessed quaked in the sky. A thousand voices collided in her mind. The nerve endings in her fingers and toes rattled madly.

Then the forest rolled up beneath her, like a canvas prepared for the tube.

Sherry bolted up in the armchair, her eyes wide open, her breath now coming in quick short gasps. She jerked her head about the room.

Her mind began to connect scattered dots into an image. She was in her apartment again; drool edged down her cheek; Marisa stood over the sink in the kitchen; daylight streamed through the windows; the clock on the wall now read seven o'clock. Those were the dots, and together they said she'd just slept through the night!

And she'd had another vision. Like the one that she'd had in the box eight years ago.

Sherry stood to her feet, still trembling. The blue blanket fell to the floor. What could be the meaning of such a vision, anyway?

"Marisa?"

"Good morning," her roommate called politely from the kitchen.

Sherry staggered over to the kitchen, running her hand over her head as if that might clear her thoughts.

Marisa turned and studied her with a raised brow. "You okay?"

Sherry ran her eyes about the room, still collecting herself. "I slept through the night," she said as much to herself as to her roommate. "Without a nightmare."

Her roommate stilled her hands in the sink.

Sherry continued, as though still in her dream. "And I had a vision, I think."

Now Marisa turned to face her, quickly drying her hands on a towel. "A vision? You mean you dreamt something."

"Maybe, but it was different from the ones on the beach. It was like the dream I had in the box when my parents were killed. I was floating above all this stuff and seeing things that were real, in real time. Like the clock, it read eleven, and I was sleeping on the chair. Did you cover me with a blanket?"

"I came out to get a drink at about eleven and saw you asleep. I didn't want to wake you, so I just pulled it over you."

"Yeah, well I saw the afghan on me."

The dream came back to Sherry in full color now. She remembered the boy and she felt her heart lift. Shannon! Only that couldn't have been real time, because he looked unchanged from the last day she'd seen him.

"I saw Shannon," she said and her voice trembled slightly.

"You always see Shannon," her roommate said.

"No. I've *thought* about him a lot, but this is the first time I've seen him." Sherry sat on a stool, her mind abuzz. "And I slept through the night—without a nightmare. That says something."

"Well, I can't argue with that. Maybe standing up to Piper yesterday did some good after all."

"That's not it. Although I think I just might agree to their three-month medical leave—somehow I can't see working with them now."

Marisa dipped her hands back into the dishwater. "So you're saying this was an actual vision. Like the kind your grandmother supposedly has."

"I don't know. But this wasn't just a dream."

Her roommate raised a brow and wiped a green plate. "You actually saw Shannon this time. Really saw him, huh?"

"He was younger than he would be now. But it felt so real."

"You never saw his body . . ."

"That's what I'm saying. I actually saw him—"

"No. I mean after he was killed. You never saw Shannon physically dead."

"Please, we've been over this a dozen times. He's dead. Period. I'm not going to open up old wounds." She'd said the same many times, but the argument didn't feel as strong in light of her dream. He had been alive there, hadn't he?

"You say that, but I'm telling you, you don't have closure. How do you know he was actually killed back there, if you didn't see his body?"

"Don't be stupid." Sherry turned to the window, remembering. It had been some government man who'd told her the plantation had been overrun, the Richtersons killed. Drug infighting. "Everyone knows that he was killed."

"Then verify it again. Track it down again. Official knowledge of his death. People have been tormented for years by lingering doubts, and from what I can see, you fall into that group. You're still having dreams about him, for crying out loud!"

"I *do* have official knowledge," Sherry said.

She clenched her eyes and tried to think reasonably. The very idea that he might still be alive cut at her like a knife. A thousand hours of therapy had placed him in a small corner of her mind—always there, always vivid, but small. Now he was suddenly coming back to the surface, and she could not allow a dead past to retake her mind. It would be worse than her nightmares.

A lump the size of a boulder pressed painfully in her throat and she cleared it. "I don't want to go there again."

But suddenly she knew that she did have to go there again. If for no other reason than the fact that she'd had this crazy dream. She had to at least verify his death again. Now that the issue had risen from the grave, she would either have to live with its haunting or bury it once again. The realization blared loud like a horn.

Sherry swallowed and steeled herself against further sentimentality. God knew she had been through worse than this. Much worse.

"How would I verify it?"

"Call the government. Living relatives."

"Most of his family came from Denmark."

"Then living relatives in Denmark. Your mother was American, right? We can find an agency who tracks foreign deaths. Can't hurt."

Sherry nodded. They would only confirm his death.

11

The twenty-four hours Director Friberg had given Casius to turn over his findings had come and gone. Casius had only gone. That was the problem. But then it really wasn't such an unusual problem—not with Casius.

David Lunow sat across from Mark Ingersol, gazing through the tinted window at the CIA complex, suddenly wishing he'd brought the car after all instead of riding his bicycle. An ominous black sky dumped rain over the hills of Virginia, masking the skyline. Ingersol sat stoically with greased hair and furrowed brow. The door suddenly opened and Friberg walked in. He didn't bother to apologize for keeping them waiting. He simply strode to the head of the table, sat carefully, and pulled his sleeves down, one at a time.

"So, we have a problem, I take it," he said and then looked up at David.

"It appears so."

Friberg glanced at the assassin's red portfolio that lay square in front of Ingersol.

"Suggestions?"

Ingersol spoke, "Maybe he's outlived his usefulness."

"Sir, if I may," David said, "Casius is the most active operative we have."

"*Active* is not synonymous with *useful,* David. An operative is only useful if he can follow simple directions. It appears your man has a problem with that. He's beyond control. Perhaps it's time we put him aside."

A chill spiked at the base of David's skull. *Put him aside?* They all knew you didn't just "put aside" assassins. You didn't just give killers lunch money and drop them off at the next bus stop. You eliminated killers. Otherwise they might very well end up in your own backyard, killing someone you didn't want killed.

David cleared his throat. "He's on the edge, but I wouldn't characterize him as out of control."

Ingersol and Friberg both stared at him without responding.

"I really don't see a reason to terminate him."

"I think the man has outlived his invitation at the agency," Friberg said.

David blinked. "If you'll pardon me, sir, I don't see it that way. A man who does what Casius does *needs* a kind of reckless confidence. We've lived with it for seven years."

Ingersol cast a questioning glance at Friberg and it occurred to David that in all likelihood neither of these men knew the facts about Casius. He reached for the red folder and opened it.

"We know who we're dealing with," Friberg said.

"And I know him better," David continued before they could stop him. "I knew of Casius's father—went by the name Micha. A sniper for hire who was best known for picking off half a dozen cartel bosses. When his father was killed in that nightclub, Casius was eighteen. He had his father's touch, to say the least. He came to us one year later. He had no living relatives, no property— nothing. Wanted a job. We put him through our training regimen, but believe me, Casius didn't need our training. We might have taught him a trick or two, but he was born to kill."

"He's unstable," Friberg said. It sounded more like a command. Like saying, *The trash is full,* when you really mean, *Take the trash out.*

"Actually, he's very much in control of his decisions."

"The man doesn't even distinguish between us and the people we pay him to kill. You heard him. In his mind we're all monsters."

"He's a killer. You accuse another killer of being a monster and you're accusing him of being a monster. That's understandable." David paused. "Look, very few agents have the ability to operate at his level. And with that come a few unavoidable consequences, I agree. But you don't just replace a man like this every day. We could go ten years without finding his equal."

"I don't care if it takes twenty years to find his equal—we can't afford a rogue agent digging around where he has no business digging." Friberg glared at him. "If Casius becomes a liability, we have no choice but to unplug him. I'm surprised that concerns you."

"If he becomes a liability, maybe. But I don't think we've reached that point. What if he does take Jamal out? Do we have a problem with that?"

"That's not the point. His motivation is personal and he's out of control."

"I disagree," David said.

The director turned to Ingersol. As the head of Special Operations the decision would ultimately be Ingersol's. "And you?" Friberg asked.

Ingersol pulled the red folder toward him. An eight-by-ten photo of Casius, with short black hair and bright blue eyes, was paper-clipped to the left flap. Ingersol studied the photo.

"You think you can draw him in?" he asked David.

"I can always draw him in. I'm his handler."

"Then bring him in again."

"And if he won't come in?" Friberg asked.

No one answered.

Friberg stood. "You've got another twenty-four hours," he said and walked from the room.

§

The room was beneath the earth, shrouded in blackness. Only one man knew its location and in reality no one knew that man. His name was Jamal. They hated him or loved him, but they did not know him.

Well, yes, there were those who knew his face and his voice and his money. But they didn't know *him.* They didn't know his loves and his desires and all the reasons why he did what he did. If they knew his passion, it was only the passion to strike out. To exact his revenge.

But then Jamal could not imagine life any other way.

A small ticking sound echoed softly through the darkness. He'd sunk the ten-by-twenty room into the earth and the water sometimes found its way through the rocks. In a way the sound was comforting. A sort of gentle reminder that the clock was winding down. The time was so close now. So very close.

The smell of musty dirt crowded his nostrils. A twenty-watt bulb glowed under a copper shade on his desk, casting a rust-colored light over the ancient wood. To his right a large cockroach skittered across the wall and stopped. Jamal stared at it for a full ten seconds, thinking that a cockroach had the best of all lives, living in its own darkness without thought for more.

He walked to the wall, snatched up the insect before it could move, and quickly pinched off its head. Jamal returned to the desk and set the roach on top of the hot copper shade. Its headless body twitched once and then stilled.

Jamal pulled on his headset and punched a phone number into the pad before him. The electronics along the wall to his right were the kind one would expect in a submarine perhaps, not here in this dungeon. But there was more than one way to remain hidden from the world and Jamal possessed no desire to sink beneath the waves every time he wanted to pull his strings. Of course, bringing the electronics here, of all places, had not proved a simple matter. It had taken him a full year to pull it off without raising suspicions.

The protected signal took thirty seconds to find its mark. The voice that spoke into his earpiece sounded as though it came from the bottom of a well. "Hello?"

"Hello, my friend."

The man's breath stilled. Jamal's voice had that strange effect on men.

A shiver rippled through Jamal's bones. "It is ready?"

It took a few seconds for the man to respond. "Yes."

"Good. Because the time has come. You will begin immediately. You can do this?"

"Yes."

"Listen very carefully, my friend. We can't turn back now. No matter what happens we cannot turn back. If anything happens that might threaten our plans, you will accelerate them, do you understand?"

"Yes."

Jamal held the man in silence for a moment. He picked the roach from the shade and pulled its wings off. The body had been slightly baked and a smell similar to burnt hair rose to his nostrils. He bit the thorax in two and rolled the one half in his mouth, allowing saliva to gather. He put the other half back on the hot shade. Only breathing sounded in his earpiece.

"Perhaps you're forgetting who you're speaking to, Abdullah," Jamal said, and then spit out the bug. "If you cease to please me, I will unmake you as easily as I made you."

"You did not make me. I did not need your interference. I could have done this without you."

A swell of black rage swept over Jamal. He blinked. "You will die, for that, my friend."

More breathing in the earpiece.

"Forgive me . . . I am anxious."

Abdullah had finally said what he had always felt, from the first day Jamal had approached the Brotherhood to give him logistical control over their plans in Venezuela. He had not come from their circles and they had questioned not only his loyalty, but his usefulness. It had taken him three months to gain their confidence and persuade them that his involvement was critical to the success of the plan. It *wasn't* critical, of course—Abdullah would have pulled it off without him. But they knew as well as he that Jamal knew too much and was too powerful to ignore. And in all reality, Jamal had altered the plan to meet his objectives. As such it was a better plan. Infinitely better.

"Please forgive me." Abdullah's voice was raspy over the line.

Jamal abruptly cut the connection.

For a few seconds he sat there, silent under the significance of what they had accomplished. A wave of heat washed through his chest. He peeled off his headset and put his face into his hands.

A mixture of relief and hatred rolled through his mind. But really it was more like sorrow, wasn't it? Deep, bitter sorrow. The emotions surprised him, and they were joined by another: fear.

Fear for allowing such emotion. He began to shake.

Jamal lowered his head and suddenly he was sobbing. He sat alone in his dungeon, trembling like a leaf and crying like a baby.

12

Wednesday

Sherry's eyes slammed open and she bolted up, her chest thumping loudly in the still morning. The sheets about her lay soaked with sweat.

For a few endless seconds the world seemed to have frozen and she wasn't sure how to make things move again. Half of her mind was still back there, in the jungle, where she'd just died.

"Marisa!"

Sherry threw the linens from her legs and swung to the floor.

"Marisa!"

The apartment echoed vacant. Marisa had already left for the university. The analog clock by her bed read 8:15, but it felt like midnight, and in all honesty, Sherry wasn't positive she was actually awake yet.

Panic swarmed around her mind. She'd come face to face with . . . what? What had she just seen?

"Dear God . . ." The prayer sounded like a groan. She ran for the kitchen and threw water on her face. "Oh, God . . ."

She had been back in the box. After eight years of nightmares, she had actually gone back. And her fingers trembled with the stunning reality of it.

Helen.

Sherry jerked up and caught her breath. Yes, of course! She had to talk to Helen!

She paced the kitchen. "Okay . . . Okay, slow down." She gripped her trembling fingers into fists and breathed deliberately. "You're awake. This is not a dream. It's morning." No, this wasn't a dream, but neither was what she had just seen. Not a dream. She wasn't sure what it was, but it was real. As real as anything she had ever experienced. As real as the box.

Sherry ran for her bedroom and pulled on a pair of jeans. Helen would know, wouldn't she? She'd had visions. *Dear God, what are you doing to me?*

Only when she pulled her Mustang into that old familiar driveway in front of Helen's two-story home did she think of calling first.

She walked to the front door and rang the bell.

No one answered. She rang again. Sherry was about to pound when the door swung open. Helen stood leaning on a cane, yellow dress swaying at her knees.

"Well, well, speak of the devil," Helen said.

"Hello, Grandma."

"You've finally decided to come."

Sherry smiled, suddenly off balance. "I'm sorry. I know it's been a while. But—"

"Nonsense. Timing is everything."

Sherry blinked. "I have to talk to you."

"Of course you do. Come, come." She shuffled back and Sherry entered. The house smelled of gardenias and the white roses Helen claimed came from Bosnia.

Sherry followed the older woman into the living room. Helen had taken her in and loved her like a daughter. But she hadn't been ready for love at first.

"Tea?"

"No, thank you."

"Do you know why I frighten you at times, Tanya?"

"Frighten me? You don't frighten me." Sherry sat and watched Helen settle into her overstuffed rocker. "And it's Sherry, remember? It was hard enough changing my name once; I have no intention of doing it again."

"Yes. Sherry. Forgive me." Helen picked up her own glass of iced tea and sipped. She set it down and looked into Sherry's eyes. A knot rose slowly up her throat. It was like that with Helen. She hadn't even said what she'd come to say, and already Tanya was feeling the significance of her presence.

"Let's not kid each other. I do frighten you at times. But then if I were in your place, I might be frightened as well."

"What place is that?"

"You're running. I ran once, you know. When I was about your age. It was a terrifying experience."

"I don't think that I'm running. I may not be as spiritual as you, Grandma, but I love God and I understand that he has his ways."

"No, you're running," Helen said. "You've been running ever since your mother and father died. But now something has happened and you're thinking twice about running."

Sherry looked at her. It was like speaking to a mirror—there was no fooling the woman. She smiled, suddenly unsure of what to say.

"I've been waiting for you," Helen said. "It's not often that God gives us visions, and when he does, they mean something."

"You know about my dream?" Sherry asked, surprised.

"So you *have* had a vision."

Sherry sat forward, excited now. "I always dream. I guess you'd call them nightmares. But now in the last two nights—"

"Tell me your vision," Helen said.

Sherry blinked. "Tell you what I saw?"

"Yes, dear. Tell me. I've been waiting a long time for this moment—I really don't want to wait any longer. You've been chosen for this and I've been chosen to hear this. So please, tell me."

A long time for this moment? Sherry looked away and settled in her chair, seeing in her mind's eye the vision as if it had just happened. A tremor took to her bones and she closed her eyes.

"I fell asleep, but then I was wide awake, in another world as bright as day. Exactly like what happened in the box. The first vision I had was two nights ago. I saw Shannon . . ."

"So he's alive."

"No. I don't think so. That's not why I came. I came about the second vision. The one last night."

She thought very briefly about the search she and Marisa had made for Shannon yesterday. Marisa had identified the International Liaison for Missing

Persons as their starting point for finding records on the Richtersons' deaths. The agency had sent them on a goose chase that had ended three hours later, on the phone with a public relations officer named Sally Blitchner. Sherry learned for the first time that, yes, there was a record of the Richtersons in Venezuela. Then she gave her a number for a man in Denmark.

The man had a heavy accent. Yes, of course he knew the Richtersons, he'd announced over the line. After all, he *was* a Richterson. The eighty-year-old man claimed his nephew had gone to the States twenty years earlier with his wife and son, Shannon. Then he'd decided that America was no longer a free country and he'd gone into the jungles of Venezuela, to grow coffee. Yes, that had been tragic, hadn't it? Should never have gone in the first place, the man said. And no, he had not heard of any living relative. They had all died. There were no survivors.

The words settled in her mind with welcomed finality. *There were no survivors.* So. Shannon hadn't survived. She'd known that all along and yet her bubble of hope had popped and her heart had dropped to her gut.

"Sherry . . ."

Sherry opened her eyes to see Helen resting, her head leaned back, eyes staring at the ceiling. Sherry took a deep breath and let the vision flood her mind.

"It was what happened last night that . . . scared me. It's not like real sleep— even though I'm asleep. I'm on a long white beach between the towering trees and the ocean's blue waters." She felt the pressure of panic rise through her throat at the vivid image, and she closed her eyes. "It's just me, standing on this long wide white beach."

She stopped.

"Please go on," Helen encouraged.

"I can actually feel the sand with my hands." Sherry lifted her right hand and rubbed her fingers together. "I could swear I was really there, smelling the salty breeze, hearing sea gulls cry overhead and the waves splashing every few seconds. It was incredible. And then I see this man walking toward me, over the water. *On* the water, like he was Jesus in that one story. Only I know he's not Jesus because he's dressed in black, with jet-black hair to his shoulders. And his eyes glow red." Sherry breathed deliberately now, feeling her pulse build momentum.

"I run behind a wide-leaf palm, shaking. I know that I'm shaking because I'm gripping the palm and its leaves are moving and I'm afraid the man might see the tree on the beach. Of course, that's ridiculous because all the trees are swaying in the breeze."

Helen remained speechless, and Sherry continued, "So, I watch the man walk right onto the beach, about fifty meters from my tree, and he begins to dig a hole in the sand with his hands, like a dog burying a bone. I watch him throwing that sand between his legs, wondering why a man who could walk on water would dig like that. And then I hear children laughing, and I think, *Yes, that's how children would dig a hole.* But as soon as I think it, real children, not just their laughter, are running onto the beach. I can't even tell you where they come from, but they're suddenly everywhere—and then adults too, thousands of them crowding the white sand, tossing balls, talking, laughing.

"But the man's still there, in the middle of all these people, digging that hole. They don't see him. And if he sees them, he doesn't show any sign of it. Then the man drops an object, like a coconut, into the hole; covers it with sand; and walks off the beach, onto the water, and over the horizon."

She continued quickly, aware that her heart now pounded steadily in her ears.

"At first nothing else happens. The people are just out there running over the sand, right over that spot. But then suddenly a plant pokes through the sand. I can actually see it grow. It just grows and the people are walking around it as if this is some everyday occurrence. They're walking around it so I know they must see the plant, or else they would step on it, right?"

Sherry paused, not really expecting Helen to answer.

Sherry felt her lips twitch and it occurred to her that most people sitting in Helen's chair would be narrowing their diagnosis to schizophrenia about now.

Her fingers were trembling and she closed them. "It grows like a mushroom. A giant mushroom that keeps growing. And as it grows, I sink to my knees. I remember that because a sharp shell dug into my right knee. The mushroom towers over the whole beach, like a giant umbrella blocking the sun."

Sherry swallowed.

"Then the rain falls. Large drops of flaming liquid, like an acid that smokes wherever it lands, pouring down in torrents from the mushroom above us." Her voice was wavering a bit. She folded her hands and struggled to sound sane.

"The drops . . . melt . . . they melt everything they touch. People are trying to leave the beach in a panic, but they can't. They just . . . they just run around in circles being pelted by these large drops—acid drops that melt their flesh. It's the most horrible sight. You know, I'm yelling at the people to leave the beach, but I don't think they can hear me. They just run through the rain and then fall in a heap of bones."

Sherry closed her eyes.

"Then I see that the acid is on my skin . . ."

Her throat seized for a few seconds.

"I begin to scream . . ."

"And that's the end?" Helen asked.

"And then I hear a voice echo around me. *Find him.*" Sherry swallowed at the lump in her throat. "That's what I think I heard. *Find him.*"

They sat in silence for a few seconds, when Sherry heard a creaking. She opened her eyes to see Helen rise slowly to her feet and hobble to the window.

Helen looked out for some time. When she finally spoke, it was without turning.

"You know, Sherry, I look out of this window often and I see an ordinary world." Sherry followed her gaze. "Ordinary trees, ordinary grass, ordinary blue sky, sometimes snow, coming and going, hardly changing from one year to the next. And yet, even though most never see it, those of us with any sense know that an extraordinary force began all of this. We know that even now that same force fills the space we can't see. But sometimes, once in a great while, an ordinary person is allowed to see that extraordinary force."

Helen turned to her now, smiling. "I'm one of those people, Sherry. I have seen beyond. And now I know that you have as well."

Sherry sat up. "I'm not a prophet."

"Surprising, isn't it? Neither was Rahab, in the Old Testament. In fact, she was a prostitute—chosen by God to save the Israeli spies. Or what about the donkey who spoke to Balaam? We can't always understand why God chooses the vessels he chooses. God knows it makes no sense to me. But when he does choose a vessel, we'd better listen to the message. He wants you to go back, dear."

"Go back?" Sherry shook her head. "To Venezuela?"

Helen nodded.

"I can't go back!" Sherry said. "I don't want to be a vessel. I don't want to have these visions or whatever they are. I'm not even sure I *believe* in visions!"

Helen returned to her chair and sat without responding.

"What even makes you think that's what this is about?" Sherry asked.

"I have this gut feeling I've learned not to ignore."

"I'm finally sleeping for the first time that I can remember," Sherry said. "I just want things to be normal."

"But you're running. You have to go."

"I'm not running! That's stupid! I want to *sleep*, not run!"

"Then sleep, Tanya." Helen was smiling gently. "Sleep and see what happens. But I have seen some things too, and I don't mind telling you that this is far beyond you or me, dear. It began long before you were trapped in a box. You were chosen before your parents went down there."

"I'm not *interested* in being chosen!"

"Neither was Jonah. But at one time, you must have agreed to this, Tanya."

Sherry swallowed. The words she had spoken in the box eight years earlier suddenly skipped through her mind—*I'll do anything.*

"It's Sherry, not Tanya," she said. "And what you're saying is crazy! I can't go back to the jungle!" Coming here had been a mistake. She wanted to walk out then. Run.

"You've been swallowed by this thing. Sleep won't be easy in its stomach. Bile doesn't sit well with the human condition. By all means, if you can stand it, sleep forever. But if it were me, I'd go."

13

Casius stood in the blue phone booth and cracked his neck nonchalantly. "I realize you think my leaving was a mistake. Is that a threat?" Of course it was, and Casius knew it well. But the verbal sparring seemed to carry its own weight in this world of theirs. He ran his hand over bunched jaw muscles and eyed the busy street outside.

"Your not coming in is obviously a problem for them," David's voice said over the phone.

"Is it?"

"Of course it is. You can't spit in their faces and just expect to walk away."

"And why are they so eager for me to come in, David? Have you asked yourself that?"

The agent hesitated. "You have proprietary information obtained on a classified mission. You're threatening to go after Jamal on your own, using that information. I see their point."

"That's right. Jamal. The man who killed my father in a nightclub. The man who has reportedly been a funding source for some of this decade's most aggressive terrorist attacks. Who has a price of $250,000 on his head. Jamal. And now I discover that he's tied to an operation in Venezuela and you expect me to ignore it? I'm going to find Jamal and then I'm going to kill him. Unless Friberg *is* Jamal, I'm not sure I see his problem."

"You don't even know if Jamal is down there. All you know is that there's a man named Abdullah down there who may or may not have ties to Jamal. Either way, it's the principle behind it," David said. "I understand why you would want to go after Jamal, but the agency has asked you to cooperate. You're breaking rank."

"Open your eyes, David. I'll tell you this because you've always been good to me. Things aren't always what they seem. They could go badly for you in the coming weeks."

"Meaning exactly what?"

"Meaning maybe your superiors don't have your best interest in mind this time. Meaning maybe you should consider going away for a few weeks. Far away." He let the statement stand.

"What are you saying?"

"I've said it." Casius eased up on his tone. "Call it a hunch. Either way, don't try to defend me. I have to leave now."

"Does this mean you're refusing to come in?"

"Good-bye, David."

§

The suburban home had been built in the fifties, a two-story farmhouse crowded by an expanding city. He'd purchased it five years ago and it had functioned as well as he'd expected.

Casius ran through the inventory quickly. He estimated the value of the contents alone at over half a million dollars. Most of it he would leave behind for the wolves. He could only afford to take what would fit in a large sports bag. The rest he would have to leave and risk losing to their searches. It didn't matter. He had millions stashed in banks around the world, most of it taken from one of his very first hits—an obscenely wealthy militant.

Casius strapped each of three canvas cash-packed straps tightly to his waist. The $700,000 would be his only weapon now. He pulled a loose black shirt over his head and examined himself in a full-length mirror, pleased with his new appearance. His hair hugged his skull in a close-cropped sandy brown matting—a far cry from the black curls he'd sported just ten hours earlier. His eyes stared a dark menacing brown rather than blue. It wouldn't be enough to

throw off a professional, but the ordinary person would have a hard time identifying him as the man in the CIA profile. The money belts bulged slightly at
his waist. He would have to wear his trench coat.

Casius glanced around the house one final time and lifted the bag. In an
ironic sort of way, leaving so much brought a warmth to his gut. It had all
come from them, and now he was giving it back. Like flushing the toilet. The
system that had spawned men like Friberg was no better than Friberg himself.
He wasn't sure which he hated more, Friberg or the sewer he had crawled from.

But that was all going to change, wasn't it?

Casius left the house, tossed the bag in the rear of his black Volvo, and slid
behind the wheel. The dash clock read 6 P.M.—nearly twelve hours had passed
since his call with David. They would be coming soon. Once the CIA discovered his absence, they would follow him carefully, knowing full well that he
would kill whoever got in his way.

And kill he would. In a heartbeat. He glanced in the rearview mirror and
turned the ignition key. The car rumbled to life. Killing David Lunow might be
a problem—he had actually grown to like the man. If there was anyone on the
globe he might call a friend, it would be him. But they wouldn't send David. It
had been five years since the man had seen the killing end of any weapon. No,
it would be contract killers. By leaving he was practically screaming for a bullet
to the head. A chill ran up his spine and he grinned softly.

Casius shoved the stick shift forward and eased the car out of the long driveway, scanning for surveillance as he left the three-acre lot behind. Of course they
knew where he was headed—but they would not know his route.

He reached the lake twenty minutes later. A deserted pier stuck over the
water like a rickety old xylophone. The moon lit a thin multicolored sheen of
oil that rested on the surface. Casius quickly removed heavy wire cutters from
the trunk, snipped the chain strapping the gates together, and eased the black
car onto the pier. He withdrew the black sports bag and started the car toward
the polluted water.

The last bubbles popped through the surface three minutes after the car's
plunge. Only a wide hole in the water's oily film showed for the vehicle's pas-

TED DEKKER

sage. Satisfied, Casius slung the bag to his shoulder and jogged toward the city—toward the crowded streets.

Within half an hour he'd hailed a yellow cab. "Airport," he instructed, climbing behind an Asian driver.

"Which airline?" the man asked, pulling into the street.

"Just the main terminal," Casius answered. He pulled the bag against his leg and gazed out the window. He had covered his bases. There was no way for them to trace him now. They would scour his house of course, but they would find nothing.

He was going down into the jungle and one way or another he would put Jamal to death.

14

Friday

The good news was that Sherry slept long and hard that night.

The bad news was that her sleep was filled with a hollow scream that could only have been shaped in hell itself.

Sherry doubled over on the sandy beach, throat raw and wailing.

Oh, God! Oh, God, save me! Oh . . .

She was running out of breath and panicking and unable to stop her shrieking. She was dying—a slow death caused by the acid that sizzled on her skin. The pain raged to her bones, as if they had been opened and molten lead had been poured into them. All around her the people were crying and toppling onto the sand, skeletons.

Sherry bolted upright in bed, still screaming. The room echoed with her hoarse voice and she clamped a hand over her mouth. She breathed heavily through her nostrils, eyes peeled at the soaked bed.

She wasn't dead.

The vision had come back. Stronger this time. Much stronger.

"Oh, God," she whimpered. "Oh, God, this is worse than the box . . . Please . . ."

Helen!

Sherry didn't bother brushing her teeth or dressing. She threw her bathrobe on and ran for the car.

Helen answered on the second knock, as if she'd been waiting.

"Hello, Tanya."

Sherry walked in, still trembling.

"You look a bit ragged, my dear." Helen looked her over and then walked for the living room. "Come on, then. Tell me again."

She walked in and sat.

"You did not like the bile, I take it," Helen said.

The bile?

Helen must have seen her expression. "The stomach of the whale. Jonah. The acid."

"The bile," Sherry said. She dropped her head and began to cry.

"I'm sorry, my dear," Helen said gently. "Really, I am. It must be painful. But I can assure you that it won't end. Not until you go."

"I don't *want* this!" Sherry cried.

"No. But you're not sweating blood yet, so I suppose you're all right."

Sherry stared at her through blurred vision, at a loss for what she could possibly mean. "I can't go through another night like that, Grandmother. I mean . . . I really don't think I can. Physically."

"Exactly."

"This is *mad!*"

"Yes."

Sherry lowered her head and shook it. Helen began to hum an old hymn and after a while it had a settling effect on Sherry.

Wiping her eyes, she lifted her head and studied the older woman.

"Okay. So what you're saying is that God has chosen me for some . . . some purpose. I have to go back to the jungle. And if I don't he'll torment me with these . . . these . . ."

"Pretty much, yes. I doubt he's the one doing the tormenting, but he isn't getting in the way. It seems that you're needed."

"Do you have any idea how absolutely stupid this all sounds?"

Helen looked at her for a few seconds. "Not really, no. But I've been through a bit."

"Yeah." Sherry's mind swam at the thought of returning to her past.

"I don't see how that would be possible," Sherry said.

"Why not?"

"For one thing, the place was overrun by soldiers! Who knows what's there now."

Helen nodded. "Father Petrus Teuwen is there. Petrus. Not where your parents were, but in Venezuela, on a mission station farther south, I believe. My husband knew him well when he was a boy. I talked with Petrus yesterday. He's an exceptional man, Tanya. And he would welcome you."

A small buzz erupted between her ears. "You talked to him? He knows about this?"

"He knows some things. And he knew of your parents."

"So you're really suggesting I pick up and go down there?" Sherry asked incredulously.

"I thought I said that yesterday. You weren't listening?"

"For how long?"

"Until you have had enough. A week, a day, a month," Helen said.

"Just up and fly all the way to South America for a day? It takes a full day just to get down there."

Was she serious? Of course she was serious! Maybe God was calling her as he had called her parents nearly twenty years ago.

But the irony of the thought. Helen was right. Sherry *had* spent eight years running from her past and now she was suggesting Sherry just step back there. Like it was some kind of booth at a fair she could walk in and out of at will. But it wasn't some booth—it was the house of horrors and the last time she'd gone in there the lid had locked shut.

But then that was Tanya Vandervan. She was Sherry Blake. The changing of her identity suddenly struck her as absurd. Goodness, her mind couldn't see what her hair or eyes looked like. The mind was on the wrong side of the skull, where the visions and nightmares wandered around at night.

The silence was stretching.

"You're free to go now that you've left the hospital," Helen said. "Do you think this is by chance? Think about it, Sherry."

She did. She thought about it, and the thought that returning might bring justification to her leave of absence from the hospital felt strangely warm. "So just buy a ticket and show up on Father Teuwen's doorstep?"

"Actually, I'd get word to him. But basically, yes."

Sherry sat for a long time and tried to wrap her mind around this call of God's. But the more she thought about it, the more its madness faded.

She spent most of the day with Helen, who took it upon herself to make some phone calls. Sherry mostly sat in the big armchair, crying and asking questions and slowly, ever so slowly, warming to the idea that something very, very strange was happening. God had his purposes, and somehow, she had been pulled into the middle of them all.

§

David Lunow sat in the director's office with legs crossed and palms wet. He had been brought in to discuss Casius, of that he was sure. The large desk Friberg sat behind was made of a wood that reminded him of oak. Of course, it couldn't be oak—oak was too cheap. Probably some imported wood from one of the Arab countries. Two high-backed chairs faced the desk. Mark Ingersol sat in one, David in the other. He couldn't remember spending so much time with the brass.

Friberg dropped the phone in its cradle and stared at them without expression. He stood up and walked to the tall window behind the desk.

"No word?" Friberg asked.

"No," Ingersol said.

"Then we move. Quickly," Friberg said, facing them. His jaw muscles flexed. "Under no circumstances can we allow this man to live."

David blinked. "Sir, I'm not sure I understand why he poses such a threat. He's off on his own, and I can understand your frustration with his pigheaded attitude, but—"

"Shut up, Lunow," Friberg said quietly. "The only reason you're sitting where you are now is because you know the man better than anyone else. You played a part in his leaving and now you'll play a part in his elimination. You're not here to express your reservations."

Heat flared up David's neck. The warning Casius had spoken on the phone rang through his head.

"Of course, sir. But without knowing more, I'm not sure I can be effective. It seems he knows more than I do about what's going on."

"He's after Jamal," Friberg said. "And to get to Jamal he's going through Abdullah Amir. That's all he knows and it's all you need to know."

"I'm not sure that's all he knows. He at least suspects more."

"Then we have even more reason to take him out."

David sat quietly now. He'd stepped into deep waters, that much was now clear.

"Perhaps it would help if we knew your concerns," Ingersol said. "I'm just as much in the dark here as David. Casius has become a liability, but I'm not sure either of us understands just how much of one."

Friberg turned back to the window and leaned on the ledge. He spoke out to the lawn. "I don't have to tell you that this is 'need to know' only. And as far as I'm concerned, you're the only two who need to know." He ran a hand over his balding head. "Casius has inadvertently stumbled into an operation we were involved in eight years ago." He turned back to them. "We know about Abdullah Amir. We know about his compound, and suffice it to say we can't allow Casius to compromise our position in Venezuela because he has some hairbrained notion that Jamal is involved."

Ingersol shifted in his seat. "We have an operation involving Abdullah Amir?"

"It was before your time, but yes. Let's leave it at that. Under no circumstance is Casius to reach that compound. Am I making myself clear? We pursue him at all costs."

David sat stunned. He wasn't sure they knew what they were getting into with Casius. He'd never known a more dangerous man. The man was born to kill. "I'm not sure pursuing him is the best option, sir."

"Because?"

"He may do more damage defensively than he would otherwise."

"It's a risk we'll have to take. This man of yours may be good, but he's not God. And now that you've blown our chances of dealing with him cleanly I need your recommendations for bringing him in."

David ignored the comment and considered the request.

"I'm not sure you can bring him in, sir. At least not alive." He lifted his eyes to Ingersol. "And there certainly aren't any operatives I'm aware of who could kill the man easily."

"That's ridiculous," Ingersol said. "No man is that good."

"You can try," David said. "But you better take the cavalry with you, because there's no way a single man will have a chance against Casius in his own backyard."

Ingersol turned to Friberg. "I've already alerted all our agents south of the border. We have eyes in every major town in the region. Why can't we insert two or three teams of snipers?"

David answered, "You could, but I doubt he'd ever give them a shot. You have to remember, the guy grew up in the region. He knows the jungle down there. His father was jungle trained, a sniper himself. Trust me, Casius would put his father to shame." David shook his head. "I still think going after him will be a mistake. You'd have a better chance taking him once he reemerges."

"No. We waited once; we won't wait again!" Friberg's face blotched red. "I want Casius dead! I don't care what we have to send in there after him; we send it all. I want some strategic options for a takeout here, not this quibbling over snipers. You just tell me how we can get to this guy and let me worry about the execution."

"What about sending troops, David?" Ingersol asked softly. "If you don't think snipers can reach him—what about cutting him off?"

"Troops? Since when does the CIA order troops around?" David asked and immediately regretted the question. Ingersol's left eye twitched below that slicked-back hairline, as if to say, *"Get off it, David. Just answer the question."*

"Yes, well supposing you could get troops, they would have to be Special Forces. Jungle trained with combat experience. You insert them in a perimeter around this plantation Casius is presumably headed for and you might have a shot at him."

"We can do that," Friberg stated flatly. "How many do you think it will take?"

"Maybe three teams," he replied uncomfortably. "Provided they're jungle trained. I think he'd have a hard time getting around three Ranger teams. But it won't be pretty."

A new light of hope seemed to have ignited behind Friberg's eyes. "Good. I want specifics on my desk in three hours. That's all."

It took a moment for Ingersol and David to realize they had been dismissed. David left with words buzzing through his head. They weren't Friberg's words. They were the words spoken by Casius a day earlier and they were suggesting he go away for a while.

Far away.

15

"Hello, Marisa. Sorry to wake you. I missed you last night and I woke early."

"It's okay. I just got up. Where are you?"

Sherry hesitated and shifted the receiver. "I had the . . . vision again last night—" Her voice broke and she cleared her throat.

The phone sat silent at her ear.

"I'm leaving for a few days. Maybe a week. Maybe longer, I don't know."

"*Leaving?* Where are you now?"

"Well, that's just it. I'm at the airport. I'm going to Venezuela, Marisa."

"You're doing *what?*"

"I know. It sounds crazy. Like going back into the snake pit. But I had this talk with Helen, and . . . well, there's a flight that leaves at eight. I have to be on it."

"What about passports or visas? You can't just hop on a plane and take off, can you? Who are you staying with?"

"My parents got me dual citizenship, so actually, yes—I can just hop on a plane. I'll be there in twenty-four hours. It's just a trip, Marisa. I'll be back."

The phone went silent again.

"Marisa?"

"I can't believe you're actually doing this! It's so sudden."

"I know. But I'm going. Something's . . . going on, you know? I mean, I don't know what, but I've got to go. For my own sanity, if nothing else. Anyway, I wanted you to know. So you don't worry."

"Don't worry? Sure, okay. You're going back into the jungle to look for a boyfriend who's been dead for ten years, but hey—"

"This isn't about Shannon. I know he's dead. This is different. Anyway, I've gotta get to the gate."

Marisa sighed. "Watch yourself then, okay? Really."

"I will." Sherry smiled. "Hey, I'll be back before you know it. No big deal."

"Sure you will."

16

Sunday

"I don't know, but I don't think it's about the boy," Helen said.

"It never was about the boy," Bill replied. "Besides, I thought he was dead."

"Yes. So they say. But it's not about Tanya, either. Not really."

"So you've said. Tanya is a Jonah, and it's really about Nineveh."

"I know, but I'm not sure it's about Nineveh anymore either."

"So now we don't even know who the players are in this chess match of yours?"

"We know who the players are. They are God and they are the forces of darkness. The white side and the black side. What we don't know is which players they are prodding and whether those players will actually move. But I have this feeling, Bill. The black side doesn't have a clue about what's really happening. This is an end run."

"As long as the players cooperate."

Helen was silent for a moment.

"Have you ever wondered what kind of man embraces evil, Bill?"

"What kind of man? Every man. What do you mean?"

"I mean, what kind of man would kill others?"

"Many men have killed others. I'm not sure I follow."

"It's just something that's been gnawing at me. One way or another Tanya is going back to confront the same evil that killed her parents. I was just thinking about what kind of evil that was. That drove those men. And I think you're right . . . I think it's the same kind of evil that's in every man. But not every man embraces it."

"And the death of Christ destroys it."
"Yes. The death of Christ. Love."

§

The valley would have looked like any other valley in Venezuela's Guyana Highlands, except for the black cliffs jutting to the sky. As it was, the stark contrast between the green jungle and the sheer rock served as a reminder to the Indians that the men occupying the valley were men with black souls. Death Valley, that's what they now called the region that had only eight years ago been occupied by messengers of God.

In a fortified complex within the mountain at the plantation's northern border, Abdullah Amir sat with folded arms, like a sentinel overseeing his brood. A shock of white split his black hair at the crown, accentuating a sharp nose that jutted from a naturally dark face. His eyes glistened black, casting the illusion that no iris, only pupil, had formed there. His right cheek blistered with a long scar rising from the corner of his mouth.

The room he occupied was nearly dark, plain, with stained concrete walls. But mostly it was damp and smelly. The smell came from the large black insects in the room. He had long ago given up with the bugs, and now hundreds of them occupied all four corners, climbing over each other to form small mounds, like hanging wasp nests. Not that he minded them. In fact, they had become like companions to him. No, he didn't really mind them at all.

What he did mind was Jamal. Or more pointedly, Jamal's orders—he had never actually met the man. As far as he was concerned, Jamal had hijacked his plan and was taking the glory for it. Yes, Jamal had made improvements, but they were not critical. It hardly mattered that he was a highly respected militant in the Mideast. He was not here, in the jungle where the plan was hatched. He had no business controlling anything.

Abdullah sat in a metal folding chair and gazed through a picture window to blazing lights illuminating the processing plant one story below. Three large vats used for cocaine refinement stood like swimming pools against a backdrop of five chemical tanks strung along the far wall. Beyond the concrete wall, two helicopters sat idle in the hangar. The operation ran like a well-oiled machine now, he thought. Here in the jungle where the days ticked by with only cicadas keeping cadence.

Sweat leaked down his temple, and he let it run. His life had been a living hell here in the jungle, but by Jamal's tone, that would soon change.

A fly crawled lethargically across his forearm. He ignored it and let his mind fall back to the first time Jamal had made contact.

Abdullah had come to this coffee plantation as part of a well-conceived plan the Brotherhood had plotted years before his arrival—a plan that would eventually change history, they were sure of it. It was brilliant for its simplicity as much as its extravagance. They would develop links within the drug trade south of the United States and exploit the traffic routes for terrorism. South America was certainly much closer to the United States than Iran. And for the kind of acts they had in mind, close was critical. The whole world had set its focus on North Africa and the Middle East after Osama bin Laden's rampage anyway. South America was a far safer home for such an extraordinary plan.

After spending two years in Cali, Colombia, Abdullah had struck his deal with the CIA to occupy this valley.

And three years after that, Jamal had entered his world. Jamal, an unknown name then, had somehow persuaded the Brotherhood to let him take control of the plan. He had the money; he had the contacts; he had a better plan.

It was then that Abdullah had begun the construction of the underground fortress, at Jamal's insistence, of course. Abdullah had already built a perfectly sufficient building, yet he had been forced to scrap it in favor of Jamal's plan.

Hollowing the caverns from the mountain near the plantation had been a harrowing experience in the terrible heat and humidity. And keeping the operation undercover meant they had to get rid of the rock without alerting air or satellite surveillance. The CIA had agreed to allow them a modest drug operation—not one that necessitated the hollowing of a mountain. The CIA had no clue what they were really up to.

They'd moved 200,000 tons of rock. They had done it by drilling a three-foot tunnel right through the mountain and depositing the dirt in the Orinoco River far below in the adjacent valley.

Using the same tunnels to deliver the logs to the river had been Jamal's idea as well. Everything, always, Jamal's. It wasn't the plan itself that bore into Abdullah's skull; it was the way Jamal held him by the neck. The way he toyed with him, demanding this and questioning that. One day Abdullah would have to kill the pig. Of course, he would have to find him first, and finding him might be harder than killing him.

A knock sounded on the door.

Abdullah answered without moving. "Come in."

A Hispanic man with an eye patch entered and closed the door. "Excuse me, sir."

"Yes?"

"The shipment is under way successfully. Three logs bound for Miami."

Abdullah turned his head slowly and looked at the man. He'd put the man's eye out for insubordination—questioning his orders about how long the men should work harvesting down in the fields. Jamal had called earlier that morning—it had been a bad day.

Abdullah turned back to the window without responding.

"We will ship again in two days," Ramón said.

"Keep an eye out, Ramón," Abdullah said.

The man hesitated. "Sir?"

Abdullah faced him quickly. "I said keep an eye out, Ramón. The spiders may try to eat us soon."

From the corner of his eyes Abdullah saw Ramón glance at the wall. After a moment of silence the man spoke again. "Jamal made contact?"

Was it so obvious? "We will send them soon. Many people will die. Let us pray that Jamal is among them."

"Yes, sir."

Abdullah resumed his stare out the window. For several long minutes they remained silent, looking down at the idle cocaine plant. It was like that out here in the cursed jungle, Abdullah thought. The world was an empty place. Damp and hot and crawling with spiders, but as empty as a deep hole. Like this prison of his.

At times he even forgot about Yuri's little toys far beneath their feet. "You may go, Ramón."

"Yes, sir."

The man left, and Abdullah sat still.

§

Five hours later and one hundred miles to the east, a cool wind whipped around the bow of a seven-thousand-ton lumber carrier pushing through choppy waters with powerful twin Doxford diesels. As far as the eye could see, whitecaps covered the sea.

Moses Catura, captain of the *Lumber Lord*, strained his eyes through the misty windows that surrounded the pilothouse. They should have been in sight by now. The evening pickups were always the worst. And in choppy waters they were nearly impossible.

"Andrew. Where the heck are the buggers?" Moses yelled through an ancient-looking intercom mounted on the wall beside him.

For three years they had guided the massive Highland Lumber transporter across the Caribbean Sea to the southern ports of the United States—over a hundred trips in all. Andrew burst through the door of the pilothouse. "One mile to port, sir. It's going to be a tough one. Wind's picking up and the tide is heading back in. I'd say if we don't get to her within half an hour, she'll be pulled back."

"Right. Twenty degrees to port." Moses barked the command into the ear of the pilot beside him, then turned and yelled down the tube, "Full steam ahead." He turned to Andrew. "Get the crane ready. How many are there?"

"Three, all grouped together so they look like one blip on the receiver." Andrew smiled. "Nothin' like a little lumber on the side, eh, sir?"

"Get going, Andrew, or you won't see a dime." Andrew slammed the door and dropped to the deck below.

The captain turned on the fog lights and gazed ahead as the huge ship slowly turned. The frequencies for the transmitters on each log had been received eight hours earlier and programmed into the homing screen that Andrew kept in his cabin. Only he and Andrew knew the stray logs contained shipments of cocaine. To the rest, the logs were just valuable lumber that they were paid handsomely to keep their mouths shut about. Most of the crew were old-timers who figured the captain deserved a few extra dollars from the smuggled lumber. Of course they didn't mind taking their share either.

Moses spoke into the intercom. "How close?"

"Two hundred meters, sir. Five degrees should do it."

"Five degrees port," Moses yelled into the pipe.

"Seventy-five yards. Just a hair starboard," Andrew barked.

"Full stop. Two degrees starboard."

The large cargo vessel shuddered as its massive twin screws thrashed in reverse. Andrew plucked each log from the ocean with the large crane and swung them carefully to the aft hold where uncut logs were transported.

Fourteen minutes later the *Lumber Lord* steamed at full power north, leaving the gray coastline of South America in its wake. Moses smiled and turned toward the comfort of his cabin. Just a few more trips and he would retire.

17

Casius had left New York under the alias Jason Mckormic and arrived twenty-nine hours later in Georgetown, Guyana.

Except for a single black bag, he carried nothing. He'd deposited $400,000 in a safe-deposit box at the Mail Boxes Etc. on the corner of Washington and Elwood—three miles from the airport in New York. Another $300,000 rested in the watertight money belts that clung to his waist under a suffocating coat. Thirty-seven hours had droned by since he'd abandoned his car to the lake, most of it crammed into window seats aboard four separate jetliners.

The yellow taxi he'd hailed at the airport slid to a stop on the gravel road by the pier. His mind hummed as if it remained at thirty thousand feet.

Casius tossed two hundred pesos over the seat and climbed out. Two cargo boats hugged the dock a hundred meters off, each loading for departure to the northern port of Tobago. From Tobago, their fruit cargo would be sold throughout the Lesser Antilles within the week. Passage would take either boat within two miles of Venezuela's coastline just north of the Guyana—on the Venezuela border.

An old man with crooked black teeth squinted at him lazily. Casius nodded and smiled gently. "Señor."

The man grunted and looked on.

Casius's deeply tanned skin favored him in this environment, as did his khakis. But the crowd serving these boats was a rough one. He spent an hour roaming the pier, mixing in and passing by the ships as if he belonged.

He boarded the larger of the cargo boats on his third pass, during an especially boisterous argument over a spilled load of bananas, found a deserted cabin belowdecks that looked by the mess as though it had been used for the drying out of frequent drunks, locked the door, and slid under the bunk.

Midafternoon, the boat left the harbor under full power. Twice in the night men tried to open the door to the cabin. Twice they retreated mumbling angrily. By midnight, the boat ran just off the borders of Venezuela.

Casius peered from the window into a dark, pouring rain. He focused his eyes through the rain but couldn't see the coastline. The thought of swimming in the dark now made his stomach turn.

He flipped the latch that secured the porthole window and pushed out. Layers of hardened varnish gave way with a snap. The window swung out to sea, immediately inviting gusts of wet sea air through the opening. He checked the gear he'd strapped to his bare body one last time—the money belts were cinched around his waist and one change of clothes was sealed in the black bag. The coat, the khakis, the shirt, and the shoes he'd worn on the flight would go out the window before him. Didn't need them.

He stepped up onto a chair, tossed the bundled clothes out into the wind, and eased his body through the opening, headfirst, facing the stars. He pushed himself out until he hung only by the backs of his calves. With one last look into the sea, he kicked his legs free of the porthole and flipped backward into the cold, dark water.

The water crashed about his ears and then he heard only the churning screws from the ship. Blackness hung in the depths below him like deep space and visions of sharks whipped through his mind. He clawed for the surface and shook his head against a sudden panic. The ship ran into the night, leaving him in the white foam of its wake. Casius struck out westward.

He swam for two hours. Three different times, when the rain thinned, he found himself swimming parallel to the distant shore instead of toward it. The waves were high and the rain annoying but the land steadily approached and Casius swam steadily toward it. When the beach finally came, it was a welcome relief.

Casius slogged from the water and sank to the sand twenty meters from the jungle wall. Trees with long vines towered along the perimeter, their menacing arms stretching out in the predawn light. He stood to his feet, adjusted the wet money belts, and walked to the edge of the black forest. He took a deep breath through his nostrils, spit to his right, and stepped once again into the jungle.

If he was right, the CIA would be waiting for him already.

§

Sherry Blake watched the helicopter twirl toward the sky, shoving gusts of wind in wide dusty circles. Her hair whipped about her face and she lowered her head until the air settled. To her left a jungle airstrip ran along the barren valley floor, carved by a freak of nature itself, not by human hands. The location was a natural choice for the station. Had it not been for the Richtersons' plantation twenty miles north, her father might have chosen this spot fifteen years earlier.

When she looked up, Father Petrus Teuwen was smiling broadly and looking at her with raised eyebrows. She liked him immediately. Bright white teeth filled his mouth like piano keys. His black hair rested long on his cleric's collar. Sherry doubted he'd been to a barber in four months.

"Welcome back to the jungle," he said. "I'm sure you must be tired."

Sherry let her eyes wander over the jungle line a hundred meters off. "Yes," she replied absently.

The trees stood tall with moss-covered vines stringing below the canopy. Green. So much dark, rich green. As the chopper's beating dwindled, the jungle noises came to her. A background of cicadas screeching nonstop, parrots calling against songs of a dozen louder hooters. The branches of a towering tree shook. She watched a furry, brown howler monkey poke its head out and study the mission.

The scene streamed through her mind, pulling her heart to her throat, and for a brief instant she wondered if she was in one of her nightmares, only in three dimensions.

"Boy, this brings back memories," she said, bending for her bag.

"I'm sure it does. Here, let me take that."

Sherry followed him toward a long structure she assumed was the station house, although it reminded her more of a dormitory. A simple tin roof covered the creosote-darkened building. The father turned to her. "I don't get much farther north, actually. Most of my work is with the southern Indians. Your parents worked among the Yanamamo up north, Helen tells me. I heard what happened. I'm so sorry."

She glanced at him and saw that he was indeed sorry. She smiled. The noises about her still rapped at her memories, and for the hundredth time since leaving the Denver airport, she wondered if this whole idea had been misguided. What could she possibly do in the jungle? Oh, yes, the vision. She had come because of the vision.

But the vision seemed a thousand miles away. It struck her as an absurd whisper barely remembered. Flying over the endless forest in the helicopter, she had decided she would leave when the chopper returned to the station again in three days. She would give this whole dream thing three days. And only because she had no choice in the matter. She could not very well step from the cockpit, glance about the mission, and climb back in, could she? That would look ridiculous. No, she would have to wait until the next trip.

She swallowed and willed her heart to lower from her throat. "And what did you hear, Father?"

"I heard that drug bandits attacked your mission. And if what the Indians say is correct, the valley is still occupied."

She looked up, surprised. "Now? You mean these people have never been brought to justice? I was told that they were!"

"It's not necessarily occupied by the same people who destroyed the mission compound, but drug merchants work in the area. The law isn't exactly swift in the jungle. Neither is the government. Half of them are partners with the drug lords. It's a sizable portion of the economy. I imagine the church raised some noise in the beginning, but memories pass quickly. Some battles are hardly worth fighting."

They came to the house and the father veered to the door on the far right. "Here we are." He went in ahead of her and set the bag in the room. "This is where you'll stay. It's not much, but it's all we have, I'm afraid."

Sherry glanced through the door and saw that it contained a single cot and a bathroom. "This will be fine. You wouldn't happen to have a drink, would you? I'd forgotten how hot this place gets." She waved her hand against her throat like a fan.

"Of course. Follow me." He led her to the middle door, which opened to a sizable living room and a kitchen beyond. The smell of kerosene filled her nostrils. Like her home eight years earlier. *God, what are you doing to me?* She plopped in a chair and waited for the father to bring her the glass of lemonade. Like the glass that had crumbled in her own hand eight years earlier. *Dear God.*

Afternoon cicadas were singing outside. It sounded like a death mass. She smiled at the priest and drew the cool drink past her lips.

"Thank you."

He sat across from her and said, "My pleasure."

She crossed her legs. "So, who told you about the attack on our mission?"

He shrugged. "The mission board, I suppose—five years ago when I first arrived."

"Did they mention the plantation next to the mission?"

He nodded, his smile now softening so she could barely see his white teeth. "They said the bandits were most likely after the fields there. The way I understood it, the mission was simply in the way." He looked out the window with a faraway stare. "From what the Indians have told me, I think that must be right. They wanted the plantation for their drugs and took the mission with it. That's what happened from man's perspective anyway. It's hard to know what God had in mind."

"And what have you heard about the plantation owners?" she asked, feeling sweat run down her blouse. "The Richtersons."

"They were killed." He looked at her. "As far as I was told, no one survived. In fact, I only learned of your survival from Helen, several years ago. I knew Helen's husband. He was with some soldiers who came to our village in

World War II. His leader killed a girl I knew very well. Nadia. Perhaps Helen told you about Nadia."

"Yes, she's told me the story."

"I was there," the father said. "Nadia was my friend."

"I'm sorry." Helen had asked her to read the book her husband had written about the episode, but she never had. "So the Indians told you Shannon was killed?" she asked. "They saw his body?"

"Most of what I have heard is hearsay. But, as far as I know, yes." He smiled apologetically. "But I'm sure I don't need to tell you that. Again, I'm terribly sorry."

"It's all right, Father. I've come to terms with my parents' death."

Father Teuwen eyed her carefully. "So if you don't mind me asking, Sherry. Why *have* you come to the jungle after all these years?"

Sherry lowered her eyes to the floor. The sound of a barking dog filtered through the thin walls. And then the dog was yelping as if it had been hit by a hurled stone or the flat of a hand maybe.

"It may sound strange, but actually Helen convinced me that I should come. Because God called me." She nodded, thinking about that. "Yes, because God called me."

She lifted her eyes to his and saw that he had both eyebrows raised—whether in eagerness or in doubt she could not tell. "Do you believe God speaks, Father?"

"Of course God speaks." He lifted a finger and cocked his ear. "Listen." She listened and she knew he meant the jungle sounds. "You hear that? That's God speaking now."

She smiled and nodded. "But do you believe he speaks specifically to people today?"

"Yes. I do. I've seen too much of the supernatural out here"—he motioned outside—"to doubt that it flies about us every day. I'm sure he speaks to the willing ear now and then."

She nodded approvingly. He was a wise man, she decided.

"Well, it feels very strange to me, I can assure you. Not only am I being peppered with memories that frankly scare me to death, but I'm supposed to find answers in the midst of them all." She shook her head. "I don't feel very spiritual, Father."

"And if you felt very spiritual, my dear, I might worry for you. It's not your duty to feel predisposed to any clear message. Think of yourself as a vessel. A cup. Don't try to guess what the Master will pour into you before he pours. Only pray it is the Master who pours. Then be willing to accept whatever message he wishes to fill you with. It's his to fill, Sherry. You only receive."

The words came like honey and she found herself wanting more. She uncrossed her legs and shifted back in her seat. "You're right." She looked away. "That makes so much sense. God knows I need things to make sense now."

"Yes. Well that's both good and bad. If your life made too much sense to you, you might forget about God altogether. It is man's most prolific sin—to be full of himself. But your tormenting has left you soft, like a sponge for his words. It's your greatest blessing."

"Suffering a blessing? I've suffered a lot."

"Yes, I can see that. Christ was once asked why a blind man had been born blind. Do you know how he answered? He said the man had been born blind so that God would one day be glorified through it. We see only the terrible tragedy; he sees more. He sees the ultimate glory." He let that sink in for a bit, but she wasn't sure how far it was sinking.

"When you're finished, Sherry, you will see that many were affected for the good because of your suffering. And because of your parents' death. I'm sure of that."

Now the words washed through her chest with warmth and she felt her heart rise. Somehow she knew that a volume of truth had just entered her mind.

She dropped her eyes, hoping he would not see the moisture there. "Sherry," he said. "Sherry Blake. I thought your last name was Vandervan."

"It used to be."

"And you changed it?"

She nodded.

He waited for a moment, regarding her with those kind eyes. "I think that when this is through, Sherry, you will embrace your past. Every part of it. You have done the right thing in coming here. A part of history rests on your shoulders."

For a few long moments neither spoke. It sounded absurd. What could this lost corner of the jungle have to do with history? Sherry sipped her lemonade without looking directly at him, and the father studied her. Then he smiled and clapped his hands, startling her.

"Now, young lady, it's growing late and I'm sure you have a lot to think about. I have some supper to fix. Feel free to rest or wander about the station—whatever suits your fancy. We will eat in an hour."

He turned to the kitchen and pulled up his sleeves.

Yes, she liked the father very much, she thought.

18

Monday

The jungle came back to Casius like thick honey—slow at first but then with sudden volume.

The roots tore at his feet until he found his rhythm, jogging with a certainty that allowed him to place his feet where he wanted. Vines slapped at his face until his eyes adjusted to the shadows of the night. The creatures screamed about him, pricking at his nerves until he managed to shove them to the bottom of his mind. When daylight streamed through the canopy, he picked his pace up considerably, and he lost his thoughts to memories of the past.

He had lived a lifetime in the years since leaving this land, and in truth he hadn't escaped it. He had lived for this day. A hundred missions had led to this one. He would live or he would die, but in the end, those responsible for his father's death would die with him.

The thoughts pounded through his mind with the cadence of his footfalls. He knew more than anyone at the CIA, including Friberg, could possibly suspect. In fact, he knew more than Friberg himself knew. And knowing what he knew, he would be surprised if they didn't hunt him down with Special Forces. The stakes were too high to rely on agents. They would take no chances, and David would tell them that meant sending in jungle-trained forces.

It was midmorning before Casius emerged from the jungle on a rise that fell slowly to the Orinoco Delta. A village below housed a small population of fishermen who also ran cargo and passenger boats up and down the river for extra income. Casius carefully wiped the calf-high mud from his legs with wet leaves and unstrapped the bag still lashed to his back. He donned a pair of shorts, and over them, slacks. Then he slipped into a pair of light brown loafers, put on a large loose-fitting, wrinkle-free shirt, and covered his head with a baseball cap. He shoved a pair of sunglasses into his shirt pocket, buried the plastic bag that had kept the clothes dry, and headed for the small village in the distance.

Casius approached a pontoon boat tended by a fisherman who sat scrubbing its hull. "Excuse me. Can you tell me how I might find a fare to Soledad?" he asked.

The man stood from the boat and regarded him. "You are a tourist, no? You like feeshing? I catch a very large feesh for you."

"No fish, my friend. I need a ride up the river."

"Si, señor. Two hundred pesos. I tek good care of you."

"You've got a deal," Casius said.

The fisherman ordered two quickly appearing sons around as if he had just been appointed the general of an army, and readied the boat in five minutes flat. Ten minutes later he piloted the screaming forty-horse Evinrude upriver toward the small but relatively modern town of Soledad. Casius sat near the rear, studying the passing jungle, arms crossed, his gaze fixed, a thousand thoughts spinning circles through his mind.

§

Abdullah walked into the concrete shipping room and saw Ramón bent over one of the logs prepared for the night's delivery. The Hispanic man caught his look and nodded, still speaking to the worker who stuffed the hollowed log with cocaine bags. Across the room, conveyor chains ran into the mountain toward the large pipe that would deliver the log into the river far below. Abdullah walked up behind the two men and peered at their work.

The shipping method had been Jamal's idea and thus far they had lost fewer than ten logs to stray currents. The logistics were simple: Fill the buoyant Yevaro logs with sealed cocaine, shoot the lumber through a long, three-foot pipe that ran through the mountain to the Orinoco River, and collect the logs when they spewed into the ocean, two hundred miles east. The river delivered with unwavering consistency, spewing its littered waters into the ocean unceasingly. Homing beacons attached to each log assisted the pickup. The logs had passed into American lumberyards without incident for five years now. The tree's thick bark hid the panel cuts exceptionally well, rendering detection virtually impossible.

"How many tonight?" Abdullah asked, and the worker started at the sound of his voice.

"Three, sir."

Abdullah nodded in approval. "Follow me, Ramón." He walked for the elevator, inserted a key for the lower floor, and stepped back. The car ground down to the restricted basement.

"You know our world will change now?"

"Yes."

"And you are prepared for whatever changes this might bring?"

"What changes do you anticipate?" the soldier asked carefully.

"Well, for one I suspect this place will soon cease to exist. We can't expect them to sit by idly. The world will come apart, I think."

Ramón nodded. His one good eye blinked. "Yes, I think you are right."

The bell clanged and Abdullah stepped from the elevator. The laboratory door was closed at the end of the hall. He eyed it without approaching.

"We must clear the surrounding jungle of any possible threat," he said absently. "There is only one base within a hundred-mile radius of the plantation. I want it occupied immediately."

"The Catholic mission."

"Yes. I want it under our control. Send a team to neutralize the compound. And I want it done cleanly. You will attack the station tomorrow night."

"Yes, sir."

"Leave me."

Ramón retreated into the elevator and the door closed.

§

Apart from Ramón and Abdullah, only Yuri Harsanyi even knew of the lower floor's existence. And Yuri knew it intimately, like a mouse would know its hole in the wall.

He wore a white lab coat, starkly contrasting with his jet-black hair that rested raggedly above his otherwise plump, pale face. "Stocky" was a word he'd decided appropriately described his build. Stocky and large. Six foot three, to be exact. It was why he tended to bend over the tables, and now his body seemed to have taken a liking to the posture.

The nature of his mission demanded he remain hidden in the basement at all times, wandering hunchbacked between the white laboratory and his adjoining living quarters. The floor housed several other rooms, but Yuri had been out to the perimeter rooms only twice. His own quarters provided all the comfort he could expect here. Besides, as far as he was concerned, the more time he spent in the laboratory, the sooner he would finish his task. And the sooner he finished his task, the sooner he would be off to begin his new life, wealthy this time.

The walls about him were white. Four workbenches holding two lathes and two molding devices lined the walls. To Yuri's right, a door led to his living quarters, and next to the door, Plexiglas sealed off a ten-by-ten room. A single chrome refrigerator-sized safe stood in the room's center, facing a single table loaded with computers.

But Yuri's focus rested on one of two steel tables dead center on the lab's concrete floor. Brackets on each table gripped oblong objects—one the size of a football, the other twice that size. Both sat with opened panels, staring dumbly at the ceiling. Bombs.

Nuclear bombs.

Yuri stood with his arms crossed as he gazed at the shiny steel objects. He felt a buzz of contentment ring through his chest. They would work. He knew without a doubt that the bombs would work. A simple collection of exotic materials fashioned in perfect harmony. He had transformed them into one of the most powerful forces on earth. To find a party who would pay a hundred million for the smaller device would not be so difficult. Yuri had thought of little else in the last six months, and with the completion of the project at hand, the pressure he felt to make a decision seemed unbearable.

The skimpy salary Russia had driveled his way for so many years would be tip money. Socialism had its price, he had decided. Not even the Politburo should expect to breed the world's most brilliant nuclear scientists without rewarding them adequately. And now it was time to pay up. He smiled at the thought.

A fly took flight from the overhead light and buzzed past Yuri's ear before settling on the larger sphere.

For him the phone call almost seven years ago had been the voice of an angel. Why the Russian Mafia had chosen him he hadn't cared to ask. All he knew was that they had offered one hundred thousand dollars up front, in cash, an additional ten thousand each month, with a million-dollar bonus upon the completion of the project. That and the small detail that the project was for the Brotherhood, a militant Islamic group. Others had talked of getting jobs in the free world, but no other nuclear scientist could hope to make even one-hundredth of the offer. He had accepted unreservedly.

Securing the basic elements had taken three years, years during which, in all honesty, Yuri felt more like a captive than a scientist. But filling his shopping list, as he referred to it, took time in the new world.

Although their timing was right; if the Brotherhood had waited until after Bush had gone after Al qaeda and clamped down on proliferation as his administration had, the task would have been much more difficult. The Clinton years had been the right time.

The list was simple enough: Krytron triggering devices, high-grade detonators, high-yield explosives, uranium, plutonium, beryllium, and polonium. Along with scores of hardware items, of course.

Clinton years or not, one didn't walk into a hardware store and pick up initiators filled with beryllium and polonium. Weapons inspectors' discovery of Iraq's extensive nuclear program had brought about the tightening of the reporting required by the Nuclear Nonproliferation Treaty. And it wasn't just the plutonium and uranium that were carefully guarded, it was any component required for a nuclear device.

Case in point, a nuclear detonation requires absolutely perfect timing between the shaped charges surrounding the plutonium. Forty perfectly timed explosions, to be exact. If even one of the forty was off by the tiniest fraction of a second, the bomb would fizzle. Only one very rare triggering device could offer such precision: a Krytron device. And only two companies in the world manufactured Krytron triggering devices. Yuri needed eighty of them. Unfortunately, each was reported to a governing body and carefully tracked.

He could have gone for a new triggering mechanism, but the chances for failure would have increased considerably. No, he needed the Krytron devices and they alone took two years to secure, and then only because of the former Soviet Union's black market, which had its share of disgruntled officers willing to turn a blind eye for $100,000. The world's supplies of beryllium and polonium were as tightly monitored. The focus was always on the radioactive elements, like plutonium, but in reality the plutonium had been the easiest. There was a lot of it around and with his contacts in the Russian Mafia, he had secured it in less than six months.

Bottom line, all of the necessary elements could be obtained, assuming money was no object. Yuri wasn't sure where these men got their money—drug trade, oil, who knew—but they obviously had what it took. All the items he'd requested eventually made it into the jungle.

And now it was time to take them out of the jungle.

Of course, there was the small matter of Abdullah, and Abdullah was no one to play with. His heart was the color of his eyes, Yuri thought. Black.

Yuri walked over to the larger of the two weapons, a fission device roughly three times the yield of the Nagasaki device. To modern standards the design itself was basic, very similar to that of the first bomb. But there was nothing simple about the sixty-kiloton explosion it would create.

A black sphere rested in the opened panel, measuring thirty-five centimeters in diameter. It was dotted with forty precisely spaced red circuits with a wire protruding from each, giving it the appearance of a hairy fruit. To the front of the sphere sat a white receiver and a small collector. The outer housing shone silver—polished aluminum—no more than an expensive case for the black bomb inside. The large fly crawled over that shiny surface and Yuri reached a hand out to chase the insect off.

Four years and untold millions and now the prize: two shiny spheres with enough power to level a very large city. Yuri walked over to the supply cabinet and stepped into it. A wide range of small tools lined three of its walls. He knelt down, pulled out a brown wooden chest, and opened its lid. There lay his ticket to $100 million—two black spherical objects, identical in appearance to those in the nuclear devices. If he proceeded now, his fate would be sealed. He would either become a very wealthy man or a very dead man.

Yuri swallowed and willed his hammering heart to be still. One of those cursed flies lighted on his hair and he impulsively smacked at it, stinging his ear badly. He wiped his sweaty palms on his thighs, lowered trembling hands into the box and withdrew the smaller sphere. "Please, God," he whispered faintly. "Let this one last thing go in my favor." Of course that was ridiculous, because he no more believed in God than he believed he would live if Abdullah discovered him.

Yuri stood, shoved the door shut with his foot, and carefully carried the black ball to the metal table on which the smaller device sat. With a final glance toward the entrance, he began the swap.

The idea was simple, really. He would take the nuclear explosives out of their casings and replace them with identical-looking explosives that contained only air. When Abdullah did get around to exploding his little toys, they would not even spark. The nuclear explosive would be safe with Yuri. It was his creation—he should reap the rewards. Let the man deploy his imitation bomb. By the time Abdullah discovered the malfunction, Yuri would be halfway around the world with two very valuable devices for sale.

He completed the swap in under five minutes. Holding the volleyball-sized nuclear sphere in sweaty fingers, he returned to the closet and eased the orb into the brown crate. Then he repeated the entire procedure with the second sphere. He sealed the lid and stood as a shiver snaked up his spine. So far so good.

He took a mop and rested it on the lid, thinking the crate might not draw as much attention in such an attitude. On the other hand, the mop normally rested on the floor like any mop. Seeing it propped up so high might actually draw Abdullah's attention. Yuri returned the mop to the floor and chided himself for being overcautious. Wiping the sweat from his brow, he closed the closet door and stepped back into the lab. He would transfer the spheres to his suitcase later that night and take it with him to Caracas on his leave in the morning.

Yuri stood with his hands hanging loosely at his sides, breathing deeply, calming himself, and looking at the tables before him. The two aluminum cases looked as much like nuclear weapons as they had thirty minutes earlier. Only a trained eye would notice the small variations. So then. He had committed himself.

The bookcase to his left suddenly scraped along the floor and Yuri started. Abdullah? He leapt over to the tables and quickly scanned for any forgotten screw, a loose bolt—anything that might alert the Arab. He brought his sleeve across his face and picked up an idle voltage meter.

Abdullah entered the laboratory frowning, his jaw jutting below gleaming black eyes. He wore a pointed frown that seemed to ask, "So what have you been up to, my friend?" A chill washed through Yuri's skull.

"They are finished?" Abdullah asked.

"Yes, sir," Yuri answered. He cleared his throat.

The Arab stared at him without changing his expression for a few long seconds and Yuri felt his palms grow sweaty. Abdullah stepped forward. "Show me the remote detonation procedure again." He walked over to the table and glared over Yuri's shoulder. "Show me everything again," he said.

"Yes," Yuri answered and hoped the man could not feel the slight tremble in his bones. "Of course, sir."

19

Scattered light bulbs lit the darkening coast when the pilot finally cut the outboard to a gurgle and coasted the small boat to a rickety dock bordering the river town of Soledad. Casius paid the man his two-hundred-peso fare and made his way into the town toward the Hotel Melia Caribe. From a dozen trips downriver with his father, he knew it was one of three hotels in which one could expect to see tourists venturing this deep into the land.

The moment Casius stepped into the lobby his eyes rested on a pale, lanky man studying a newspaper in the corner. The man's eyes lifted and met his own. They held for a moment and then returned to the paper. Casius glanced about the room and quickly decided the man was the most likely prospect for a CIA agent. He returned his gaze to the man, willing him to look up again. If the man was an observer, fingering Casius with short brown hair and dark eyes might prove a challenge. But any man with his profile would be reported, and Casius wanted Friberg to know that he had spotted them as well. The man's eyes had grown still; he was no longer reading.

The man glanced up again and met his gaze. Casius nodded and winked. Recognition passed between them. His jaw firm, Casius turned and walked to the front desk, keeping the man in his peripheral vision. So Friberg had reacted quickly as expected. Forty-eight hours and they already had men in place.

He took a room on the second floor. He ruffled the bed, cracked a few drawers, tested the shower—leaving the shower curtain pulled—and wet a towel. Satisfied that the room looked used, he slipped into the hall. The back stairs led into the lobby below, but an old wooden fire escape led into an alley behind the hotel. Casius climbed through the fire escape, dropped into the alley, and made his way down the dark passage. No sign of the agent.

He walked through alleys to a small shop on the south side of the city. The gray cinder blocks splashed with dirty white paint looked unchanged from his last visit to this alley. Casius stepped up to the shop's back entry door, found it unlocked, and stepped into Samuel Bonila's gun shop.

He paused in the entryway, letting his eyesight adjust to the dim light.

"María?" a gruff voice called.

Casius stepped into the lighted shop and eyed Samuel evenly. The man blinked and returned the gaze.

"What are you doing?" Samuel demanded. "We do have a front door for customers. And we are closed."

"You are Samuel Bonila?" Casius asked, knowing the answer.

The man hesitated.

"I'm not going to hurt you," Casius assured him.

"Yes, that is my name. And who are you?"

"My father was known to you, Mr. Bonila. A foreigner who knew how to shoot. Perhaps you remember him?"

"A foreigner who—"

Samuel suddenly stopped and stared at Casius, searching. "You are . . . ?"

"Yes."

The storekeeper blinked and took a step forward. "But I can't see the resemblance. You've changed. You're nothing like the boy I remember."

"Time changes some people. I need you to keep my coming here to yourself, Mr. Bonila. And I need to purchase a few knives."

"Yes, of course." He glanced to the door. "You have my full confidence." He smiled, suddenly pleased. "And you will be needing a gun? I have some very fine imports."

"I'm sure you do. But not this time. I need two knives."

"Yes, yes." He took one more long look at Casius and then hurried to a case behind him.

Casius left the shop five minutes later with Samuel mumbling behind him. Ten minutes later he checked into a cockroach-infested joint that had the gall to call itself a hotel and took a room on the third floor. He shed the money belts, withdrew five thousand dollars, and hid the rest in the ceiling above the bathroom mirror. It had been over twenty-four hours since his last sleep. Exhausted, he fell onto the bed and slept.

He awoke six hours later to the sound of insects shrieking in the nearby forest as the city slept in silence. Without lighting the room, Casius splashed water on his face and stripped to his black shorts. The jaguar tattoo blackening his thigh would give him away in the jungle so he covered it with a wide band of medical tape. He withdrew a tube of camouflage paint from his pouch and applied the green oil to his face in broad strokes. It was a habit of stealth that successfully masked his face beyond possible recognition.

He shoved the bowie knife he'd purchased from the gun shop into the back of his waistband and strapped the Arkansas Slider around his neck. The waist pouch and the rest of his clothes he shoved under the bed.

Dawn broke over Casius's shoulder as he left the city on foot and entered the towering jungle. The plantation lay thirty miles due west. It would take him a day and a half to circle the valley and make an approach from the south. The route would add another thirty miles to the journey, but he'd decided the strategic advantage of the longer course outweighed the inconvenience. For starters, the CIA would expect him to take the quickest route now that he had been spotted. But more importantly, the cliffs would be relatively easy to guard. A southern approach, on the other hand, consisted of a hundred thousand acres of heavy jungle inhabited mostly by Indians. It would be more difficult to protect.

As he passed their nests, macaws and herons took flight—squawking at his intrusion into their world. Twice he stopped in his tracks as thousands of brightly colored parrots scattered to the skies, for a moment blacking out the rising sun. Spider monkeys gazed down, screeching at him. The air felt clean; the vegetation glistened with dew. Everything was untouched by human hands here. His bare feet were quickly covered with surface cuts but his pace remained unbroken. During the next thirty-six hours he would sleep only once, for a few hours. Otherwise he would stop for food—mostly fruits and nuts. Maybe some raw meat.

He grunted and cracked his neck as he ran. It felt good to be in the jungle.

20

Sherry Blake awoke from her first night of sleep in the jungle with a start. The vision had reoccurred. In terrifying colors and screaming sound.

It took her a few seconds to understand that she was in the mission house, alive and well—not on a beach trying to dig a hole in the sand to escape the acid. She ripped the damp sheet from her legs and reached the door before realizing she wore only a loose, oversize T-shirt. She wasn't in her apartment with Marisa, for heaven's sake. She was in the jungle with the priest. She returned for a pair of shorts and her shoes.

Outside, the jungle was shrieking its way into another day, but the noise in Sherry's mind came mostly from the people on the beach, as the acid rain fell from the mushroom, like brown globs of searing molasses. She shook her head and pulled on the boots.

When Sherry entered the common room adjacent to her sleeping quarters, Father Teuwen had already perked coffee and fried eggs for breakfast. "Good morning," he said, beaming a smile. "I thought you might enjoy—" He saw her face and stopped. "Are you all right?"

She lifted a hand to her hair, wondering what he saw. "Yes. I think so. Why?"

"You look like you saw a ghost. You didn't sleep well?"

"Like a baby. At least my body slept like a baby. My mind decided to revisit this crazy vision I keep having." She plopped onto the couch and sighed.

The father brought a steaming cup to her and she thanked him. "Yes, Helen mentioned them," he said.

She sipped at the hot coffee and nodded. "I think I might prefer a whale to this."

Father Teuwen smiled and sat opposite her in an armchair. "Even Jonah eventually decided that speaking the truth was better than the whale."

"And if I *knew* that word, I'd be all mouth. Here we are talking about messages from God and yet I don't have a message, do I? Not even close. All I have is some dreadful vision that plagues me every night. Like a game show in the heavens, daring the guest to crack some absurd riddle."

"Patience, my dear." His voice was soothing and understanding. "In the end, you will see. Your path will lead to understanding."

She leaned back and stared at him. "And maybe I don't *want* to go down this path. God is love—so where's all the love?"

He crossed his legs and spoke deliberately. "The path between the natural and the supernatural—between evil and good—is not such an easy path, Sherry. It's usually accomplished with things like death. With tormenting. Why do you suppose Christianity waves a cross on its flag? Do you know how cruel the cross was? You would think there might be a simpler, more humane means for God to bring about the death of his Son. But before fruit can grow, a seed must die. Before a child is born, a mother must wail. I don't see how a few sleepless nights is such an impossible price," he said, still smiling.

Sherry set the cup down, spilling a splash of coffee on her thumb. "A few sleepless nights? No, I don't think so, Father. I wouldn't call being locked in a box while your parents are butchered above you and then living through eight years of nightmares a few restless nights!"

The priest didn't flinch at the words. "Let me tell you a story, Sherry. I think it may bring this into perspective for you.

"One day not too many years ago, near the end of World War II, a common man—a doctor—was detained and brought to a detention camp with his wife. His twelve-year-old son was in the safekeeping of his grandmother, or so the doctor thought. In reality his captor, an obsessed man named Karadzic, had also found the boy. Bent upon breaking the doctor's spirit, they placed the man in a cell adjacent to two other cells—one holding his wife and the other holding his son. Of course he did not know his son was in captivity—he still thought he was safe with his grandmother.

"The wife's and son's mouths were strapped shut and each day all three were brutally tortured. The doctor was told that the screams from the cell on his left were his wife's screams, and those on his right were the screams of a vagrant child, picked from the streets. He was told that if he ordered the child's death, both he and his wife would be spared, and if he refused, they would both be killed on the eve of the seventh day.

"The doctor wept continually, agonizing over the groans of pain from his wife's cell. He knew he could spare her with the death of one stray child. Karadzic intended on dragging the son's body in after the doctor had ordered his execution, in the hopes of breaking his mind.

"But the doctor could not order the child's death. On the seventh day both he and his wife received a bullet to the head, and the boy was released." The priest paused and swallowed. "So the doctor gave his and his wife's lives for another, not even knowing it was that of his own son. Does this seem fair to you, Sherry?"

Sherry's head swam in the horror of the tale. Another emotion muddied the waters of her mind—confusion. She didn't respond.

"We don't always understand why God allows one to die for another's life. We don't easily fathom God's Son's death. But in the end"—he swallowed again—"in the end, Sherry, we will understand what Christ meant when he said that in order to save your life you must lose it."

Petrus looked away and shrugged. "Who knows? Maybe my parents' death saved me for this day—so that I might speak these words to you."

Sherry dropped her jaw. Father Petrus was the boy? "You were—"

The priest looked back to her and nodded, smiling again. "I was the boy." Tears wet his cheeks and Sherry's world spun. Her own eyes blurred.

"One day I will join my parents," the father said. "Soon, I hope. As soon as I have played my role in this chess match."

"They both died for you."

He turned away and swallowed.

Her chest felt as though it might explode for him. For her. She had lived through the same, hadn't she? Her father had died for her above that box.

The father had found love. Love for Christ. In some ways, she had as well.

"What is it with death? Why is the world filled with so much violence? Everywhere you turn there is blood."

He turned back to her. "In living we *all* eventually die. In dying we live. He has asked us to die. *Take up your cross and follow me.* Not a physical death necessarily, but to be perfectly honest, we of the West are far too enamored with our own flesh. Christ did not die to save us from a physical death."

"That doesn't remove the horror of death."

"No. But our obsession with life is as evil. Who is the greater monster, the one who kills or the one who is obsessed with their own life? A good strategy by the dark side, don't you think? How can a people terrified of death climb up on the cross willingly?"

The statement sounded absurd and Sherry wasn't sure what to make of it.

"In the great match for the hearts of men, it isn't who lives or dies that matters," Petrus said. "It's who wins the match. Who loves God. We each have our part to play. Do you know what the moral of my parents' story is?"

She looked at him.

"The moral of the story is that only true, selfless love will prevail. No greater love hath a man than to lay down his life for a friend. Or a son. Or a stranger in a cell next to you."

"Your parents *died.*"

"We *all* die. My parents defeated Karadzic. Their love set me free to do what it is I must do."

"So do you think I've been brought to the jungle to die?" she asked.

He tilted his head down slightly. "Are you *ready* to die, Sherry?"

A ball of heat washed over her skull and swept down her spine. It was the way he asked the question.

Are you ready to die, Sherry?

No.

It all swam through her mind—her parents' deaths, the father's story, her own nightmares—they all swirled together to form this lump that swelled in her throat.

She stood and walked into the kitchen. "What's there to eat?"

§

David Lunow handled the paper cup gingerly. Someone had told him that coffee grew acidic once its temperature fell below 170 degrees. He supposed real connoisseurs could gauge this with the dip of their tongue. All he ever managed was a blister and a curse. Either way, in his opinion, good coffee was always piping hot.

Mark Ingersol stood next to him on the arching park bridge and stared at the brown water below. "I know you hold some reservations about going after Casius, and frankly, I share them. But that doesn't mean we don't follow our orders. Neither does it mean we slack off. If the director wants us to take Casius out, then we take him out. Period."

"In my opinion, you're begging for problems," David said. "This is the kind of thing that blows up in your face." He felt Ingersol's stare, but he refused to look. "We've been at this two days and already Casius has walked in and out of our fingers, stopping just long enough to let us know that he was fully aware of our pursuit. We're lucky he didn't lure our man into some alley and kill him."

"Maybe, but that doesn't change our objective here. And that objective is to kill Casius."

Ingersol picked up a pebble that rested on the railing and flicked it into the water. It landed with a *plunk* and disappeared. "Well, we'll find out soon enough. The Rangers will be inserted before nightfall."

David leaned on the railing. "If they fail, I suppose you could always carpet bomb the jungle. You might get lucky." If Ingersol saw any humor in the statement, he showed no reaction. "Actually, if the teams fail, you wait for Casius to come out and hope to catch him on the rebound. Like I initially suggested."

"What are the Rangers' chances?" Ingersol asked.

David turned to Ingersol. "You mean chances of walking out of that jungle alive, or chances of killing Casius?"

Ingersol looked up at him blankly.

"Either way, some people are going to die. The only question is how many," David finally offered, and then added for Ingersol's benefit, "and who ends up taking the fall for it all."

§

Captain Rick Parlier blinked at the sweat snaking into his eyes. His square jaw sported three days of stubble, efficiently covered by a healthy layer of green camouflage paint, accentuating the whites of his eyes. His right hand gripped a fully loaded M-16. His left hand vibrated loosely to the thumping Pratt and Whitney above them. His last cigar protruded from curled lips. He was going back in, and he wasn't sure how he felt about that.

Parlier glanced at the others sitting expressionless in the dimming light and turned his head to the trees rushing below. The blades of the DEA troop carrier beat persistently above him as the helicopter carried his team farther and farther into the uncharted jungle. He'd taken Ranger teams into the jungle three times before, each time successfully accomplishing the objective laid before him. It was why he'd been selected, he knew. He could count the number of men with active jungle combat on a few hands. Now desert, that was different—a whole flock of them had tasted battle in the desert. Not that they'd actually fought much, but at least there had been real bullets flying around. Neither environment was what most would call a blast. But then, except in literal terms, war never was. He preferred the jungle anyway. More cover.

He'd thought the use of three teams to take out one man a bit hyperactive at first. But the more he read up on Casius, the more his appreciation for the two helicopters chopping in the sky behind them grew.

Three teams: Alpha, Beta, and Gamma, he'd dubbed them. Eighteen of the best jungle fighters in the Rangers' arsenal. The plan was simple enough. They would be dropped off on the summit of a mountain overlooking the valley Casius was supposedly headed for. The teams would set up observation posts and send scouts into the valley. Once positive identification had been made, they were to terminate the target at the earliest possible opportunity. Until then, it would be a game of waiting.

Only one restriction hampered their movement. Under no circumstances were they to pass the cliffs. Why? Why did the bureaucrats place any of their nonsensical constraints on them?

He glanced over his men, who sat unmoving. Behind those closed eyelids lives were being lived, memories recalled, procedures rehearsed. His first lieutenant, Tim Graham, looked up. "Piece of cake, Cap'n."

Parlier nodded once. Graham was their communications man. Give him a diode and a few capacitors and Tim could find a way to talk to the moon. He could also wield a knife like no man Parlier had ever seen, which was probably the single greatest reason the army had managed to steal the boy away from eager electronics firms.

The rest of the team consisted of his demolition expert, Dave Hoffman; his sniper, Ben Giblet; and two other light-fighters like himself: Phil Crossley and Mark Nelson. The team had trained and fought together for two years. There could hardly be a tighter fit.

His mind wandered to the target's portfolio. Casius was an assassin with "numerous" confirmed kills, the report said. Not ten or sixteen, but "numerous," as though it was a secret number. A sharpshooter who favored a knife, which meant he had the nerves of a rhino. Anybody who had the skill to take out a target at a thousand yards yet chose to get up close, eyeball to eyeball, had a few screws loose above them eyeballs. The worst of it was the man's apparent adaptability to the terrain. Evidently he had grown up in this jungle.

"What odds you put on this guy lasting the day?" Graham asked.

Phil scoffed. "As far as we know the guy's back in Caracas smokin' a joint and laughing his head off at the Rangers streaking off to pop some white man in leech country."

Someone chuckled. Hoffman eyed Phil. "They wouldn't send three teams to a drop point unless they had it on good intel this guy would show up."

"You don't get good intel this deep, my friend."

"Ready the drop line," Parlier barked as the helicopter feathered near the summit of their drop zone. The troop carrier hovered over a break in the canopy. Hoffman threw the two-hundred-foot rope overboard. Parlier nodded and he dropped into the trees, disappearing below the canopy. One by one the Rangers lowered themselves into the trees.

§

Deep within the mountain, Yuri Harsanyi sat shivering with excitement. In less than an hour a helicopter would take him away to safety. And with him, the large black suitcase that held his future: two thermonuclear weapons.

He had carefully stored the devices in his case the night before and then secured the straps tightly around the leather bag. The replacement bombs sat powerless in Abdullah's casings. When he tried to detonate his bombs, he would get nothing but silence. By then Yuri would be far removed, living a new life, squandering away his newfound wealth. He had rehearsed the plan a thousand times in the last three days alone.

Yuri saw that the left strap had loosened slightly in the humid heat. He cinched it tight and hoisted the suitcase from the floor. If they decided to inspect him now, he would have a problem, of course. But they'd never checked his bags before. He glanced around the room he'd lived in for so long and stepped away for the last time.

An hour later, precisely on schedule, the helicopter wound up and took off with Yuri sweating on its rear bench.

21

Casius plunged through the dense foliage, sweating bare chested, with mud plastered up his legs and streaking his chest, his black shorts now clinging wet and torn down the right thigh. He'd covered forty miles in the twenty-four hours since entering the jungle, tracking by the sun during the day and by the stars at night. He'd slept once, eight hours earlier. His father would have been proud of him.

But then his father was dead.

Casius halted at the edge of a twenty-foot swath cut from the forest floor, surprised to see the wide scar so deep in the jungle. The canopy above had survived and now grew together, creating the appearance of a large tunnel through the underbrush.

He pulled out a wrinkled topographical map. The compound lay ten miles to the east, in the direction of this wide overgrown path. Casius crossed into the jungle and resumed his jog.

Since his departure from the city, he'd eaten only papaya and yie palm cut on the run, but hunger pains now slowed his progress. Without a bow and arrow, killing a heron or a monkey would be difficult, but he needed the protein.

Ten minutes later he spotted the root that would give him red meat. Casius took his knife from his belt, cut deep into a twisted *mamucori* vine, and let the poisonous sap run over his blade. Under normal conditions the Indians dissolved the poison in boiling water, which would evaporate from any dipped surface, leaving only deadly residue. But he had neither the time nor the fire necessary for the application.

Finding the howler monkeys was like finding a traffic light in the city.

Approaching them undetected wasn't nearly as simple. The small animals had an uncanny sense of danger. Casius slipped behind a tree and eyed a group of five or six howlers shaking branches fifty meters away, high in a Skilter tree. He slid into the open and crept toward them. The approach was painstakingly slow, and for fifteen full minutes he inched forward, until he came to rest behind a large palm. Four monkeys now sat chattering unsuspecting on the end of a branch that hung low, no more than twenty meters from his position. Casius slipped from behind the tree and hurled his knife into the group.

They scattered in terror as the knife flipped toward them. The blade clanged into the branches, grazing one of the monkeys. It was two minutes before the poison reached the monkey's nervous system and sent it plummeting from its perch high in the tree, unconscious. He picked it up, snapped its neck with a quick twist, and resumed his push south. The poison would be harmless to him, and the meat would replenish his depleted energy. He had always preferred meat cooked but he had learned to eat it however it came. Today a fire was out of the question, so the meat would remain raw.

The sun had already dipped behind the horizon by the time Casius reached the rock outcropping overlooking the Catholic mission station, twenty miles south of his destination by the map. A scattering of buildings rose from the valley floor—it was inhabited then. Once the valley had been vacant. Now, even from this distance, a mile above, Casius could see a cross at the base of an airstrip flying a limp windsock.

A slow river wound its way past the end of the airstrip and then lazily wandered through the flat valley toward the south. If there was one thing Casius needed now it was information, and the mission might give him at least that.

He dropped from the cropping and began the descent. He'd seen no one on the station. Odd. Where were the Indians? He'd think they'd be loitering all over the place looking for whatever the missionaries might give them in exchange for their souls.

Half an hour later, he stepped from the jungle under a black sky and jogged for a long house lit with pressure lamps from the interior. The night sang with overlapping insect choruses, and the memory of it all brought a chill to Casius's spine.

Casius ran up to the house in a crouch and flattened himself next to a window. He looked through and saw two people seated at a wooden table, dipping spoons into their evening meal. A priest and a woman. The priest's collar was missing, but there was no mistaking his black-and-white attire. The woman wore a white T-shirt, the sleeves rolled once or twice baring her upper arms. Her dark hair fell shoulder length and for a moment he thought she reminded him of a singer whose music he had once purchased. Shania Twain. He had put the CD through his sound system only twice, but her image had made an impression. Or was it that actress . . . Demi Moore? Either way she brought images of a soft-souled American to his mind. Somehow misplaced in this jungle.

He watched the two eat and listened to their indistinguishable murmur for a full minute before deciding they were alone. He slipped around the house.

§

Sherry started when a knock sounded on the door. *Rap-rap-rap.*

The evening had been quiet. There were the comforting sounds normal to jungle living: the forest's song, a pressure lamp's monotonous hissing, clinking silverware. Following the father's confession of his parents' sacrifice, the day had floated by like a dream. Perhaps the most peaceful day she'd experienced in eight years. They talked of what it meant to lose life and what it meant to gain it. They talked of real love, the kind of love that gave everything, including life. Like her father had given, and according to Father Teuwen, the kind they were all asked to give. She let herself go with him, remembering the passionate words of her own father—reliving the best of her own spiritual journey, before the box.

It brought her peace.

For the last twenty minutes her mind had come full circle, to the box, to suffering. She had cried, but it wasn't a cry of remorse. It was the cry of a heavy meaning. A head cold was coming on, she thought. Unless it was only the day's crying that stuffed her sinuses.

And suddenly this *rap-rap-rap* on the door.

She glanced at Father Teuwen and swiveled in her seat to see the door swing open. A well-muscled stranger stood in the frame, his arms hanging loosely to his sides, his legs parted slightly, his shoulders squared. But this simple realization quickly made way for the dawning that the man wore only shorts. And torn shorts at that.

Sherry felt her jaw part slightly. His face was painted in strokes of green and black that swept back from his nose, casting the odd illusion that his head belonged on a movie screen, not here on a mission station. Brown eyes peered from the paint. A sheen of moisture glistened on the intruder's dirtied chest, as if he'd worked up a good sweat and then tumbled to the dust. Short-cropped, dark wet hair covered his head. If she didn't know better, she would have sworn that this man had just come from the jungle. But she did know better. He was a white man. And white men didn't come from the jungle during the night. It was too dangerous.

The stranger stepped into the room and pulled the door closed behind him. Now other details filled her mind. The sharp edges to his clenched jaw, the hardened muscles, the muddied legs, the wide band of browned tape around his thigh, the bare feet.

He was dripping on their floor.

"Good evening," he said, speaking evenly as if they should have expected this visit.

The father spoke behind her. "My goodness, man. Are you all right?"

The man shifted his eyes from Sherry to the priest. "I'm fine, Father. I hope I'm not intruding, but I saw the lights and hoped I could ask you a few questions."

Sherry stood. His voice moaned through her skull like a howling wind. She saw that Father Teuwen was already on his feet, gripping his chair with one hand. "Ask a few questions? Heavens, you sound like the jungle patrol or something, popping in to ask a few questions. Where on earth did you come from?"

The man shifted his dark gaze to Sherry for a moment, and then back to the priest. He looked suddenly lost, she thought. As if he'd crossed over from another dimension and mistakenly opened their door. She noted that her pulse raced and she assured herself that the man meant no harm.

"I'm sorry, perhaps I should leave," he said.

"No. You cannot leave, man!" the priest objected quickly. "Look at you.

It's night out there! A bit dangerous, don't you think?" He paused, catching himself. "But then I suppose you already know that. You look like you've just spent the day in the jungle."

For a moment the man did not respond and Sherry thought he had indeed made a mistake and was now looking for a graceful exit. A hunter perhaps. But what would a hunter be doing running around barefoot at night? The whole thing was preposterous.

"Perhaps I've made a mistake by coming here," the man said. "I should leave."

The father stepped up beside Sherry now. "This is a Catholic mission," the priest said evenly. "I'm sure you know that. I'm the priest here—I think I have the right to know the identity of a man who calls on my door in the middle of the night, don't you?"

The man's arms still hung loosely at his sides, and Sherry noted that the knuckles on his right hand were red with blood. Perhaps he was a drug runner, or a mercenary. Her pulse quickened.

"I'm sorry. I should leave." He shifted his feet.

"And why do you insist on withholding your identity, sir?" Father Teuwen asked. "I will have to report this, of course."

That stopped the man. He eyed the priest long and hard. "And if I tell you who I am, you won't report me?"

So the man was on the run! A fugitive. Sherry's pulse quickened again. She glanced at Father Teuwen and saw that he was grinning knowingly.

"That would depend on what you tell me, young man. But right now I can tell you that I'm imagining the worst. And if you tell me nothing, I will report what I imagine."

The stranger slowly smiled.

§

The moment the priest stood, Casius knew coming here had been a mistake and he cursed himself.

He had wanted to leave then, before the father asked any questions. Perhaps a missionary would hold his curiosity. But the priest had proved otherwise. And now he had no choice but to either kill them or take them into some kind of confidence. And killing them wasn't really an option either, was it? They had done nothing; they were innocent.

The woman's eyes were ringed in red, as if she'd been crying recently. He smiled at the father. "You're a persistent man. You don't give me much choice. But trust me, you may wish you'd let me go."

"Is that a threat? I suppose that goes for the sister as well."

He noted the woman's quick glance at the priest. So she was a nun then. Or at least she was being cast as a nun by the father. "Did I threaten your life, Father?"

The father glanced at the nun. "You don't have anything to fear from us."

Casius decided he would give them a bone, a herring—just enough to draw out their knowledge of the region. Sooner or later they would call on the radio, of course. But by then it would no longer matter.

"I work for the DEA. You know the agency?"

"Of course. Drug enforcement."

"We suspect a significant operation south of here. I'm on a reconnaissance mission. I was inserted a mile from here, at the top of the western ridge."

The priest nodded.

Casius paused, searching their eyes. "I'm planning to take the Caura River south tonight." In reality he was headed north, of course. "As for my dress, I realize it's not every day you see a westerner traipsing through the brush near naked. But then I'm Brazilian, from Caracas."

"You don't sound so Brazilian," the father said.

Casius ran out a long sentence of fluid Portuguese, telling him he was wrong before switching back to English. "I attended university in the United States. Now, if you don't mind, I have a few questions of my own."

"And your name?" the father asked.

"You may call me Casius. Anything else, Father? My GPA perhaps? My ancestry?"

The woman chuckled and then launched into a cough. Casius smiled at her.

"You're quite bold, Sister. Not many women would willingly choose the jungle as a place to live."

She nodded slowly and spoke for the first time. "Well, I suppose I'm not most women, then. And not many men, Brazilian or not, would run through the jungle, half naked, in bare feet."

She sounded as if she had a cold from her husky tone. He ignored the comment. "Have you heard rumors of any drugs south?" he asked, turning back to the father.

"To the south? Actually no. Which is surprising, because most of the Indians we serve are from the south. How far did you say?"

"Thirty miles, along the Caura River."

The father shook his head. "Not that I am aware of. They must be well concealed."

"Possibly. But I suppose that's why they pay me. To find the difficult ones," Casius responded.

"What about up north?" the nun asked.

He blinked. "Up north? Caracas?"

"Not the city. The jungle up north."

Casius glanced at the father. So they had their suspicions of the north.

"We've heard occasional rumors of drug running farther north. I think the sister refers to those rumors," the priest said.

Casius felt his pulse surge. "How long ago did you hear these rumors?" he asked, trying to sound casual.

"How long? They come sporadically." The father turned to the woman. "Wouldn't you say, Sister? Every few months or so." She nodded, her eyes a bit too wide, Casius thought.

"Interesting. Farther north, huh? How far north?"

"Twenty miles or so. Wouldn't you say, Father Teuwen?" the woman said.

"Yes."

Casius looked from one to the other. "Well, I'll definitely report it. Any unique details?"

They both shook their heads.

"I'm sorry, but what are your names?"

"Forgive me. Petrus Teuwen. And this is Sherry Blake. Sister Sherry Blake."

Casius nodded. "It's a pleasure meeting you," he said. He turned and reached for the door.

§

Sherry thought the man who called himself Casius knew more than he admitted and she thought to ask him about the assault on their mission. But the incident at the plantation occurred eight years earlier, and judging his age, he would have been too young to be involved with any agency at the time.

The longer she looked at him, the more she thought he resembled some outrageous drugstore action figure. Or one of those Wrestlemania wrestlers, snarling at the television cameras and flexing their muscles for the kids. Either way she had seen his kind before, and they had always made her cringe.

She saw the knife at his back as he turned. A large bowie shoved into his waistband. Casius could do more than observe, she decided. His image couldn't have stood in greater contrast to the day's discussion with Father Teuwen. A small knot of disgust churned in her belly.

The man suddenly turned back. "I'm sure you can understand my need for your silence," he said evenly. "At least for the next day or two. Drug merchants aren't well-bred men. They would think nothing of slitting your throats."

He said it so casually, so evenly, that Sherry wondered again if he himself were a drug runner, lying to gain their confidence and planning to return later and do just that. Slit their throats. But that made no sense. He could have done it already.

Casius turned from them, stepped through the door, and was gone into the night. She let out a breath of relief.

"Do you believe him?" the father asked to her left.

"I don't know. He smells like death to me," she replied, still staring at the closed door. Muddy water spotted the floor where the man had stood.

"Yes, he does," Father Teuwen agreed quietly. "Yes indeed, he does."

22

Casius left the mission house feeling a surge of blood lust pull at his pulse. He cut northeast through the jungle, his thoughts suddenly full of the woman. A nun possibly, but more likely a visitor by her wide eyes, posing as a nun for her own protection. If so, it had been the father's doing. Strong man, the father, worthy of his post. Hardship had visited the priest often, he guessed. The woman might not have the father's weathered soul, but her own soul wasn't as soft as Casius had initially guessed. Odd for such a feminine-looking woman. He pushed the thought from his mind and pressed forward.

A faint sound suddenly registered in his mind—a distant, abstract contradiction in the jungle. He caught himself midstride and stilled his breathing. A cough, perhaps? It didn't repeat itself, but now a rhythmic thumping drifted through the trees, from the direction of the mission.

Boots! Running for the compound!

Casius cursed under his breath. This deep in the jungle the heavy clodding of boots on the run was a sound rarely heard. Definitely military. He stood still and spun through his options. He was too close to his objective to ignore an attack.

He swore again and cut back through the jungle toward the mission station. The father and the nun had their own lives to live and defend—they weren't his concern. But those boots, they came from men who had no business in this part of the jungle—that made the priest and nun his concern.

Casius leapt over a log and sprinted down the jungle path, withdrawing the bowie as he ran. The mission clearing came abruptly, and he pulled up behind a wide tree on the compound's edge.

His pulse settled quickly and he slid around the tree, knowing the dark trunks at his back would keep him concealed.

A bright moon drifted between clouds, revealing two groups of men, clearly paramilitary by their khaki dungarees. A band of three or four ran doubled over for the utility shack at the airstrip's turnaround, possibly headed for the radio. Four others ran directly toward the mission house.

Without thinking through his options, his heart now pounding in his ears, Casius crouched low and ran for the mission house. They clutched rifles that jerked in cadence to their run. The sound of spare clips rattled with each foot-fall. They had come to kill.

Worse still, he was running after them. Racing right across this wide-open field in plain sight now, jeopardizing his whole mission for the sake of two mis-sionaries he hardly knew. No, he was protecting *his* mission. Yes, protecting his mission.

Two of the soldiers veered toward the living quarters on the left; two ran for the far right. Keeping those on his right cleanly in his peripheral vision, Casius cut left, wielding his knife wide, underhanded. The lead soldier smashed his rifle butt against the door with a loud *crack!* that split the night air. The door snapped open.

Casius reached them then, just as the first man lifted his leg to step inside. He crashed full tilt into the second man's back, propelling him chin first into the doorjamb. The soldier's jaw snapped with a crunch. The other man dis-appeared inside, unaware of his partner's troubles.

Casius saw the others to his right spin toward him. He operated solely on instinct, from the gut, where killing was born.

With his left arm he caught the man who'd crashed into the doorjamb under his arm before the man slumped to the ground. With his right he slashed his blade across the soldier's neck. He swiveled him like a shield to face the other two now fumbling with their weapons. One had his rifle at his cheek, the other at his waist. Casius slung his knife at the first man and released the man in his arms. He snatched the rifle from the dead soldier's hands and threw himself to his right.

Two sounds registered then: The first came from his bowie, drilling that first man in the neck. He knew that because he glimpsed it as he rolled not once but twice, chambering a round as he tumbled. The second sound came from within the building. It was a single gunshot. He knew immediately that someone had died inside.

Another boom crashed on his ears—that second man across the yard, next to the one with a knife in his neck, was firing at him. Casius came to his knee with the rifle at his shoulder, pumped two slugs into the soldier's chest, and spun to the first door again. To his right, both soldiers crumbled to the earth.

The night fell eerily silent and Casius knelt frozen, the rifle against his shoulder, trained on the dark doorway through which the first solider had disappeared. On the lawn, three of the man's compadres lay in heaps. Casius felt his heart thump against the wooden stock and he breathed deep, keeping that black doorway in focus.

Across the compound shouting came now. The other men had secured their objective and were coming. Casius watched the steel barrel sway with each breath, a throbbing cannon begging for a target.

But the target was taking its time, in there feeling for a pulse, gloating over spilt blood, no doubt. Heat flashed up his spine at the thought. Saving lives never seemed to come easy to him. Killing, on the other hand, was second nature. He was a killer. Slayer. Not savior. He should just waste them all and get on with it!

The door to his right suddenly burst open. At the same moment the dark doorway in his barrel sights filled with a beaming Hispanic male. He squeezed the trigger three times in rapid succession, slamming the man back in a silent scream.

The yelling rushed closer now.

Casius spun to his right and saw the woman standing there wide-eyed and gaping. Which meant the father had probably been shot.

"Wait there!"

He bounded across the lawn and into the living quarters. A figure ran out of the back room—Father Petrus, white-faced and haggard, but somehow alive.

"What . . . ?" the father began.

"Not now! Run!" Casius snapped.

The priest ran past him and Casius followed.

The woman hadn't moved. A glance told him that she'd been coherent enough to pull on work boots. She wore the same white T-shirt and shorts she'd worn earlier.

Casius crossed the lawn in four long strides and snatched the woman's hand. "Follow me if you want to live! Quickly," he said and tugged at her arm.

She refused to budge for a moment, her eyes scanning the dead bodies. A small guttural sound came from her throat. A moan. Her cold hand trembled badly in his own.

"Move!" Casius snapped.

"Sherry!" Petrus had spun back.

She sprang over the bodies, staggered once, nearly planting herself facedown, and then regained her balance.

They ran like that, Casius leading, pulling Sherry by an outstretched arm toward the looming jungle ahead and Father Petrus to their side. Voices began shouting behind, but at each other. Casius remembered the woman's white shirt. It would be an easy target. He ran faster, now literally dragging her behind. But honestly, he wasn't thinking of her. He wasn't thinking of himself either. He was thinking of that dark jungle just ahead. Once he reached that dark mass of brush he could resume his mission.

They plunged past the first trees, pell-mell. No shots rang out behind and he glanced back. No pursuit. Casius slowed to a quick walk.

A soft sob filtered into his ears. He blinked. For the first time a strange notion took shape in his mind. He had a woman in tow, didn't he? A woman and a priest. A small buzz droned between his ears.

He realized he still held the woman's hand. He dropped it and instinctively wiped his sweaty palms on his shorts.

He couldn't take them with him. The sob came again, just behind, through clenched teeth, as if she fought a losing battle to keep her emotions in check. A haunting from America, trailing him into the jungle like his own personal ghost, he thought.

Casius swallowed hard, refusing to look back. He could set them in the direction of a nearby village and send them packing with a slap on the back. But he might as well be sending them to their deaths.

And there's a problem with that?

No, of course not.

Yes.

Heat flushed his face at the thought and he veered from the path into the jungle. The men behind weren't pursuing, but there was no telling what else might show up on a marked path.

He mounted a large log bordering the trail and dropped beyond it. The woman's boots scuffed the log's bark. They were following without protesting. Fingers of panic raked his mind.

Casius spun around. The black canopy masked the moon high above. Sherry froze ten feet behind as if she were his shadow, staring at him with white eyes in the dark. Petrus stopped beside her. For a few long moments neither moved.

His options spun through his mind, calculated for the first time. On one hand he was tempted to leave them. Just bolt now while they stood like mummies, leaving them to crawl back to the path and survive on their own. Back to the mission perhaps. The men might have left.

On the other hand, she was a woman. And he was a priest.

Then again, that was why he *should* leave them. He could hardly make the plantation, much less penetrate it with them stumbling behind.

They still hadn't moved, a fact that now dawned on him with a glimmer of hope. Maybe the woman wasn't some soft-souled talker, but one of those athletic types. She'd kept up with him easily enough, it seemed. And she had just witnessed him shoot a man in the throat while the blood from two others flowed under her boots. Yes, she'd cried, but she hadn't screamed or wailed as some would.

In reality, leaving her would be killing her. His shoulders settled and he closed his eyes briefly.

When he opened them, he saw that the woman had taken a step toward him. The priest followed.

"Sherry and Petrus, right?" His voice sounded as though he'd just swallowed a handful of tacks.

"Yes," the priest said, voice steady.

He exhaled and squeezed his hands into fists. "Okay. Sherry and Petrus. Here's the way it is. You want to live? You do exactly as I say. No talking, no questions. Out here it could mean life or death. You take all those feelings in your chest and you stuff them. When we get to safety, you can do what you want. I'm sorry if that sounds harsh, but we're just trying to survive here. Not save souls."

"I'm not a nun," she said.

"Fine. Follow me as close as possible. Watch where I place my feet; it'll help. Father, you follow her. If you become too tired, tell me quietly." He turned from them and waded into the brush. Sherry followed immediately.

He slid over another waist-high log, thinking she might need help over. But from his sideways glance he saw that she mounted the log quickly and followed in step with Petrus right behind.

He would take them to the plantation's perimeter, stash them safely, and return after a quick penetration.

23

Abdullah Amir leaned over his desk, picking a scab that had formed over an infected mosquito bite on his upper lip. White miniblinds covered the window that overlooked the processing plant. Behind him a dilapidated bookcase housed a dozen books, haphazardly inserted.

Abdullah sucked blood from his lip and returned his attention to the Polaroids spread on the desk. He had taken them of the bombs in the lab below, their panels opened like two spacecraft waiting to be boarded while the Russian scientist slept. Beside the photographs, a hardcover book titled *Nuclear Proliferation: The Challenge of the Twenty-first Century* lay open.

It had been nearly a week since Jamal had made contact. He'd simply said that it was time and then vanished. The thought that the man might be on his way here to the compound had not escaped Abdullah. The thought both terrified and delighted him. He'd decided that if Jamal came, he would kill him.

A knock startled him. Abdullah shoved the photographs into the book and dropped the evidence into his top drawer. "Come."

Ramón opened the door and guided the captain of the guards, Manuel Bonilla, into the room.

The captain's eyes skirted him and beads of sweat covered Manuel's forehead. "Yes?" Abdullah said.

"We successfully took the compound, sir."

But there was more. Abdullah could see it in the man's tight lip. "And?"

"We suffered four casualties, sir."

It took a moment for Abdullah to understand the words clearly. When he did, heat surged up his spine and washed through his head. "What do you mean, you suffered casualties?" Abdullah felt his voice tremble.

The man stared directly ahead now, not making eye contact. "It was highly unusual," Manuel replied awkwardly. "There was a woman . . . She escaped with the priest."

Abdullah stood slowly. A wave of dizziness washed through his head. The infection on his lip stung. Not so long ago he would have lashed out in a moment like this, but now he only felt sick. What he was about to do loomed like a giant in his mind.

"I am sorry—"

"Shut up!" Abdullah screamed. "Shut up!"

He sat, aware that he was trembling. Where was Jamal?

"Find her," he said. "When you find her, you will kill her. And until then, you will double the guard in the valley."

Manuel nodded with an ashen face, sweat now running in small rivulets down his cheeks. He turned to leave.

Abdullah stopped him. "And if you think they are alone, you are an idiot."

Manuel nodded again, turned, and left the room.

"Have you heard from Jamal?" Abdullah asked Ramón.

"No, sir."

"Leave."

§

Parlier lifted his hand and peered over the rim with the night-vision goggles sticking from his eyes like Coke bottles. The valley dipped below him several miles before breaking abruptly at a formation he thought might be the cliffs they had been warned about. But in the jungle night, the formation was difficult to make out clearly.

Graham dropped to his belly next to him. "You see it?" he asked in a hushed voice.

"Not sure. I think so. We got us a valley and some kind of rock formation halfway down there." He pulled away the glasses and swiveled to Phil. "What do we have on the GPS, Phil?"

"That's gotta be it. We're 5.2 clicks north, northeast of the compound."

Parlier twisted back on his elbows. The others joined him along the rock outcropping. He peered through the glasses again. "Then that has to be it. We have, say, a couple miles to the cliff and then another couple to the bottom of the valley. There must be a clearing in there somewhere, but I'm not seeing it with these things. Anyone else see a clearing?"

They peered ahead, some through goggles, others dumbly into the night. A mile behind them Beta and Gamma teams waited for their first intel report before taking up their positions. By the look of things, the airdrop had put them on the money.

"Nothing," Phil said. Someone slapped an insect from his skin.

"So our man is supposed to come out of this valley?" Graham asked. "He'll have to cross those cliffs. That's where we nail him."

Phil grunted. "And we're supposed to sit and wait for this guy up here? I say we cover the top of the cliffs."

"Can't," Parlier said. "We have orders to stay back. Graham, get on the horn and tell Beta to make for a position one mile due east. And Gamma one mile west. I want twenty-four-hour surveillance on that cliff, starting now." He turned to his sniper. "Giblet, you think you could put a round where it needs to go from this distance?"

Ben Giblet studied the jungle below them. "It would be tight. Yeah."

Graham looked at Parlier with skepticism. "We gotta get down there, Rick, and you know it. What's the big deal? We got us a compound with a bunch of druggies down in the valley. I don't see the danger in taking the cliffs."

"That's not the point. We have our orders."

Parlier peered into the dim light below. Graham was right, of course. But the orders had been to stay away from the cliffs. Meaning what? Meaning the *face* of the cliffs or the *lip* of the cliffs? If it came down to it, he might do some interpreting of his own on this one, he thought.

§

The *Princess* cruise ship rested in the green harbor waters under a black sky. The ship bustled with passengers who scurried up and down her planks like ants to and from their nest. Yuri Harsanyi boarded the luxury cruiser bound north for San Juan and headed quickly for his cabin. The short-notice fare had cost him three thousand dollars and he had barely made the ship before its scheduled departure at 10 P.M. But he was safe. And the suitcase was with him.

He glanced nervously down the narrow hall before opening the door to his assigned cabin on the third level: #303. There was no way anyone would find him here. He fumbled with his key, unlocked the cabin door, picked up the heavy bag, and entered his room. He boosted the case onto one of the double beds and walked across the cabin to the small bathroom. He looked in the mirror and stretched his neck, thinking he should shower, shave, and then go for dinner. He stepped from the cramped room and removed his shirt.

He shed his slacks and eyed the black case. It contained enough power to vaporize the ship in less than two-thousandths of a second. One minute here, the next—*poof*—gone. Six inches of steel hull disintegrated like the sides of a soap bubble. That man had ever discovered how to harness this incredible power was a miracle. He wondered briefly if any damage had come to the devices during the trip out of the jungle. But the suitcase hadn't left his side.

Yuri reached into the shower and turned the hot water on. His dirty clothes lay strewn on the floor. After testing the water, he stepped into the shower.

But his shaving kit was still in the suitcase.

Yuri stepped from the shower and walked quickly over to the suitcase. He hesitated, watching water drip from his wet face onto the hard case. Then he reached down, released the straps, sprung the latches, and opened it.

For a brief moment Yuri's eyebrows scrunched at the sight within. The two spheres he had placed in the case were gone. Instead a square box rested among the clothes. And then his eyes sprang wide. Abdullah had found him out! Taken his bombs and put this . . .

In that moment, two tungsten contacts fell together, sending a surge of DC current into a detonator that ignited C-4 explosive. An explosion shredded the room precisely three seconds after Yuri opened his case. No nuclear explosion—just plastic explosive that had been substituted for Yuri's bombs.

Even then the explosion was no laughing matter. Ten pounds of high explosive incinerated the cabin in a single white-hot flash. The explosion rocked the port side of the ship. Fire, smoke, and debris spewed out of the porthole that had erupted under the impact of the blast. Amazingly the flame-resistant mattresses, although gutted of their stuffing, did not burn.

But then Yuri Harsanyi could not be aware of these small details. His life had already ended.

24

Sherry kept to the painted man's heels, depending on his movements to guide her through the brush. What sight they did have in the dark seemed more instinctive than a function of sensory perception. An instinct the man had obviously developed. An instinct that neither she nor Petrus had. The father was strong and he kept up, but at this pace, he was hardly better than she.

She was a medical intern from Denver, Colorado, who should be following a doctor on his rounds through whitewashed halls right now. Not running through a nightmare, behind some crazed lunatic. Maybe it was just that— another nightmare grabbing at her boots and slapping at her face instead of real tree roots and leaves clawing at her. She prayed she would bolt up in bed soon.

Actually the dream idea made some sense. She couldn't remember waking, which could mean she still slept. She'd gone to her room to retire; she remembered that. And then the gunshots and the images of killing and now this man leading her like a rabbit through the jungle. The thoughts careened through her skull as she struggled to keep him in sight.

Hadn't he said something about going south on the river? She had no idea where they headed, but this was no river. An image of Father Petrus popped into her mind. *Living is about dying.* His words echoed in her mind. *We all live to die.*

"So do you think I have been brought to the jungle to die?" she'd asked, barely serious.

"Are you ready to die, Sherry?" The words suddenly struck her with clarity. Was she ready to die? No, she wasn't. Right now all she felt was a strong urgency to survive. *God, save us. Please save us.*

Casius had killed with the ease of a man shooting pool, she thought. Which made him what?

On the other hand, he had saved them. Without Casius she would be back in that yard now, lying in her own blood. Which made him her angel in the night. But could an angel kill the way this man had killed?

She suddenly slipped hard to her seat and grunted. Mud oozed through her denim shorts. She scrambled to her feet before Petrus reached her. She ran forward, realizing that Casius hadn't even paused to see if she was okay. He was there, not ten feet ahead, his back still rising and falling like a shadow. A branch smacked her face and she threw an arm against it, tempted to rip it off the tree and stomp it underfoot. She swallowed the frustration growing like a knot in her throat and pushed forward.

Sherry followed relentlessly, stumbling quite regularly, several times to her seat. Twice she lost Casius and was forced to call out. Each time Petrus ran into her and muttered apologies. When it happened, the man had been no more than five yards from them. If he made more noise, it would have been much easier, but he seemed to glide like a ghost. Tracking both him and the ground proved nearly impossible.

She explained the problem to him defensively the second time. He stared at her through the dark for a few seconds, as if trying to comprehend. Then he turned and continued, but this time awkwardly brushing his hands against the foliage to make some noise as he passed. That helped her. But then the rain came, and what had seemed nearly impossible became downright ridiculous.

Sherry let the tears come to her eyes again, wiping constantly to clear her vision. But she would not let the man hear her silent sobs as she pushed on.

Oh, God, please let me wake up.

§

The journey had been an easy one until the rains began. And even that wouldn't have been such a problem if it hadn't come as they began a sharp descent into a valley. The dark, steep jungle, now wet, proved to be the limit. Their pace slowed to a crawl. Casius stopped frequently and waited for the woman to catch up, slipping and sliding her way down the mountain.

He pitied her, after a fashion. Poor woman had come to the jungle probably thrilled to visit, and now she had been thrust into this impossible world. And led by him of all people. He was no ladies' man. If she didn't already know it, she would soon enough.

Her strength surprised him. She might not have developed the skills to navigate through the foliage with ease, but she had the will of a jaguar.

Midpoint down the descent, Casius admitted bitterly that reaching the plantation before dawn would not be possible with the two. Fortunately, the rain would wash most of their tracks away, which was good considering the jungle would certainly be searched at first light. The attack had been no random pillaging. On his own he would press on, night or day, search or no search. But not with this woman and priest crashing through the brush behind him. They would be spotted from the sky, smashing into trees and shaking their limbs.

Which meant they would have to hide out during the day. With a woman. And a priest.

"All right, mister," the woman suddenly snapped through the darkness. "*This* is too much. We're cut, we're bruised, and we're exhausted. Will you stop for just a minute and let me rest?"

He spun. "Why don't you hoist a flag above the trees while you're at it? Just in case they missed your voice." She peered at him angrily through the darkness. "We will rest soon," he said and turned back down the hill.

They had traveled seven or eight miles from the mission when Casius found the cave. Overgrown vines coated with moss covered its mouth but the lay of the rock clearly suggested a break. He walked past it twice before pulling the matted brush aside enough to make out a small cavern. He pried the covering aside to create a hole for them to crawl through. "Crawl in," he said, waving them forward.

The woman came close, her mouth wide, gazing into the damp darkness. "In there?" she asked.

"You wanted to rest. You can't just flop on the ground and fall asleep.

They'd find you for sure. We'll be safe in there." He jabbed a finger into the blackness.

"It'll be safe? What if something else is in there?" Her voice came ragged and breathy; her cold was worsening.

"Just don't threaten it. Go in slow," he said.

She pulled back and shifted her hazel eyes to his.

Father Petrus stepped up, looked up at him, and slid into the cave without a word.

"You go," Sherry said. "I'll hold this for you." She slid behind him and grabbed the tangle of vines at his hand, gripping his forefinger with them.

He pulled himself free and shrugged. "Suit yourself," he returned and slipped through the opening. The cave immediately opened up to a small enclave, perhaps seven feet square. A damp moss blanketed the ground, providing for a fairly comfortable bed. The sound of critters scurrying confirmed that they were not alone—spiders by their light ticking. But most spiders would scatter, not attack. They would be safe enough. He could barely see her outline against the dark sky as she entered haltingly.

"As long as we're stopped, we should sleep," he said matter-of-factly. "In the morning I'll try to get you something to eat. As soon as we're sure the jungle is clear, we'll leave."

"I want to thank you for what you did back there," Father Petrus said.

"I wouldn't thank me just yet, Father. We're not exactly in the Hilton yet."

"Actually, I'm not thinking of my own comfort. But God—"

"This has nothing to do with God."

That shut the man up. Casius found himself wishing he'd left the priest in his bungalow.

"Get some sleep," he said.

Sherry sat cross-legged, quiet for a moment, peering around in the darkness. "I'm not sure I can sleep," she finally rasped. "I said I was tired and bruised, not sleepy. I'm not sure if you happened to notice with all of that testosterone floating through your veins, but we've been just a bit traumatized here."

No, not soft-souled at all. Not this one. "Suit yourself," he said as calmly as possible. He patted the moss with his open palm and turned his back to her, as though she were already the furthest thing from his mind. He dropped to his side and closed his eyes without the slightest interest in sleep now.

The priest followed his example, whispering encouragement to the woman. For several minutes the cave remained quiet behind him. And then the woman lay down, but by her ragged breathing, he knew she was not acclimating well. In fact, she now seemed at her worst. Surely, at some point exhaustion would take her.

Casius ground his teeth and forced his mind to run through his options for the hundredth time.

§

Sherry woke to the smell of burning wood. She started and pushed herself to her arms. Three feet away a small fire managed to burn through damp wood, filling the cave with smoke.

The vision had come again and raged with its intensity, soaking her with sweat. And now she had awakened. Which clearly meant that the rest of this was not a vision or a nightmare or any other such supernatural episode. The attack, the escape, and now this cave—they were all real. Sherry swallowed and sat all the way up.

Father Petrus slept on one side, head facing the wall away from her.

How Casius had managed a fire of all things, she didn't know, but he bent over it now, blowing into the coals as rising white ash filtered through his hair. A single small flame flickered lazily over red embers. Smoke drifted past him, bent at the cave's ceiling, and then wandered out the small opening through which they had crawled in the night. The tiny firelight flickered amber on the rough stone walls, highlighting a dozen plum-sized insects fixed to the cave's interior. Sherry swallowed again and turned her eyes to a dead lizard lying limp next to the man.

"Good morning," he said without looking up from the flame. "The fog is thick outside, so I lit a small fire. It will mask the smoke. You need some food, and I didn't think you'd want to eat it raw. We'll wait here until the search parties have come and gone."

"What search parties?"

"They know we escaped. They will send out search parties."

Made sense. "Where are we going?" she asked.

"I'm taking you to safety," he replied.

"Yes, but to where?"

"The Caura River. We'll find a boat that can take you to Soledad."

His voice tweaked a raw nerve in Sherry's spine, reminding her that she had decided she did not like him. She stared at the wide yellow strip running from the creature's snout to its tail. If she had woken hungry, her appetite had already made a hasty retreat. She looked up at the man as he quickly skinned the lizard with a large knife and lay strips of its flesh in the coals.

The firelight danced off broad, muscled shoulders. He knelt over the coals and she thought his calves must be twice the size of her own. The broad band of tape still clung to his thick thigh. A makeshift Band-Aid perhaps. Dark hair lay close to his head. His eyes glimmered brown in the dim light. Camo paint was still plastered on his face, unwashed by the rain.

Whoever he was, she doubted he was simply a DEA scout who'd grown up in Caracas. In another world he could easily bear the title "the Destroyer" or "the Emancipator" or some other such stage name. The likeness resonated.

Smoke stung her eyes. "Is there a way to get rid of the smoke?" she asked. Her cold had worsened through last evening's rain. She cleared her sore throat.

He looked at her and blinked once. "No." He returned to the preparation over the fire, and she realized he would probably insist she eat the meat.

She unfolded her cramped legs and stretched them before her, leaning back on her hands. Mud had dried on her shins and thighs, no doubt covering a dozen cuts and bruises. She rested one boot over the other and edged close to the fire, watching the man's face. He glanced at her legs quickly and then back to the lizard meat now simmering in the red coals.

"Look, Casius." She cleared her throat again, thinking she sounded like a husky man with the cold. Her chest felt as though a vise had moved in over night. "I realize this is all a terrible inconvenience for you. We've crashed some terribly important mission you were dying to complete. Life-and-death stuff, right?" She flashed a grin, but he merely glanced at her without responding. A wedge of heat rose behind her neck.

"The fact is, we are together. We might as well be civilized."

He pulled the meat from the fire, laid it on the moss, and sat back to his haunches. "You've thrown a kink in my plans." He lifted his eyes and studied her for a moment.

Sherry shoved herself up and crossed her legs. "Is that how you see us? A kink?"

He dropped his eyes to the fire and she saw his jaw muscles clench. *Now that was good, Sherry. Go ahead, alienate the man. He's obviously a brute with the social skills of an ape. No need to enrage him. Just toss him a banana and he'll be fine. He saved your life, didn't he?*

Then again, she wasn't exactly the queen of social graces either. "You know, the thing of it is, I didn't choose this. And I don't mean just *this*, as in running through the jungle with some . . . Tarzan, but coming to the jungle in the first place."

He didn't respond.

"A week ago I was a medical intern, studying with top honors. And then my grandmother convinces me that I have to get to this mission station two hundred miles southwest of Caracas. Something terrible is about to happen, you see. And I'm somehow a part of it. I'm having terrible nightmares about something that's going to happen. So I rush down here, only to be thrown into a bloodbath. Do you know how many men you killed back there or don't you count?"

He looked up at her. "Some men need to be killed."

"Some?"

He held her eyes for a few seconds. "Most."

The word seemed to fill the enclave with a thick silence. *Most?* It was the way he said it, as if he really meant it. As if in his opinion, most people had no business living.

"You are right," Father Petrus said. Sherry turned to see that he'd awoken and faced them. "In fact, all men need to be killed—one way or another. But not by you they don't. You are the hand of God?"

The corner of Casius's mouth lifted. "We are all the hands of God. God deals in death as well as life," he said.

"And to whom do you deal death?" Father Petrus asked.

Casius looked as though he might break off the conversation. He dropped his eyes and stirred the coals. But then he looked up.

"I deal death to who he tells me to kill."

The fire crackled.

"*Who* tells you to kill?"

Casius stared, eyes blank. "Your God, as you call him, doesn't appear to be so discriminating. He slaughtered whole nations."

"Are you directed by God?"

No response.

"Then, you are against him," Petrus said. "And in the grand scheme of things, that's not such a good place to be. But still, we are grateful for what you did. Now, what's for breakfast?"

Casius glared at him. Looking at the man, a small portion of sorrow spread through Sherry's chest. There was a whole history there that neither she nor Petrus could possibly know.

She dropped her eyes to the fire, suddenly feeling heavy. "I was told yesterday that life comes through dying." She lifted her eyes and saw that Casius stared at her. "Are you ready to die, Casius?"

She had no idea why she asked the question. Really she was asking it of herself. A knot rose to her throat and the flames suddenly swam. She swallowed.

Casius tossed a stick onto the fire, sending a shower of sparks to the ceiling. "I'll be ready to die when death defeats me."

"So . . ." She was speaking again, and she still wasn't sure why. "Death hasn't put its claws into you yet? You yourself haven't felt the effects of death—you're too busy killing."

"You speak too much," he said.

This was all wrong. She didn't mean to insult this man. On the other hand, he reminded her of everything she'd come to believe was offensive. Men like Casius had killed her parents.

"I'm sorry. It's not that I'm not grateful for your help—I am. You just bring back some pretty . . . awful memories. I've seen enough killing." She looked at Petrus. "The father told me that for every killing, there is a dying. There were two sides to the crucifixion of Christ—a killing and a dying. Like in some grand chess match, there are the black players who are the killers, and there are the white, who are the die-ers. One kills for hate, while others die for love. I was just coming to understand that . . ."

"You show me someone—anyone—who dies for love, and I'll listen to you. Until then, I will kill whom I have to. And you should learn to keep your mouth closed."

"You are CIA?" Father Petrus asked.

He pulled back into himself then and breathed deliberately. "I've said too much already. I'll be back as soon as I check the perimeter." He stood abruptly, walked to the entrance, and slid out, leaving Father Petrus and Sherry alone with the fire.

And the lizard.

25

Wednesday

They spent the rest of the morning in an odd silence, waiting for signs of a search, huddled speechless in the small cavern. Several times the woman made comments in hushed tones, but Casius immediately lifted a finger to his lips. As long as they were in the cave, they wouldn't have the advantage of being able to hear an approach. Their own silence became critical. He was glad for the restriction.

Casius made the fifth perimeter sweep of the day, stepping lightly from tree to tree, eager to confirm the direction of any search party and resume their journey north. Eager to step beyond the strange dichotomy that seemed to rear its head as the day progressed.

He decided that the priest's and woman's presence was simply an inconvenience. A *kink,* as he'd said. As long as he ignored them, they wouldn't be much of a threat to his mission. He'd soon dump them in the arms of safety and continue. He pulled into the shadow of a large Yevaro tree and scanned the slope before him. Several times helicopters had beat low over the trees, possibly carrying men to the search. So far, none had ventured this deep.

He leaned on the tree and thought about the woman. Sherry. She was an enigma. For reasons out of his grasp, ignoring her was more difficult than he had imagined. She kept popping into his mind like one of those spring-loaded puppets. Only she was no more a spring-loaded puppet than he was her monster. The talk had put a spur in his chest. A small ache. *And what about you, Miss Sherry Blake? You and your mission from God, come to the jungle to die with your priest. What kind of heart do you have?*

A good heart. He knew that and it gnawed at his mind. She'd surprised him with the questions earlier and he had surprised himself even more by engaging her. An image of her leaning back in the dim firelight rose in his mind's eye. Her dark hair lay on her shoulders; her hazel eyes glistened like marbles in the flickering flame. The white T-shirt was no longer white, but muddy brown. She had well-muscled legs and a silky smooth complexion under the dirt. Her cold had turned her voice husky and her eyes a little red. She'd slept again—stretched on her side, her head resting on her arm. Sherry Blake.

He'd seen someone who looked like her before. Not Shania Twain or Demi Moore, but someone from his past. Someone from Caracas maybe. But he had shut out his past. He couldn't even remember what his father or mother looked like. They said the stress of the killing had done that. Washed out portions of his mind.

Casius left the tree and scaled the hill to his right quickly. He paused at its crest and listened carefully. Far off, possibly as far as the mission, another helicopter whacked at the sky.

The snap of a twig interrupted his thoughts and he shrank back into the tree's shadow. Down the slope, slogging away from them, three men headed back toward the mission. So they had come and gone then. He watched them step carefully through the brush, dressed in khakis and a mismatch of paramilitary garb. They held their course and disappeared through the jungle.

Casius turned and retreated to the cave quickly. He found Sherry on her side and the priest poking a stick at the ashes, attempting to revive the dead fire. Light streamed in through the vines at the entrance now.

"I'm sorry, but I had to extinguish the fire when the fog lifted," he said, dropping to one knee. "They're gone. We'll go now."

He slid through the opening, followed by the woman and then Father Petrus. It dawned on him that if a guard had been waiting in the open he would have hardly noticed. He swore under his breath. For all their talk of killing, the pair might be the death of him.

He looked at Sherry, suddenly struck by her beauty in the full light. "Let's go," he said.

§

"Where did you last have them in sight?" Abdullah asked. It was late and he was tired. Tired from the lack of sleep, tired of incompetent men, tired of waiting endlessly for Jamal's call.

Ramón leaned over the map in the security room. Other than the laboratory below, this room contained the only real sophistication in the compound. There was the processing plant, of course, and the conveyors that took the logs to the chute through the mountain, but those were relatively basic operations. Security, on the other hand, was always a matter of the highest regard in Abdullah's mind. Not even Jamal knew what he had here.

The map showed the boundaries of the perimeter security system, a sensitive wire buried several inches under the forest floor. Using radio waves, the system showed the mass of any object that crossed over, allowing them to distinguish animals of smaller mass from humans.

"They crossed here." Ramón pointed to an area south of the compound. "Three persons. Traveling fast, I think."

Abdullah blinked, letting the last statement settle. Who could possibly be in the jungle so close to the compound? Hunters maybe. The infection on his lip throbbed and he ran his tongue over it gently. "How can you know they are traveling fast?" he asked.

"They crossed the perimeter here and then exited here, ten minutes later. At first we thought they had left, but within a few minutes they reappeared here."

Heat spread down Abdullah's neck. Hunters? Yes, hunters might move about like that. But so deep in the jungle? It could just as easily be a sniper with his spotter. Or a reconnaissance mission, launched by some suspecting party. The Russians, perhaps, somehow tipped off as to Yuri's location after all these years. Or the CIA.

Or Jamal.

"And what have you done?" he asked.

"I have ordered Manuel to pick them up."

Abdullah whirled to the man, his eyes glaring. "Pick them up? And what if it's a sniper? How do you plan on picking up a trained sniper? You don't just pick up trained men; you take them out!"

Ramón stepped back. "If we kill them and they are in contact with some authority, then their absence will be a warning. I thought they should be taken alive."

Abdullah considered that, turning from the man as he recognized the validity of the man's point. "But you don't just pick them up as if they were stray dogs. You saw how well Manuel did with the mission compound. How can you possibly—"

A rap suddenly sounded on the door and Ramón opened it.

Manual stood, winded and breathing hard. "We have spotted them, sir. Two men and a woman."

"Good!" Ramón said. "Take them with the tranquilizers."

Manuel turned to leave. "And Manuel," Abdullah said. "If you let these three escape again, you will die. Do you understand?"

The guard stared wide-eyed for a moment and then dipped his head.

§

Casius led them through the jungle at a punishing pace. To make a statement, Sherry thought. The statement that he wanted to leave her and her big mouth for the animals. They moved steadily through the trees, down one slope, over the next, up a cliff, through a creek, only to begin the cycle again.

The man dragging her through the brush was a killer many times over, that much was now painfully obvious. Like the men who had killed her parents. Killers for some abstract cause, ignoring the simple fact that for every one they killed, someone else was sentenced to live with that death. A brother, a sister, a wife, a child. No telling how many nightmares Casius had spawned in his years. She detested the man.

On the other hand, he had saved her life. And every time he spoke she found herself chasing away an absurd sentimentality. As if he were her guardian. God forbid.

But true enough. It was why she had become so angry at him, she decided. It was as if her parents' killer had stepped out of her nightmares and come to save her with a flashing smile. One last twist of the knife.

The muscles in his calves balled and flexed with each stride. His bare feet moved effortlessly over the forest floor. Sweat glistened on his broad shoulders. At one point she found herself wondering what it would feel like to run a finger over such insanely massive muscle. She quickly dismissed the thought.

Father Petrus took up the rear, and Sherry thought about his suggestion that she was now on God's path, waiting for God to reveal truth as he saw fit. And if so, then this man was also a part of God's grand plan. Maybe somehow connected to the vision. Yes, the vision that came around each night like the falling of a pole-driver. That mushroom growing huge, night after night.

Casius had paused three times in the last fifteen minutes, surveying the land ahead carefully. Now he stopped a fourth time and raised his hand for silence.

A flock of parrots squawked into flight above them. Sherry held a hand to her chest, feeling her thumping heart beneath her fingers. "What is it?" she whispered.

He jerked a finger to his lips, listening.

§

Casius had felt it four times now—that hair-raising sense of prying eyes. They had progressed to within two miles of the compound, the last three hours under cover of darkness. He would leave Sherry and the father there under the shadow of several large boulders, scout the plantation quickly, and return for them within a few hours. He would then take them to the Caura River and return depending on what he found at the compound.

At least that had been in his mind. But now this tickle at the base of his brain unnerved him.

He had seen no sign of men. And yet that fourth sense—as if they'd been monitored by invisible eyes for the past fifteen minutes. In the dark, the man who used surprise wielded the biggest weapon. As an assassin he had relied heavily on sudden surprise in darkness. Losing it now with the woman and the priest would force him to abort his plan until he could get rid of them.

On the other hand he had been careful, staying under the heaviest canopy and avoiding ridges. Only a lucky observer could have picked them out and then only with powerful scopes. If there had been men stationed on the ground, he would have discovered them; he was confident of that.

Casius lowered his hand and stepped forward. Behind him, Sherry and Petrus followed. Although they hadn't talked, Sherry's disposition toward him had changed in the last few hours, he thought. Less animosity. Sharing the struggles of life and death united even enemies, it was said. Maybe that accounted for his own growing apprehension over leaving her alone while he scouted the plantation. In fact, it could have been her presence that brought that tickle to his neck.

Within ten minutes, they came to the edge of a clearing. Twenty yards out a small pond shone with the moon's reflection. Three large boulders jutted from the ground at one end. He turned to them and nodded. "All right. See those boulders? I want you to wait under them for a few hours while I scout ahead."

Sherry stepped next to him, breathing steadily from exertion. He could smell her breath, like only a woman's breath could smell, although he could not imagine why—she hadn't worn lipstick or gloss for at least twenty-four hours. She peered ahead, her lips slightly parted, apprehension clear in her round eyes. Her shoulder touched his arm and it startled him.

She faced him and he shifted away as casually as possible. "A few hours? For what?" she asked.

Casius opened his mouth, not sure what he intended to say. It was then, with his mouth gaping and she looking like a puppy up at him that the faint coughs carried to him on the wind.

The instant before the darts reached them, he knew they were coming. And then they struck, *whap, whap*, the first in his arm, the second in his thigh. Thin and hairy and buried to their hilts.

Tranquilizer darts!

Whap, whap! Sherry was hit!

His first thought was of Friberg's face, grinning back in Langley. His second was of the woman. He had to save Sherry.

He slung an arm around her waist and pulled her back, deeper into the jungle's cover. She was saying something. He could smell her breath, but he could not make out her words. He faced her and saw her wide eyes, inches from his face.

Casius staggered back as the drug swept through his veins. He fell, still holding the woman, breaking her fall with his own. Far away a shout rang out. Spanish, he thought. So he had been followed. But how? Something heavy rested on his chest.

Then his world went black.

26

Rick Parlier stood over Tim Graham, who fiddled with the tuning dials on the satellite transmitter. They had been in the jungle one night, and already the insects were taking their toll. The satellite dish had been set up in the canopy within minutes of their securing a base on the mountain's crest. Contact had been established with Uncle, Rick's designation for their U.S. link, and Graham had confidently settled down next to his toys. The receiver was left on at all times, and the frequency altered every thirty minutes to a schedule followed by all three parties.

It had been an hour since the receiver had first started sputtering, refusing either transmission or reception.

"There it is." Graham withdrew what looked like a giant winged ant from the opened receiver. "Bugger chewed right through the variable volume resistor. Made a mess. Should be all right now."

Five minutes later, Tim Graham hit the power switch and handed the mike to Parlier. "Should work now."

Parlier took the mike and depressed the transmission lever. "Uncle, this is Alpha, Uncle, this is Alpha. Do you copy? Over."

Static sounded over the speaker for a moment before the response came: "Alpha, this is Uncle. Read you loud and clear. Where the heck you been?"

"Sorry. We had a little problem with our radio. Over."

There was a pause and the voice came back on. "Copy, Alpha. What is the status of the target? Over."

Parlier looked out into the jungle. Uncle had reported a disturbance at some mission station twenty-five miles south and had speculated that it might be connected with their target. Then nothing. No action, no word, no nothing.

He pressed the toggle. "No activity on this side. Beta and Gamma report no movement. Will advise, over."

"Roger, Alpha. Keep to the schedule. Over and out."

Give me equipment that works in the jungle and I will, Parlier thought as he handed the mike back to Graham. "Good work, Graham. Keep this radio clean. We can't afford another break like that."

"Yes, sir."

Parlier stood, walked to the boulders cropping from the crest, and glanced over his men. Phil and Nelson were on glass duty, peering diligently through the high-powered field glasses to the cliff lip below. Next to them, Giblet rested on his back, shooing away various flying insects with his hands. His sniper rifle sat propped on a tripod beside him, readied for a shot. Of course, even if they did spot the man, it was highly unlikely that Giblet would have the time to get a shot off. And even if he did, it would be a quick one—he could miss.

Graham's recommendation that they descend to the cliffs had gnawed in his gut all night. Beta and Gamma had established similar observation posts from which they studied the forests in the valley below. In addition to the cliff, they watched the canopy, looking for anything unusual that might indicate the passage of humans below them. So far they had observed nothing.

Except for insects, of course. They had observed plenty of those.

Parlier walked back to his radioman. "All right, Graham. Tell Beta and Gamma to hold tight. I'm taking this team to the cliff."

Tim Graham grinned and snatched the mike from its cradle. "Immediately, sir."

"Make sure you explain that we're not going *to* the cliffs. We're just going *near* the cliffs. You got that? And tell them I want them on the horn if they hear so much as a monkey fart."

"Yes, sir. Anything else?" The radioman grinned.

"Pack up. We're headed down."

§

David Lunow knocked once and walked into Ingersol's office without waiting for a response. The man looked up, staring past bushy black eyebrows. His hair slicked back nicely, David thought, the kind of hairdo he could wear without washing it for a week.

David walked up and eased into a wing-backed chair facing Ingersol's desk. He stroked his mustache and crossed his legs.

"If you don't mind, I have to express my concerns. In the fifteen years I've been at the agency, I don't remember a single occasion when we've gone after anyone like we're going after Casius. Except in situations where we had full knowledge of a specific intent to damage. Now, correct me if I'm wrong here, but Casius isn't exactly on a course to inflict any real damage. He may take out some rogue drug operation, but so what? Explain to me what I'm missing."

"He broke ranks. A killer who breaks ranks is a dangerous man."

"Yes. But there's more, isn't there?"

"You're his handler, David. Someone suggests taking out your man and you have a problem. I can understand that. Haven't we covered this?"

"It's more than that. Casius can take care of himself. Actually, that's its own problem. We're gonna end up with blood on our hands whether we like it or not. But it's this dogmatic insistence that we take him out instead of considering other alternatives, alternatives that seem much more reasonable to me, that has me baffled."

Ingersol stared at him judiciously. "Not all issues of national security are put out in broad distribution memos."

David flashed a smile at the man. "Look, all I'm saying is that nobody knows Casius like I do. Going after him this way is liable to create precisely the kind of problem we're trying to avoid by killing him. And the director must know that."

He studied Ingersol's face at the first mention of the director. Nothing. He continued, "Evidently someone figures that risk is warranted, given what Casius might uncover down there. I think they're trying to protect something."

"Pretty strong words for a man in your position," Ingersol said. "You wanna rethink that?"

"I have. A hundred times. I think Casius is headed for a deep-cover operation, and I think someone wants him dead before he discovers whatever's being hidden down there in that jungle."

"The world's full of deep-cover operations, Lunow. And if they weren't worth protecting, they wouldn't be deep cover, would they? It's not your position to question whether there is or isn't something to hide. It's your job to follow orders. We've been over this."

"You're trying to take him out. I just wanted to make my position clear for when this thing hits the fan. And you know it will, don't you?"

"Actually, no, I don't."

"If I'm right, it will. Because whatever is down there, it's about to be exposed."

"All right. You've made your point. Finished. And, for the record, I think you're overreacting because it's *your* man down there breaking ranks. Go have a drink on me, but don't come waltzing into my office accusing the agency of negligence."

David felt his cheeks flush. A trickle of sweat broke from his hairline.

"Are we clear?" Ingersol asked.

27

Sherry's eyelids felt heavy, as if they had been coated with lead while she slept. She applied pressure to them, wanting light to fill her eyes, but they weren't cooperating because the darkness did not roll back.

An image of Casius running barebacked through the brush filled her mind. Muscle rippled across his shoulder blades with each footfall.

She should open her eyes. And then another thought struck her: What if her eyes were already open?

She shoved herself to her elbow, lifted a finger to her eye, and recoiled when it contacted her eyeball. A chill broke over her head and she threw her arms out. They collided with cold stone. Or cement.

She was in a dark cement room—a holding cell. She must have been thrown here after the dart.

Sherry turned and extended an arm, afraid it would contact another wall. But it swished harmlessly through the stuffy air. She leaned forward and it touched the opposite wall. Five feet.

She was in a holding cell. Blacker than tar. It all came crashing in on her like a wave hitting the beach. In that instant Sherry became a girl again, trapped in her father's box with no way out.

Panic surged through her mind. She whirled about, whimpering, lurching in all directions, feeling the air and cold cement surfaces. The whimper rose to a wail and she fought to her knees, shaking.

Oh, God, please!

The blackness felt like syrup over her face. A heavy, suffocating syrup. Waves of dread slammed into her mind, and she thought that she might be dying. Again. Dying again like she had in the box.

Her wail changed into a dreadful moan that lingered on and on. She knelt there in the dark, moaning, crumbling, dying.

Oh, God, please, I'll do anything.

She suddenly froze. Maybe this wasn't a cell! It could be a dream. One of her recurring nightmares. That had to be it! And if she just opened her eyes, it would all be gone.

But her eyes were already open, weren't they?

Sherry pulled her legs up and hugged them. An ache filled her throat. "Oh, God, please."

Her words whispered in the small chamber. She bobbed back and forth, groaning. "Please, God . . ."

Are you ready to die, Sherry?

The father's words rolled through her mind, and she answered quickly, "No." Then rocking, feeling the terror freeze her bones, she suddenly wished for death to come. She swallowed again. "Yes."

But she didn't die. For an hour she sat trembling and rocking in the cold, damp space, mumbling, "Please, God." She had no idea what lay above her. She had no desire to find out. Her body had shut down except for this rocking.

It occurred to her through the fog that she had come full circle. Eight years ago she had been trapped like this. She had made a vow, and now God was testing her resolve. She was in the black belly of a whale and the vision was her acid.

Will you die for him, Sherry?

For who?

The light lit her mind abruptly, without warning, while she was still rocking. Her first thought was that a strobe light had been dropped into the cell, but then she saw the beach and she knew she was in the other world.

Sherry stood shaking to her feet and sucked hard at the fresh sea breeze. A smile spread her mouth wide and she wanted to scream. Not with terror, but with relief and joy and the pleasure of life.

The waves lapped against the beach and then hissed in retreat. She lifted her eyes and felt the wind cool against her neck as the palm branches swayed above. She spread her arms wide, turned slowly on the soft sand, and laughed aloud.

On the third twirl she saw the black-cloaked man walking over the water, and she knew he was coming to plant his seed in the beach, but she didn't stop. Let him do his deed. She would enjoy the sun and the wind while she could. When the acid rains came, she would stop. And die.

Are you ready to die, Sherry?

Yes.

The familiar vision rolled forward in stunning reality.

But one thing changed this time. Not in the vision, but in her understanding of it. This time when the mushroom grew, she saw that it wasn't a mushroom at all. No, of course not! How could she have missed it? It was a cloud.

The kind of cloud that grew out of a bomb blast.

28

Casius awoke on a cot and slowly sat upright. The events of the night came to him haltingly as he lifted his hand to the bruise on his right shoulder. His captors had used a tranquilizer dart. And they'd also shot the woman and the priest. They held them elsewhere.

Sherry.

A small ache burned in his chest at the thought. He'd led the woman into the jungle; she was now his to deal with. It was a wrinkle to this whole operation he could do without. But a wrinkle that was beginning to haunt him.

Casius swept his eyes around the prison. The room was ten by ten—cinder block. Empty except for this one bed. No windows, one door, all white. A brazen bulb glared on the ceiling. The bare mattress he sat on looked like something they'd found in an alley, grayed with age and stained with brown rings. It smelled of urine.

He carefully checked his body for wounds or breaks but didn't find any. They had taken him easily. They had either been exceptionally lucky or they possessed a security system far more advanced than he would have expected.

Casius leaned against the wall and rested his head back.

His wait ended within the minute. A scraping sounded at the door.

So now the game would begin in earnest. He settled his stiffened muscles and let them come.

The soldier who entered came in gripping a nine-millimeter Browning revolver in both hands. An eye patch rested like a hole over his right eye. He was Hispanic.

Another man stepped past the door and Casius felt his chest tighten. Short-cropped, black hair with a streak of white topped the man's hollow face. He was looking at Abdullah Amir. The man bore a surprising similarity to his brother. Casius's hand twitched instinctively on his lap and he calmly closed his fingers.

The man stood with his arms limp at his sides, eyeing Casius with drooping eyes. He wore a white cotton shirt with short sleeves and tight maroon pants that ended an inch above black leather shoes. Casius felt a thin chill break down his spine, and he suddenly wondered if he could pull this off. The whole thing.

A corner of his mind had expected this, of course. But now looking at Abdullah, the truth of it all hit his head like a sledge and he wondered if he'd overestimated his mental strength and patience.

By Abdullah's raised eyebrow, he saw Casius's fear. "You think I'm a ghost?" he asked.

Casius swallowed and regained composure, his mind still reeling. The man could have no clear fix on his identity. At least not yet.

Abdullah stared, unwavering. "Who are you?"

Casius suppressed the instinct to launch himself into the man now and be done with it. He glared at the man without answering, gathering his resolve to play his cards as planned.

"Abdullah," Casius growled softly.

The Arab's eyes registered a flicker of doubt. For a moment he looked non-plussed.

Casius spoke before the man could utter a word. "Your name is Abdullah Amir. I killed your brother ten days ago. You look very much like him. Your brother was an effective terrorist—you should be proud."

Casius smiled and the man blinked, stunned to silence. Every muscle in his thin body went taut, baring veins at his neck and forearms.

"You killed . . . Mudah is dead?" Abdullah sputtered. For a moment Casius thought Abdullah might shoot him there, on the spot. Instead he regained his composure slowly as if he could flick it on and off between those ears. It spoke well of his strength, Casius thought.

"CIA." Abdullah spoke as if he'd just swallowed a bitter pill. Now a different glint flashed through the man's eyes. "And what is your agency doing so deep in the jungle?" he demanded.

"We're looking for a killer," Casius said. "Perhaps you, Abdullah. Are you a killer?"

The man found no humor in the question. He looked at Casius carefully. "What is your name?"

"Your family is in Iran. In the desert. What brings you to the jungle?"

The Hispanic guard shifted his one good eye to Abdullah, his gun still leveled unwavering at Casius's head.

"Why did you kill my brother?" Abdullah asked.

Casius considered the question. "Because he was a terrorist. I despise terrorists. You're monsters who kill to feed a blind lust."

"He had a wife and five children."

"Don't they all? Sometimes wives and children die too."

Moisture beaded the Arab's upper lip and glistened under the ceiling bulb. Casius felt his own sweat trickle past his right temple. His vision clouded with that familiar black fog and then cleared.

"You yourself are a killer," Abdullah said. A fleck of spittle stuck to his curled pink lip. "The world seems to be full of monsters. Some of them kill for God. Others drop bombs from ten thousand feet and kill for oil. Both kill women and children. Which kind are you?"

A small voice whispered in his mind. *You are the same as he*, it said. *You are both monsters.*

Casius said the name slowly, before he realized he was saying it. He felt a tremor take to his bones, and he fought for control.

When he spoke, he could not stop the anger that tightened his voice. "You,

Abdullah Amir, are a monster of the worst kind. How many have you killed in your eight years on this plantation?"

§

A small warning bell was ringing in the dark, Abdullah thought. Set off by the agent's last statement. But he could not place it. What he could place was the simple fact that the CIA must now suspect his extracurricular activities. It was why they had sent this reconnaissance. Maybe his brother had talked under this assassin's knife. Either way, the operation was now in jeopardy.

Jamal's order had new meaning now.

The dark-haired man reminded him of a warrior, displaced in time, stripped of his clothing for some ungodly reason, still covered in his war paint. They had found only a knife on him. Well, then, he would have this man killed with a blade. Across the neck, perhaps. Then he would have his gut ripped out. Or maybe in the reverse order.

"According to the CIA's records you put a few people down, coming to this valley," the man said to Abdullah. "This was once a coffee plantation and there was a mission station nearby—both of which had to go. But it seems that fact bothered the CIA as little as it did you."

The last statement made Abdullah blink. This agent knew about the CIA's involvement? And by the flicker of the man's eye, he obviously did not approve.

"But that's not my concern," the assassin said, holding his gaze. "Jamal, on the other hand, is my concern."

Jamal? This man knew of Jamal! "What is your name?" Abdullah asked again.

"Casius. You know of Jamal."

Abdullah felt his pulse pound. He did not respond.

"I'm not sure you realize what kind of trouble has just landed on your doorstep, my friend, but trust me—your world is about to change."

"Perhaps," Abdullah said evenly. "But if so, then yours as well."

"Tell me what you know about Jamal, and I'll walk out of this jungle without a word. You realize my absence alone will raise red flags."

Abdullah felt a smile form slowly on his lips. The man's audacity struck him as absurd. He was here, under a gun, and yet he seemed comfortable issuing threats? "If I could give you Jamal's location right now, believe me, I'd do it eagerly," Abdullah said. "Unfortunately, Jamal is thinner than a ghost. But then I'm sure you know that, or you wouldn't be chasing him through this god-forsaken jungle. He is not here, I can assure you. He has never been here. You, on the other hand, are. A fact you don't seem to appreciate."

"Jamal may not be here, but he *is* your puppeteer, Abdullah, isn't he? Only an idiot would think differently."

Heat flared up Abdullah's neck. What did the man *know?*

Casius shifted his gaze. "Your brother spoke quite freely before I cut him. Evidently your competence was of some concern to him. But really, if you read between the lines, I think it was more Jamal who regarded you as stupid." The man looked back into Abdullah's eyes. "Why would Jamal feel obligated to take over an operation you had perfectly under control? This was all your idea, wasn't it? Why did he take over?"

But Abdullah could not dismiss the words easily. In fact, he knew this to be true. Jamal *did* think of him as stupid—every communiqué dripped with his condescension. And now this assassin had forced the same information out of his own brother before slicing him open.

A tremble ran through Abdullah's bones. He had to think. This man would die—that much was now certain—but not before he told Abdullah what he knew.

The fool was staring at him as if he were the one doing the interrogating. His eyes glinted fierce, not in the least cautious. He obviously knew more than he was saying.

"I want Jamal," Casius said. "His offense of me dates back eight years and has nothing to do with you. You tell me how Jamal makes contact with you, and I will make sure your operations stay well covered."

Abdullah raised an eyebrow. "If it's true that this operation is really under Jamal's thumb, why would I give a killer information that might lead to him?" he asked.

Casius drilled him with an unblinking stare. "Because if *Jamal* isn't killed, I'm quite sure he'll kill you. In fact, if I were a betting man, I might say you were already dead. Your usefulness is finished. You're now a liability."

Abdullah came very near to grabbing Ramón's gun and shooting Casius then. Only the man's arrogance kept him alive. That and the tiny voice that whispered in his ear. Something was amiss.

His face twisted with contempt. He turned his back on the man and left without another word. If Casius had any useful information, it was now immaterial. The man was dead already.

Abdullah spoke as soon as the door slammed shut. "Prepare the bombs. Have them ready to ship," he said, and his voice held a tremor.

"So soon?"

"Immediately! Jamal is right; we cannot wait."

"Send them to detonate?"

"Of course, you idiot. Both. We send both and then tell their government they can stop their detonation by complying with our demands, as planned. But we will detonate them anyway, after the Americans have had a chance to wet themselves. Injury to insult—the best kind of terror. Release our people or we will blow a hole in your side." He grinned. "We will shove in the knife and then turn it. Just as planned."

"And the others?"

Abdullah hesitated. He'd nearly forgotten about the woman and the priest. "Kill them," he said. "Kill them all."

29

Casius needed a distraction.

As soon as the door had closed, he was pressed against it, willing his heart still so he could hear unobstructed. They had clicked off ten paces before pausing at what could only be the elevator by the faint whir that started just after their final step.

It took him ten minutes to settle on his course of action. His cell probably lay beneath the ground, on the basement level. The steel door had been bolted, leaving him hopelessly penned in. The only movable objects in the room were the wooden bed, the thin mattress, and the glaring light bulb. Otherwise the cell provided nothing usable.

An hour after Abdullah and Ramón left, two others that Casius assumed must be guards descended on the elevator and took up positions in the hall— one opposite his cell and one next to the door.

He knew he had very little time. As long as Abdullah thought he worked for the CIA, the Arab might hold him alive, hoping for leverage. But the minute the man learned that he was on the run from the CIA, Abdullah would kill him. And Casius doubted the CIA would have any problem forwarding the truth.

Working very quietly, Casius removed the mattress from the bed and propped the wooden frame on its end, directly under the light, so that anyone entering the room would see only the frame at first look. He then ripped strips of cloth from the mattress and mounted the frame under the light. He unscrewed the white-hot bulb until the light blinked off and let it cool before removing it completely.

Working by feel in the darkness, Casius wrapped the bulb in the cloth strips and then squeezed the glass in his palm. It imploded with a snap, slicing into his forefinger. He bit his tongue and carefully removed the cloth, taking the broken glass with it. He felt for the tungsten wire. It remained intact. Good.

Casius reached for the ceiling, found the light fixture, and guided the bulb into its socket. The tungsten wire glowed a dull red without the vacuum.

He tore another strip from the mattress and wound it around his bleeding forefinger. He took a deep breath and mounted the frame again. He grabbed a handful of stuffing from the mattress and lifted it to the glowing wire. The dry material smoldered for only a moment before catching fire.

Casius dropped to the concrete, shoved the flaming material into the mattress, and set it against the far wall. He retreated to the wall behind the door and watched the fire grow until the room blazed orange. Waiting until the last possible moment, he drew a last deep breath of clean air from the room and waited.

So now he would either live or die, he thought. If the guards did not respond, the smoke would suffocate him. His heart began to pound like a piston in a freightliner. His temples throbbed and he squelched the fleeting temptation to run over to the mattress and extinguish the deadly flame.

Within seconds the room billowed with thick smoke. The guard's alarm came then, when the gray clouds seeped past the door. It took them another full minute to decide on a course of action, most of it spent calling to him for a response. When none came, a muffled voice argued that the prisoner must be dead and they would be too if Ramón thought they had allowed it.

The keys scraped against the metal lock and the door swung open, but Casius remained crouched behind, his lungs now bursting in his chest. The guards called into the smoke for a full thirty seconds before deciding to enter.

Casius sprang then, with every remaining ounce of strength. He crashed into the door, slamming the first guard against the doorframe and shoved his palm up under the man's jaw, snapping his head back into the wall. The guard crumpled to the ground. Casius snatched his rifle from his limp hands, slid behind the wall, and gasped for breath. Smoke filled his lungs with the draw, but he bit against a cough.

Gunfire thundered in the hall. Holes punched through the wall above him. Casius shoved the AK-47 around the corner and shot off six scattered rounds. The gunfire ceased. Casius slid into the doorway on one knee, lifted the rifle to his shoulder, and put a bullet through the other guard's forehead, smashing him to the ground with a single shot.

Adrenaline throbbed through his veins. He coughed hard now, bent over, ridding his lungs of the smoke. He scanned the hall, saw there were four other doors, and then ran for the steel elevator at the end.

It took him five seconds to understand that the car would go nowhere without a key. The other doors then—and quickly. An alarm had been raised.

Casius ran to the first door, found it locked, and fired a slug through its lock. He kicked it in, hit a light switch, and stepped into the room under stuttering fluorescent tubes. The room lay bare except for a single table and three chairs. Charts lined the walls. There was no exit from here.

Blueprints, darkening purple with age, were taped to the wall on his left. The architectural drawing nearest him showed a cross section of the black cliffs. And nestled in the hill between the plantation and the cliffs, a cross section of a three-story structure. This structure. Casius shifted his eyes to another blueprint, next to the first. This one showed an expanded view of the underground construction, complete with an elevator at one end.

No less than twenty drawings lined the walls, detailing the complex. Long blue lines shaped a passage that ran through the mountain. Red-dotted rectangles showed the tunnel's purpose. Cocaine was refined in a large plant on the second floor and then loaded into logs that were shot through the mountain into the Orinoco River and carried out to sea.

Casius left the room and closed the door.

The next door opened easily with a turn of its knob and revealed a utility closet. He snatched a machete from the corner and ran back to the elevator.

Surprisingly, the red indicator still had not lit, which caused him pause. Either they hadn't bothered to install any alarms in the lower level—figuring that any threats would come from above—or they waited for him, knowing that the elevator was the only way out.

But they were wrong.

With the *clank* of steel against steel, Casius shoved the blade between the doors and leaned into the machete. The doors resisted for a moment and then yielded. He surveyed an empty shaft that fell to another basement level and rose to the bottom of the car, one story above.

He had to find the woman. Sherry. It was ironic—he had stalked a terrorist like Abdullah for years and he had planned for the fall of the CIA nearly as long. And yet here was a woman and he knew he had to save her. She was somehow different.

Or was she?

The black fog lapped at his mind.

He grunted and dropped down to the bottom of the shaft. He pried open the dormant elevator door and entered a dark, damp hallway formed in concrete, empty except for a single doorway on the left. Like a root cellar, although in the jungle there was no need for a root cellar.

A faint cry echoed above him, far away. An alarm! His heart bolted and he leapt into the hallway.

A picture of Sherry filled his mind—her gentle features, her bright eyes, her curved lips. She was the antithesis of everything he had lived for. He was driven by death, she by . . . what? Love?

The door was concrete and he found it bolted. But no lock. He jerked the bolt out and shoved the slab. It grated open to a pitch-black room.

His breathing echoed back at him from the emptiness.

"Sherry?"

Nothing.

Casius spun around. He had to get out before the place swarmed with Abdullah's men. He'd taken a step back toward the elevator shaft when he heard a groan behind him.

"Hel . . . hello?"

Casius whirled around. A strange rush surged through his veins.

"Sherry?" His heart was hammering and it wasn't from fear.

"Casius?"

§

Sherry saw the silhouette standing in the open doorway like a gunslinger and she wondered what Shannon was doing in her dream. Shannon was dead, of course. Or maybe it was her captor, the terrorist with the bomb, if the vision of the mushroom was right. Abdullah. He'd visited her a few hours ago—now he'd come back.

She felt sluggish and she knew that she was waking. The figure turned to leave and it struck her that maybe this *was* someone real.

"Hello?"

The figure spun. Was it Casius? Had Casius come to save her? She climbed out of her dead sleep.

"Sherry?"

It *was* Casius!

"Casius?"

She pushed herself up and Casius swept in. He dropped to one knee and placed an arm under her back. He lifted her up like a rag doll and ducked out of the cell.

He smelled like sweat, which was no surprise—he was wet with it. His face was still green from the paint.

"Where's the priest?" he asked quietly.

He was still holding her. "I don't know. What happened?"

It must have occurred to him that he was holding her because he dropped his left arm and let her stand on her own.

"Come on. We don't have much time."

Casius ran for a set of steel doors at the end of the hall and pressed his ear against them. It was an elevator, resting closed.

He stepped back and lifted the machete. "It's clear. Stand back," he said in a hushed voice.

The assassin jammed the blade into the crack and pried the doors open. A cable ran up the dark elevator shaft. He wedged the machete kitty-corner in the doors and stepped into the shaft. Without speaking to her, he hauled himself up the cable, right past the doors where Sherry peered in with wide eyes.

"Where are you going?" she asked. Sherry looked up and saw the bottom of the car twenty feet higher. Casius was now parallel to a large opening on the opposite side of the shaft, ten feet up. He swung into the causeway without answering her, but she had her answer already. He dropped to his belly and reached down the shaft for her.

She edged forward and, clasping the pried elevator door with her left hand, she stretched her right hand up for his arm, wondering if she had the strength to hang on.

But he seized her wrist like an iron claw and the question fell away. She gripped nothing but thin air. He literally snatched her from her feet and hauled her up to the opening. She threw her leg over the lip and rolled into him.

He repeated the process, taking them another floor higher, just below the elevator itself. And then they were standing and scanning the tunnel they had entered.

A long line of lights hung from an earthen ceiling stretching both ways several hundred feet, maybe longer. To their right the tunnel ended in a glowing light; to their left the tunnel dimmed to darkness. An idle conveyor belt ran waist high the length of the passage.

A shout suddenly echoed down the tunnel and the sound of boots thudding onto packed earth reverberated past them. Casius grabbed her wrist and pulled her into a stumbling run toward the dark end of the tunnel. She pulled her hand free and tore after him, pumping her fists in panic.

"The priest!" she panted.

"Just run!" he said.

Cries of alarm suddenly filled the air. A shot crashed around her ears. Casius slid to a stop and Sherry almost ran through him. She threw her arms up and felt her palms collide with his wet back. Her hands slipped to either side and she smacked into his wet flesh. But neither seemed to notice.

They had reached a steel platform, she saw, and Casius had managed to unlatch its gate. He leapt over the threshold and yanked her through. When he punched something on the wall, the whole contraption trembled to life and began to rise. They were on a freight elevator of some kind. Flashes of fire erupted down the tunnel, chased by shouts of anger. Sherry instinctively crouched.

Then they were past the earth ceiling and rising through a vertical shaft lit by a string of bulbs along one wall.

Casius was madly searching the floor with wide eyes. Something about his jerking movements sent a chill down Sherry's spine. He was afraid, she thought. And not just afraid of the guns below. He knew something she did not, and it was sending him scampering about in fits.

She grabbed the rail and watched him, too stunned to ask what he was doing. He rounded the floor twice and evidently found nothing, because he ended with wide eyes raised to her.

He glanced above and she followed his gaze. A dark hole yawned ten feet higher. And above it—dirt. The end.

"Take your shirt off!" he snapped frantically.

"Wha . . . ! Take my what?"

"Quick! If you want to live through this, take your shirt off. Now!"

Sherry clawed at the T-shirt and pulled it over her head. She wore only a sports bra. Casius snatched the shirt before it had cleared her head and pulled it over his own. He'd lost his mind, she thought.

"You're gonna have to trust me. Okay?" Her shirt barely stretched over his chest, and one shoulder ripped at its seam. He had lost his mind.

"We're going for a ride. You just let go and let me carry you. Understand?"

She didn't answer. What could he possibly . . . ?

"You understand?" His face was white.

"Yes."

And then the gears ground to a halt and the floor began to tilt toward a hole waiting like an open mouth. It was a steel tube maybe three feet in diameter, disappearing into blackness.

Casius swung an arm around her waist and threw himself to the floor, pulling her with him so that she lay on top of him, faceup. Their heads were pointed into the gaping steel tube. He was taking her into the shaft, headfirst!

Sherry closed her eyes and began to whimper then. "Please, please, please, God." The smacking of steel colliding with steel suddenly crashed in her ears. Bullets! Like heavy hail on a tin roof. The men below were firing their guns up the elevator shaft and their bullets were slamming into the steel floor. She clenched her eyes and began to scream.

And then they were falling.

It was why he'd searched the floor frantically, she realized. It was why he insisted on taking her shirt when he'd found nothing else. Because his back was sliding against steel. She didn't know how long this ride would last or where it would take them, but she imagined that her thin cotton shirt was already giving way. His skin would be next.

Like breakaway tobogganers, they gained speed. Sherry pried her eyes open and lifted her head. Far away now, the dwindling entrance glowed between her jerking feet. Below her, the man suddenly tensed and squeezed her like a vise. His arms were wrapped around her midsection, coiled like a boa constrictor.

He grunted and she knew the T-shirt had given way. His forearms wound tight, forcing the air from her lungs. She grabbed at them in panic—but to no avail. And then he was screaming and white-hot terror streaked up her spine. She opened her mouth, wanting to join him. But she had no wind for a scream.

He went suddenly limp; his scream fell to a soft groan and she knew he'd lost consciousness. She sucked a lungful of air and then another. Casius's arms bounced limp. She imagined a long smear of blood trailing them. Oh, God, please!

And then the mountain spit them out, like discarded sewage. Sherry heard the rushing water below them and it occurred to her that they were headed for a river. And under her, Casius was unconscious. She instinctively reached for the sky with both arms. Her scream echoed off the towering canyon walls above.

Cold water engulfed her and sucked the breath from her lungs as if it were a vacuum. Sound fell to murmuring gurgles and she clenched her eyes tight. *Oh, God, help me. I'm going to die!* She instinctively clutched the assassin's arm.

He came to life then, shocked by the water, disoriented and flailing like a drowning man. Sherry opened her eyes and struck for the lighter shade of brown, hoping she would find the surface there. She tugged at his arm once and then released him, hoping he would find his own way. Her lungs were caving in.

She nearly inhaled water before her head cleared the surface. But she held on and gasped desperately before her bottom teeth broke water. Casius shot through the surface next to her and she felt a rush of relief wash over her.

Sherry looked about, still pulling hard at the air. They were in a fast-flowing river, deep and smooth where they were, and crashing over rocks on the far side. She felt a hand grip her shoulder and propel her toward the nearest bank. They landed on a sand bar two hundred meters downriver, like two grounded porpoises, belly down, heaving on the shore. Sherry flopped her head to one side, and she saw Casius with his face in the mud. His shoulder blades oozed red through her T-shirt and her heart rose to her throat.

She tried to go to him, but a black cloud settled over her eyes. *God please,* she thought. *Please.* Then the black cloud swallowed her.

30

Abdullah bolted from his chair, sending it clattering to the wall. Heat rose through his chest in one suffocating wave, and he felt his face flush red.

"Both? Impossible!" How could they escape? Even if the agent had found another way out of his cell, the lower level was sealed!

Ramón shook his head. A dark ring of sweat soaked into his black patch. His voice quivered when he spoke. "They're gone. The priest is still in his cell."

Abdullah's head spun. "I thought I told you to kill them!"

"Yes. I was going to. But considering—"

"This changes everything. The Americans will try to destroy us now."

"But what about our agreement with them? How can they destroy us with the agreement?"

"The *agreement*, as you call it, is worthless now. They've never known the extent of our operation, you idiot. Now they will." He hesitated and turned his back. "They will turn on us. It's their nature."

Abdullah suddenly slammed his fist on his desk and clenched his teeth against the pain that shot up his arm. Ramón stood still and stared past him. Abdullah closed his eyes and bowed his head into his other hand, gripping his temples. A haze seemed to be drifting over his mind. *There now, there now, my friend. Think.*

For a moment Abdullah thought he might actually burst out in tears, right there in front of the Hispanic fool. He took a deep breath and cocked his head to the ceiling, keeping his eyes closed.

There, there. He wagged his head, as if to crack it. *It is nothing more than a chess match. I've made a move and now they have made a move.* He ground his teeth.

A CIA agent has penetrated my operation and escaped to tell. The same agent who killed my brother.

Heat flared up his neck again and he shook his head against it, pursing his lips and breathing hard through his nostrils.

It had been a mistake not to kill the man immediately. Maybe the fall had killed them.

"Sir?" He heard the voice, knew it was Ramón's, but chose to ignore it. He was thinking. *There, there. Think.*

An image of a thousand marching boys, all under the age of thirteen, suddenly popped to mind. Good Muslim boys on the Iraqi border, chanting a song of worship, dressed in colors. Going to meet Allah. He'd watched the scene through field glasses fifteen years earlier with a lump the size of a boulder lodged in his throat. The mines began erupting like fireworks, *pop! pop!* and the children's frail brown bodies began flipping like sprung mousetraps. And the rest walked on, marching into the arms of death. He remembered thinking then that this was the sole fault of the West. The West had armed the Iraqis. The West had spawned infidelity, so that when he saw an example of purity, such as these young boys marching to Allah, he cringed instead of leaping for joy.

So then, think. Ramón was calling him again. "Sir."

Shut up, Ramón. Can't you see that I am thinking? He thought it, maybe said it. He wasn't sure. Ramón was saying something about the agent not knowing about the bombs. *Yes? Says who? Says you, Ramón? You're a blind fool.*

A buzz droned above him and he opened his eyes. The black bugs in the corner were crawling over each other in a writhing mass. One small firecracker in that ball would decorate the wall nicely. He dropped his head to Ramón. The fool *was* actually saying something.

Abdullah cut him off midsentence. "Ship the bombs immediately." Ramón's mouth hung open slightly, but he didn't respond. His good eye was round like a saucer.

Abdullah stepped forward, a quiver in his bones. The agent's escape could well be the hand of Allah forcing him forward. If Jamal was coming, the bombs would be gone when he got here. It would be he, not Jamal, who ended this game.

"Tonight, Ramón. Do you understand? I want both bombs sent tonight. Pack them in the logs as if they were drugs. And do it yourself—no one else can know of their existence. Are you hearing me?"

Ramón nodded. A trail of sweat now split his eye patch and hung off the corner of his lip.

Abdullah continued, noting that he would have to watch the man. He snatched a pointer and stepped up to a dirtied map of the country and the surrounding seas. His voice came ragged.

"There will be three ships. They will pick up the logs tonight, just outside the delta." Abdullah followed the map with the pointer as he talked, but it only ran in jagged circles from his taut nerves and he dropped it to his side. "The fastest of the three ships will carry the larger device to our drop point at Annapolis near Washington, D.C. The second will take the inoperable device to the lumberyards in Miami, just like any other shipment of cocaine." He paused, still breathing heavy. "The freightliner will carry the smaller device to a new drop point there"—he stabbed with the pointer again—"near Savannah, Georgia." He turned to face Ramón.

"Tell the captains of these vessels that it is an experimental shipment and that they will be paid double the normal rates. No, tell them they will be paid ten times the normal rate. The shipments must arrive at the destinations as planned, before the Americans have a chance to react to the news they will receive from this agent."

"Yes, sir. And the priest?"

"Keep him alive. A hostage could be useful now." He grinned. "As for the agent, we will use him as our demand instead of the release of prisoners as Jamal planned. Either way the bombs will go off, but perhaps they will deliver this animal to us." Abdullah felt a calm settle over him.

"I want the logs in the river by nightfall," he said. He suddenly felt strangely euphoric. And if Jamal appeared before then? Then he would kill Jamal.

Ramón still stood, watching him. Abdullah sat and looked at him. "You have something to say, Ramón? Do you think we have lived in this hellhole for nothing?" Abdullah smiled.

For a brief moment he pitied the man standing before him as if he were a part of something important. In the end he, too, would die.

"Do not disappoint me. You are dismissed."

"Yes, sir," Ramón said. He spun on his heels and strode from the room.

§

Sherry awoke on the riverbank with the vision once again stinging her mind. Casius glanced up at her from a rock where he worked over a palm leaf, twisting a root. He motioned beside her. "Your shirt's right there." Two holes had been worn through to his shoulder blades. She pulled it on and walked over to him.

"That stuff on your face doesn't come off very easily," she said, noting the camo paint had survived the river.

"Waterproof."

She looked at a small puddle of salve he'd forced from the root onto the palm leaf.

"And what is that?"

"It's a natural antibiotic," Casius said.

She winced, remembering the slide. "For your back?"

He nodded.

"Can I see?"

He twisted his back to her. His shoulder blades were worn to glistening red flesh.

"Here." He handed the palm leaf back to her. "This will help. I've seen this stuff work miracles."

She took the palm. "Just wipe it on?"

"You're the doctor. It has a mild antiseptic in it as well. It'll help with the pain."

He flinched when she touched the seared flesh. Sherry smeared it on, tentative at first, but then using the whole palm leaf as a brush. He groaned once, and she let up with an apology. A sense of déjà vu hit her like a sledge when he winced, and for a moment she felt as though she were in a hospital working with a patient in the emergency ward—not here in the jungle bent over the assassin.

But then she was seeing things strangely these days. *Everything* was one big déjà vu. Casius just fell into the pot with the rest.

They left the river with Casius insisting they get to a town as soon as possible. He had to get her to safety and return for the priest, he told her. He took to the jungle as if he knew exactly where they were. A hundred questions burned through her mind then.

They had just escaped some terrorist who planned to do something with a bomb, if she understood the vision now. She was supposed to *die* for this? No, that was only Father Petrus's talk.

An image of a nuclear weapon detonating filled her mind and suddenly she wanted to tell Casius everything. She had to—even if there was only the smallest chance of it all being true.

She swallowed at her dry mouth and held her tongue. What if he was part of this? But of course, he *was* part of this. So then, which side was he on?

They walked for a long time, in a dumb silence. When they did talk, it was her doing. She asked small questions, mostly, pulling short but polite answers out of him. Answers that seemed pointless.

"So you work for the CIA, right?" she finally asked.

"Yes."

"And you said that they were after you? Or are you after Abdullah?"

He glanced at her. "Abdullah?"

"Back at the compound. I could be wrong, but I think he's a terrorist. He's got a bomb, I think."

Casius walked on, mumbling something about everyone having a bomb.

He led her to a small village while the sun still stood overhead. Despite the availability of phones in the town, he insisted that she not contact anyone yet. He would call and alert the right people to Abdullah's operation, he said.

He made his call and then convinced a fisherman to lend them a small pontoon boat. They were soon rushing downriver, accompanied by a whining twenty-horse outboard and a backdrop of birds squawking in the treetops.

"Thank you for what you did back there," Sherry said, breaking a long stretch of silence. "I guess I owe my life to you."

Casius glanced at her and shrugged. He stared off to the jungle. "So what makes you think this Abdullah character has a bomb?"

She considered the question for a moment and decided she should tell him. "Do you believe in visions?" she asked.

He looked at her without responding.

"I mean supernatural visions. From God," she said.

"We've been over this. Man is God. How can I believe in visions from man?"

"On the contrary, God is Creator of man. He also is known to give visions." It sounded stupid—something she was just really believing for the first time herself. She could almost hear him mocking now. *Sure, honey. God speaks to me too. All the time. He told me just this morning that I really need to floss more regularly.*

She plunged ahead anyway. "That's how I know Abdullah has a bomb."

"You saw that in a vision?" He spoke in a voice that might as well have said, *Yeah right, lady.*

"How else?" she said.

He shrugged. "You saw something at their compound and pieced it together."

"Maybe brilliance isn't something that comes with seven years of higher education. But then neither is stupidity. If I say I had a vision, I had a vision."

He blinked and turned his head downriver.

"I had a vision about a man planting something in the sand that killed thousands of people. That's the reason I'm here in this jungle instead of back in Denver. The only reason." She swallowed and pressed on, hot in the neck now. "Did you know that building is built on an old mission site? Missionaries used to live there."

She waited for a response. She didn't get one.

"If there is a bomb . . . I mean like a nuclear bomb, it would make sense that he's planning on using it against the United States, right? You think that's possible?"

Casius turned and studied her for a long moment. "No," he said. "The facility is a cocaine processing plant. He's a drug runner. I think nuclear weapons are a bit beyond his scope."

"You may be a pretty resourceful killer, but you're not listening to me, are you? I saw this man in my dreams and now I've met him personally. That means nothing to you?"

"You can't actually expect me to believe you were drawn to the jungle to save mankind from some diabolical plot to detonate a nuclear weapon on U.S. soil." He looked back at her and forced a smile. "You don't find that just a bit fantastic?"

"Yes," Sherry said. "I do. But it doesn't change the fact that every time I close these eyes this Arab keeps popping back onto the stage and planting his bomb."

"Well, I'll tell you what. As it turns out, I'm going back into that jungle to kill that Arab of yours. Maybe that will stop him from popping into your mind."

"That's insane. You'll never make it."

"Isn't that what you want? To stop him?"

How could he go back in there knowing they would be waiting for him? Could God use an assassin? No, she didn't think so. Then she knew what she had to do and she said it without thinking.

"You have to get Father Petrus out. I have to go with you."

"That's out of the question."

"Father Petrus—"

"I'll get the priest. But you're not coming."

"It's me, not you who—" Sherry pulled up short, realizing how stupid it was all sounding.

"Who has been guided by visions?" he finished for her. "Trust me, I'm guided by my own reasons. They would make your head spin."

"Killing never solved anything," she said. "My parents were killed by men like you."

The revelation took the wind out of him. It was fifteen minutes of silence before they spoke again.

"I'm sorry about your parents," he said.

"It's okay."

It was the way that he said, "I'm sorry," that made her think a good man might be hiding under that brutal skin. A lump came to her throat and she wasn't sure why.

31

CIA Director Torrey Friberg stood in the east wing of the White House, staring out the window at the black D.C. sky. It was a dark day and he knew, without a question, that it would only get darker. Twenty-two years in the service of this country, and now it all threatened to blow up in his face. All on the account of one agent.

He turned away from the window and glanced at his watch. In less than five minutes they would brief the president. It was insane. Less than a week ago it had been business as usual. Now, because of one man, his career teetered on the edge of disaster.

He glanced over at Mark Ingersol, sitting with crossed legs. The man had pretty much figured things out, he assumed. With David Lunow's help he could hardly not. But his new appointment to Special Operations would ensure that he keep this one to himself—he had too much to lose.

The door suddenly banged open and the national security advisor, Robert Masters, walked into the room with Myles Bancroft, director of Homeland Security. Bancroft held the door for the president, who walked in ahead of two aides.

Friberg stepped past Ingersol and extended his hand to the president, who took it cordially but without greeting. His gray eyes didn't sparkle as they did for the cameras. They peered past a sharp nose—all business today. He swept a hand through his graying hair.

The president seated himself at the head of the oval table and they followed suit. "Okay, gentlemen, let's skip the formalities. Tell me what's going on."

Friberg cleared his throat. "Well, sir, it appears that we have another threat on our hands. This one's a little different. Two hours ago—"

"I know about the threat we received," the president interrupted. "And I wouldn't be here if I didn't think it held some water. The question is how much water."

Friberg hesitated and glanced at Bancroft. The president caught the glance. "What can you tell me about this, Myles?"

Bancroft sat forward in his seat and placed his arms on the table. "The message we received two hours ago was from a group claiming to be the Brotherhood, which, as I'm sure you know, is a terrorist organization. They originate out of Iran, but they've been largely inactive over the past few years—since our crackdown on Afghanistan. They're a splinter group outside Al qaeda gone underground. They're reportedly giving us seventy-two hours to deliver a recently defected agent to the Hotel Melia Caribe in Carabelleda, Venezuela. If within seventy-two hours the agent isn't delivered, then the group threatens to detonate a nuclear device that it claims to have hidden in the country."

The president waited for more, but none came. "Is this a real threat?"

Friberg answered, "We have no evidence whatsoever of any nuclear activity in the region. We've handled dozens of threats, which, to use your words, hold more water than this one. The chances that the Brotherhood has anything resembling a bomb is highly unlikely. And if they did, a threat like this would make no sense."

The president turned to Bancroft. "Myles?"

"Frankly, I agree. My guess is that they don't have it, but I'm basing that on nothing more than my gut. Nonproliferation has had nuclear components under the highest scrutiny since the Gulf War. Despite all the experts who insist suitcase bombs are available on any black market street corner, assembling all the components to actually build a bomb is, as you know, nearly impossible. I can't see it, especially not in South America."

"But it still involves a weapon of mass destruction," the president said. "We treat them all the same. What were the chances of Iraq getting the bomb? Tell me about the man who issued the threat. This Abdullah Amir."

Friberg answered, "We have no idea how Abdullah Amir came to be in South America, or whether in fact he *is* in South America."

The president just looked at him.

"It's more likely that the threat came from one of the drug cartels in the region." Friberg made a decision then, hoping desperately that Ingersol would follow his lead. Sweat wet his brow and he took a deliberate breath.

"We recently sent an agent operating under the name Casius into the jungle to take out a powerful drug cartel in the region. A black operation. Our information is a bit sketchy, but we believe that the agent attempted an assassination and failed. We believe the cartel is responding with this threat. But it's important to remember what Bancroft said, sir. It's highly improbable that the cartel has anything resembling a bomb at their disposal."

"But it is possible."

Friberg nodded. "Anything is possible."

"So, what you're saying is that you initiated black operations against a drug cartel and your guy, this Casius, missed his target. So now the cartel is threatening to blow up the country?"

Friberg glanced at Ingersol and caught the glint in his eye. "Isn't that pretty much your assessment, Mark?" His nerves ran taut. Ingersol's next few words would cast his position. Not to mention Friberg's future.

Ingersol nodded. "Basically, yes."

"And this Brotherhood threat is just to throw us off? We're not dealing with Islamic militants at all but some drug runners?"

"That's our assessment," Ingersol answered.

The president looked at his security advisor, Masters. "Make sense to you, Robert?"

"Could be." He looked at Friberg. "DEA involved in this?"

"No."

"If this agent of yours failed in his assassination attempt, why is the cartel so uptight? Seems like an unusual reaction, doesn't it?"

Friberg had to get them off this analysis until he and Ingersol had time to talk. "Based on our information, which I should reiterate is still sketchy, Casius took out some innocents in his attempt. He has a history of high collateral damage."

Friberg threw the lies out, knowing he had now committed himself to a far more involved cover-up than he'd imagined. His mind was already isolating the potential leaks. David Lunow topped the list of potential snitches. He would have to be silenced.

And as for the Rangers, they were puppets without political agendas—even if they stumbled into something down there, they wouldn't talk. Mark Ingersol had just committed himself to going along for the ride. It could be done. It had to be done—as soon as this bomb foolishness passed.

It dawned on Friberg that the other three were staring at him. "I really think it's as simple as that, sir. They know how excited we get over things like nuclear threats. They're playing us."

"Let's hope you're right. In the meantime, we treat this thing like any other threat of terror. So let's hear your recommendations."

Friberg took a deep breath. "We deliver Casius and defuse the demand."

"Beyond that. Myles?"

"We activate full Homeland Security measures and put all law enforcement on alert. And we look for a device, particularly in the path of recognized drug routes. Despite the unlikelihood of there actually being a bomb, we follow full protocol."

Friberg wanted to get past this foolishness. Seventy-two hours would come and go and there would be no bomb. He'd seen it a hundred times, and each time they'd had to run through this nonsense. A year ago in the wake of the big attack it had been one thing. But getting all worked up every time some nut yelled *Boo* was getting old.

Myles Bancroft continued, "We've already made a preliminary search plan that starts with the southeast coast and the West Coast and expands to all major shipping points in the country. The Coast Guard will bear the heaviest burden. If the cartel did manage to land a bomb in our borders, it was most probably through a seaport."

The president frowned and shook his head. "It's like trying to find a needle in a haystack. Let's pray to God we never actually have to face a real nuclear bomb."

"No system's perfect," Masters said.

"And if they have managed to get a device through, you honestly think we have a chance of finding it?" the president asked, turning back to the director of the CIA.

"Personally?" Friberg asked.

The president nodded.

"Personally, sir, I don't think we have a bomb to find. But if there is a bomb, finding it in seventy-two hours will be extremely difficult. Every bill of lading identifying merchandise which entered our country from South America during the past three months will be reviewed, and those that indicate merchandise which could possibly harbor a bomb will be traced. Merchandise will be tracked to its final destination and searched. It can be done, but not in seventy-two hours. That's why we start with southeastern and western seaports."

"Why not just take the cartel out?" Masters asked.

Friberg nodded. "We're also recommending positioning to move on the cartel's base of operations. But as you say, if the threat is legitimate, all it would take is a flip of a switch somewhere and we could have a catastrophe on our hands. You bomb them, and you'd better be sure that first salvo will kill them or they might twitch their finger and detonate. You don't play strongman with someone who has a nuclear weapon hidden somewhere."

"No? And how do you play?"

He paused. "Never been there."

The president stared at a window across the room. "Then let's hope we aren't there now."

No one spoke. Finally the president stood from the table. "Issue the appropriate orders and have them on my desk right away. You'd better be right about this, Friberg." The president turned and walked toward the door.

"This is only a threat. We *have* been here before, sir," Friberg said.

"Keep this sealed. No press. No leaks," the president said. "God knows the last thing we need is media involvement."

He turned and left the room, and Friberg released a long, slow breath.

32

Sherry followed Casius up a long flight of stairs behind the hotel he'd taken earlier on a weekly basis. She was certain the assassin's mind had left him during the trip.

On the river they had talked only once about their captivity. A riveting conversation in which he mostly stared off to the passing jungle, grunting short replies. He had shut her out. She had once again become baggage.

Now his eyes remained open only as a matter of courtesy to his brain, which was thoroughly engrossed with what he would do next. And what he would do was return and kill Abdullah. Destroy the compound and slit Abdullah's throat. When she asked him why, he had simply drilled her with those dark eyes and told her the man was a drug runner. But the explanation hardly made sense.

She asked him again what he thought she should do if there actually was a nuclear weapon in the jungle. But he dismissed the notion outright, so strongly that she began to question her own memory of the vision.

In the end it all came down to their beliefs. He'd come to the jungle to kill. Nothing more complicated than that. Just kill. Like the skull-man in her visions, like a demoniac. She, on the other hand, had come to die—if not literally, as Father Teuwen seemed to suggest, then to die to her past. To find life through a symbolic death of some kind. Maybe she had found it already in the prison back there. A reliving of her death as a child.

They talked about the jungle, finally. It seemed like a common bridge that did not lead to some allusion to life or death. Casius seemed more knowledgeable about the local jungle than anyone she could imagine. If she didn't know better, she might assume the man had grown up here, in this jungle instead of the ones north by Caracas.

For a terrifying moment she even imagined that if Shannon had lived, he might have become a man like this—tall, rugged, and handsome. Shannon would be a gentler, kinder man, of course. A lover, not a killer. She shoved the comparison from her mind.

At some point floating over the brown waters, she had finally decided that he struck a chord of familiarity with her because he was meant to play this part in her mission. He, too, had been drawn by God and the fact resonated with her like a memory.

Maybe he had been right in saying their worlds were not so far apart. Like heaven and hell kissing up against each other, but separated by some impenetrable steel plate. Maybe that explained the growing ache in her heart as they approached the sleepy town of Soledad in the afternoon.

They walked into a grungy room on the third floor. He shut the door.

"This is your room?" she asked, looking about the dimly lit hotel pad. Other than a queen bed and a single dresser, the room was bare. Soledad had a dozen hotels with far better accommodations than this, but at least the dresser had a mirror.

"It's not exactly the Hilton, but it has a bed," he said, fumbling for something in the bathroom. "I've paid through tonight. You probably want to find something a little cleaner."

Casius stepped out of the bathroom and tossed two well-stuffed money belts onto the bed. Evidently killing paid well. He dropped to his knees, pulled some folded clothes and a waist pouch hidden under the bed, and tossed them next to the money belts.

"Travel light, do we?" Sherry asked, grinning at the small pile of possessions.

The assassin looked at her without smiling. "I'm not exactly on a vacation."

"I could use some clean clothes and a shower," Sherry said.

Casius motioned to the pile of clothes on the bed. "You'll find those a bit large, but they'll do until we can get some clothes from the market. Go ahead, clean up. The water's hot and there are towels in the bathroom."

Sherry nodded and took the clothes. A bit big indeed. She would float in his clothes. On the other hand, the white T-shirt hanging from her own body was literally falling apart. Her denim shorts had survived in remarkable condition, considering the jungle. A good wash and they would do. She tossed his pants back onto the bed and turned, holding his white cotton shirt.

"Thank you," she said and stepped into the bathroom.

Sherry took a long shower, relishing the steaming water, scrubbing the dirt from her pores. She washed and wrung out the jeans, donned his shirt, and ran her fingers through her hair. Not exactly fit for a prom, but at least she was clean. She debated removing her colored contacts. They normally stayed in place for a month at a time, but the journey through the jungle had worn on her eyes and she decided to remove them despite the questions a sudden change in eye color might draw from the man.

"Thank God for hot water," she said, stepping from the bathroom.

Casius kneeled at the dresser, writing on a tablet. "Good," he said without looking up. His mind was obviously buried in that tablet. She plopped onto the bed and lay back, closing her eyes.

"I'm going to shower," he said, and when she looked up, he was already gone.

Sherry lay back down and rested for a while. At the moment the man planting his little silver sphere in the sand seemed far away. Like a dream fogged by reality.

What was she to do now? Contact the authorities with her version of what had happened? Tell them that she had been captured by a *terrorist* holed up in the jungle? *And there's more,* she'd say.

Really? And what would that be, miss?

He's got a nuclear bomb that he's going to blow up in the United States, she'd say.

A nuclear bomb, you say? Oh, heavens! We'll activate the bat-signal right quick, miss. What did you say your address was?

She rolled to her side and groaned. Maybe she had read too much into the dream. Other than being taken hostage for a day, nothing concrete had happened to lead her to the conclusion that anything remotely similar to a bomb was involved. Only her dream. And really, it could mean that her life was about to blow up, rather than a real bomb.

Get a grip, Sherry.

Father Teuwen's face filled her mind. He was still back there. She swallowed. That had been real. The father's words came to her. *Think of yourself as a vessel. A cup. Do not try to guess what the Master will pour into you before he pours,* he had said. *Your life of torment has left you soft, like a sponge for his words.*

But you have poured, Father. Every night you pour, filling me with this vision. Are you ready to die, Sherry?

Sherry sat upright on the bed, half expecting to see Father Teuwen standing there. But the room was empty. The sound of splashing water ceased— Casius was finishing his shower.

Helen had said she was gifted. That she played some part in God's plan. Like a piece in some cosmic chess match. Heavens, she felt no more like a knight or a bishop than she felt like Father Teuwen's sponge.

She pushed herself from the bed and walked to the dresser. Her image stared back from the mirror. She scratched at her hair, trying to make some order out of it. Her eyes stared back at her, bright blue again. It struck her that with wet hair she looked like her old self—like Tanya. The door to the bathroom opened and she looked up to the mirror, her hair forgotten. In the reflection, the bathroom door opened and Casius stepped out.

Only it wasn't Casius she was seeing. It was a blond-haired man, still shirtless, still wearing the black shorts, but clean.

Something clicked in her memory then—something painful and buried deep. A déjà vu in three dimensions that made her blink. Sherry whirled around. He stood, ruffling his hair.

He saw her stricken face and froze.

"What?" he said. "What's wrong?" He looked quickly around the room, saw no danger, and returned his questioning eyes to her.

Sherry looked from his hair to his face, cleaned of the camo paint for the first time. His eyes were green. Her knees began to quake. Her throat froze shut, and she felt suddenly dizzy. His likeness crashed in her mind like a ten-ton boulder.

But it was an impossibility and her mind refused to wrap itself around this image. A thousand pictures from her early years streaked across her mind's eye. Her Shannon grinning above the falls; her Shannon shooting from beneath the surface to smother her with kisses; her Shannon popping a shot off at that rooster above the shed and then turning to her with a sparkle in his eye.

A reincarnation of that image stood before her now. Taller, broader, older, but otherwise the same.

She found her voice. "Shannon?"

S

Shannon stood staring at Sherry. Her mouth gaped as if she were looking at a ghost. And he had already opened his mouth to tell her to get a grip when he saw the change in her eyes. They were blue. They were not hazel.

The words stuck in his throat. He could not place the significance of the change in her eye color, but the detail spun crazily through his mind. She was now clearly a dead ringer for someone he knew. Problem was, his mind had misplaced the identity. For three days her image had whispered to him; now it had tired of its suggestions and it began to wail. *You know this person! You really do know her!* Another assassin? CIA? The warning bells blared through his skull.

Then she called him. "Shannon?" she said. As if it was a question.

The way she said his name, "Shannon," threw a face up in his mind. It was Tanya's face. His legs went weak. But it had to be the wrong face, because this could not be Tanya. Tanya was dead.

She said it again. "Shannon?"

Heat surged up his neck and burned at his ears. He dropped his hand and swallowed, feeling that if he did not sit, he might fall. "Yes?" he answered, sounding like a child, he thought.

She wavered and what color remained in her face drained. "You—you're Shannon? Shannon Richterson?"

This time he barely heard the question because a notion was growing like a weed in his head. Sherry had known the jungle too well for an American. Her eyes were bright blue. Could it possibly be?

"Tanya?" he said.

Two large tears fell from each of her blue eyes and her lips quivered. Then Shannon knew that he was looking at Tanya Vandervan.

Alive.

His heart lifted to his throat and the room shifted out of focus.

Tanya was alive!

§

Tanya felt the tears fall down her cheek. She grabbed at the chair beside her. It was either that or fall.

It was Shannon! "Tanya?" The voice soared in from a thousand memories and she suddenly wanted to throw her arms around him and flee all at once. Casius. The assassin! Shannon? This man who had dragged her through the jungle on a mission of death was really Shannon. After all these years. How was it possible?

"Yes," she answered. "What's happening?" The question echoed through the room. It was him! She stepped to the bed as if on a cloud and sat down, numb.

Shannon wavered on his feet. "I . . . I thought you were dead," he said. She could see small pools of tears in the wells of his eyes.

"They told me that you were killed," she said and swallowed against the stubborn lump in her throat.

"I came to the mission and saw the bodies. I . . . I thought you were dead." He backed up a step and ran into the wall. She saw his Adam's apple bob. He was hardly in control of himself, she realized.

"How did you . . . get out?"

"I . . . I killed some of them and escaped over the cliffs," he said. "What . . ."

She stepped toward him, hardly realizing she was doing so. This man had become someone new. Someone from her dreams.

"Shannon . . ."

He rushed toward her. His arms spread clumsily before he reached her. She felt as though her chest might explode if she did not touch him now. Their bodies came together. Tanya embraced his broad chest and she began to weep. Shannon held her carefully with trembling arms.

They swayed, holding each other tight. For a few moments, he became the boy under the waterfall once again, strapping and young with a heart as big as the jungle. He was falling in a swan dive, arms spread wide, long blond hair streaming behind. Then they were tumbling under the water and laughing, laughing because he had come back for her.

She buried her face in his neck and smelled his skin and let her tears run down his chest.

The next thought fell into her mind like a stun grenade, obliterating the images with a blinding flash.

This wasn't Shannon holding her with his flesh pressed against her. This was . . . this was Casius. The killer. The demoniac.

Her eyes opened. Her arms froze, still encircling him. A panic ripped up her spine. *God, what have you done to him?*

She pushed herself away slowly, carefully, suddenly terrified. He had gone rigid. He stood there and faced her, his thick muscles winding their way around his torso like vines. Angry scars bulged over his chest, like slugs under his skin.

This wasn't Shannon.

This was some beast who had taken over the body of the boy she had once loved and transformed it into . . . this! A sick joke. With her at its brunt. *Oh, dear Tanya, we have decided to answer your prayers after all. Here is your precious Shannon. Never mind that he is twisted and spewing bile from the mouth. You asked for him. Take him.*

"No," she said aloud, and her voice trembled.

Shannon's eyes flashed questioning.

She took a deep breath and tried to settle herself. She still couldn't believe that this was happening. That this killer, Casius, was somehow connected to her Shannon. *Was* Shannon!

"You . . . you've changed."

He stood and she watched his chest expand with heavy breathing. But he did not respond. He seemed suddenly as confused as she.

"What *happened* to you?" She didn't mean them to, but the words came out accusing. Bitter.

His upper lip curled to an angry snarl. Like a wounded animal. But he recovered immediately. "I escaped . . . to Caracas. I took the identity of a boy who was killed with his father, the same year my parents were."

"No! I mean what happened to *you?* You've become . . . them!"

The words somehow reached in and flipped a switch in him. His eyes dimmed and his jaw flexed. She took another step back, thinking she should turn and run away. Leave this nightmare.

"Them? I *kill* them!" he said.

"And who's them?"

"The people who killed my mother!" He said it with twisted lips, bitter beyond himself. "Do you know the CIA ordered it? To give that man in the jungle a place to grow his drugs?"

"But you don't just kill! That's why we have laws. You've become like them."

He spoke quietly now, trembling all over. "My law is Sula."

The name echoed through her mind. *Sula.* The god of death. The spirit of the witch doctor.

"I will do *anything* to destroy them. Anything! You have no idea how long I've planned this." Spittle flecked his lip. "And you have no idea how sick they are."

She blinked. "What are you saying? How can you say that? You're insane!"

"They killed my . . . our parents!" His face was twisted into an ugly, terrifying scowl.

"How could you do this to me?" she whispered.

"I've done nothing to you!" Shannon said. He turned from her and strode for the door. Without looking back, still wearing only his pants, he stepped from the room and shut the door.

Tanya backed to the bed in shock. She sat heavily, hardly able to form coherent thoughts now. When one did string through her head, it said that this was madness. That the world had gone berserk and she along with it.

She lay back, acutely aware of the afternoon silence. Outside, horns honked and pedestrians yelled muted words. She was alone. Maybe even God had deserted her.

Father, what's happening to me? I'm losing my mind.

Then Tanya began to cry softly on the bed. She felt as abandoned and destitute as she had those first weeks after her parents had been killed.

Will you die for him, Tanya?

For him? Shannon.

She curled up in a ball and let the grief swallow her.

33

"Yes, that's right, Bill; we don't have a clue what's going on down there. But what-ever it is, it's changing the world."

"I'm preparing for my Wednesday evening teaching at the church, my son is at soccer practice, and Tanya is down in the jungle changing the world."

"Yes. She's loving and she's dying and she's changing the world."

"And who's she loving?"

"The boy."

"Shannon. So he is alive?"

"I think so. I think that she was called down there to love him."

"How does that change the world?"

"I don't know. But it's all I get now. To pray for her to love the boy. In fact, I really think that's what this is all about. Tanya loving Shannon. I really do think maybe Tanya's parents were called down there twenty years ago so that Tanya could fall in love with the boy."

The line was silent.

"And I think Father Petrus was brought to the jungle years ago for this day."

"Important day," he said.

Six hours after Shannon and Tanya fell through the tube into the Orinoco River, three large Yevaro logs followed them. The mountain spit them out like torpedoes and they rushed through muddy waters toward the coast. They reached the Orinoco Delta and bobbed out to sea.

A clipper bearing the name *Angel of the Sea* plucked the first log from the ocean at eight that evening. The log sat snug, among twenty other similar exotic logs bound for the coastal port of Annapolis, twenty miles from Washington, D.C., thirty miles from the CIA headquarters in Langley. *Angel of the Sea* cut north at a steady forty-knot clip. Barring any unforeseen storms, she would arrive at her destination within thirty hours.

Marlin Watch, bound for Miami, hauled the second log from the waters an hour later. This log contained a silver sphere that consisted of nothing more than a small ball of plutonium. Enough to set off a Geiger counter if one were run along the log's surface, but otherwise it was harmless.

Two miles behind her, the *Lumber Lord* stowed the third log in its forward hold and steamed north behind the other two ships. Captain Moses Catura leaned over his map in the pilothouse and spoke to Andrew, who stood beside him.

"Two degrees to port, Andrew. That should compensate for the winds." He looked up into the darkness ahead and swore under his breath. It was the first time he had taken the freighter north on such short notice, but Ramón had insisted. And for a single log! They must have a million dollars of cocaine packed into the tree.

"All set, Captain," Andrew said. "We should make good time if the weather holds."

Moses nodded. "Let's hope so. I don't like the feel of this one. The sooner we get these logs off-loaded the better."

"They're paying well. More than we make in a year. It's one log—what could go wrong with a single log?" Andrew referred to the $100,000 they were being paid for the run. In Senegal where his family waited, his share would make him a wealthy man.

"Maybe, Andrew. Did you know that the Coast Guard is larger than South Africa's entire navy? They're not friendly to drug runners."

Andrew chuckled. "We're not drug runners. We have no idea how that log got on board. We're stupid sailors." He turned to face the darkness ahead with the captain. "Besides, this will be our last run. It's fitting that we make so much on our last run."

Moses nodded at the thought.

Below him the Yevaro log they had plucked from the water slowly dried. In its belly a silver sphere sat dormant, housing a black ball cradling enough force to vaporize the seven-thousand-ton ship with a single cough.

§

Jamal turned his back on the busy street and spoke into the phone. "Hello, Abdullah."

Silence.

"Do you have anything to report, my dear jungle bunny?"

"I have followed your directions."

"Good. They are on their way, then?"

He could almost hear Abdullah's mind spinning on the other end. "I was told to prepare them," Abdullah said. "Not to send them."

"Unless there was a problem. Isn't that what I told you? Hmm?"

"What problem—"

"Don't be an imbecile!" Jamal spit into the phone. "You don't think I know when you eat and when you sleep and when you pass gas?"

His hand was shaking and he took a breath to still himself. He had two men in the compound who reported to him regularly. Not that he needed them often—he knew Abdullah's moves before the fool did.

"I am on my way, my friend. If you have not done precisely as I have said—"

"The bombs are on the way," Abdullah said tightly.

Jamal blinked. "They are." The words stopped him cold.

"Good."

He slammed the phone down and walked from the phone booth.

§

Sweat glistened on Abdullah's face under the fluorescent lights. He set the phone down, poured another splash of tequila into his shot glass, dipped a quivering tongue into the burning liquid, and then tilted his head slowly back until it drained empty into his mouth. Although he'd never been a drinking man, the last twenty-four hours had changed that. He and Ramón had done little except sit at his desk and wait. And drink.

The alcohol made him perspire, he thought. Like a pig. "Where are the ships now?" he asked again.

"Coming to Cuba maybe," Ramón answered.

So, Jamal was coming. And when he did arrive, he would die. Abdullah felt a chill tickle his shoulders. He honestly wasn't sure which thought gave him more pleasure, killing Jamal, or detonating a thermonuclear weapon on American soil.

He ran a finger along the edge of the transmitter lying on the bar beside him. It was a simple 2.4 gigahertz transmitting device, impossible to isolate quickly. But it tied into a far more sophisticated transmitter hidden one mile away, secured in the jungle canopy in a protective housing. From there a tiny burst masquerading as a television signal would be simultaneously relayed through commercial communication satellites. Not all would fail. Not all could be stopped.

And by the time the authorities detected the burst, which they would, it would be too late. The detonation of the first bomb would automatically send a signal to set the second bomb on a twenty-four-hour countdown to detonation. Two green buttons rose from the black plastic like two peas. He circled first one button and then the other. Below the buttons, nine numbers made up a small keypad. Only he and Jamal had the codes to stop the inevitable.

Abdullah spoke without lifting his head. "You are sure the logs arrived at the boats intact?" He waved the question off with a nod of his head. "Yes, of course, you have said so."

"Do you think they will give us the agent?" Ramón asked.

Abdullah thought about Casius and blinked. A widening thought in his mind suggested it might be best if they did not deliver the agent. Then his hand would be forced—it would be Allah's doing.

Abdullah glanced at the clock ticking on the wall opposite them. It had been twenty-four hours and not even a breath from the fools. A chill suddenly spiked at the base of his skull. What if they had ignored the message entirely, thinking him a madman? What if they hadn't even received the message? It had been relayed through the same relays he would use for the bombs. Five million dollars of technology—all from Jamal, of course.

Abdullah grunted and shoved himself back from the bar. "Something isn't right. We'll send another message."

He walked for the door with Ramón on his heels. His fingers were shaking badly. Power was its own drug, he thought, and it was coursing through his veins. At the moment he might very well be the most powerful man in the world.

§

Friberg jerked in his seat when the knock came on his door. He lifted his head, but the door opened before he could say anything. Mark stepped in.

Ingersol's greased hair flopped to the right side. He threw it back with a hurried hand and rushed forward. "We received another message!"

Friberg stood and snatched the message from the man. "Settle down, Ingersol." But he was already reading the typed communiqué in his fingers.

Ingersol sat in one of the chairs facing his desk. "This guy's dead serious. He's adamant that he has a bomb. I thought you said—"

"Shut up!"

Friberg slowly sat. "Forty-eight hours," he read. "He's cutting the time from seventy-two hours to forty-eight hours because we have been *insufficiently responsive?*" He lowered the paper. "That's absurd! This guy can't be serious."

Ingersol's greasy black hair had fallen to his cheek again. "This isn't the kind of communiqué a man who's bluffing sends, sir. He's either a total imbecile or he *does* have a bomb. And the fact that he's survived Casius this long does not bode well for the imbecile theory." Ingersol stopped and took a long pull through his nostrils.

The director felt a ball of heat spread over his skull. And what if Ingersol were correct? What if . . . ?

The note was signed Abdullah Amir. Disconnected fragments of information fell together in his mind and he blinked. Jamal. Casius was after Jamal.

What if Casius had actually stumbled onto more than the cocaine plant?

"What's going on?" Ingersol repeated. "It seems to me that I've stuck my neck out with you. I deserve to know what I've gotten into, don't you think?"

Friberg eyed the man. Ingersol was a wreck. If he didn't pull him in, he would destroy them both.

"You and me, Mark. It goes no further than this room, you understand?" Ingersol didn't respond.

"All right. You want to know? Ten years ago Abdullah Amir approached us with a plan to infiltrate the Colombian cartels in exchange for his own piece of the operation. We agreed. He disappeared into their networks. Two years later he reappeared, this time with enough information to wipe out two drug cartels. In exchange, he wanted our cooperation, allowing him to establish and operate a small cocaine plant next-door in Venezuela. We agreed. We pointed him to a coffee plantation and gave him some assistance in taking it over. Nothing major—minor casualties. He's been operating there ever since. Small stuff. We got the DEA to sign off on the deal, but I was the agent who put it together. It was highly successful, all told. We shut down nearly a hundred thousand acres of production in exchange for a hundred."

Ingersol blinked. "That's it?"

Friberg nodded.

"And what does that have to do with this bomb?"

"Nothing. Unless Casius was right and Jamal is connected with Abdullah Amir. Or unless Abdullah isn't who we think he is. South America would make a good base for a strike against America." The sense of it occurred to Friberg even as he spoke it.

"And none of Abdullah's money has found its way into your retirement account, right?"

Friberg didn't respond.

Ingersol shook his head and stared off to the window. He had no choice, Friberg realized. He had already committed himself in front of the president. The money was only dressing.

"I've been suckered into this," Ingersol said and Friberg did not object. "I wasn't looking for this. It's not what I do."

"Maybe, Mark. But we all face the choice at some time. You've already made yours."

Ingersol's eyes fell to the note and Friberg lifted it up. Yes, there was the matter of the bomb, wasn't there? That could be a real spoiler. "So you think we're dealing with a madman who actually has a bomb?" Friberg asked.

"I don't know anymore," Ingersol returned.

"I don't either. But if we are, we now have twenty-four hours to deliver Casius and defuse the situation. Or find this bomb." The idea of it sounded absurd. A suicide mission or even a biological attack was one thing—they had all seen it. But a nuclear bomb? In Hollywood movies, maybe.

"Who else knows about this?" Friberg asked, lifting the transcript.

"No one. It just came over the wire less than ten minutes ago."

"And what's the current status of the search?"

"The Office of Homeland Security is working through its protocol. Law enforcement's on full alert. They're looking—the import documents in question have been identified, and traces are being done now. But it's only been twenty-four hours. We're nowhere near the discovery phase in this thing. In twelve hours we may have traces complete, but very few searches, if any." Ingersol bit his lower lip.

"No one hears about this last message, you understand?"

Ingersol nodded and flipped his hair back again.

"Good. Give the Rangers the clearance to sweep the valley. We go for anything that lives in that compound. If Abdullah does have a bomb, we're risking him detonating it the minute we attack, but I don't see our choice at this point. Anything from the satellites yet?"

"Nothing except cocaine fields. If they have anything else down there, it's hidden."

"And no word of Casius?"

"None."

"Then we go for Abdullah Amir or whoever is sending these crazy messages. I'm going to recommend that all southern ports be closed until we get a better feel for the situation. We'll call it a drill or something. We've got to shake something loose." He lost himself in thought for a moment. They all knew it was simply a matter of time before a terrorist finally found a way to get a nuclear bomb into the United States. The World Trade Center collapse would look like a warm-up exercise.

Ingersol stood. "I'll get on this. I hope you know what you're doing."

34

Shannon Richterson ran through the jungle barefoot, under a black fog of confusion. Above the canopy, the sun shone in a blue sky, but in his mind light barely reached his thoughts.

Sherry was Tanya. Tanya was alive. He could hardly manage the notion. Tanya Vandervan alive. And filled with anger at him. Couldn't she see that he was doing what so few in the world had the stomach to do?

What would she have him do? Kneel beside Abdullah and pray that he lie down and kill himself. Shannon grunted at the thought.

She only knew the half of it. If she really knew what was happening here, she might kill Abdullah herself. Or kill Jamal.

Jamal had to die. If he did nothing else here in the jungle, he would put Jamal to death.

Shannon pulled up near the edge of Soledad, breathing heavy, hands on hips.

In reality it was *he* who made the difference in the real world. The world was filled with treachery and the only way to face such an evil was with treachery itself. It had been one of the first lessons he'd learned from the natives as a boy. Fight violence with violence.

But Tanya . . .

Tanya had come up with this nonsense about dying.

Shannon spit into the dirt and jogged on. Eight years had come down to this moment, and no person—no woman—would have a say now. Not even

Tanya. He had held her and kissed her and at one time would gladly have given his life for her—but she'd changed. And she hated him.

Shannon's mind grew dark and he groaned above the pounding of his feet. He closed his eyes.

He would show her.

He pulled up at the thought. She wasn't Tanya any longer. Not really. She'd become Sherry.

He doubled back and ran for the town.

And now he would show Sherry how things worked in the real world. Why he was doing this. How to deal with a world gone sick. Maybe then she would understand.

He would return to the jungle and finish what he had started, and he would let Sherry see for herself.

§

Graham keyed the radio. "Roger, go ahead."

"The mission has changed. Sweep the valley compound and eliminate any unfriendlies you encounter. Copy?"

Graham looked up at Parlier. Parlier nodded. "Ask him what he means by unfriendlies," he said.

Graham depressed the transmit toggle. "Roger, sir. Request you clarify unfriendlies."

Static sounded for a moment.

"If you don't know their name, then they're unfriendly. Understood? You take out anything that walks."

Parlier nodded at Graham. "What about the agent?"

"Copy that. What about the agent?" Graham asked into the mike.

"Take him out."

"Copy. Alpha out."

Parlier was already walking toward the other men stationed on the cliff. He turned back to Graham. "Get Beta and Gamma on the horn and tell them to follow our lead. I want to be at the base of the cliffs by morning. There Beta spreads east and Gamma spreads west."

He swung back to the cliff. "Pack up, boys. We're going down."

§

Tanya had drifted for over three hours, lying on the hotel bed. Her thoughts spun lazy circles around the notion that she had really lost her mind this time. That this whole thing might well be an extended dream episode in which she had flown the coup and revisited South America only to find Shannon a mad killer instead of her innocent love. After eight years of nightmares a mind could imagine that, couldn't it? She'd read somewhere that if all the power of the brain were harnessed, it could rearrange molecules to allow a person's passage through walls. Well if it could walk through solid objects, surely it could conjure up this madness.

A knock on the door about launched her into orbit. She sat up and nearly slipped from the bed.

He walked in then. Shannon. Or Casius, or whoever he really was. The tall, rugged killer with green eyes and firm muscles. She wanted to shrivel into the corner.

He walked to the dresser, snatched a small backpack from it, and fastened it around his waist. "Okay, lady," he said. "Pull yourself together. We're taking a walk."

"A walk? To where?"

"A walk to hell. What does it matter? We both survived, fine. Now you're going to see how things work in this screwed-up world of ours. Get up."

He walked over, grabbed her by the arm, and yanked her to her feet roughly, eyes flashing.

Tanya felt a stab of pain rip up her arm and she gasped. He relaxed his grip and pulled her toward the door. She stumbled after him.

"I've *seen* your world. Let go of me!"

"And now you're going to see why I do what I do. I owe you at least that much, don't you think?"

"You don't have to hurt me. Let me go!"

This time he did. She followed. She would play his absurd game for the moment. She wasn't sure why. But she had to find out what had caused the love of her life to be transformed into this . . . creature. Shannon led her from the hotel. She stopped at the street, but he continued walking. He shot her an angry glare and she followed.

They walked to the outskirts of Soledad. She expected him to turn into a side street and show her his "screwed-up world" at any moment. But he didn't. He walked past the last road and turned onto a thin path snaking into the jungle.

"Wait a minute," she objected. "I'm not about to go back into the jungle with you. Are you nuts? You think you—"

He spun back, grabbed her by the arm, and propelled her before him.

She fought an urge to whirl around and slap him. "Okay!"

Then she lost comprehension of what his intentions might be. He passed her once they entered the forest and she followed, thinking she would turn back at any moment and return to the town.

But she didn't. For one thing they had switched paths several times and she quickly realized that she could hardly navigate her way back. For another thing, she was drawn by the bare-chested man ahead of her, leading her like a wild savage. Not drawn *to* him, of course, but *by* him, like a homing beacon faintly red in the distance.

That it was Shannon leading her into the jungle and not Casius made her think that she might follow him to hell if he asked her to. Deep in her heart, Shannon was still her lost love.

But she hardly considered the notion before replacing it with the notion that *he* deserved to be sent to hell.

Dear God, help me!

She was panting within the hour. Shannon didn't bother looking back to check on her. If anything he walked faster, more deliberately, intent on punishing her maybe. She determined then not to give him the satisfaction. She had kept up with him once—she could do it again. As long as he let her, of course.

Tanya walked behind him, watching his muscles roll over his bones with each footfall. To think she had once loved this man so passionately. Shannon. How had he grown so strong? Not that he wasn't strong before, but this . . . this man ripping through the jungle ahead of her was as powerful as they came in the human species.

And she hated him for it because those once tender fingers had been replaced by claws. Those emerald eyes she had once gazed into with a weak heart now slashed and cut with an unquenched fury.

And what would you expect from a boy traumatized by his parents' slaughtering? Eight years of nightmares?

No. That would be you, Tanya.

Tanya gritted her teeth and rebuked the sentiment. He had become one of them. Walking the world seeking whom he might destroy. This demoniac now leading her into hell.

The thoughts whirled unchecked.

The moon rose behind them and highlighted his glistening back. Still he refused to look at her. He could smell her perhaps, like some ruthless animal who knew when it was being followed. And she could smell his sweat—musky and sweet in the humid night.

She stopped in the trail and spoke for the first time since entering the jungle. "Where are you leading me? It's dark."

He walked on, ignoring her.

"Excuse me!" Anger flashed up her spine. "Excuse me, it's dark, if you hadn't noticed."

His voice drifted back amid the screaming of cicadas. "I suggest you stay close if you don't want me to leave you here."

She mumbled angrily under her breath and ran to catch up. He had led her into danger without consideration for her safety and now he was threatening to leave her behind.

Tanya caught him and pounded on his shoulder. "Stop it!" she shrieked. "What are you trying to prove? This is crazy!"

He swung around, fists clenched. "You think so? You think *this* is crazy? Then listen to me, Tanya. *This* is nothing!" She could see that he was trembling. "This is two people walking along a path in the real world. I'll tell you what's crazy. Watching a bunch of men shoot holes into your mother and father while you stand by powerless. *That* is crazy. And that's the real world. But then you're not used to the real world, are you? You're too busy running from your nightmares, I suppose. Explaining away the death of Mommy and Daddy. Trying to make sense of it all? There's only one thing that makes sense now and it's got nothing to do with your God."

He turned around and left her standing, her mouth agape. *Running from my nightmares?* She followed quickly, fearing the dark alone.

And he had called her Tanya.

He's wounded, Tanya.

He's an animal.

He's a wounded animal, then. But he needs my love.

They walked in silence for hours, stopping only periodically for rest and water. Even then they did not talk. Tanya let her mind slip into a numb rhythm that followed the steady cadence of her feet.

In the end it was only prayer that soothed her frazzled spirit.

Father . . . dear God, I'm lost down here. Forgive me. I'm lost and lonely and confused. I hate this man and I hate that I hate him. And I don't even know if that's possible! What are you doing? What is your purpose here?

She stepped without caution on the path behind Shannon now, trusting his leading.

I hate this man.

But you must love this man.

Never!

Then, you would be like him.

Yes, and I'm a fool either way.

A picture of Jesus spread on the cross hung in her mind. *Forgive them, Father, for they know not what they do.* The image brought a knot to Tanya's throat.

Then her mind returned to the vision. What significance her life now played in this insanity was far beyond her. The thought of a bomb's mushroom cloud barely registered out here in the heavy forest. For all she knew the whole notion was absurd. Shannon certainly thought so.

Her mind returned to him. *God, help me.*

With each step, she resigned herself to the knowledge that this was indeed a part of some symphony conducted by God himself. In some absurd way it did make sense. In the end she would see that. The realization gave her strength.

35

Saturday

They had come far in the eight hours—farther than Shannon would have guessed the woman would last. He stopped by the Caura, five miles downriver from the plantation, and stood in the morning sun with a clenched jaw. The river was only twenty feet wide here and it curled around this meadow. It would be the safest place to leave her. She would have greater visibility of any approaching animals, and if he failed to return, she could find her way to safety down the river. It would also give him a way to reach her quickly once he'd finished.

Tanya.

She hardly registered as Tanya any longer. She was "that woman." It was what his mind called her now. And then on occasion the other part of his mind would call her "Tanya," and his heart would break a little. The voices pushed him at a relentless pace.

Ahead, the mountain rose and then fell over the cliff to the plantation. A *Year* bird cawed long and sober above him, and Shannon lifted his gaze to the canopy. The black bird's foot-long beak rested open. A yellow eye studied him. Shannon lowered his head and looked at the trees cresting the rise ahead. Abdullah waited there. A killing waited there—a throat begging for the blade. He imagined the thick brown cords of Abdullah's neck, parting under the edge of his knife. The man's eyes were smiling.

Shannon's breathing thickened. The plan was well laid and ticking along like a clock. Friberg would be moving by now. A chill flashed up his spine. He wanted to be there, facing the man who'd killed his mother and father, feeling the pounding of his heart, tasting his blood.

"Can we rest?" The sound of the woman's voice jerked him back to the river. Yes, that woman. Tanya. He could hardly remember why he had brought her. To share this part of his life with her, of course. To bring her into a holy union with death. To hate her so that she could love him. It was something that made no sense to weak minds, but to others it made perfect sense.

In the black fog.

You've lost your sanity, Shannon.

Have I? The world is insane.

He turned to her. She stood twenty feet off, haggard and dripping wet and looking near collapse. She gazed at him steadily. Her mind wasn't as weak as her body, he thought.

"You'll wait here," he said. "If I don't return, take the river east to Soledad."

He heard his voice from a distance, as if he were floating over his own body, and it sounded strange. Like the words of some dark priest summoning a body for sacrifice.

"Why are you doing this?" she asked softly.

"To help you understand," he said.

"Understand what? That you're a tortured soul?"

Shannon forced a grin. The fog swam in his mind.

"You see? Even now you insist on berating me," he said. "Don't you want to understand how your beloved Shannon turned out to be so wicked? I'm going to show you how."

"Shannon . . ." She stopped.

She called you Shannon.

"You're showing me only one thing," she continued. "You're showing me that you need help. I'll admit that I may have overreacted back there, but you've gone over the edge. You need help."

"Maybe it's you who need help. Have you considered that possibility? Or is your mind too full of nightmares to consider that?"

He saw her swallow. "Be careful what you say. My name's Sherry. Or Tanya. You remember that name, don't you?"

"And my name is what?"

"Shannon," she said softly. "We've both had a difficult time with things. I'll give you that. I've spent eight years reliving the nightmare of those three days, trapped in the box. But now there's only one right way. You think our meeting out here in the jungle is purely chance? You think my dreams are stupid?" She paused. "I suppose you do. But that doesn't change what we should do."

"And what should we do?"

"I don't know. But not this."

"*This?* You don't even know what *this* is," he said. "This, *Tanya*, is the shedding of blood. This, *Tanya*, is the bull and I hold the sword. Without the shedding of blood there can be no forgiveness of sin. Isn't that in your Bible? Half the world sits on padded pews singing pretty songs about the blood of Christ. Well, now you will see what it means to shed blood in the real world."

As he spoke, threads of confusion wrestled in his mind. He should not talk to her like this. She was extending a hand of peace. Maybe more. And what was he offering her? Only anger. Hatred.

"You've given yourself to Satan, Shannon. Can't you see that?" Her voice sounded deeply saddened. "I was wrong to be angry with you. Forgive me. I pity you."

Pity? Any illusion he harbored about her offering him peace shattered with her words. Revulsion swept through his gut like a wave crashing to shore.

He knew he couldn't allow her the satisfaction of seeing the impact of her words, but his hands were shaking already. Surely she could see that. The knife was at his waist—he could flip it out to her in the space of a single breath—pin her to the tree behind.

He blinked. What was he thinking? It was *Tanya* there!

Shannon lifted a trembling finger. "We'll see who should pity whom. I don't have time for this. Stay here by the river. I'll be back tonight."

He spun away and broke into a jog, knowing he should tell her how to avoid the crocodiles, but too furious to bring himself to it. She would have to depend on her God.

§

Thoughts crashed through Shannon's mind as he ran under the trees, confused and furious. Slowly the images of the woman were replaced by images of Abdullah. Slowly the lust for his blood crept through his mind, like an antiseptic numbing this other pain. Slowly Shannon climbed back into his old skin and prepared himself for the end of this long journey.

The first indication that he wasn't alone on the mountain came at the base of the black cliffs. A flock of parrots took to the air down valley, squawking loudly. He immediately pulled up and changed direction.

Shannon eased his way through the bush to the right of the disturbance. He moved from tree to tree, carefully measuring the jungle before him. The wind shifted and a light breeze brushed his face. He dropped to the ground as the strong smell of fish—tuna fish—filled his nostrils.

Humans. Whites.

Then he saw the soldier. Through the brush, still about fifty yards off, to his left, a single man dressed in the stripped-down military garb typical of the Special Forces. Close-cropped hair topped the man's camouflage-painted head. An automatic rifle crossed at his waist.

Shannon stared through the foliage at the hidden warrior and quickly considered his options. This was probably the perimeter guard of a post farther ahead. The cliff likely.

He studied the man carefully for a full five minutes before moving forward. He slowly edged his way closer to the shifting guard. For Shannon, armed with only a knife, stalking a trained killer armed with an automatic weapon, stealth would be the difference between life and death.

He stopped, crouched low behind the foliage, and studied the husky man. Regardless of their confidence, most of these white boys didn't belong in the jungle—at least not *this* jungle.

Shannon drew back his knife, held it for a second, and then hurled it at the man's exposed head. The startled soldier had barely started his turn when the butt of the knife smashed into his temple and dropped him. Shannon waited for a few moments, allowing the adrenaline in his veins to ease. Confident that no alarm had been raised, he slid next to the unconscious Ranger, retrieved his knife, and quickly removed a nine-millimeter revolver from the man's waist. He left the man on his back and slipped through the trees toward the cliff pass.

Laying the Ranger out hadn't been necessary, of course. He could've just as easily made his way past the team unnoticed. But since the CIA had gone as far as inserting Ranger forces to stop him, the least he could do was let them know he appreciated the gesture.

He thought of the woman briefly, like a distant memory now. *No, you can't change what I am, Tanya. And I am a killer. It's what I do. I kill. I do not die. There has been enough dying. Dying is for fools.*

36

Lumber loading dock D on the southern tip of Miami Harbor received the order to close six hours after the director drafted the recommendation. Three of those hours had been spent chasing down the proper naval authorities, who were evidently indisposed at a convention in Las Vegas. It had taken the port authorities another two hours to implement the orders. In sum total, the ports along the southern tip of Miami closed their doors to business eight hours after the decision had been made to do so.

Not bad for a monolithic bureaucracy. Too slow, considering the stated operational goals of Homeland Security.

During the last two hours of operation at loading dock D, a large converted fishing vessel bearing the name *Marlin Watch* unloaded the last of her cargo and pulled back out to sea for its return voyage to Panama. No one paid much attention to the unmilled Yevaro log set among the others. It was, after all, just a log.

Thirty minutes after it had been unloaded from the ship, the mid-size log was put aboard an eighteen-wheeled lumber rig with six other imports and transported to the Hayward Lumberyard on the outskirts of Miami proper.

Six hours later, an eighteen-wheel International rumbled into the yard, loaded the log, and left without filing any paperwork.

Farther north a clipper named *Angel of the Sea* moved steadily up the northeastern coastline of the United States.

Farther south, just entering U.S. waters, another ship, a larger one called the *Lumber Lord,* steamed up Florida's eastern coastline.

§

"How many?" Abdullah demanded, dropping his empty glass on the desk.

"Eighteen. The men passed the perimeter security line at the base of the cliffs three minutes ago, three groups in single file."

Abdullah whirled around and slammed his fist onto the desk. "They don't believe me? They're attacking?" He glared at the wall map. "Eighteen men, single file—they are professional soldiers. How long until they reach us?"

"An hour, if they move quickly. An hour and a half if they are careful," Ramón responded.

So then, they were coming for him. Eight years of waiting and now it was happening. The Americans weren't taking him seriously.

He shuddered, as if a nerve had been touched in his back. But then a nerve had been touched by the heat that rose through his spine. Maybe it was better this way. They would have their guard down and the blasts would rock their smug little world. Even if they did bring him down in the process, they would still feel a little heat.

He turned to Ramón, who stood waiting anxiously. "Tell Manuel to take his six best men and position them for surveillance near the northern edge of the compound. They are not to engage the soldiers unless they reach us." He twisted his head and looked at the map that outlined the perimeter's defense system. The old Claymore mines were buried just beneath the surface of the jungle floor in a three-meter band that circled the entire complex. It had taken them over two months to lay the three thousand mines, and for three years now, they had remained undisturbed.

"Activate the compound mines and inform the men to stay clear." He swung to Ramón. "Do it!"

Ramón left quickly.

Abdullah rounded his desk and sat carefully. The room was silent except for a slight scraping sound that came from the bugs in each corner. They were hard-shelled species that clung to each other's backs with long bipeds.

It was time to send another message. The Americans had never felt terror, not really. Not lately. They had never had their limbs severed or their wives raped or their children killed. So now he would change that.

Where was Jamal?

What if Yuri's bomb did not detonate? Abdullah shuddered and closed his eyes. Sweat soaked his collar, and he ran a hand across his neck.

Someone walked into his office and Abdullah opened his eyes. The room seemed to shift off center before him. Everything doubled—two doors, two Ramóns. He twisted his head and blinked. Now there was one. He lifted wet palms to the desk and set them before him. A fly settled on his knuckle but he did not bother it.

"Where are the bombs?" he asked.

"The boat with the larger device should be entering Chesapeake Bay now. It will be in place with time to spare." Ramón's voice quaked—he was afraid, Abdullah thought. Imagine that, afraid.

"The *Lumber Lord* is still off Florida's coast, going north."

Abdullah nodded. At his right hand the black transmitter sat facing the ceiling.

"Send a message to the Americans," he said quietly. "Tell them that they have thirty minutes to withdraw their men from the valley."

He ran a finger over the green knobs. His world had slowed. A drug had entered his body, he thought. But even the thought was slow. As if he had slipped into a higher consciousness. Or possibly a lower consciousness. No, no. It would have to be a higher state of mind, one that approached greatness. Like those boys marching off to their death on the minefields.

"Tell them that if they do not withdraw the soldiers, then we will detonate a small bomb. Don't tell them it will trigger the countdown for the larger one," he said, and his fingers trembled on the box.

§

Mark Ingersol stood with his arms dangling, sweating as though it were a sauna and not a situation room he and Friberg had retreated to.

They had received a third message.

A thousand books lined oak bookcases, wall to wall, surrounding the long conference table. But no amount of book learning would help them now. The crisis had gone critical and Friberg should have gone ballistic. The tall leather chairs around the wood table should be occupied with a dozen high-ranking strategists. Instead, there sat only one man and he slouched, numb, barely able to move.

"Do we tell him or not?" Ingersol asked.

Friberg lifted his eyes, looking more like a puppy than top shop man. "Tell who?"

"The president! You can't just sit on something like this. That madman down there has given us thirty minutes—"

"I know what that madman down there has given us. I'm just not sure I believe it."

"Believe it? If you don't mind me pointing out the obvious, we're way past believing here. We'll find out soon enough whether or not they have the bomb. In the meantime, we should be briefing the president."

"I've been in this game long enough to know what is obvious, *Ingersol.* What's obvious here is that you and I are in a hot spot if this idiot has the bomb. You think there's anything anyone can do about this in thirty minutes? How about putting out an all-points bulletin, flood the news channels with the message—'Get out, 'cause a nuclear bomb is about to explode down the street from you!' We'd lose more to the panic than to the bomb."

"Either way, the president should know."

"The president is the *last* person who should know!" Friberg had come back to life. His face twisted in a red snarl. "The less he knows the better. If there is a detonation, we have a problem. Agreed. But we don't need to draw attention to the issue now. There's been a threat and we're handling it—that's all he needs to know. I updated him less than three hours ago. We're proceeding systematically. Just a routine threat, that's all. Get it through your head."

Ingersol blinked and took a step back. "And how will it look if this thing goes off and it's discovered that you withheld information?"

"We, Ingersol. *We* withheld information. And it won't be discovered—that's the whole point. Not if you pull yourself together here."

A chill descended Ingersol's spine. "We should at least pull the Rangers back. Sending them in now is crazy. Abdullah will detonate!"

The director nodded. "You're right. Pull them back immediately."

Ingersol lingered a moment, thinking he should say something else. Something that would diffuse this madness, make his heart ease up. But his mind had gone gray.

He turned from the table and left the room. They should have sent the message to the Rangers ten minutes ago. As it was, the men would have less than fifteen minutes to retreat before Abdullah did his thing.

Whatever that was.

37

Tanya collapsed under a tree at the perimeter of the river clearing within minutes of Shannon's hasty departure. It occurred to her that there might be creatures in the brown water a hundred feet off, but she'd lost interest in her own safety.

The madness of eight years was slowly unwinding in her mind; she could feel it as though it were a snake uncoiling. She did not know how just yet, but somehow this was all forming a collage with meaning. The notes were beginning to make music. The words were carrying a message. And it was all flowing through her.

She spent the first few hours in a haze, barely aware of the curious birds squeaking above or the parade of insects crawling over her shoes and legs.

The words she had spoken to Shannon were not her own. Oh, they had come from her own mouth and even her own mind, but her spirit had handed them off to her mind. She knew that because a warmth had started to glow in her spirit and it wasn't her own.

God was warming her. He was holding her and breathing his words of comfort into her like a father whispering to a crying baby.

And with his breath came a new understanding of Shannon. An ache for him that burned in her bones. He had been tormented for years, she saw, much like she had been. But his tormentor had been from hell, grinding him into the ground. Her torment had been a gift from heaven, a seasoning to soften her spirit, as Father Teuwen had suggested. A thorn in her flesh, preparing her for this day. This colliding of worlds. This crescendo of clashing cymbals, like the finale in a grand symphony.

There was the matter of the dream and the bomb and all that, but in reality none of it seemed important to her anymore. Now it was all about Shannon.

Tanya lay her head on her forearm and closed her eyes. "Shannon, poor Shannon," she whispered. Tears immediately flooded her eyes. That ache in her heart swelled for him. It wasn't love as in the classical sense of romantic love, she thought. It was more like empathy.

"I'm so sorry, Shannon." The sound of his name coming softly from her lips threw her mind back to a time when they spoke in hushed tones to each other. I love you, Shannon. I love you, Tanya.

What's happening, Father? Speak to me.

Then Tanya tumbled into an exhausted sleep.

§

Shannon knelt on the edge of the jungle, breathing hard from the run. Before him the old plantation sprawled with awful familiarity, like a landscape pulled from an old nightmare and shoved before his eyes. He caught his breath and swallowed. The mansion had deteriorated to flaking boards several hundred meters to his right. The once manicured lawn on which his mother and father had been ripped apart now swayed with waist-high grass.

Tanya's voice whispered in his ear. *Are you ready to die, Shannon?* An absurd question. A wedge of heat ripped through his skull.

Are you ready to kill, Shannon?

Yes.

He jerked his gaze to the left, where the entrance into the mountain processing plant sat closed off by a large hangar door. Apart from two guards standing on either side of the overhead door, no other humans were in sight. The field hands probably lived in the old mansion, he thought. God only knew what they had done in there, who had slept in his bed all these years. He should burn it as well. To the ground.

Shannon stepped back into the forest and ran along the perimeter toward the hangar. He had encountered another set of guards earlier and found them incompetent—lazy from years of facing no trained adversaries. They might be able to butcher natives in their sleep, but today he would advance their training. He dropped to his knees now thirty meters from the nearest guard.

A single entry door opened, and Shannon pulled back into the shadows. A man dressed in a white lab coat stepped out briefly, talked to the guard, and then retreated back inside.

The grass between the jungle and the hangar stood two feet high, uncut in recent months—a foolish oversight. Shannon slid the green backpack loaded with explosives to his chest and lowered himself so that the bag dragged on the earth. He snaked from the tree line, keeping just below the grass.

He'd covered half the distance to the two guards before he stopped and eyed them carefully. Using the gun he'd taken off the Ranger would be like waltzing in with a marching band, but then he'd always preferred the knife anyway. Both guards leaned against the tin siding, their rifles propped within easy reach.

Shannon rubbed a small stone he'd brought from the jungle and waited. A full five minutes passed in sweltering stillness before the guards both faced away.

Shannon hurled the rock to the far side of the hangar door, in the direction they faced but to the tin eaves. The stone clattered and they jerked.

He came from the grass then, while their senses were taken by the initial start. Before the stone thumped harmlessly to the ground twenty yards past the guards, Shannon was halfway to them, a knife in each hand. The bowie he hurled at the closest guard, while he ran; the Arkansas Slider he flipped to his right hand while the bowie was still in flight.

From his peripheral vision Shannon saw the bowie take the first guard in his temple. The second guard whirled then, but Shannon's throwing arm already swept forward with the Slider. It flew through the air and buried itself in the man's chest, to the right of his breastbone. Neither man had cried in alarm; both gasped and sank to their seats.

Shannon veered for the single door, snatched the bowie from the closest guard, and flattened himself against the wall, adrenaline pounding through his veins. The euphoric buzzing that always accompanied his killing tingled up his spine. He swung the pack at his chest onto his back, gripped the doorknob, and pulled out the Ranger's nine-millimeter Browning.

One of two things would happen when he opened the door. They might spot him, in which case he would find himself in a full-scale firefight. Or he would slip in unnoticed. He couldn't remember the last time he'd left the success of a mission to such poor odds, and he ground his teeth thinking of it now. Either way he was committed.

Shannon twisted the knob and pushed very slowly. Sweat dripped from the end of his nose and splashed onto his knee. The door opened a crack and he held still.

No response.

He stretched his neck and peered into the slit. His heart thumped in his chest like a basketball being dribbled in an empty gym. A single helicopter rested in his narrow view. He pushed the door wider. Two helicopters. And beyond, a door that led to the processing plant.

But the dimly lit hangar was still, unguarded. Shannon drew a breath of the humid air, slipped through the door, and eased it shut behind him. Without pausing, he ran to the cover of a tall, red tool chest and crouched behind. Working quickly now, he pulled the pack off his chest and withdrew three charges. He set each timer to thirty minutes and slung the bag over his shoulder.

Shannon peered around the tool chest, saw that no one had entered the hangar, and eased over to the nearest helicopter. He shoved a bundle of C-4 under the fuel tank and went for the other one. The third bundle he tossed behind a large fuel tank at the hangar's rear. When the explosive detonated in twenty-eight minutes, the hangar would come down. If they managed to get one of these birds airborne, it would go off like a bomb in the air. Shannon shook the sweat from bangs hanging like claws over his forehead.

The door leading into the processing plant rested closed. Shannon ignored it and ran for the corner beams that arched to the ceiling. His luck so far had been good.

Maybe too good.

§

The Ranger teams penetrated the jungle in a conventional three-pronged fork foray. Rick Parlier led his team up the center, stepping through the brush light-footed. A dozen insects droned around him, but only those honing in on his neck bothered him and then only after an hour of high-stepping through the valley and finding nothing. He would have preferred to move much faster—take the team in on the run. But three self-repeating facts kept tumbling through his mind.

One, they didn't know the geography. This wasn't like picking a point over a few sand dunes and racing on over. It was more like crawling through a thicket of thorns. At night.

Two, although they knew that the valley was occupied, they didn't know precisely *where* that helicopter had come from or how many others hid beneath the canopy.

And three, the agent was still at large, running about these trees like some kind of maniac. Best they could figure, he'd laid Phil out cold back there a few hours ago. Nothing else made any sense.

Parlier slipped behind a large palm and slapped at his neck, thinking it was time to speed things up when Mark snatched his fist to the air behind him, motioning a full stop. He dropped to his knees and waited for Graham to reach them from the rear of the file.

Graham slid in beside Parlier. "We got a problem, sir. Uncle has ordered us back."

Parlier stared at the communications man. "Are they nuts?"

"You got me. They refuse to give an explanation. Just get out and get out fast. We got five minutes to get back to the cliffs."

"What did you tell them?"

"I told them that was impossible."

Parlier stood and snatched the transmitter from Graham's hand. "We've got some imbecile ordering us around! I'm—"

An explosion suddenly shattered the air no more than a hundred meters to their right. Parlier whirled toward the sound.

The jungle shrieked with the response of a thousand creatures. "That was Gamma!" Graham snatched the transmitter back. He fingered the mike and spoke quickly into it. "Come in, James. What was that?"

The radio hissed its silence.

Graham's hand trembled, and he depressed the transmission lever again. "Gamma, Gamma, this is Alpha. Come in!"

The receiver shrieked to life. "Alpha, we got trouble here! We got a man down. Tony's down. I repeat, we got a man down from some kind of mine!"

Parlier grabbed the microphone from Tim. "James, this is Parlier. Now listen carefully. Get your man and get back to the cliffs. Do not, I repeat, do not proceed forward. Do you copy?"

"Copy that. Retreating now." The radio fell silent.

A land mine? To protect what? "Beta, you copy that last transmission?"

"Copy, Alpha. Standing by."

"Get the heck out of there, Beta. Get back to the cliffs, you copy?"

"Copy, sir."

Parlier tossed the mike back to Tim and signaled a retreat to Mark, who passed the signal back to Ben and Dave in the rear file.

"Go." Graham slung the radio over his arm and moved out quickly.

Parlier turned and took one last look at the jungle that descended into the valley. Four days in the jungle and they'd seen only one other human being—and him for a brief moment before being cold-cocked. Now they had a man down. If they didn't get some clarification by nightfall, he was coming back to finish this job on his own. Maybe bring Graham.

Parlier turned and retreated toward the cliffs.

Abdullah sat at his desk and watched the clock. He'd never noticed its faint ticking before, but now it was louder than the soft clicking of the bugs.

Sweat trickled slowly down his chin and dripped onto a white sheet of paper on which he'd scrawled his first transmission. Several flies sat unmoving on his knuckles, but he hardly noticed them. His eyes remained fixed on that clock as his mind crawled through a fog.

He breathed steadily, in long pulls, blinking only when his eyes stung badly. Ramón sat cross-legged, staring at Abdullah through his one good eye, breathing, but otherwise motionless.

Something had changed. Yesterday the notion of detonating a nuclear weapon in the United States had been exhilarating, to be sure. But it had been a project. A plan. Even an obsession. But always more Jamal's obsession than his.

Now it had become his own. A desperate craving—like a gulp of air after two minutes under water. He felt as if *not* pushing this little plastic button might suck the life from his bones.

The effect seemed surreal. Impossible, actually. His mind skipped through the chain of events as Yuri had described them so many times.

Who was he to change the world? Abdullah Amir. A tremor ran through him at the thought. He almost pushed the button then. A high ringing sound popped to life in his head and the clock shifted out of focus for a moment. Then his vision was back.

The Rangers now had five minutes to pass the perimeter defense wire. Abdullah mumbled a word of prayer for their failure. It was in Allah's hands now.

38

Ramón watched Abdullah and felt a new kind of fear overtake his soul. His right leg had fallen asleep fifteen minutes ago and his back ached from his static posture.

Abdullah sat there sweating profusely, dripping on his desk, unmoving. His reddening eyes slowly shifted from the clock on the wall to the transmitter at his hand. His right cheek twitched every few seconds, as if a fly had lighted there. His lips twisted in an odd grimace, one that might just as easily be fashioned from delight as bitterness.

Ramón glanced up at the wall clock and saw the second hand pass through the bottom of its arc to the top. He swallowed, suddenly struck by the absurdity of it all. It would not just be this plastic button pushed in thirty seconds; it would be a fist down the throat of an unsuspecting world. Not one but two atomic weapons detonated twenty-four hours apart. In the name of God no less.

The second hand climbed, and Ramón suddenly thought that he should stop the man. He should lift his pistol and shoot him through that wet forehead. The thought screamed through his mind, but Ramón couldn't get the message out there, to his extremities where frozen muscles waited.

Then the red hand was at the top.

It occurred to Ramón that he had stopped breathing. He jerked his eyes to the Arab. Abdullah's face quivered, shaking a final drop of sweat free of his upper lip. His eyes bulged at the clock like two black marbles.

But he hadn't pushed that green button.

Ramón pried his eyes to the wall. The second hand was falling, past the large five, then the ten. Then he heard a loud exhale and he jerked his eyes back.

Abdullah sat slumped in his chair, his eyes closed, expressionless. Ramón dropped his gaze to the man's hand. The Arab's forefinger still rested on the green button.

It was depressed.

§

Daytona Beach had always been known for its beaches and worshiped for its sun. On most Saturdays the sky stretched blue. But today clouds had swept in from the west on cool winds, shielding the tourists from the rays. Consequently the beach lay gray and nearly empty. Where thousands of tourists normally slouched on the white sand or splashed in the surf, only the bravest slogged along the beach.

Twenty miles out to sea, the *Lumber Lord* steamed steadily north, up the coast of Florida. A flock of sea gulls fluttered over the ship, snatching up whatever morsel they could find. A dozen crew members were engaged in an enthusiastic water fight led by Andrew. Captain Moses Catura had assumed his typical position in the pilothouse and watched the men below drench each other. He smiled to himself. It was the kind of moment that made him glad to be alive.

It was also his last moment.

A single signal, invisible to the human eye, boosted and relayed from the coast of Venezuela to the southeastern coast of Cuba, found the *Lumber Lord* then. It penetrated her hull, located the small black receiver resting in one of the logs, and triggered it.

The detonation in the *Lumber Lord* started innocently enough. Krytron triggering devices released their four-thousand-volt charges into forty detonators that surrounded the core of the silver sphere. The detonators simultaneously fired the fifteen kilograms of shaped charges that Yuri had meticulously positioned around the uranium tamper. With absolute precision, just as the Russian had designed them to perform, the shaped charges crushed the natural uranium tamper into an orange-sized ball of plutonium.

It was an implosion rather than an explosion at this particular point.

The implosion compressed the plutonium core so forcefully that an atom at its core split and released a neutron. At exactly the same moment, the shock from the initial implosion broke the initiator housed within the center of the plutonium. When the initiator was crushed, beryllium and polonium contained in its core combined and released a flood of neutrons into the surrounding plutonium.

Within three-millionths of a second, the first neutron split from its parent atom—generation one.

In fifty-five generations the mass of plutonium reached a supercritical state and the little plutonium sphere shredded the boundaries of nature.

The entire episode lasted for less than one-thousandth of a second.

Suddenly the little orange-sized sphere of plutonium was no longer a sphere at all, but a 300 million degree sun, reaching out at over a thousand miles per second. Twenty miles off the coast of Daytona Beach, history's third offensive nuclear explosion had been detonated.

In one moment the *Lumber Lord*'s massive steel hull was lumbering through calm seas, and in the next, a blinding ball of light had vaporized the ship as though it were made only of crepe paper.

The explosion lit up the horizon like a sputter of the sun. A huge fireball rose from the sea and stared the unsuspecting bathers in the face. In the first millisecond, a thermal pulse of light reached to the beach, effectively giving nearly a thousand onlookers what amounted to a bad sunburn. A dozen fires ignited along the coast.

An electromagnetic pulse from the blast cut off electricity and communications in the city. A huge mushroom cloud rose over the ocean and rumbled for several long seconds.

Then all went silent.

After an endless pause, the city slowly began to fill with sounds once again. Police sirens wailing up and down the streets, aimless and desperate without radio contact. People running helter-skelter, screaming.

The tidal wave rippling in was a small one by tidal standards, but enough to surge a hundred yards inland. The water spread past the beaches roughly ten minutes after the blast.

Then the vacuum created by the blast caved in on itself and the winds, which had earlier brought the clouds, resumed their push out to sea. The radiation fallout drifted away from the land, for the moment.

The detonation was a mere sniff of the destruction within the grasp of the much larger sister device, now already in a countdown to its own detonation.

Twenty-three hours, forty-eight minutes and counting.

§

Tanya slept beneath the towering trees, ignorant of the passing jaguar, unaware that not one but three crocodiles eyed her from the far shore; oblivious to the little sun that had lit the sky off of Florida's coast. For her it was darkness. The sweet darkness of sleep.

Until the sky opened up suddenly, like a tear in space. The beach lay before her and the surf lapped at sandy shores. The vision was back. Only this time Shannon was there calling for her to come.

Shannon. Sweet Shannon. I love you, Shannon.

She flinched in her sleep. I love what he was.

Come, Tanya. The boy was calling to her. *Please save me.*

The sky in her mind erupted then, like a flash grenade. The wind was sucked from her lungs by a white-hot fire and the world returned to black.

Tanya bolted upright, panting under the towering tree. Sweat streamed down her neck. The bomb had gone off!

The bomb had just gone off!

39

Mark Ingersol stood in the basement room among the computers and teletype machines with one arm across his belly and the other lifted to his chin. He had never been the type of man to bite his nails, but for the last twenty minutes he had managed to draw blood from his right forefinger. He had spoken directly to the Ranger team this time, bypassing the regular communication channels. A soldier named Graham had told him they couldn't withdraw in time.

"What do you mean you can't withdraw in time? You're a Ranger! Hightail it, man!"

Twice he'd been tempted to call back—check on their progress. But in the end he just paced. The operator on duty had come over once and asked if he could be of help. Ingersol had sent the man packing.

And now the clock on the wall had ticked off two minutes past the deadline and nothing had happened. That was good. That was real good. Ingersol felt this shoulders ease.

Ingersol blew some air from his lungs and walked for the bathroom.

Regardless of this crazy bomb threat, a few annoying loose ends still dangled in his mind. David Lunow for instance. He relieved himself, thinking already of what it would feel like to take out someone like David. A rogue agent was one thing, but David? He was a friend.

He pushed through the bathroom door, turned for the exit, and glanced at the teletype machine. White paper rose past its roller like a tongue. A chill fell down Ingersol's back.

The message could have come from a hundred different sources. A thousand sources. He veered to his right and leaned over the machine.

At first the words didn't place clear meaning in his mind. They read quite simply:

If you do not deliver the agent as requested, then another bomb will detonate. In Miami. A much larger device, which is already triggered. You have precisely twenty-four hours.

The Brotherhood

It was that word—*another*—that suddenly came to life like a siren in Ingersol's skull. His knees went weak and that chill washed right down to his heels. He reached trembling fingers for the white sheet and ripped it from the teletype. He whirled about and ran from the room.

Ingersol reached the director's office four stories higher in twenty-five seconds. Friberg was on the phone, his face white, his eyes wide. He did not look up when Ingersol shook the message at him. His mind wasn't in the room.

" . . . Yes, sir. I understand, sir. But that was under different pretenses. Things have obviously changed."

He's talking to the president, Ingersol thought. *It's happened!*

Friberg spoke again. "Well, if he had one, yes he could have more."

"He does," Ingersol said. Friberg's face went white. Ingersol swallowed and lowered the message.

Friberg listened for a moment. "Yes, sir." He then hung up.

They stared at each other for a few seconds, silent.

Friberg's face suddenly settled before he said, "NORAD recorded a twenty-kiloton blast two miles off of Daytona Beach five minutes ago."

Ingersol blinked rapidly several times. He sat in the guest chair, numb.

Friberg looked out the window, still white but otherwise expressionless. "Fortunately it was a bad beach day; no reported casualties yet. They've reported heavy structural damage on the beachfront."

"This wasn't supposed to happen."

"It happened. Get used to it."

"What is the president doing?"

Friberg faced him. "What do you expect he's doing? He's going ballistic. Calling in the troops. He's ordered the closing of all airports. The Europeans are already screaming about the fallout headed their way. They've got a squadron of F-16s on the tarmac and they're screaming for a target, and now I suppose they'll begin the evacuation of southern Florida. Like I said, they're going ballistic."

"You gave the F-16s a target?"

"No."

Ingersol shoved the message to Friberg. "Well, you'd better. We've got another bomb."

Friberg took the communiqué and glanced over the message. "You see, this is precisely why we can't give the Air Force their target."

"What do you mean? This changes everything! I'm not going to just sit by and watch—"

"Shut up, Ingersol! Think, man! That device was remote detonated. We can't just sweep in and carpet bomb the jungle. Anybody crazy enough to set off one bomb because we didn't deliver someone's head on a platter is crazy enough to detonate a second at the first sniff of an attack!"

"The second bomb is already triggered."

"So he says. Could be a bluff. If it is, we're pretty much done."

"We should suppress any signals coming from the region."

"We're on it."

That set Ingersol back. So the man was thinking beyond his own problems finally. "Can't they drop a smart weapon on the compound? Something that hits them before they know it's on its way?"

"And accomplish exactly what? If he *has* already triggered the second device, killing him now would only remove any chance of terminating this twenty-four-hour countdown of his. If he hasn't triggered it, we can't afford to set him off."

"So what, then?"

Friberg glanced at the message again. "We evacuate southern Florida. We look for the bomb in every nook and cranny surrounding Miami. We curse the day we allowed Casius to live. We locate Abdullah Amir using whatever resources exist and we hope we can isolate any signal he's using for the detonation."

A thought dropped into Ingersol's mind. The thought that a highly skilled operative dropped into that jungle might be their best bet.

"Then we should send Casius after him."

Friberg blinked. "Casius?"

"He's the best operative we have, he knows the lay of the land, and he's already there."

"He's also AWOL. We have no way of contacting him." Friberg stood. "Forget Casius. We've got some briefings to run. We'll give the president an update from the car."

He headed for the door.

"Where are you going?" Ingersol asked, still short on breath.

"*We,* Ingersol. We are going to Miami."

§

The simple fact that very few United States residents had ever seen the effects of a nuclear blast rendered the news that a detonation had just occurred off the coast of Florida at first impossible to believe. The terrorist activities in New York had been horrifying; this was simply incomprehensible. When the pictures finally flashed on the tube, the nation came to a literal standstill.

The first live images came from a jetliner flying high enough to avoid the electromagnetic pulse. They showed a coastline dotted by a thousand small trails of smoke that news commentator Gary Reese of CBS said were scattered fires. By the time the first helicopter flew over the region against specific orders to clear the air space, 90 percent of the country hovered around television sets, gawking at images of fires and gutted buildings.

A hand-held video taken from a hotel room in Daytona Beach was first played by a local ABC affiliate. But within minutes the networks had picked it up and the simple image of the eastern horizon lighting up, midday, replayed itself a thousand times on every television set across America.

The largest freeways ran bare through silent cities. Bars with televisions were crowded with customers, their necks cocked to the sets.

All regular programming was canceled and the talking heads began their analysis to a gaping public. The president begged the country's patience and vowed swift retribution. It was a terrorist attack, everyone quickly agreed. Some analysts suggested responding with nuclear weapons immediately and overwhelmingly. Others insisted on a surgical strike. Against whom or where seemed almost beside the point.

Then news of another kind came and a new terror spread through the nation like a raging fire. Residents of south Florida were being asked to evacuate their homes. In a calm manner, of course, controlled by the National Guard along five selected routes running north. But leave quickly and take nothing. Why? Well, there could only be one reason regardless of what the official word insisted.

There was another bomb.

And if there was another bomb in Florida, then who was to say that the same terrorists hadn't hidden one in Chicago or Los Angeles or any other city? Wouldn't it make more sense to spread the weapons for greater impact?

Within three hours of the detonation, the nation ran amuck in panic. The truth settled in like a gut punch—the impossible had just happened and no one knew what to do.

40

Shannon dropped into the processing plant behind one of the five large white tanks, each marked respectively with the chemical that it held: calcium bicarbonate, sulfuric acid, ammonium hydroxide, potassium permanganate, and gasoline. Chemicals used to refine cocaine. He peered around the tank marked "gasoline" and scanned the room. Pipes fed from the tanks to the mixing vats clustered in the room's center. The vast operation was controlled from the glass room that hugged the east wall opposite the tanks.

Two armed guards loitered by the door leading from the lab. An additional eight to ten men worked in the lab. As things now stood, crossing the room without raising an alarm would be impossible. He had roughly twenty-four minutes before the first helicopter exploded.

Shannon slipped the pack from his back, set a timer to twenty-two minutes, and wedged the plastic explosive under the gasoline tank. He slipped to the ammonium hydroxide tank on the far left, laid a small bundle of C-4 on the cement floor behind it, set the timer for one minute, and retreated back to the right side.

He crouched and waited. Directly across the room from him, the tunnel through which he and the woman had escaped ran into the mountain. Tanya. Her name was Tanya, come back from the dead to speak to him about her God. She was as beautiful as he remembered. Possibly more. His heart pounded steadily.

And the priest? It was too late for the priest.

The air shattered with an explosion. Immediately all heads jerked to the far corner and Shannon bolted from his cover. Steams of ammonium hydroxide jetted from the ruptured tank to his far left. Yells of alarm filled the air as pipes hissed the potent gas. Before any of the men had fully registered the nature of the accident, Shannon was across the room and in the tunnel, sprinting down the earth floor toward the elevator shaft he and Tanya had used.

He tossed a single bundle of C-4 under the conveyor track as he ran. It would close the tunnel. Then he was at the gaping elevator shaft—clear to the bottom with the car resting above him. He looked back toward the processing lab from where the ruckus now carried. If he'd been spotted, they weren't pursuing.

He reached into the shaft, grabbed the thick steel cable, and lowered himself to the basement level, ten feet above rock bottom. He withdrew the bowie knife, jammed it between the elevator doors, and wrenched hard. The steel doors gaped and he shoved his foot through the opening. Five seconds later Shannon tumbled into the hall that had sealed him in just two days ago.

§

Abdullah stood slightly hunched in the upper room, drenched in sweat, his facial muscles twitching spastically.

He considered calling the coast for confirmation of his blast but the fidgeting Hispanic before him was right. They couldn't trust anyone now. In fact, they should leave, before a fighter jet dropped one of those bombs on them that drilled through mountains. Before Jamal arrived by helicopter.

"But they can't attack us. They know the second device is already on a countdown. They will assume that only I can stop it. You see, that's the power of true terror." He couldn't remember such a feeling of satisfaction.

The room suddenly shook under the rumble of an explosion and Ramón bolted from his chair, terrified.

Abdullah sprang to the window. A dozen men scrambled about below, fleeing what appeared to be the contents of a ruptured tank. An accident? It was too coincidental. The seconds slogged off in his mind with the surreal pace of a huge pendulum.

And then he saw the half-naked man disappear into the tunnel to his far left and he swallowed.

The agent. Casius!

He spun to Ramón. "It's the agent!" For a moment he couldn't think. He stared at Ramón, who'd already drawn his gun.

"Casius?" Ramón said.

The Americans had sent the killer after him again! Instead of withdrawing, the CIA was going for the jugular.

It was time to leave. "Bring me the priest!"

He leapt over to the desk and snatched up the transmitter.

"The priest?"

"The priest, you idiot! The hostage! I need a hostage!"

§

Shannon placed four charges in the basement where they'd held him before swinging back into the elevator shaft and climbing hand over hand to the second level.

Using the bowie again he pried his way into the middle floor, gun in hand. Apart from three closed doors, the hall lay empty.

Shannon slid up to the two doors on his left, listened for a brief moment with his ear pressed to the wood, and cracked them open only to find each empty. The men had probably rushed to the explosion in the lab. A barroom and a mess hall each received a timed explosive.

He ran back to the elevator and pressed the call button, ignoring the third door, which he knew must lead to the large processing lab. Only the third floor remained above him. Abdullah would be there.

The elevator whirred to life behind the door. Shannon blinked at the sweat leaking into his right eye and took a deep breath. He would go up there and kill Abdullah as he had always planned. And then he would leave the jungle forever. A picture of Tanya flashed through his mind and his head twitched.

Are you ready to die, Shannon?

Soon. I will be soon.

He flattened himself on the wall, leveled his gun at the elevator doors, and exhaled.

§

Ramón pressed himself into the elevator car's corner, squatting low. He'd taken the priest up to Abdullah and then he'd been sent to deal with Casius. The agent had eluded him once, but he wouldn't escape again. The elevator bell rang loudly and he shrank farther down.

The elevator jerked to a stop and the doors parted. Ramón's gun hand wavered before his eyes. Nothing. He held his breath and waited, straining for the first glimpse of movement.

But there was nothing. The doors slid closed and the elevator sat still, waiting further instructions.

Now what? If Ramón pressed any button, he might very well give himself away. Unless the agent was on the basement level. But then why didn't the car descend? Someone else had called the car, not he.

For a few moments Ramón remained crouched in the corner waiting, undecided. Meanwhile the agent was no doubt below or above. He wouldn't be on this floor. The thought finally prompted him to lean forward and press the "open" button.

The doors spread again and Ramón trained his gun on the opening. Still nothing. He stood and eased to the door's edge.

§

Shannon smelled the musty scent of sweat the moment the doors opened and he was back-pedaling to the corner before they stopped. He sighted down the wall and waited.

The doors closed on the occupant, but the elevator sat still. He waited with his gun arm extended. The charges in the hangar would explode in less than five minutes. He didn't have all day.

The door opened again and after a moment a gun poked past the wall. Still he waited, his patience wearing thin.

A hand followed the gun. Shannon shot then, into the hand. The slug took it off at the knuckles and he ran forward. The hall filled with the gunman's wail.

Shannon's mind echoed with another wail—a wail suggesting that he didn't have the time for this. He stepped into the elevator just as the doors began to close. The man he'd wounded knelt in a gathering pool of blood. It was the one-eyed man. Shannon shot him through the forehead and had a hand on his collar before the head lolled back. The man's eyes remained open. He angrily jerked the body from the car, leapt over it, and stabbed the third-floor button.

Too slow. Any minute the mountain would begin its collapse under heavy explosions.

The elevator groaned upward. Shannon cursed the heat flashing along his spine. Anger blurred his thinking. What if Abdullah waited in ambush on the third floor? Had he thought *that* through? No. He only wanted to kill the man, a blind desire that ran through his blood like molten lead. Eight years of plotting had finally come to this moment.

And what if Abdullah wasn't up there at all?

Shannon ground his teeth. The bell sounded and the door slid open before his extended gun.

The hall was empty.

He stepped from the car, thinking even as his foot cleared the threshold that he was in a fool's game now. Acting before thinking.

The hall lay vacant and white-walled excepting two brown doors. Shannon ran for the first, tossing the Browning to his left hand midstride. The door was locked. Any minute now that C-4 would start blowing the helicopters. Grunting against a surge of panic, he stepped back, pumped a single slug through the handle, and smashed his foot against the door. It snapped open and he jumped through, gun extended.

The contents of the room barely registered. Some kind of storage. What did register was that they did not include Abdullah.

Shannon spun around and ran for the second door. This time he didn't bother trying the handle. He simply shot through the lock and crashed it open with the sole of his foot. He leapt through and fell to a crouch, swinging his weapon in a quick arc.

A desk strewn with papers was on one end of the office; a tall bookcase stood against the other. The office was empty! Impossible!

Shannon stood, at a loss, his mind spinning. This could mean only one thing: Abdullah had escaped! A growl started in his throat and rose past his gaping mouth in a ferocious snarl. A red surge swept through his mind, momentarily blinding him.

He looked back to the desk. A book on nuclear proliferation lay facedown. The bomb.

Yes, the bomb.

Across the room a glass picture window was shaking and it occurred to him that the explosions had started. Then the sound came, deep-throated booms that shook the floor under his feet.

Shannon's mind snapped then as instinct took control of his body. He bent low, snatched a thin rug from the wood floor, and ran from the room. When the gasoline tank went, the main complex would collapse. Screams drifted over another detonation, still in the hangar, he thought. Those helicopters were popping.

He punched the call button and the elevator doors sprang open. The car suddenly quaked badly and he knew one of the basement explosives had detonated early. If the one in the tunnel went, he would be finished.

The elevator ground down a floor and opened to the tunnel that housed the conveyor. Shannon sprang from the car and sprinted away from the processing lab. The ground suddenly shook with a string of explosions and the overhead lights winked to black. The gasoline tank had gone! The caverns would come down around his ears!

He pelted forward. The freight elevator waited in darkness thirty yards ahead, powerless now. But he could still take the shaft up to the tube.

It was suddenly there, barely lit by the flames raging in the lab far behind. He vaulted over the rail and grabbed at the framework built into the vertical shaft. He flung the rug over his shoulder and clawed his way up, knowing that at any moment the explosives in the tunnel below would blow.

And then they did, with a steel-wrenching thunder. Stone crumbled and fell past him. Shannon slung the rug into the tube and scrambled over the lip for the second time in as many days. This time it would be belly down—he had no time to adjust his position. The rug slid forward and the elevator framework behind him tore loose from the rockface.

Shannon gripped the rug with both hands and fell toward the river far below.

41

"It appears that we might, and I want to stress the word *might*, have another device located somewhere in southern Florida." The president's face looked white on the tube, despite the makeup CNN had hurriedly applied, David thought.

It was happening. And he was learning about it with the rest of the department—heck, with the rest of the country. He had suspected something, but never this. The briefing room was silent.

"It is very important that any residents within a fifty-mile radius of the pier head north using the recommended routes as quickly and as calmly as possible. This is only a precaution, mind you, and we can't afford panic. I cannot tell you how important it is for you not to panic. Everything in the realm of possibilities is being done to search the area with highly specialized sensors. If another nuclear device is located near Miami, we will find it. But we must take the precautions the Office of Homeland Security has laid out."

The president was talking, but another voice was whispering in David's mind as well. It was Casius, and he was telling David to leave town for a while. Far away. Which meant that Casius knew, or at least suspected more than any of them.

§

While America glued its eyes on Miami, a U.S. registered clipper bearing the name *Angel of the Sea* slipped up the Intracoastal Waterway best known as

Chesapeake Bay. It was one of hundreds of boats on the water that day. The small cargo vessel had made the trip from the Bahamas to Curtis Point—just south of Annapolis and a stone's throw from Washington, D.C.—dozens of times, each time with a variety of imported goods on board, usually with at least a partial load of exclusive lumbers that sold by the pound rather than by the foot.

The small business had made its owner—best known as John Boy in the local bars—quite wealthy. Or more accurately, the *extracurricular* business he conducted with *Angel of the Sea* had made him well off.

For every week John Boy spent traipsing back and forth to the Bahamas, he spent two dealing the coke. His price from Abdullah was half what every other dealer paid to get their hands on the white powder—the benefits of establishing this new route.

Fine by him. The less he paid, the more he made and, judging by the ease of his trips, this route could hardly be safer. Jamal had done his homework. Heck, on more than one occasion he had waved to the Coast Guard while steaming through the bay. They all knew John Boy.

John Boy had been nursing a beer behind the wheel when news of the nuclear blast off Florida's coast reached him. He stared dumbfounded at the tube for half an hour and his beer had gone warm. He had just cut through those waters himself, less than twenty-four hours earlier. If he'd stopped off in Freeport as was his custom, he might be . . . toast. Literally. But Ramón had insisted on making the trip a straight shot this time.

"You see, you can never tell, John Boy," he muttered to himself at the wheel. "You live and let live, and you die when it's your time." That's the way he'd always lived his life.

"Holy Moses." Next you know, some mad man'll be wheeling a bomb up to the Capital. Maybe it was time he thought about moving west.

He glanced at the chart spread out before him. If the weather held, he'd make Curtis Point in four hours, anchor in the bay, and head home. The log with the goods would have to wait this time. He always waited until all eyes were firmly off the ship before unloading that last log—forty-eight hours at least. But now with this Florida thing . . .

"Holy Moses."

§

Abdullah had just stepped from the underground passage, dragging a blindfolded priest, when the mountain began its trembling. Around him the jungle came to life with fleeing creatures and Abdullah crouched low. The escape passage behind the bookcase had been his idea from the beginning, but he'd always imagined using it to flee his own men, or Jamal, not some assassin from the CIA. Either way, he had chosen well in sending Ramón down in the elevator to deal with Casius.

The Caura River's current waited half a mile to the south. He had pushed the button on Yuri's transmitter and if all had gone well, the bomb aboard the *Lumber Lord* had detonated. But had it? He ground his molars, desperate to know this one detail.

Nothing here mattered now. The second bomb would soon detonate and nothing would make him stop it.

Actually, nothing *could* stop him.

Yes, that was right, wasn't it? He had the codes, but he hadn't memorized them. And now they had just gone up in smoke because of the American's own foolishness. So no one could stop the second bomb. Other than Jamal, of course. But Jamal wasn't here to stop it. He had only to make his way out of the jungle now.

He shivered and suppressed the urge to send the second signal, detonate the second bomb, in case the first had failed.

Abdullah closed his eyes. It was the second bomb that would make history—not this little firecracker he'd sent them. The second bomb was now close enough to Washington, D.C., to destroy the CIA. And the Capital. The thought pushed a soft groan through his chest.

He considered shooting the priest and leaving him here—it would be much simpler than taking him. But another thought stopped him. There were others out there, the ones who'd crossed the perimeter sensors. American soldiers. A hostage would be wise. He would kill him downriver, after the Caura joined the Orinoco.

42

At ten thousand feet, peering from a military transport's bubble, David Lunow thought metro Miami looked like an octopus with long tentacles of creeping automobiles reaching out from the bloated city. The lines stretched north two hundred miles along five major routes that had hemorrhaged into several hundred smaller escape routes.

Based on reports from the National Guard, the scene on the ground brought new clarity to the meaning of "chaos." Driven from their homes at the president's urging and by relentless television images of a blackened Daytona Beach, twenty million city dwellers scurried like rats from a rising tide. Honking cars clogged the streets within hours. Bicycles wobbled in and out of stalled vehicles. Some of the more fit jogged. In the end the runners led the exodus. No mode of transportation moved as fast as they.

And where were they all going?

North. Just north.

David glanced at his watch. Ten hours. Across the aisle, Friberg gazed out another window with Mark Ingersol. David caught Ingersol's attention and thumbed outside. "There's no way they're going to get away in time. You know that."

The man's eyebrow lifted. "They're doing better than I imagined. If they had any brains, they'd just leave the cars and walk."

"For the record, sir, I want to make it clear that I believe we're going about this wrong. We should be looking north as well."

"You've said that. We don't have the time to check Miami and you want us to spread ourselves even thinner? You have a hunch. We have a threat on paper that puts a bomb in Miami. I'm not sure we have any choice."

He had a point, of course. But David's hunch was making his skin crawl. The plane dipped a wing and began a quick descent to Miami International. They were the only plane on pattern and within ten minutes they were down.

The air seemed thicker than David remembered and he couldn't help but wonder if the detonation out to sea had affected the weather. They were ushered into the terminal where a solemn gray-haired Lieutenant John Bird met them with an outstretched hand.

"I hope you have some information for us," Bird said, taking each hand quickly. "I've got a thousand men scattered over southern Florida and we don't even know what we're looking for. A picture or a description wouldn't hurt." He spoke without smiling. By the rings under his eyes, he hadn't slept for a while, David thought.

"If we knew what you were looking for, you would know by now, wouldn't you?" Friberg's tone earned a hard stare from the National Guard officer.

"Tell me what you've got," Friberg demanded.

Bird hesitated only a second before spitting out his report in staccato fashion. "We're sweeping every port south of the blast site in ten-man teams with Geiger counters. So far, nothing has turned up. We're manually picking through every storage bin waiting for customs inspection, but like I said, without a specific description the process is slow. We've isolated every shipment received in the last three days and are currently searching their deliveries, but again, we're shooting in the dark. If we at least had a size on this thing—"

"But we *don't* have a size on this thing. What about the DEA leads? Have you traced the suspected trafficking routes?"

"Not yet, sir. We—"

"Not yet? I thought the DEA gave that top priority. These terrorists are operating out of drug country, Lieutenant. Don't you think it would make sense for them to use trafficking routes?" The director's face flushed red. "Bring me the DEA intelligence."

"Yes, sir." Bird eyed Friberg for a moment.

"Now, Lieutenant."

Bird turned and strode for the door.

"Excuse me, sir," David interjected. "But have we established contact with Casius?"

Friberg faced him. "What would Casius have to do with this, Lunow? If we'd made contact with him, he'd be dead, wouldn't he?"

"Maybe. Maybe not."

Friberg's nostrils flared.

"But I was referring to his knowledge of the situation, not his elimination. You put the word out to him?"

"He's a rogue agent. Our intentions are to kill him, not court him. And we don't exactly have a direct line to the man's head."

"He's been in contact with these terrorists, for crying out loud! He may have information you need," David said. "And if you wanted to get word to him, I would think a few well-placed helicopters with loudspeakers might be a start. But you're not interested in bringing him in, are you?"

Friberg trembled when he spoke. "You are out of line, Lunow! But I don't have the time to address your obvious lack of understanding right now. We've got a deadline here."

The director turned his back on David and strode for the window.

"Ingersol!" he snapped.

Ingersol flashed David an angry stare and followed the director over to the window. Bird burst through the doors, gripping the DEA report. He joined the men at the window.

David swallowed. "We're toast," he mumbled. "We're toast and they know it."

§

Shannon crawled from the Orinoco River, feeling a deep desperation he'd rarely felt. It was the same vacuum that had sucked at his chest eight years earlier. The emptiness he thought might precede suicide.

His back stung badly and he wondered if the skin was drawing infection. He was a good ten miles from where he'd left Tanya on the banks of the Caura River.

Shannon stood for a moment on the shore, his hands dripping limp at his sides. For the first time in eight years he had failed to kill a man he'd pursued. Abdullah had escaped.

He gripped his hands to fists, glanced up the mountain, and lumbered forward. He would finish this. It was all he knew, this drive to kill. And it wasn't just about Abdullah, was it? He was showing them all.

The feeling couldn't be too different from what a trapped animal felt, pounding relentlessly into a concrete wall, oblivious to the blood seeping from its head.

Shannon blinked the sweat from his eyes and crashed through the underbrush, not caring who heard him now. If this was his last mission, so be it. It would be a fitting end—to die having killed the one who had taken the life of his mother on the lawn.

Are you ready to die, Shannon?

Tanya.

Her face rose up in his mind, out of the black fog. A seventeen-year-old blonde, diving from the cliff into his arms. A twenty-five-year-old woman, running through the jungle at his heels. His vision blurred and he grunted.

You're a fool, Shannon.

He pulled up and gripped his head, suddenly terrified. For a few long breaths he shook on the path. What was he doing? What had he *done?*

The black fog settled into his mind slowly.

A thought stuttered through his mind. An image of his blade crossing Abdullah's neck. He shook again, this time with a familiar eagerness.

Shannon dropped his arms and ran. He would kill Abdullah and then he would kill Jamal.

43

Tanya was sleeping dreamlessly when the blow caught her midsection. She instinctively coiled up, coughing. A voice screamed above her.

"Get up!"

Another blow slammed into her back and she scrambled to her knees. Above her, a figure slowly shifted into focus, backlit by the afternoon sun. Her head spun, and she thought she was going to faint. But the feeling passed, and she blinked at the man.

A man with the white wedge through his hair still stood over her, grinning with twitching lips. Abdullah. She knew him immediately.

He held a silver pistol in his right hand. A small aluminum skiff tied to a muddy stump bobbed on the current behind him. The man's white shirt had been browned by river muck and his black shoes were caked with mud. He'd saved his pants by rolling them up above his socks to hairy, bony shins that looked as though they hadn't seen the sun in years. The angry scar on his cheek curled with his grin. He'd come down the river from the plantation, which meant Shannon had failed to find him.

"Well. What a surprise. It's the assassin's woman," Abdullah said. His tongue seemed dark in his mouth when he spoke, like an eel hiding in its black cave. His wet lips quivered spastically.

"It appears that you'll die after all." The Arab's eyes glistened black and bulging, and Tanya thought that he had lost himself. She stood slowly.

She saw Father Petrus then, kneeling in the mud by the skiff, blindfolded, hands tied behind his back.

"Father Petrus!" She instinctively moved toward him.

"Shut up!" Abdullah struck her shoulder, and she fell back to her seat.

She scrambled around. "What have you done to him?"

"It's okay, Tanya." The priest's voice was hoarse.

Tanya? He knew her real name?

Abdullah smiled, amused. "You want your priest, don't you? Yes, of course, you are about to die and you want your priest." He turned to the river. "Priest, come here."

Petrus did not move.

"Come here!" Abdullah screamed. "Are you deaf?"

Father Petrus got his legs under him and staggered toward them. The Arab stepped out impatiently and shoved him the last few yards. Petrus collapsed beside Tanya.

She ripped his blindfold off and threw it to one side. Petrus blinked in the light, and she helped him to his seat.

Abdullah looked at them, an amused expression on his face, momentarily lost, it seemed. He lifted his black eyes and studied the tree line above the clearing. "Where is your man now? He's not here, is he? No. He couldn't have come this far so quickly. But he'll come. He'll come for his lover."

Please, God . . . Tanya started the prayer but didn't know where to go with it.

Abdullah rested his eyes on her again. He motioned to her with the pistol. "Do you know what I've done?"

His face held such a look of pure evil that Tanya instantly knew. The bomb. He had detonated the bomb in her vision. Fear squeezed at her heart.

"Yes?" A twisted grin lifted his left cheek, the one without a scar. Sweat snaked from his temples. "Do you know?"

"You're the devil," she said.

His lips snapped shut. His eyes glared round. "Shut up!" Spittle flecked on his lower lip.

She looked at Father Petrus seated beside her. Their eyes met and his were bright. His face sagged and his clothes were torn but his eyes were bright. A smile tugged gently at his mouth. She blinked. A lump rose in her throat.

She looked up at Abdullah. "You're the hand of Satan."

The Arab's gun hand began to tremble and she spoke again, gaining confidence now, "Yes, I do know what you've done. You've detonated a nuclear bomb."

He stopped, surprised. "It worked?"

He didn't know? "Yes, I think so."

"And how would you know this?"

"I saw it," she said simply. "In a dream."

He cocked his head slightly and examined her face carefully. "You saw it, did you? And what else did you see?" His lips twisted. "Do you see what will happen now?"

She hesitated. She only knew that it would be good for Shannon to come through the trees now. And she didn't necessarily want him to save her, although that seemed reasonable enough, but she wanted him to be here. Shannon.

"I'm sure you want to kill," she said.

He blinked. "And will I succeed?"

"I don't know."

"Then you don't know anything."

"I know that you're death."

"Shut up!" he screamed. His voice echoed about the trees.

She looked past him to the tree line. *Shannon, do you hear that, my love? Come quickly. Please, there isn't much time.*

My love?

"If you speak again, I'll kill him," Abdullah said, pointing the gun at Petrus.

She looked back at him. "You can't kill him."

Abdullah's face quivered with anger.

"He would hear the gunshot. My Shannon would hear it," Tanya said.

The Arab's black eyes seemed to hollow with hate. Like two holes drilled through that skull of his.

"Lie down on your stomach."

Petrus protested. "Please, I must—"

"Shut up!"

Tanya hesitated and then did as he asked. His knee dropped into her back and she waited for something to happen. The fear returned then, as she lay on her stomach. A panicking terror that ripped through her bones like white-hot lead. Nausea swept through her and she imagined his blade reaching forward and slicing through her neck.

Oh, God, please! Please save me! Her heart crashed in her chest and her muscles strung tight. Behind her Abdullah's breathing thickened.

And then Abdullah simply stood and walked away.

§

Tanya lay on her stomach for a long minute before moving. Petrus was still seated beside her, staring at the river. She followed his eyes. Abdullah squatted on the muddy bank, twenty meters off. He stared at them, rocking, gun limp in his right hand.

Tanya pushed herself up to her seat and faced Abdullah.

"Father Petrus?"

He answered without turning. "Yes, Tanya?"

"I'm . . . I'm very sorry, Father."

He turned his head and raised a brow. "Sorry? Don't be sorry for me, my dear. We are winning. Can't you see that?"

"Winning? We're sitting on a river a thousand miles from anywhere with a madman staring us down. I'm not sure I'm following."

"And to be honest, I'm not necessarily following either. But I do know a few things. I know that your parents were drawn to this jungle twenty years ago so that you could be here today. I know that a young girl named Nadia died in my homeland of Bosnia forty years ago so that I could be here today." He offered a smile. "This is far beyond us, my dear."

"My parents were *killed*, Father."

Father Petrus looked up to the canopy to his left and sighed. "So were mine. And I think we may be as well. As were all the disciples and Christ himself."

Tanya's mind spun. Something in her belly told her that his words were spun of gold. Her vision swam.

"God's chess match," she said.

She expected him to comfort her. To reason with her or something. But he didn't.

"Yes."

For a full minute they just stared out to the trees, hearing a sea of cicadas, watching Abdullah's glazed-over stare from across the way. He was squatting and waiting for something. He was insane.

"You're saying that my parents died so that I would end up in a box and pledge my life to God to come back here and lay on a riverbank and die myself."

"Perhaps. Or so that you could do something only you can do." He looked at her. "Do you know what that might be?"

She considered the question. "It sounds crazy, but maybe to love . . . Shannon."

"The boy."

"Yes, the boy. You know him better as Casius. The assassin."

The father's eyes widened with the realization. "Casius." A smile tugged at his lips. "Of course."

A tear pooled in her eye. "It may not make any sense to you, but my heart is crying for him."

"So then he is a part of this too."

"He was the man I loved."

"Yes, but more."

"What?"

"I don't know. But nothing is without a purpose. For all we know *his* parents were somehow drawn to the jungle so that he could become who he has become."

"An assassin? Doesn't sound like God to me."

"And the man who killed Hitler, was he raised up by God?"

"You're saying that one of the reasons God brought our parents to the jungle was so that Shannon and I could fall in love and become who we are today for some reason somehow connected with this . . . this attack on America by these terrorists."

"The chess match. I'm saying that the black side has had something up its sleeve and God has known for a long time. Yes. It happens a thousand times a day."

"We are hardly pawns. What if my parents had not responded to God's call?"

"Then you wouldn't have fallen in love with Shannon, would you?"

"And what if Helen hadn't persuaded me to come back?"

"Then . . . then you wouldn't be able to love Shannon again."

"And?"

He paused. "And I don't know."

A knot rose in her throat and she swallowed against it. "Part of me does still love him. But he's changed. I'm not sure I know how to love him."

"Love him the same way you are loved," he said.

She looked at Petrus and he held her gaze for a long time. His brow lifted mischievously. "I knew a priest who died for a village once. He was crucified. Would you like to feel the love he felt, Tanya?"

Feel love? The silky voice of B. J. Thomas crooned through her ear, *Hooked on a feeling.*

"Yes," she said.

Petrus smiled and closed his eyes.

Tanya looked away. Abdullah still sat across the way, staring at them. The birds still called in the afternoon heat. A warm breeze swept over her—a breeze laced heavily with the odor of sweet gardenia flowers. Like the gardenias around Helen's house. The ones from Bosnia.

Tanya's heart hammered. She felt the scent caress her nostrils and then sink into her lungs. Heat surged through her bones, like an electric shock.

She gasped and fell back to the grass.

The euphoria followed almost immediately, swallowing her whole. An ecstasy unlike any she had ever felt. As if her nerves had been injected with this drug—God's love flowing through her.

But it wasn't simply her nerves or her bones or her flesh. It was her heart. No, not her heart, because her heart was just flesh and it was more than a drug that wrapped itself around flesh.

It was her soul. That thing in her chest that had long ago taken to hiding in her bowels. Her soul was doing backflips. It was leaping and twirling and screaming with pleasure.

She threw her arms wide on the grass and laughed out loud, thoroughly intoxicated by the love. She felt hot tears run down her cheek as if a tap had been turned on. But they were tears of ecstasy. She would give her life to swim in a lake of these tears.

In that moment she wanted to explode. She wanted to find a lost orphan and hug him tight for a whole day. She wanted to take her tears and sprinkle them on the world. She wanted to give. Give everything so that someone else might have this feeling. It was that kind of love.

Then an image of a cross stuttered through her skull and she caught her breath. Her arms were still spread wide in laughter, but her chest had frozen. A man bled on the towering wooden beams. It was a priest. No, it was Christ! It was God. He was loving. All of this came from him. These tears of joy, this euphoria that had raged through her bones, her soul doing backflips—all because of his death on those beams.

The image burned into her mind like a red-hot branding iron.

And then it was gone.

Tanya lay prostrate, shaking in sobs. She wept because for the first time in memory everything was starting to clear. The purpose of life lay before her, crystal and breathtakingly beautiful. It all made sense. It not only made sense; it made lovely sense. And she was reduced to this . . . this blubbering lump in the face of it all.

Yes, something terrible had happened. But God was taking care of that. It wasn't her concern now. What mattered now was that she had been loved. That she was loved.

That she had been called to love.

Shannon, oh Shannon! How her heart ached for him. It was as though this breath flowing through her body had given her a transfusion of love. Love for Shannon.

Tanya lay on her back and stared past tears at the sun. She was barely aware that Father Petrus was crying softly beside her. The jungle slept in the noon heat. To think that history lay cradled in the bosom of a young woman lost here in the deepest of jungles while the rest of the world went mad seemed absurd. High above, a macaw flapped lazily through the blue sky. It showed no concern for the humans by the river. Maybe it didn't even see them.

Tanya closed her eyes, once again consumed with an image of the tall, muscular man who had dragged her here. Shannon Richterson.

Father, I will do as you will. I will do anything. I will love him. Please bring him back to me.

Will you die for him, Tanya?

Tanya heard a rustle and opened her eyes just in time to see Abdullah grinning, swinging his gun down. Its butt struck her head and her world exploded with stars and then went black.

§

By the time David Lunow followed his superiors into the final transport out of Miami International, less than three hours remained until the Brotherhood's twenty-four hours expired. And Bird's men had found nothing.

The Bell helicopter rose slowly and then skimmed north over deserted streets. Stragglers could be seen wandering the main streets of the downtown districts and farther north the highways were clogged, effectively shutting down any retreat for the millions of stranded motorists. One thing became crystal clear as the helicopter wound its way out of danger's way: If another bomb did detonate inland, a lot of U.S. citizens would die despite the evacuation. A million. Maybe more. And if the bomb went off in another city, then many more.

David turned to Ingersol and noted that the man had been watching him with a hazed stare. "If this thing goes, you're toast; you know that, don't you?"

For the first time in many days, Ingersol did not respond.

"In fact, regardless of what happens, you're toast."

Still no response.

"If you would have listened to me a week ago, we might not have had the first blast and we probably wouldn't be running for cover now. Someone's gonna take the fall."

When he received no response to his third charge, David turned back to the window.

"God help us," he mumbled. "God help us all."

§

Of the nearly three hundred million people living in the United States of America, the only ones *not* awake and watching the real-time satellite picture of southern Florida were those fleeing southern Florida.

It was an event that shut down the world. The cities near Miami had been deserted, the hospitals had been evacuated, and the air space had been cleared. It was a looter's paradise down there and nobody cared. Not even the looters. They were too busy trucking north.

The talking heads hosted an endless lineup of experts who stammered their way through hours of speculation. In the end, nobody looked good; nobody looked bad. They all pretty much looked desperate.

Someone in the White House had leaked the twenty-four-hour detail and every station now had a clock on-screen, ticking down the time from the last blast. Give or take a few seconds, the clocks now read one hour, thirty-eight minutes.

John Boy sat eating a sandwich in his home in Shady Side, watching NBC's coverage of the nation's meltdown, shaking his head. All seaports had been closed, but not before he'd lowered anchor in the bay. The terrorists had finally done it.

John Boy's boat, *Angel of the Sea*, sat in silent waters, and if anybody had been listening with a highly specialized listening device, they might have heard the faint electronic ticking in the bowels of her hull. But nobody was listening to *Angel of the Sea.* Nobody was even thinking of her.

Except Abdullah, of course.

And Jamal.

44

Lost in the madness, barely aware of himself, Shannon came upon the bank where he'd left the woman.

The sun was dipping in the west. Ahead lay an endless sea of foliage, rolling and climbing and falling and plunging. And under it somewhere crept a single man running from him. The Arab Abdullah. It was madness. They both were mad.

But deep in his mind, beyond the madness, an image replayed itself in an endless loop, drawing Shannon forward despite it all. An image of a thick green lawn, and on the lawn his father. And beside his father, his mother. Father was cut in two; Mother's head was missing. And in the machine hovering over them, Abdullah was grinning. And beside the Arab, a thousand men in brown suits, with plastic grins.

The miles passed underfoot steadily, with pounding monotony. But the thoughts were anything but monotonous—they were hell.

As his feet ate up the miles, a few new frames joined that clip running through his brain. They showed a young woman trapped screaming in a box while her own father soaked up the bullets above her.

Tanya.

She had latched her claws into him. He couldn't shake the images. In fact, they seemed to work their way deeper into him with each footfall, like barbed spurs.

She was as beautiful as the day he'd last seen her, swimming in the waters beneath the waterfall. His mind drifted to old memories. To tender moments that seemed grossly out of place in his mind. Snapshots from a fairy tale of happy endings. Pages filled with laughter and gentle embraces. Sweet delicate kisses. Windblown hair across a fair neck. Soft words whispered in his ear.

I love you, Shannon.

Tears blurred his eyes and he gave a grunt before clenching his teeth and shoving them back.

Abdullah, Abdullah, Shannon. Think of Jamal. Think of the plan.

Tanya, oh, Tanya. What has happened? We had paradise.

But Abdullah had snatched it away, hadn't he? And the CIA. They would all die. All of them.

Shannon ran under the canopy, desperately fighting the terrible ache lodged in his throat. Then years of discipline began to win him over to his mission. He had come to this jungle to kill. He had waited eight slow, agonizing years for the perfect timing, and now it was here.

Sula . . .

He lowered his head and replayed the brutal slaying of his parents, isolating each bullet as it spun through the air and landed into flesh. With each slap of his feet, another bullet bit deep. With each breath, the helicopter's rotors rushed through the air. A knife to the throat would be too good for Abdullah. His death would have to be slow—the blood would have to flow long.

When Shannon came upon the bank where he'd left Tanya, he was barely aware of himself. He swam through a black fog.

He entered from the south, through tall trees and scarce brush. The murmur of flowing water carried in the stillness. A gentle breeze played over the grass.

Tanya lay in the grass.

Shannon pulled up.

She was on her back in the middle of the grass. Not that he expected her up and working, but she lay folded with one leg under her torso—odd for sleep.

Shannon scanned the tree line quickly. He tested the air but the wind was at his back. She could be sleeping, still exhausted from the long trek.

He watched her chest rise and fall with each breath. For a long time, he watched her and the ache in his throat returned.

Dear Tanya, what have I done? What have I done to you? He closed his eyes. When he opened them, his vision was blurred.

You are wounded, my dear Tanya. Thinking like that—using those words, *dear Tanya*—released a flood of emotion in his chest. *A stake was driven into your heart when you were a tender woman. And now I have pushed it deeper. I just wanted to show you, Tanya. Can you understand that? Killing is all I have. It is what Sula gave me. I meant to show you that. I didn't mean to hurt you.*

Shannon leaned against the tall Yevaro tree beside him and let the pain roll through him. The jungle sounds fell away and he allowed himself to wallow in the strange sentiments. The field before him lay in surreal stillness, peaceful with Tanya resting on the grass. He stood at the perimeter, wreaking of blood. Like a foul monster peering from the shadows at a sleeping innocent beauty.

He clung to the bark and felt his torso buck with a dry sob.

It was the first time he'd ever felt such ravaging sorrow. She lay out there so innocent, breathing like a child, and he . . . he had nearly killed her.

Kill her, Shannon.

He blinked. The fog was washing through his mind and for a moment he thought he might be dying. Kill her? How could he even think of killing her?

Sula . . .

Shannon closed his eyes and swallowed hard. He stepped out into the clearing and then saw the dark stain in her hair when he was halfway across the clearing.

His instincts took over midstride, before he formed the clear thought that this was blood on her head. He dove and had the knife from his belt before he hit the grass.

"Stand up, you fool!" a voice sneered across the clearing.

That voice. A chill flashed down Shannon's spine.

Tanya was still breathing—the wound hadn't been fatal. A blow to the head had left her unconscious. And now Abdullah was screaming at him.

"Stand up or I will shoot your woman!"

Abdullah had found his way here! In a thousand square miles of jungle he had stumbled upon Tanya. It was the river, of course. He had taken the river as most would. The crocodiles hadn't gotten to her, but Abdullah had.

Shannon's mind had already climbed back into its killing skin. Now he would kill Abdullah. And he would do it in front of Tanya.

He stood slowly and saw Abdullah step from the trees, dragging a man by the collar. The priest! He had Father Petrus.

Shannon cursed his own carelessness. He had given Abdullah the upper hand. It was the insanity plaguing him, the voices screaming in his skull, the foolish sentiments—they had made him weak. Now he faced a man bearing a gun at a distance of twenty meters without the least element of stealth in his favor.

The terrorist's white teeth flashed through a wicked grin and he forced the priest to kneel. Father Petrus's head lolled—he was barely coherent.

He shifted his gun to cover Tanya. "Throw your knives down. Slowly. Very slowly. And don't think that I won't kill her. If you even flinch, I will kill her, do you understand?" He held the gun three feet from Tanya's prone body, which still rose and fell in deep sleep.

Shannon ground his teeth. If he moved quickly enough, he could flip the knife backhanded and stick Abdullah in the throat. From this distance he could kill the man easily. Bleed him like a pig.

But Abdullah would have time to squeeze the trigger. If the gun had been trained on him, he might avoid the bullet, but Abdullah had the gun on Tanya.

"Throw them down!"

Every muscle in Shannon's body begged to hurl the knife now. He hesitated one last second and then tossed the knife. It landed with a soft thud. He clenched his jaw.

"The other one. Or are there two others?" Again that grin.

Shannon bent slowly and withdrew the Arkansas Slider from an ankle sheath. He threw it aside. It landed on the bowie and clanked.

"Turn around slowly."

Shannon glanced about the perimeter, his mind racing for alternatives, but they came slow just now. He turned as Abdullah asked. If he could coax the man into arm's reach, he could kill him without risking the woman. Quickly, before the butcher had time to know he'd been outwitted. Or slowly to give him time to feel his death.

"Turn around."

When Shannon turned back, Abdullah was kicking Tanya in the ribs. Shannon flinched.

"Back!" Abdullah screamed. Spittle frothed on his lips. Bulging veins wrapped his taut neck.

"I told you to move slowly. Next time I will put a bullet in her thigh."

The Arab was quick. Very quick. He had anticipated—possibly even provoked—the reaction from Shannon and snapped back with amazing speed. Like a snake.

Tanya stirred on the next kick to her midsection. She moaned and pushed herself to her knees. A thin trail of dried blood stained her temple.

Kill him, Shannon. Kill them both. Kill them all.

He hated the thought.

Tanya stood and faced Abdullah. She hadn't seen Shannon yet. The priest still knelt, between them, eyes closed.

"Turn and greet your visitor." Abdullah grinned with childish pleasure at his cleverness.

Tanya turned. Very slowly. As if she were in a dream.

Their eyes met. Hers were blue and round, the eyes he remembered from the pool. Her lips sprang open. The same lips that had kissed him, dripping wet on the rocks. Something had changed in her face since he'd left her here. He saw more there than a cry for help. Actually, it wasn't a cry for help at all.

Shannon's heart stopped beating for a few long moments. She was pulling him back to the pool and he wanted to go.

The Arab stepped to the side and smiled at them. "You are reunited, yes?" He shoved a coil of fishing string at Tanya. "Hogtie him! Do you know what a hogtie is?"

She shook her head.

"Of course not. It's a tie for pigs." He jerked his pistol toward Shannon. "Tie him."

Shannon looked at Abdullah and saw that his eyes danced with fire.

He looked back at Tanya. She walked toward him, holding his eyes with her own. She stared at him like a child looking upon a magician performing an illusion—with utter awe. As if the last eight years were nothing more than one of her vivid dreams, and she was looking at him for the first time after finally waking.

A slight smile lifted the corners of her lips.

"Shannon," she said, and her soft voice echoed through his mind.

"Shut up!" Abdullah screamed. His voice rang about the perimeter and a flock of startled parrots took flight with screeches of protest. Abdullah kept his gun trained on her, sidestepping to match her pace.

"Did I tell you to talk to him? No, I told you to tie him!" He made a crazy circular motion with his free hand. "Tie his hands behind his back, to his ankles."

Stunned, Shannon watched her approach. She was hardly hearing the Arab—he knew that now. He had studied a hundred men under extreme trauma, more often than not trauma provoked by him. And he knew this: Tanya was barely aware of the man to her right. She was thoroughly engrossed with *him*, with Shannon.

The realization made him dizzy.

She had reached him and was gazing up at his face now. She lowered her eyes to his neck, his shoulders, his chest, studying each muscle as though for the first time. Tenderly, like a lover.

"Tie him!"

A voice was screaming in Shannon's mind, way back where his ears could barely hear it, but his mind was bending over in pain.

"Tie my hands behind my back and then to my ankles when I kneel down," Shannon said, his voice trembling. He suddenly wanted to cry. As he had cried just a few minutes earlier. What was happening to him?

Tanya.

Sula. Both names took hold of his thoughts, warring for dominance.

He was no longer thinking as clearly as he had a week ago.

Tanya pulled her eyes from him, still smiling softly. She slid around him and took his hands in hers. Spikes of heat ripped up his bones and he felt his fingertips quiver.

She was touching them gently; feeling his fingers, his palms. She ran her fingers down his arms. She was speaking to him with her tender touch. His heart raced.

Tie me, Tanya. Please, just tie me.

She wrapped the string around his wrists loosely, still touching his hands lightly, tracing his palms. She cinched her knots and he knelt. She knelt behind him and passed the line under his ankles.

He could feel her hot breath on his shoulders as she worked, leaning over him. The heavy aroma of flowers—gardenias—caressed his nostrils and he trembled once.

What's happening to me?

Kill her, Shannon! Kill her, you spineless worm!

He let his head loll to one side. Stillness settled over the clearing. Even the wind seemed to pause. Tanya's chin approached and then lightly touched his back, and his flesh quivered at her nearness.

A lump swelled in his throat, and for a terrible moment he thought he might burst into tears. For no reason at all.

Dear Tanya, what have I done to you? I am so sorry.

Kill her! Kill—

"Shannon," she whispered.

He froze.

She whispered it again, barely audible yet tender. "Shannon. I love you." Her breath played over his shoulder, and he could smell it. Musky and sweet. Gardenias.

The last of his control left when the scent of her reached his lungs. She was breathing love into him. He went limp—all but his heart, which was slamming against his chest desperately.

And then she was done with her tying.

"Step away from him," Abdullah said.

Tanya did not move. Maybe she hadn't heard him.

Abdullah shrieked this time. "Get back!"

Tanya stood slowly and stepped aside. Abdullah swept in and yanked the ties tight. Shannon bit his lip against the pain and gathered his senses. Any illusion he'd harbored of freeing himself from Tanya's loose bonds fell away.

Abdullah jumped back and cackled like a hyena. "There, you pig. You won't be so difficult to kill now, will you?"

He grabbed Tanya and shoved her back toward the center of the clearing. She stumbled forward and spun to him, flashing a vicious glare. For a second, Shannon thought she might yell at Abdullah. But the moment passed and she returned her gaze to him.

Abdullah stood halfway between them and stepped back to study his victims. He spread his legs and grinned wide.

He licked the spittle from his lips and shifted the gun to his left hand and then back to his right. "Well, well." He glanced at his watch. "We have time. Do you know what I have done, assassin?"

Tanya was staring at Shannon again, oblivious of Abdullah. Her figure distorted in the tears that hung in his eyes.

"I have detonated a nuclear device in your country, gringo. And another is set to go off soon. It's on a countdown that will end in less than an hour. A countdown that can only be stopped by me now."

Shannon stared at the man without expression.

"I have the power, and the world can do nothing." He tapped his temple. "The only code to stop it is locked in my mind."

"Shannon." It was Tanya, speaking in that soft, milky voice again. "Forgive me. I'm so sorry."

Abdullah jerked his head toward her. "Shut up!"

Shannon blinked the mist from his eyes, feeling as though he might crumble from the insanity of her words.

Tanya ignored Abdullah. "I know some things now, Shannon. I know that I was made to love you. I know that you need me to love you. I know that I always have loved you, and that I love you desperately now."

Abdullah took three leaping steps to her and brought a heavy hand across her bare cheek. The air resounded with the sound of flesh smacking flesh.

Crack!

Heat flared up Shannon's neck. He grunted and jerked against the bindings in sudden rage. Tanya's face turned a bright red. But her smile didn't waver.

"Leave her alone!" Shannon screamed. "You touch her and I'll rip your heart out!"

Pain shot down his spine and his head swam, and he knew now that it was Sula's doing. He closed his eyes against the agony.

"Shannon." She was speaking again and her words flowed like a balm flows. "Shannon, do you remember when we used to swim together, in the pool?"

He opened his eyes.

The Arab stood, dumbstruck.

Shannon remembered.

"Do you remember how I fell into your arms? And how you kissed my lips?"

Her deep blue eyes held him.

The Arab spun his head to Shannon, off balance now.

Tanya ignored him. "Do you know that it was for today that we loved each other then? It was beyond us, Shannon. Our parents—they died for this day."

The words made no sense to him, but her eyes and her lips and her voice—they all crashed in on him at once. Her breath seemed to flow to him again.

She was loving him with an intensity he did not know could possibly exist. The blood drained from his head, and he let her words wash over him.

Something she had said made Abdullah step back.

"We're a part of God's plan, Shannon. You are. Like Rahab. God's trump card."

Shannon's mind spun in wild circles.

"Those bonds of love have never been broken. Tell me that you love me, Shannon. Please, tell me."

The pressure on his chest felt like a dam set to burst. Tears ran down his cheeks. Blood roared through his ears, and his face twisted in anguish.

"I love you desperately, Shannon."

I love you, Tanya.

A ball of anguish rolled up his chest, swelling as it rose.

Kill her—

"No!"

The pain roared in his ears, and for a moment he thought he was passing out. Tears spilled from his eyes and his face contorted in agony.

"Nooooo!" He let the cry run out and he gasped. "No, you sick spineless worm. I *love* her!" Sobs robbed his breath. He sucked in a lungful of air, tilted his head back, and screamed full throated at the sky.

"I love her!"

His cry echoed, silencing the jungle.

And then the ball of pain ripped up through his skull. His muscles tensed in a seizure and then released him. He groaned and sagged to a huddle.

For an endless moment, the world was blank to him. The river stopped rushing by, the ground no longer pressed into his knees, the breeze seemed to freeze. And then slowly his mind began to crawl out of its hole.

" . . . when I say something, I mean what I say!" The Arab was screaming and his face was red. Shannon turned to Tanya beyond him.

Tanya? He felt oddly as though he had stepped into a new world. Or out of one.

Tanya! What was she doing? She was smiling at him.

He began to sob softly. "I . . . I love you, Tanya," he said. He knelt there lost, like a child. "I love you. I love you so much. I'm sorry. I'm so sorry."

"Shut up!" Abdullah screamed.

She began to cry. "Shh . . . no, don't cry, Shannon. We're together again. It's okay now. Everything will be okay now."

"Tanya," he sobbed. The forest echoed with his cry. "Oh, God!" he wailed. "Forgive me. I've been so wrong. Oh, God, help me!"

And what have you done, Shannon? What have you gone and done? Panic skirted through his mind. *I've got to stop—*

Boom!

The gunshot echoed through the trees and Shannon snapped his eyes open. Father Petrus lay on his side, blood leaking from a head wound. *Oh, dear God, what have I done?*

Tanya was crying.

"Shut up!" Abdullah said as his face twisted with rage, and he leapt for Shannon. A knife glistened in his right hand. He slashed forcefully, slicing Shannon's chest to the ribs.

Shannon sat back to his haunches. His head swam.

The Arab trembled from head to foot. His eyes shone black and eager. He stood like a rabid dog over a rabbit. He reached down and cut again—across Shannon's shoulder.

Shannon moaned. Nausea swept through his gut. He looked at Tanya, pleading. Not for her help. For her love.

"I love you, Tanya," he said.

Tears streamed silently down her face as she mouthed her answer. *I love you, Shannon.*

The Arab slashed again, spittle flying from his lips. The blade flashed across Shannon's chest, forming a cross of sorts. He brought his arm back for another thrust.

"Sula!" Tanya's voice cut across the clearing.

The Arab spun, arm still cocked. Shannon's mind was only half here, at the river. The other half was thinking that he had to stop something. Something only he could stop.

Tanya was staring at Abdullah. She'd called him *Sula*. The corners of her mouth slowly rose. "I know you. We've met. Remember? You're called Sula and it means death."

Yes, death. Known as Sula to some. Lucifer to others. They were the same. Abdullah was frozen, holding the gun in his left hand and the knife now dripping with blood in his right. His face went white.

Tanya stood with her arms at her side, a new boldness in her posture. "And how are you stopped, Sula?"

The Arab slogged forward three steps. He stared dumbstruck at Tanya.

"You know that I can't let you kill him," Tanya said softly.

The world began to slow down. Things were going topsy-turvy. He had to stop something. Something much worse than this. And she was going to make sure that he did it.

Abdullah shook like a leaf now. Somehow this strange encounter between him and Tanya had flipped a switch.

Tanya spread her arms, still barely smiling. "You've done this before, haven't you?"

Shannon screamed then. "Abdullah! Take me! Leave her." He strained against the line, feeling it cut into his flesh. Blood from his chest and shoulder wounds ran down his belly.

The Arab looked at him, his facial muscles quivering. He held the gun at his side.

"No. Take me instead," Tanya said. She had lifted her arms to form a cross.

The Arab swiveled his head and lifted the pistol to her head in one smooth motion. The world fell to blurred images. Tanya shifted wide blue eyes to Shannon and they poured love into him.

She was giving her life for him!

Shannon's mind lost coherence then. He roared to his feet, snapping the line as he did so. The jungle was screaming.

His head hit Abdullah's back and the man's gun bucked. *Boom!*

From the corner of his eye, Shannon saw Tanya standing, her arms spread wide, her head tilted back. Abdullah had shot her! He'd shot Tanya!

The jungle was still screaming, long wails of desperation screeching around his ears.

And then the Arab hit the ground and Shannon crashed down on top of him. He shoved his knees forward, so that he straddled the man's chest. His left hand had found Abdullah's black hair. He snatched his bowie from Abdullah's belt.

Then it occurred to him that the screaming came from his own throat, not the jungle.

For a moment Shannon thought that he had died as well. His soul had been sucked clean of his body, leaving only a vast empty hole. But he knew that couldn't be true, because he was still screaming. "Noooo! Noooo!" Just that, over and over.

Only then did he realize that Tanya wasn't falling. The realization snatched the wind from him and he pulled up.

For a moment Abdullah shifted out of his focus. He jerked his head up and he stared into Tanya's blue eyes. She lowered her arms.

She was alive. Shannon's arms began to shake.

"Don't kill him, Shannon."

The Arab coughed beneath him.

Shannon breathed heavy, his lungs burned. His worlds were colliding. For a few moments no one moved.

He released his grip on Abdullah's hair. He would follow this woman over a cliff if she suggested it.

You have to stop it, Shannon. Only you can stop it.

He snatched up Abdullah's gun and scrambled to his feet. "Tanya! There's a bomb!" He was frozen by this strange panic that swept through him. He felt oddly vacant. *Tanya, there's a bomb?* What was he saying?

She looked at him dumbly. "It went off already—"

"No. Another bomb!"

Dear God, what had he done!

Abdullah struggled to his elbows, coughing again. The man should be dead already. But Shannon had changed somehow. The fog was gone and that realization was dizzying.

Abdullah backed up slowly, staring. Then he turned and stumbled toward the skiff.

"Stop!" Shannon lifted the gun and fired it into the air. "The next one won't miss."

The Arab halted.

Shannon ran for him. He wasn't sure how much time he had, but that no longer mattered. Either he would make it or he wouldn't.

The Arab turned around and Shannon shoved the gun under his chin.

"Give me the transmitter!"

The Arab didn't flinch. "It's useless without the code, you fool. I don't even know the code—"

"Give it to me!" Shannon screamed.

Abdullah dug in his pants pocket and pulled out the black transmitter. Shannon grabbed it and shoved the man away. He turned it on end, activated it with a familiar flip of the power switch, and stared at the number pad.

He lifted an unsteady hand, entered a five-digit code, pushed the green button on the left, and waited. In less than three seconds the red light on the top blipped once.

Transmission confirmed.

Tanya had come up and stood with her arms limp at her sides. The Arab stared at him white faced.

"Only Jamal—"

"I am Jamal."

Abdullah's face slowly went white. His lips suddenly twisted to a snarl and he launched himself with a scream. Shannon reacted without thinking. He stepped into the charge and brought his right palm across the man's head. The impact dropped Abdullah like a sack of grain.

For a long moment Shannon just stood there, staring at the fallen terrorist.

"You are Jamal?" Tanya asked. "Who is *Jamal?*"

The strength left Shannon's legs. He backed away from them then, suddenly horrified. "Jamal," he said.

She took a step toward him. "Yes, who is Jamal, Shannon?"

A desperate urge to run rushed through his head. His limbs began to shake.

"Shannon . . . Nothing Jamal has done will change my love for you." She smiled.

It was too much. Shannon dropped his head and sobbed.

She came at him and placed a hand on his shoulder. "It's okay—"

"No!" He spun away.

"Please . . ."

Shannon turned back and flung both arms wide. "I am Jamal! Don't you see? The bombs are mine!"

She blinked. Her face turned white.

He took a breath. "I made a vow, Tanya . . . Everyone who had a part in the killing of . . . our parents. The terrorists, the CIA." He paused . . . it was sounding absurd.

She stared at him for a long second. "A nuclear bomb?"

He looked at her desperately. "Sula . . ." was his only explanation.

"He took you."

Sorrow boiled over, and he turned from her, sobbing again. "Oh, God . . . Oh, God," he prayed. He caught his breath. He sat hard to his seat and put his head between his knees.

Her hands were suddenly on his shoulders, and he wanted to pull away.

"Tell me what you did," she said.

He closed his eyes.

"Tell me."

How could he tell her?

He lifted his head and swallowed. He spoke, only half hearing himself. "I found out that the Brotherhood had sent Abdullah to South America for the purpose of building and smuggling a bomb into the United States. That's why they established the drug routes. And the CIA helped them, without knowing about the bomb. They wanted Abdullah out of Colombia, so they suggested Venezuela. That's why my parents were killed. Your parents."

"And how did you become Jamal?"

"I decided the best way to destroy them was to take over their plan. Hijack it and use it to destroy the CIA. I persuaded the Brotherhood to let me coordinate parts of the plan. I took a good plan and made it better."

"A bomb wouldn't have killed just the CIA," she said softly.

"I know. I don't know. It didn't matter." He could hardly remember why he had done it now.

The Arab had stopped his groaning and lay still, perhaps unconscious. The jungle screamed about them, oblivious to all of this. They sat still for a while. She was stunned; he was numb.

"But it's okay now," Tanya said softly. "If you hadn't become Jamal, the second bomb would have gone off." She paused and her fingers began to work on his shoulders.

He turned to her.

"And if I hadn't loved you," she continued, "the bomb would have gone off. Father Petrus was right. If my parents hadn't come to the jungle, or if we hadn't fallen in love, or if Abdullah had chosen a different location, the bomb would have gone off. It was all God's leading, his turning evil to good."

Shannon understood what she was driving at, but the notion seemed impossible.

"If our parents hadn't been killed?"

She nodded. "Yes, if our parents hadn't been killed, the bomb would have gone off. They would have done it without you and today three million people would have died around Washington."

Movement caught the corner of his eye, and he jerked his head.

Abdullah was halfway to them, face snarled and black, a bowie knife in his right hand. His scream began then, when he was only ten feet away.

Shannon rolled to his right, away from Tanya, palmed the pistol he'd taken from the man, and came up on one knee, gun leveled. Killing had been like breathing for the last eight years. He'd lived to kill as much as he'd lived to breathe. He'd hunted and he'd slaughtered and always he'd relished each death. Sula.

But now Sula had been overcome by love, and with Abdullah tearing at him like a rabid dog, pulling the trigger came hard. At the last moment, he inched the barrel down. The gun bucked in his hand.

Boom!

The slug took Abdullah in the hip.

The force of the impact spun him into the air and he landed with a thump to his back.

Shannon dropped the gun and slumped to his seat. He closed his eyes and moaned. *Father died for this? Mother died for this, so that I could become the one man who could stop the bomb?*

He had fallen madly in love with a seventeen-year-old woman in the jungle for this?

Tanya's arms slipped around his neck and her hot breath brushed his cheek. She was crying very softly.

"I love you, Shannon. And God loves you desperately."

He draped his arms over her as she buried her face in his neck.

Then they were crying together, swept back to the pool, lost in each other's embrace, lost in love reborn.

EPILOGUE

One Month Later

Tanya stood by the square oak table fidgeting nervously, watching the door through which she assumed they would bring Shannon. It was her first visit to the Canyon City Correctional Facility and she hoped it would be her last.

Helen eased herself into a chair with a sigh. "Not bad for a prison."

Tanya shifted on her feet. Yes, but it was still a prison.

"Don't worry, dear," Helen said softly. "From what you've told me, Shannon will have no problem handling himself here. Besides, he's practically a national hero. He stopped the bomb, for goodness' sakes. He won't be in here long."

"He's not who he used to be," Tanya said. "I'm not sure what he can handle anymore."

Tanya had remained by Shannon's side during the indictment and the sub-sequent grand jury hearing. It was a strange case to be sure. The media had a field day with the CIA agent who was really Jamal, the terrorist, who was really a boy from the jungle who had watched his parents die at the hands of terror-ists *and* the CIA. Would the real Shannon Richterson please stand up?

If you asked the man on the street, the real Shannon was the man who saved America from the most horrific terrorist plot ever to be conceived. Driven mad by his parents' deaths, he had become complicit in the plot, true enough. But once he had come to his senses, he had also stopped that very plot. Without him, the plan would have been executed successfully. That's what the man on the street would say. In fact, the whole county was saying it.

But technically, Shannon had assisted terrorists. All of those he himself had killed over the years, he'd killed in the service of the United States. But thirteen people had died on the *Lumber Lord* as a result of the nuclear detonation in which Shannon had participated. They were mostly a criminal lot themselves. But that did not excuse the man most Americans wanted to see set free.

An armed guard walked past the window across the room and Tanya's heart leapt. The man who followed the guard was dressed in orange prison clothes like every other convict in the high-security building. But she hardly saw the bright color; she was looking at Shannon's face. At his hair, at his jaw line—

And then Shannon was out of sight again—for a moment. The door swung open and Shannon stepped through it. His green eyes lifted, focused on her, and held steady. He stopped just inside the door, which closed with a hush behind him.

Tanya's heart thumped and for a moment they stared at each other. She wanted to rush up to him and throw her arms around him and smother him with kisses, but somehow the moment seemed too heavy for lighthearted kisses. This was Shannon, the man whom she had been led into the jungle to love. The man she had always loved. The man who was wrapped in muscle and hardened like steel and yet as gentle as a dove.

Her Shannon.

A sheepish smile nudged his lips, and it occurred to Tanya that he was embarrassed.

"Hi, Shannon," she said softly.

"Hi, Tanya." He broke into a wide grin and walked toward them. Yes, the sight of her did that to him, didn't it? It melted him.

She stepped out to meet him. Sorrow swelled through her chest and she knew she was going to cry. He took her into his arms and she buried her head into his shoulder and slipped her arms around his waist.

"It's okay, Tanya. I'm okay."

Tanya sniffed once and swallowed hard. "I miss you."

They held each other and Tanya wanted to spend the whole hour just holding him. Behind them, Helen shifted in her chair. Shannon kissed Tanya's hair and they sat across the table from each other.

"Well, young man, you look larger in person than on the tube," Helen said. "And easily as handsome."

Shannon blushed through a smile and glanced at Tanya.

"I'm sorry, I should have introduced you. This is Helen."

Shannon looked at Tanya's grandmother. "So you are Helen. I've heard a lot about you. All good, of course. It's a pleasure meeting you." He dipped his head.

"And you." Helen grinned approvingly.

They exchanged some news and talked lightly about prison life. Tanya told Shannon about the latest positive spin on *Larry King Live* that was gathering steam. Shannon joked about the food and talked kindly about the guards. Within ten minutes they began to run out of small talk, and an awkward silence engulfed them.

Looking at the shy, gentle man across from her now, Tanya's heart ached.

"You are still confused, Shannon," Helen said.

"Grandmother," Tanya objected, "I'm not sure this is the time."

Shannon looked at Tanya and then lowered his eyes to the table.

"I can hardly remember who I was," Shannon said. The room felt charged with electricity. *You don't have to do this, Shannon.*

He closed his eyes and took a deep breath. "Actually I feel more lost than confused." He looked up at Helen, who wore a faint smile. They seemed to look into each other's souls.

"Then tell me what you remember," Helen said.

Shannon hesitated and looked away.

"I remember what happened. It just seems like a whole different person did those things." He paused. When he spoke, it was introspectively.

"When my parents were killed by the Brotherhood, something snapped. I went to the cave . . ."

"Sula," Tanya said after another pause. "The witch doctor's grave."

"Yes. And I . . . I changed there."

"What changed?" Helen asked.

"Things went fuzzy. I could hardly remember what Tanya looked like, or what my parents looked like. I became obsessed with death. With killing. Mostly with killing whoever had ruined my life."

"Abdullah and the CIA," Tanya said. He'd told her everything already, but hearing him tell Helen, it sounded new. Somehow different.

"Yes. But more than that." He shook his head and his eyes went moist. "Things got cloudy. I hated everything. When I learned about the CIA's involvement, I just began to hate everything that had anything to do with the CIA."

"But if you were driven by evil, why would you want to destroy Abdullah, who was also evil?" Tanya asked.

He shrugged. "Evil isn't so discriminating. I went back into the jungle within a year of my parents' death, intent on killing Abdullah. But while I was there, I learned that the CIA had done it as much as Abdullah had. Then I learned about the Brotherhood's plan to take a bomb into the U.S. I decided then to become Jamal and destroy both of them in one blow."

"Why didn't you just kill them and then expose the CIA?" Tanya asked.

He looked at her. "That wasn't enough. I think I could have blown up the whole world and not thought it was enough." He swallowed. "You have to understand, I was very . . . I was consumed with this thing."

"He was possessed," Helen said.

The simple declaration silenced them.

"But the powers of darkness forgot something," Helen said. "Or perhaps they've never really understood it. The Creator is the ultimate chess master, isn't he? Why he allows evil to wreak havoc, we can hardly understand. But in the end, it always plays into his hands." She paused. "As it did this time."

"It's hard for me to accept," Shannon said. There was a deep sadness in his eyes, and Tanya reached her hand out to him. "I did so much . . . damage. It feels impossible now."

"I've been there myself, Shannon," Helen said. "Believe me, I've been there. Evil is great, but not as great as God's love and forgiveness. You are freed, child. And you are loved."

Tears pooled in Shannon's eyes and one broke down his right cheek.

Tanya leaned forward and cupped his hand in both of hers. "Listen to me,

Shannon. I am madly in love with you. I have always been madly in love with you. God brought my parents to the jungle so that I could fall madly in love with you. And he did it all for a purpose. You think any of that was a mistake?"

He shook his head, but the tears were slipping down his face now.

"And the love I have for you is only a fraction of the love he has for you."

His shoulders began to shake and suddenly he was sobbing silently. Tanya looked at Helen in desperation. She smiled, but there were tears in her eyes as well.

Tanya looked back at Shannon, and it struck her then that there was more than sorrow in those tears. There was gratitude and relief and there was love.

She pushed her chair back, stepped around to him, and put her arms around his shoulders. His head rested on her shoulder and he shook like a leaf as he cried. He suddenly reached over and encircled her with his arms.

"I love you, Tanya."

"I know. I know. And I love you."

They held each other and wept. But it was most definitely a good cry. The kind that cleansed the soul and bound hearts as one. The kind that healed deep wounds. Tears of love.

At some point Tanya saw that Helen had left them. She could see the older woman standing by a large window, staring out to the blue sky. She was smiling. And if Tanya wasn't mistaken, she was humming. It was an old tune she had heard a hundred times before.

Jesus, Lover of my soul.

In the end it was always about love, wasn't it?

More selections from *Ted Dekker*

Heaven's Wager

He lost everything he ever wanted—and risked his soul to get what he deserved. Take a glimpse into a world more real and vital than most people ever discover here on earth, the unseen world where the real dramas of the universe— and of our daily lives—continually unfold.

"[*Heaven's Wager*] is genuinely exciting . . . fast paced . . . Spine-tingling . . ."
PUBLISHERS WEEKLY

When Heaven Weeps

A cruel game of ultimate stakes at the end of World War II leaves Jan Jovic stunned and perplexed by the demonstration of love by the victim. This love haunts him and springs to life in his own heart as he falls in love with a woman determined to learn love the hard way.

"*When Heaven Weeps* displays more of God's love than any other book I've read, save the Bible. It'll make anyone who is forgiven stand up and shout. It is a beautiful story . . . exquisite."
STEVEN BLACKMON, ConsumingFire.com

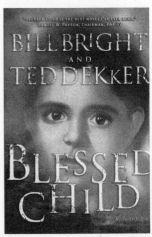

Blessed Child

Caleb, a child from Ethiopia with extraordinary powers, challenges a nation's view on the supernatural and its attempt to control it.

"A fast-paced thriller of apocalyptic dimensions. The book will move you to wonder . . ."
CHARLES W. COLSON

W PUBLISHING GROUP™
www.wpublishinggroup.com